Searching
for
Johnny

Thomas Dunne Books

St. Martin's Press   New York

Searching
for
Johnny

JAMES GIBBINS

THOMAS DUNNE BOOKS.
An imprint of St. Martin's Press.

www.stmartins.com

Library of Congress Cataloging-in-Publication Data

Gibbons, James.
  Searching for Johnny / James Gibbins.—1st ed.
    p. cm.
  ISBN 0-312-28184-6
  1. World War, 1939–1945—Motion pictures and the war—Fiction. 2. Women motion picture producers and directors—Fiction. 3. Motion picture industry—Fiction. 4. Air pilots, Military—Fiction. 5. Americans—England—Fiction. 6. Yorkshire (England)—Fiction. 7. Time travel—Fiction. I. Title.

PR6107.I23 S43 2002
823'.92—dc21

                                                                2001055570

First Edition: April 2002

10 9 8 7 6 5 4 3 2 1

For Doris

Acknowledgments

I want to thank those senior scientists at Cambridge University who so patiently answered my questions and indulged my ignorance about the broader dimensions of time and its manifestations.

Equally, I am grateful to the US Eighth Air Force veterans I talked with who flew from England in World War II. As a guest at one of their reunions in Lincolnshire, I acquired valuable background material—everything from slang to technicalities and diets—of that era. I send a particular salute to Captain (jg) "Top" Taylor, now sadly dead, who filled me in on the intricacies (and the capriciousness) of in-flight radio communications.

On another wavelength, I note with appreciation, the hike across the so-called Wuthering Heights moors in Yorkshire in which I was escorted by Japanese members of the Brontë Society.

Beverly Hills
and Yorkshire

One

IT BEGAN IN YORKSHIRE WHERE WE WERE SHOOTING—WHAT LIT-
tle there was of it—that doomed movie, that would-be epic about
American fliers in Britain in the early 1940s. Phil Cowell, very much
in his cinema-verité mode, was the director.

An airfield of the period, a former bomber base, had been located
and, half a century on, re-created in detail, right down to the siting of
a Stage Door Canteen. World War II was back in business and had
invaded the seventeenth-century manor house whose over-turreted
bulk sloped in subsidence, like history with a hangover, a couple of
hundred yards from the end of the runway. The production crew, of
which I was one, lived in that house and in its great hall the Andrews
Sisters were live, albeit look-alikes, and sang "Chattanooga Choo
Choo" from the minstrels' gallery, while the madrigals were canned
and relayed on old Wurlitzer jukeboxes.

This particular setup was for the off-duty relaxation of the crew,
though the unit publicist, an intense young man from Wisconsin
with a doctorate in the psychology of communication, insisted that it
served the cause of "creative ambiance in keeping with the ethos of

this major motion picture." To me, this literal and simultaneous clash of cultures was Chattanooga Choo Choo Hey Nonny No. A Hollywood absurdity. I would have been prepared to go along with it, if only Phil Cowell had been truly getting on with the shooting of the movie.

We were in our fifth month in Yorkshire. We arrived in mid-November and had fewer than fifty significant takes in the can and needed at least three hundred more just to come in at average length.

Only this wasn't an average movie. This was a movie in which I was one of three producers (the other two were tucked away in Los Angeles) and also the director of the second unit, but I had not seen more than a few pages of the script at a time. This was a movie financed by Middle East oil sheiks with, so it was rumored on the set, "secondary collateral" put up by Mafia figures in Las Vegas.

And, much more to the point, this was a movie in which Phil Cowell felt he had reached the Orson Welles zenith of his work. He had directed a string of tightly budgeted pictures which, one after the other, had gone on to be box-office hits and had saved at least two studios. Now, in his words, he was ready to "put aside the doodling pad and turn to the master canvas."

He was still doodling, though—doodling with miles of film as he shot and re-shot the simplest scenes over days, sometimes weeks. And he was doodling with my life: this was my first movie and I had sacrificed much to make this career switch.

"Trust me, sweetie," he would say, his arm around my shoulder, when I protested. And even though I realized he had brought his own calculated patent to plausibility and trademarked it with his hazy indigo eyes, the overdone integrity of his graying beard and a voice that creaked like old leather, I would end up trusting him. For ten minutes. An hour. Even a day. I, the total feminist, even let him get away with calling me sweetie.

Always, though, there was the unassailable evidence that the regular hell-raising in the great hall was a counterpoint to the fiasco of the movie. The crew were bored and frustrated and so they roared into the ritual of revels. The booze tended to be drunk from battered old

Eighth Air Force mess cans—more "creative ambiance"—and the cocaine did communal rounds in antique snuffboxes which someone had found in a bureau in the house.

I drank little and stayed away from the cocaine altogether. I am not abstemious on either count, but I felt I had to make a stand against this expression of the larger waste. At the same time, as one of the few non-Americans there, I felt I couldn't be seen too openly as the snotty Englishwoman who would not, or could not, hack it with the rest of "the gang". I made a point, then, of chatting, smiling, making an occasional contribution to the dirty stories. At least for two or three hours.

I was hanging in, I felt, as gamely as the Andrews Sisters, up there in the minstrel gallery, cute in their WAC uniforms, indefatigable in their energy in which not one jived finger-snap ever lacked éclat. I grew to admire them. Maxine, Patty and Laverne. In particular, I liked the way they sang "Chattanooga Choo Choo": the way, linked together at the waist, they simulated the train taking a bend, the way the symmetry of their arm movements essayed the rhythm of the pistons and the wheels, the way the widening of their eyes accompanied their warbling of the train's whistle. It was sheer virtuosity.

To this day I retain an affection, a nostalgia, for "Chattanooga Choo Choo." Somehow, it made all those occasions in the great hall bearable, though even that song's charms were not proof against the night three celebrations took place—two birthdays and the news, phoned in from Oregon only hours before, that Del Wimont, the lighting director, was the grandfather of twins.

That night Chateau Mouton Rothschild was sloshing in the mess cans, and though I had joined in the toasts the grogginess I was feeling was down to the noise. Our happy new grandfather was engaged in a hog-calling contest with Steve Lothe, the second-unit cameraman. One of the birthday boys, Howie Stollen, the stunt coordinator, was trying to break the sound barrier on a hunting horn, and the other one, Willie Stirk, head of wardrobe, was happily, and to resonant effect, rolling a ten-pin bowling ball down the full length of the hall. All this and the Andrews Sisters and the madrigals, the whoop-

sie cushions and the bursting balloons—and finally, to mark the birth
of the twins, the exploding cigars.

I was seated next to Merv Scill, the sound recordist, and it was he
who told me, after he had passed one of them under his large and
apparently expert nose, that the exploding cigars were hundred-
dollar-apiece Havanas. "He's got class, uh, ole Phil?" he asked.

Phil Cowell, as always, sat at the top of the table in a high-backed
chair that was topped on each side by carvings of stags' heads. He was
sweating and beaming and in that baronial setting, and given his
prizefighter's shoulders and his beard, looked like a well-pleased
King Henry VIII. This was his court and these were his jesters and
his was the kingdom of the big budget. And he was bankrupting it.

All I could do, I reflected helplessly, was sit it out. In the broader
sense, the movie. In the immediate sense, the party: two birthdays
and twins demanded my steadfast presence for once. Then a cigar
went off only two or three seats down from where I was sitting and I
got up abruptly and left.

I ended up by taking a walk along the runway. I simply had to get
away from the lunacy—though I was to decide there was no escaping
it. For my solitude out there was encroached on by a young American who, preposterously, told me he was newly returned from a
bombing raid over Germany.

Two

A CLEVER-CLEVER TELEVISION DOCUMENTARY I DID ON POPULAR romantic fiction made the point that the only cosmic thing about the genre was the eclipse of the sun. Researchers dissected a number of these novels and found that virtually all of the key scenes took place in moonlight. I wrote the narration, which concluded, "The sun also rises in so-called women's stories—but only just. On average, only every eighty pages. As for the rest, it's pure moonshine . . ."

With due irony, then, I acknowledge that the moon was out when I met him that night on the runway . . .

I had thought of going to the village, but in the darkness that would have involved a stumble on rutted lanes. So the runway it was, and that near-mile stretch of asphalt was its own proof of Phil Cowell's spendthrift ways: as in some archaeological dig, it had been hacked out of the undergrowth of the years and resurfaced with asphalt. We could have hired a functioning airfield, but he wanted this one. He liked its all-American vibes, he said, overlooking the fact that it had been an RAF bomber command base. "You could string a college ukulele with those vibes. Trust me, uh, sweetie?"

Trust Phil Cowell? Striding down the runway, my hands thrust into the pockets of my old blue woollen anorak, a reliable remnant from my student days, I cursed my folly for doing just that. But he had been *so* persuasive, right from the outset.

I met him for the first time at a television awards ceremony in London and he said the little globe I had picked up was cute, but wasn't it time I switched my sights from fairground trinkets to the prizes in the big arena? He was talking Oscars, sweetie, and he had a gut feeling about my talent. He amused me, and I let him take me on to a nightclub. There, as we danced, he told me of his newest movie project. The working title was *The Last of the Good Guys* and it would encapsulate the spirit of a bygone America through the experience of a squadron of American airmen in England during the war. That movie, he swore, was his destiny, his chance to be a legend.

"As in Leonardo," he said.

"Da Vinci?" I said, twitting him.

"Is that the guy's second name?" He winked, beamed, then went on almost fiercely. "I *mean* to make a masterpiece. A *classic*. Something that'll truly define the war and the ideals it inspired through the eyes and the souls of the guys who flew in it."

"*Memphis Belle* did that."

"*Memphis Belle* wasn't the *Mona Lisa*."

He beamed and winked again, but there was no doubting the intensity of his cause. I had assumed our date would end in sex. He seduced me in another way: I signed up for his movie.

I could say he caught me at a vulnerable moment. For months I had been coordinating a planned documentary series about the political aspirations of women across the world. Only a few days before I had learnt it had been shelved. So I was in the mood to quit my job in television. Still, I believe I went for that movie because, for a time, Phil Cowell made me believe in it.

Con man! Hustler! Though even on the runway that night, I had to concede that in the pinpointing of the period at the airfield he had created a World War II time capsule. Apart from the physical layout and the old military aircraft—no scale models for Phil Cowell—the place fizzed with young men shipped in from the States and, it almost seemed, from another generation. From the style of their hair to the very set of their faces—the kind of faces you see in minor roles in American black-and-white movies of the thirties and forties—they *looked* different and were generally smaller and wirier than the young men of today. And they sounded different as they exchanged such dated slang as, "You're in the groove, Jackson," "Jeepers Peepers!" and "What's buzzin', cousin?"

These actors, more than one hundred of them, wore their GI uniforms jauntily and in the same spirit, I take it, bunked down in the draughty Quonset huts and followed orders to "think, feel, talk and scratch the war." They slept under military issue blankets, read the *Stars and Stripes* and the *Saturday Evening Post*—reprinted copies corresponding to the specific period, 1943, of the movie—shaved with old-fashioned razors, wore wind-up watches, ate the food of World War II GIs—Spam, corned beef hash, the occasional steak, a lot of ice cream—and smoked, even the non-smokers, cigarettes and cigars in the packaging of the 1940s. (A clause in their contracts meant they could not later sue for health risk.) Television was forbidden: one young man was sent home for smuggling in a tiny portable. For entertainment they relied mainly on the phonograph and, typically, offerings on old 78 records of Glenn Miller, Tommy Dorsey, the Andrews Sisters of course and Alice Faye, and, in the Stage Door Canteen, a twice-weekly showing of the "latest" movies, featuring stars like Abbot and Costello and Dorothy Lamour.

Phil Cowell defended this approach and its attendant costs—90 percent of the cast were extras and British actors would have been much cheaper—as empathy and bonding in the cause of re-creating a quintessential and vanished American spirit because the bottom line, sweetie, was that this was a renaissance picture. He actually believed that. And once or twice, when I saw the rushes, so did I. Fleetingly. His work was finely textured, evocative. But there was so *little* of it. Hey, now, not to worry, sweetie, this was no off-the-peg movie—this was a movie that was gonna be dressed in the robes of posterity.

I thought of those words as I huddled in my old anorak. I had reached the end of the runway, which gave way to arid fields. I stood there, at a loss, and tried to resist the temptation to feel sorry for myself. I could quit, of course. Now. Simply go back to the house, pack my bags, cut my losses—but also pick up a reputation for unreliability that could keep me out of movies. On the other hand, to be associ- ated with a production that clearly had no chance of recovering its costs could be just as damaging. It was a perfectly balanced dilemma, a catch-22. My career, I reflected, had no script. Just like this movie. Several million dollars had been spent on scripts from some of the top hands in Hollywood, but other than Phil Cowell no one on the set had seen their work, which he was rewriting on yellow scratch pads and, judging from the paucity of scenes shot, at the slowest possible rate. None of us knew the exact story line any longer—he kept changing it—and there was one rumor on the set that he had decided on an "extemporaneous" movie and another, even more dismaying, that he actually was intent on a glorious flop that would give him bad-boy celebrity in Hollywood, a town that, though grudging, has not lost its residual respect for truly egregious behavior, as long as it's classy enough. For once in my life, I had no idea what to do.

I shivered suddenly; I had stood there too long and now I felt the full chill of the night in which the thin overcast of the sky showed the drifting frosty sheen of a concealed moon. I shrugged, pulled up the hood of my anorak, and began my walk back. It seemed a long way. A trudge. And it didn't help when the moon emerged through the clouds.

And then the moonlight broadened, became as bright as a flarepath and struck a small apprehension in me as it showed a still figure about thirty or forty yards ahead. I made out a man. He stood on the edge of the runway, to the left of the center on which I was walking.

I couldn't be sure immediately, but I thought he might be in uniform. I saw the outline of a peaked cap and what could have been a flying jacket. In which case he was only one of the actors and therefore too self-absorbed—that was my convenient reasoning—to be any kind of a nuisance.

Only he was looking at me. Intently. I saw that as I got closer. At the same time his right hand was extended at about the level of his chin and, the way his hand moved swiftly, I had the curious feeling that he was taking notes. Then I was near enough to see that he was holding a pad and that he did indeed seem to be writing on it.

I saw too (it shone in the moonlight) the metal US Eighth Air Force insignia in the middle of his cap and I knew for sure he was an actor. Just another face in the cast of bit players and extras. A face I scarcely looked at when, as I passed him, I inclined my head in the merest acknowledgment.

Almost at once he called after me. "It's me. Johnny."

His tone was harmless, a mild bemusement which implied we already knew each other and I had failed to recognize him. It occurred to me that probably we had met, though only in the tenuous circumstances of a minor second-unit take on the set—I had worked with most of the cast—and now that encounter had been inflated to friendship by his actor's ego.

I'd had enough of egos that night, thank you, and so I didn't even bother to turn my head. I quickened my pace to a cool briskness that was meant to distance him socially.

And then he caught up with me and he was by my side and falling in step with me with a familiarity I took as audacity. Though for a while, as he tagged along, he said nothing.

Nor did I. Exploding cigars and the totality of my ensuing demoralization seemed to have stunted my flair for the put-down that could have gotten rid of him or at least asserted my lead in the situation. All I was up to was cold aloofness, the contempt of ignoring him. Or seeming to. Circumspectly, from the cover of my hood, I eyed him. He was smaller than I imagined when I first saw him on the runway and when, though that was no more than an affronted glance, he

joined me. At most he was five nine and, even in the bulk of his flying jacket, slim. A lean face, a high forehead. Mid twenties, I supposed. A bit older than the rest of the cast. Then I had a momentary
impression—it took me unawares—that he was without the raw
boyishness of the other actors and that in him I sensed a seniority, a
matureness, a . . . Come on! He was a nonentity called Johnny and
anyone with such a mom's-apple-pie name had to be thoroughly
gauche. Thus I checked the onset of a wandering reflective interest
in him. But almost immediately I was musing on the fact that I didn't
at the moment recognize him, that I wasn't able to place him in the
ranks of the cast, and I had seen those faces every day for months.
Still, I hadn't exactly studied them, had I? They were the extras, at
most the one-liners, and I viewed them no more than peripherally.

On that reasoning note, my small curiosity faded—but returned a
moment or two later when he lit a cigarette. I glanced, in reflex, as
his lighter flared. As he lowered his head slightly, the flame showed
clearly an S-shaped scar on the right side of his face. The scar looped
diagonally from the middle of his cheek to the corner of his mouth
and from there to the edge of his jawbone. It was distinctive, almost
ornamental, like an insignia. None of the actors had such a scar. Or
not that I could remember right then. Besides, a scar—such a cliche!
Even so, I was curious.

He flicked the lighter shut and my renewed inclination to place
him in my memory was forestalled when, almost immediately, he
spoke to me.

"I'd sure value your opinion," he said. (Or something close to
that; my paraphrasing takes over at this point.) He was holding out to
me the pad I had seen in his hand only moments before. I hesitated.
Then, with a shrug of remote condescension, I took the pad; after
exploding cigars, I told myself, I might just as well face up to the rest
of the bad joke of the night.

The pad turned out to be a small rectangle of white cardboard,
about eight inches long and four across, and on it, courtesy of the
simpering moonlight, I recognized at once a pencil sketch of myself.

True, he had transposed my humble anorak into a hooded cloak and though my face was little more than a blank outline my mood was fully visible: in a fluency of simple lines he had caught not just the full extent of my head-down look but also, it seemed to me, all the uncertainties that had caused me to be out there that night. Even his rendering of the runway, flowing behind and ahead of me in a few telling strokes, appeared to place me at a crossroads.

Finally, and I must have gazed at it for some moments, I looked up. Indifferently, I thought, but almost at once I was aware that in my concentration on his work my footsteps had slowed and I had lost the paced advantage of disdain. That didn't seem to matter so much now. I was still holding the drawing.

"So," he said, "is it any good?" I picked up on the quiet anxiety behind his question and knew that a smirk on my part—a tight, contemptuous little smirk—would be an easy way of scoring points. Too easy. Too cheap. I owed more to myself, and maybe even to him, than that; perhaps I owed honesty.

"It . . ." I paused for an instant, reconsidered the tempting smirk. Rejected it. "It has a certain quality of perception."

"You mean that?" In seeming jubilation, he tilted his cap back on his head. "Of course you mean it! You've always been straight with me about my work. And I really tried with this one. I did what you taught me right from the start—to look *into* and not *at*. Guess maybe I brought it off this time. Just a lucky break. I don't kid myself that I'll ever be in your league as an artist."

I looked at him. Had he really mistaken me for someone else? Or was this a gambit, a play for my attention? He looked back at me and smiled—an open, non-opportunistic smile. I reminded myself that he was an actor.

"Very first time we met you were wearing that cloak," he said. "Out here on the runway too. Same hour, I guess. Same old moon."

Same old bullshit! I implied that verdict in the curt turn of my head, though immediately I found myself gazing down at his drawing and its fine execution of lines and the way they accreted in a seeming interpretation of my brooding. I didn't want to appear too interested, though, and since the other side of the cardboard had a soft feel I turned it to see what was there. It was a section of map behind a transparent laminated cover. A circle crossed by three red dots had been drawn in the middle of the map and at the top, on the left, the name Bremerhaven had been written and underlined.

"That's where we were tonight," he said, tapping the map with his finger. "Bremerhaven. The flak was heavy and we had to make two runs before we sighted the marshalling yards. Our target. On the way home we were jumped by night fighters over the Dutch coast. We came back with a slice of the tailplane shot away."

Actors, I thought. Role immersion. They were children. Though this one—my concession took me by surprise—was quite a likeable child.

"On our future missions, I figure we're gonna have better luck with you as our figurehead," he said.

"Me?"

"Moonmaiden," he said, taking the drawing from my hand. "We fly by night and so the name's right. I'm having the stencils done in the morning and next time we take off you'll be on the side of the ship."

"Thank you, kind sir." Let him have his little game; it was better than exploding cigars.

"I've had it in mind for some time—I wanted it to be a surprise—and when I spotted you tonight I had this hunch that the moment was right to do the drawing. I also have another hunch—that Madge is gonna be trouble. I mean, I'm gonna have to write and tell her. And you know what Madge is like."

"I'll take your word for that." Was I, I wondered, humoring a drunk?

"It's just that it means a lot to her—being up there on the side of the ship as Miss Scarlett." (Scarlett with two t's, as I was subsequently to discover.)

"I suppose we all need our place in life," I said: What on earth was he talking about?

"Still," he went on, "the rest of the guys are all in favor of the new name—I can 'fess up now and tell you we've discussed it for some time—though Harry, and I don't have to tell you how Harry rags me, says it oughta be Miss Emily." He chuckled. "Can you just imagine Emily Brontë riding the nose of a B17?"

"If she's the Emily Brontë I have in mind, I think she has altitude enough in *Wuthering Heights*!" I laughed, though not at what I said; I laughed at his nonsense. For once lonely and off-guard, I needed to laugh that night, needed, however briefly, the silly and simple "let's pretend" company that only an actor could offer. And of course he had to be an actor: with that obvious explanation, I entered further into what I saw as a mere diversion.

We walked on slowly and he talked of his "ship" and his crew (he spoke warmly of the Harry he had already mentioned) and his regular visits to the village of Haworth (he claimed to be doing some kind of literary research there into the lives of the Brontë sisters) and the volatile ways of the girl back home in Atlanta, the Madge who fancied herself as Miss Scarlett.

I thought I was lightly amused. Looking back, I realize I was hugely, and quite irrationally, happy. Happier than I had ever been before in my life.

Until then I had counted happiness as professional triumph and the spoils of a private life in which I always had to be better in bed than any man. I am not claiming any moral redemption as a result of that night and what it betokened; I am simply putting it down as fact.

Likewise it's a fact that I thought I was content enough to have his company merely as far as the ornamental iron gate of the house. A telling little thing happened at that gate, though, or so it seems in retrospect. The lock had a tiresome idiosyncrasy in which the brass handle needed to be turned sharply twice to the left and then a slow half turn to the right before the gate would open; even so, it never opened at once—everyone had complained about this—and a lot of fiddling was involved. He, though, in a way that suggested the familiarity of long practice, made those movements with the handle and the gate opened immediately. But what registered at the moment was that he seemed to expect—the way he stood against the open gate to let me go first—to enter the grounds with me and then wondered, almost gravely polite, if I would like to carry on to his room in the house to listen to the new phonograph records he had received from the States only the day before. I smiled and thanked him for escorting me back, said good night, formalized that farewell with a handshake and eased the gate closed on him.

I stepped out briskly up the gravel drive.

There must have been a relative lull in the partying in the great hall for I could hear the Andrews Sisters singing the finale to the "Boogie Woogie Bugle Boy from Company B." At that distance the words were muted and seemed to mist the night with nostalgia, the echoes of a remote era.

The song ended. I paused, considered, then turned and looked back—and he was still standing there in front of the gate. Maybe it was because the Andrews Sisters had now struck up with "Chattanooga Choo Choo"—they were warbling the opening down-the-track whistles—that he struck me as having the lost air of someone stranded at a railway station after the last train of the night had gone.

Actors! I picked up my pace and headed firmly for the house.

I didn't sleep that night. I blamed the noise of the party, five floors below, and when that stopped I blamed the dense silence of the old house.

Finally, I put on the bedside light. Three fifty-five. I looked around my room, with its sloped ceiling and oak beams, and decided anew that the wallpaper, with its motif of cherries and purple plums, was hideous. I switched on the transistor radio and tried to take an intelligent interest in a talk on the BBC World Service about the geopolitics of Greenland. I snapped it off. I picked up *Shaw's Collected Essays,* which had entertained me well enough the night before. I gave up after a page.

"Actors!" I said aloud. And finally acknowledged the cause of my insomnia.

With that dismissal, I turned off the light. But, as if darkness had endorsed a total and spontaneous honesty, I remembered instantly what I had been suppressing—the beauty of his hands. That beauty was apparent to me when he handed me the drawing and, a few moments later, when he pointed out the details on the map on the other side. Such slender hands, the fingers long and semi-squared at the tips, the thumbs unknobbled. There were no lies in those hands. No cheating. No menace.

I was ten years old when my uncle and legal guardian—I was an only child and my parents had died in a ridiculous yachting accident on Lake Windermere—pressed his hands to my nascent breasts. I was in my room, wearing a cotton slip his wife had made for me. That's all he did, before sidling out of the room, his finger to his lips as if we were sealed in an oath; he was a magistrate. He had pressed my breasts in hard, circular motions—I remember the black hairs on the knuckles of his fingers—as if moulding me to the kind of person I became: tough, self-sufficient, skeptical. I am not invoking trauma over that incident, which occurred as I was packing to return to boarding school, but I did go on to become a wary observer of men's hands. To this day, they are the first thing I look at in a man.

And tonight, I had seen perfect hands. Could it be (I was drifting into a fractured sleep and open to naive and unguarded questions) that all my life, as a result of what happened to me as a child, I had been searching for trustworthy hands? Hands I could reach out to openly and without doubt?

Nonsense! I drew back from sleep to rebut that gaucherie. But the late hour and the darkness were their own tribunal and I, a drowsy witness, conceded that those hands had essayed the rest of him in a symmetry that flowed from his broad forehead to a straight nose that was almost feminine in its lines and—a wry nod to the romantic novelists of the world as I write this—what was known as a strong mouth, the strength somehow all the greater because of that S-shaped scar. His eyes, I imagined, were hazel, though I couldn't be sure. Who was he?

I'd find out at first light. Shortly after dawn, as he had every day for almost the last month, Phil Cowell would be resuming his bid for the perfect ensemble shot: a slow pan of the actors as they stood, from one wingtip to the other, against a B17. This shot was for the opening credit sequences. Every member of the cast was in it. So he *had* to be there . . .

Three

YOUNG FACES. AMERICAN FACES. DEAD FACES. THE WHITE GLARE of the arc lights gave the actors a stiff and embalmed look, an exaggerated pallor in which pink cheeks—and it was a frosty morning—stood out like the cosmetic ministrations of the funeral parlor and eyes seemed fixed and staring and final.

The men were lined up rigidly to meet the requirements of the first phase of the shot: a slow pan of their inertia and then a repeat of the process to show them relaxed and wisecracking.

It was a good, imaginative opening to the movie, or it would be if Phil Cowell ever got round to considering costs and putting it in the can. But that morning I had no time for such considerations—my concern was that the young man on the runway last night was not part of this fully assembled cast.

He *had* to be. Standing on the podium next to the center camera, I began yet again to examine those faces, one by one . . .

I had turned up in front of the B17 a little before six thirty, while it was still dark, merging with the technicians and the other assistants as they set up the scene. At that stage, the actors were arriving. They

were checked in by floor staff who ticked off their names on clip-
boards and made sure that their appearances—some had to be in full
flying dress, others only partly so; some had to be newly shaved and
others had to have a day's growth—were correct. They were then
shown to their appointed positions where assistant directors re-
coached them briefly and urgently on posture and attitude and all the
other things Phil Cowell had decided were missing from yesterday's
takes.

Twenty minutes after my arrival the arcs were turned on, clamp-
ing the scene in incandescence, defining every face uncompromis-
ingly: as a mug shot, as a corpse.

And he wasn't there.

He *had* to be. With this insistence, I kept doing my re-check, my
survey of a human map ranging from the broad country boy faces of
the Midwest to the narrowed, knowing ones of the big cities on the
eastern seaboard, telling myself to go more slowly, reminding myself
that I was tired and so felt the cold more keenly and therefore my
attention was "off".

I also tried to believe that last night's encounter was today's
detached curiosity, that I simply wanted to take a look at the man
who had disarmed me for a little while the night before and, as it
were, put him in a frame, so that the silliness of the night could be
challenged by the reality of the morning.

Only he wasn't there.

At seven, and as I continued with my search, the star, Joel Merton,
was in place dead center under the B17's perspex nose; he had swaggered onto the set a few minutes earlier, surrounded by a retinue of
makeup and wardrobe staff, exploiting his prerogative to be the last
actor to arrive. He, too, stayed in a Quonset hut, though on a daily
hardship allowance that would have rented two or three times over
the best penthouse suite at The Savoy.

At five past seven Phil Cowell ambled into sight, wearing a beige
shoulder cape—he really thought he was Orson Welles reincar-
nated—over his brown corduroy jacket. As ever, he was beaming: no
doubt his pre-breakfast snort of cocaine had cleared up last night's

hangover. "Swell day for it," he said, looking up at a dawn sky as gray as a freight yard. "Swell day." His movie, he said, would present war as a cold emotional winter, which was why we were in York-shire at that inhospitable time of year.

As he sat down in his director's chair he got a "Hail to the Chief" in the form of megaphone announcements from the young graduates of film school who now became town criers in this little community of make-believe—"Director present!" "Quiet on the set!" "Stand by for take one!"

The clapper boy moved in front of the center camera as Phil Cowell swept the lineup with his hand-held viewfinder. I went up to the chief floor manager. "There's an actor missing," I said.

"No way."

"I tell you . . ."

He held up the master clipboard. "Listen," he said, "there's one hundred and eleven names here. Entire cast. And every one is ticked off. All present and correct."

"He has a scar, three or four inches long, at the side of his face. An S-shaped scar."

"I don't care if he has the Stars and Stripes on his butt, we still got a full turnout here."

I stayed to watch the first take. It was abandoned after less than a minute when Phil Cowell decided that an actor near to Joel Merton needed a pimple on his nose to prevent any diminishment of Merton's smooth good looks. "Kid with the lucky rabbit foot hanging round his neck. Handsome kid, in a boondocks way. We need him just where he is, between those two plainer guys, but he comes into frame just before Joel so why don't we give him a pimple to bring out the, uh, pubescence—the country boy juices—in him, uh? Pimple on the bridge of his nose, I figure."

Normally, I would have been exasperated by this typical prodigal-ity—one pimple was costing many thousands of dollars in production time—but as the makeup team moved in with tubes and brushes I instead reflected, as indeed I had during the night, that the scar could have been manufactured. Even so, there was no one in that whole

lineup who looked like him. There were some of his approximate
height and build, but none, scar or otherwise, who resembled him
facially. And, of course, the floor manager was right—the whole cast
was present. I turned and walked away.

It was, I reasoned, an interloper I had met last night, possibly a
film-struck individual who had read about the making of the movie
and was scouting the chances of work as an extra. It was just the kind
of thing an out-of-work actor would do. Or a simple crank. Or an
out-and-out madman. There was no shortage of such persons. I
wondered also, though doubting it from the start, if it had been a
hoax by the crew. But to what point? If they had wanted to do that
they would have devised something much richer than a stranger
accosting me on the runway. I decided to forget it all.

What I could not ignore was the drizzle of tiredness and headache
that moved in on me as I made my way to the apron in front of the
control tower where the members of the second unit, shuffling in
front of a Mitchell bomber, waited to resume work on a sequence of
scenes once the six or seven actors involved were freed from the
ensemble shot with the B17.

I had set up those scenes several weeks earlier, after coaxing pages
of script out of Phil Cowell. Since then, the second unit had assembled daily, like a platoon behind the front line, waiting for the release
of its modest squad of actors held hostage to Phil Cowell's ego. The
scenes involved some detailed aircraft interiors and exteriors and so
the movie's technical consultant, Colonel Bob Crinkle, was in full-
time attendance.

I arrived as he was demonstrating the niceties of entering and exit-
ing the Mitchell through its belly hatch. As he levered himself up, he
curved his back and rolled inside. A moment later, he emerged with
similar fluidity, bouncing lightly on his heels. He was seventy-six.
The crew applauded in a scattered way and Colonel Crinkle did a
mock bow.

He was small, as trim as a swagger stick. A fighter pilot in the war,
he had gone on to establish himself as a military historian. Consider-

ing the way he leapt nimbly in and out of aircraft, he could also have passed off as a stuntman.

In fact, he was a lumbering old bore.

In our early days in Yorkshire he had lectured us, a formal lecture in the great hall, on the history of the base and why Phil Cowell had been so right to follow his blind hunch and set his movie there. (The lecture must have been Phil Cowell's doing.) For though home to an RAF bomber squadron, he said, the base had the *most crucial* (he was free with his italics) link with US Eighth Air Force. No doubt we knew—his arch lecturer's manner implied that perhaps we didn't— that during the war the RAF bombed by night in Europe and the Eighth Air Force by day. With *one* exception. A pause. *Here. On this base.* From here, a lone B17, a Flying Fortress, crewed by "American boys," had flown in a liaison and familiarization role with the RAF as a contingency in case the overall strategy was switched—an option that was forever under review by Supreme Command—and the British started to bomb by day and the Americans by night. That B17 flew sixty-one missions—*sixty-one,* he repeated—as it fulfilled a role instigated, and closely monitored, by both Churchill and Eisenhower. Another pause, to let this magnitude sink in. Any questions?

None. We were bored. And though the lecture was over, the boredom had only just begun. Colonel Crinkle was his very own drone zone on the subject of the war and promised us "more insights" into the history of the American presence on the base the moment he uncovered them. He was unfailingly amiable, but such was his tedium, especially after he'd had a few drinks, that at dinner in the great hall there was an informal rota system in which we'd take turns sitting next to him in order that no one should suffer disproportionately.

Now, though, on the second-unit set, I had been stuck with him for long stretches on a daily basis as we waited for the actors. So as I slouched in the control tower that day I was, more than usual, in no mood to take Colonel Crinkle, especially since I knew exactly what to expect. For true to his word, he had indeed come up with "more insights" into the base. His scuttlings in the mouse runs of research had led to his discovery of a room in the house given over to World War II memorabilia, most of it, he said, American.

He genuinely could not understand why his enthusiasm over the find was not shared by anyone else. Two or three members of the crew, humoring him on account of his years, had gone along to see the room. Though there was no doubt he had expected whole groups, like visitors to an ancient site.

He wasn't giving up, however. The obstinacy of age and the passion of his calling as historian had given a new dimension to his boredom. "But it's *history*!" I would hear him insist as he lobbied his glazed companions at dinner, and I would be glad not to be sitting there.

For the last three or four weeks, though, I had been totally exposed to Colonel Crinkle and no matter what my evasions—script pages to be studied, a camera angle to be carefully and needlessly checked—and no matter what his general talk about the technicalities of the scene to hand I knew he was waiting to renew his obsession with that room.

"At first glance, I grant you, it's not much to look at. Kinda small. But I know you'll find it fascinating, my dear."

He looked at me expectantly that morning and his enthusiasm seemed to shine in his deep tan—he lived in Arizona—and sparkle in the silver of his perfectly squared crew cut. We were seated on canvas chairs around a card table in the control tower. He had joined me there, bearing a flask of coffee and doughnuts. About two weeks ago, in a bid to assuage his rambling about that damned room, I had half-promised to go and take a look sometime. Now, obliquely, he was reminding me of that. "You'll find it a most rewarding experience, my dear."

My dear! Sweetie from Phil Cowell and my dear from this old man: I was sick of the patronage. I was sick of everything that day, especially myself. I saw my headache and fatigue as unforgivable weakness; I wasn't a headachy-and-tired person. Meantime, it was getting colder and there was no heating in the control tower. Through the windows, the arc lights at the other side of the airfield, where the ensemble shot ground on, reared in the shape and hard white burn of an iceberg and on that glacial surface Colonel Crinkle's voice seemed to slither and tug at my nerve ends as if they were tow-ropes.

". . . Okay, that room's a jumble, but war's a jumble. Right? Poke around up there and you'll find, as well as the RAF stuff, *personal* evidence of the American boys. Birthday cards. Letters. Cables. Clippings from old newspapers. Photographs. Things like that. Now if I'm boring you, my dear, just holler for me to stop."

"Stop," I said. Quietly. A plea.

"Uh?" He smiled. "Why, there's even an Eighth Air Force issue bible there imbedded with a chunk of shrapnel and—"

"I said *stop*."

"So what gives, my dear?" He was still smiling, puckishly amused, and that released a shrillness in me, though my next words were stone hard.

"What gives, since you ask, is that you *are* boring me. You bore *everyone*. Without exception. In fact, Colonel, if boredom had a rank you would be a five-star general."

He blinked, and I noticed how blue and childlike his eyes were. He blinked a second time, as if to scoot the smile that for a moment or two, out of sync with realization, had hung uncertainly around his mouth.

"I see," he said.

He got up, stood erect, his fingertips on the edge of the table. Irrelevantly, it struck me that even in his padded mauve-and-yellow track suit and his trainers he was managing to look ambassadorial.

"Do please excuse me," he said. And left.

I groaned. Why hadn't I just hit him on the head with something hard?

The actors turned up a couple of hours later and we actually got in a fair amount of work. Colonel Crinkle took care to avoid looking at me. The final scene of the day was that of the belly entrance into the Mitchell bomber, but in his demonstration he lacked his earlier aplomb; he miscalculated as he hauled himself up and for a moment his skinny legs flayed from the hatch and his loss of dignity blazed in the exposure of a vivid tartan sock and the chalky old man's flesh above it. Still, we completed the scene on only the fifth take.

By way of amends, I made a point of thanking him for his help. He said he was only doing his job and besides—his smile had a thrown-together look—he hadn't exactly made a ballet dancer's leap into that bomber, had he? He paused. "Guess I'm getting old," he said. And I had a sudden guilty thought that until a few hours ago he had never contemplated that possibility.

At dinner I noticed he said practically nothing and left early. Let him sulk! But I came to realize, though this took perhaps two weeks, that he wasn't sulking. We all have our illusions about ourselves and I believe he, with his researcher's thoroughness, had taken a conscientious look at his self-standing as captivating company and natural raconteur and had seen the truth—that he was old and a bore. Now he was tedious in another way, in his diffidence. He was polite and helpful to me on the set, and we had a few more days together, but he was strangely quiet. It was the same at dinner. A few words if someone said something to him, otherwise silence. At first everyone was relieved, then gradually discomfited. They also started to miss the one part of his showing off he was admired for—his way of consistently hitting the jackpot on the fruit machine in the great hall. He put this down to mentally researching the sequence and frequency of the combinations and a crowd would gather round him to see if they could learn from his method. Now the crew were talking better than even odds that the "old guy" was sickening for something. One night even Phil Cowell and the unit doctor made a point of sitting next to him at dinner.

And that's when I decided, though not without a certain exasperation, to visit his dreary war room—a penance instead of an apology.

It was too late to say sorry now, and in any case I've never apologized for anything; it's a trait I picked up in boarding school when I realized the nuns were intent on promoting subservience rather than intelligence. Still, I could mention to him that I had been to the room, throw in one or two details, fake enthusiasm, and perhaps jolly him out of his present state. I was prepared to make that compromise.

I went to the room that night, after dinner. And he was right—it was fascinating. Though not in the sense that he had in mind, or could even have conceived.

Four

THE ROOM WAS ON THE THIRD FLOOR OF THE EAST WING, THE
last door on the corridor: Colonel Crinkle had impressed the location
on me ad nauseam. A brown door, smaller than any of the others,
and oval at the top. I opened it and a smell like dry leaves reminded
me of the times I had spent in the Latin legal archives at Oxford.

I felt for a light switch on the inside wall. I had to work the switch
three or four times before a ceiling bulb glowed feebly from the
recesses of a perfectly dreadful multi-layered shade of tortoiseshell
colors and configurations.

The current was faulty, an endemic failing in that house, and it
whirred like a time exposure on a camera as the room formed round
me like a sepia print.

It wasn't a big room and it was circular. It had two slatted windows and I realized it had to be one of the house's turrets. I shrugged,
started my little inspection.

I took in a framed painting on the wall to my right of a camou-
flaged bomber. Under the painting was a small table, its surface

crammed with bits and pieces. A flying helmet. Goggles. A compass. What looked like a gun for firing distress flares. Things like that.

A small stack of newspapers, yellow and brittle as old straw, was at the side of the table. I picked up the top paper and its edges flaked in my fingers. I took it under the light so I could read it better and I saw it was the *Stars and Stripes,* dated May 15, 1942, and banner head-lined CORREGIDOR FALLS TO JAPS! I put it back on the stack.

The wall to my right was crowded with photographs that were tacked on felt boards. I could see they were of men in uniform, but in that scant light I couldn't make out any details. I tetched. No doubt this twilight might have been part of the room's mystique for Colonel Crinkle, but he was a silly old man adrift in the fog of the past. Or certainly he was well and truly adrift now. And that was my fault. I can't be sure that I actually made that acknowledgment, but I changed my mind about leaving after a perfunctory look-see. I deter-mined that I was damn well going to find something a mite more specific than what I had so far seen; it was—I've always been tena-cious—a tiny personal challenge.

There was a longish metal container on the floor; it looked like a drawer from a filing cabinet, and it was uncovered and showed a lumpy and indeterminate sprawl of contents. It was more or less in line with the light and, with my hands and the shovings of my foot, I edged it over until it was directly under the bulb.

Kneeling by the container, I began to sift through what was in it. The first thing I saw was a military ordnance map of England date-stamped 1942. I moved on to log books, a diary (empty) for 1943, a wallet (empty except for a dollar bill and a photograph of a pretty girl in a sweater and bobby sox), then—and that was something positive to mention to Colonel Crinkle—a few old gramophone records in brown sleeves, including one of the Andrews Sisters, the originals, singing "Don't Sit Under the Apple Tree with Anyone Else but Me." A small blue bundle, I unfurled it, turned out to be a beauty queen sash. MISS SEATTLE 1940. The words, once a gaudy wing flash of youth, were now faint and spectral under a feathering of dust.

I wondered, and still do, why such riffraff memorabilia had been stored and retained. Sentiment? A hoarding for hoarding's sake? (God knows, that house was full of junk.) But I have an enquiring mind, it comes with my tenacity, and I pressed on through that container and its hectic and hodgepodge history.

Betty Grable was on the cover of a calendar for 1943 and she was aiding the war effort in a pose in which she fastened a black suspender belt on one of those legendary million dollar legs and, her head raised, she pouted, the tip of her tongue on her lower lip. The baseball player Joe DiMaggio flashed an all-American grin in an autographed photo. An unopened package of nylons was labelled Sheerly Yours, 35 cents. A large menu for Ricky's Diner in Thunder City, Colorado, advertised Gala Dinner, New Year's Eve, 1942, and was inscribed to "Walt, in old England" and scrawled over with dozens of signatures. A booklet was entitled "Over There—a Guide for the GI in Wartime Britain." A Western Union cable—curiously, I remember its exact words—was now, in its message, an age-yellowed certificate of superannuated passion: *Married Brad in Reno tonight stop Forget about me and find a nice English girl stop But I will always love you stop Arlene.*

So it went on—the past as an amusing enough cartoon strip, a diverting enough collage. And then I saw an old oil painting.

At first, I merely glanced at the painting, the latest job lot in the miscellany uncovered by my briskly moving fingers. Then I took it out. It was small, about ten inches by six, and unframed. The canvas had been fixed to a thin wooden backing by tacks that were now rust-blurred. It was a head and shoulders study of a young man.

I recognized him instantly. I would have known him, I think, even without the S-shaped scar on the side of his face.

Though on television I trashed pulp romantic fiction, it occurs to me now that a stock maidenly gasp and a heart flutter were my due as I looked at the painting. Instead, I was utterly detached.

I honestly can't remember any initial reaction—no bewilderment, not even a momentary surprise—and all I can venture is that my total matter-of-factness was my instinctive way of avoiding larger questions.

Those questions were addressed later by an eminent physicist—a Nobel laureate, no less—I sought out at Cambridge. Among other things, he mentioned a specific Einstein quotation which I have never forgotten: "Adults never question time and space. Children do. My secret is that I remain a child." And although I am drawn to the simplicity of those words and what they imply and encompass, I cannot pretend to any childlike virtues—not even when I was a child did I have any—and in the room that night, looking down at that painting in my hands, I was my knowing and adult self.

I remember thinking I was right in my earlier surmise about the color of his eyes—the painting showed them to be hazel—though this seemed at the time no more than neutral observation, a technical note in a general appraisal of the picture.

The paint was old and in places cracked, but it had been applied with skill and feeling and in the sitter—and that's how I thought of him at that moment, as *the sitter*—the artist had discerned and interpreted a quiet grace, almost a serenity. Again, this was my dispassionate critique. An analysis. He was not, in the accepted sense, good-looking, but what he lacked in ruggedness and any other standard male attribute was supplanted by the strength of that understated grace—there in his eyes, in the slight inclining of his head, in a half-smile that self-deprecated his role as the object of the artist's attention.

This, I must repeat, is what I saw in a balanced way and not what I *felt* on any personal level of involvement. Not then. Or not that I was prepared to concede then. I concentrated on the art itself and, from this focus, approved of the way the artist had neither toned down the scar nor tried to embellish it as some evidence of male derring-do. It was there as a simple fact, part of the total honesty of the painting, along with his cap, worn slightly to the side, the beige of his collar and tie and the twin silver bars on the lapels of his jacket. The artist had understood him. The artist, I felt strongly, was a woman.

I looked for a signature, found only the initials A.M. They were written at the foot of the painting, on the right. In the middle, the work had been titled and dated—*Johnny. February 1943.*

Johnny. The letters were small and, against the wash of the paint, hard to make out at first. But they were there and unmistakable—just as surely as the fact that I had, after all, been hoaxed. I wanted to believe that, wanted to slap the backs of those who had devised it and be a general good sport about their ingenuity.

Simultaneously, though, I knew there had been no hoax. I knew, an inner certitude, that this young man in the painting was the same young man I had met that night on the runway. No one had tricked me into going to that room. I was there entirely of my own volition and as a result of perfectly logical and straightforward circumstances.

Still, I resisted. Rationalized. I told myself that while I did not for one moment doubt the authenticity of the painting and that someone called Johnny had indeed sat for it back in 1943, he was simply like hundreds of thousands of others who had been in the war and no more mysterious than the young men in the photographs on the wall.

I glanced over at those photographs and, quite against my will, wondered if his face might be among them, though the withered light of the room ruled out a search. But, a nagging, *was* his photograph there? A corroboration of the painting. A double check in another perspective of my memory of the young man on the runway. The further proof that all of this was too elaborate to be a hoax.

Nonsense! I put the painting back in the container, made an efficient show of rubbing my hands together to get rid of the dust and, satisfied with the conclusion of my finale, left the room and went upstairs to bed. It was time to be firm with myself.

About half an hour later I was back in that room in my robe and carrying the flashlight I kept at the bedside table against the frequent power failures of the house. I shone the flashlight on the wall of photographs.

There were scores of them, possibly more than a hundred, and they were mounted in tiers.

At first the beam showed me only shot after shot of young men in RAF uniform. They seemed to have regarded the camera as an instrument of official inspection, for whatever the settings—aircraft, a sports field, a bar, the house itself—they tended to a correctness in which they lined up in semi-formal poses in which no one lounged, no one had his hands in his pockets or a button undone. The effect suggested a protocol, though it may have been no more than an unfamiliarity in those days with casual photography, in which even their smiles, precise and standard, were "on duty".

Not so, though, the young man who lounged across the wing of an aircraft as he played a harmonica. His legs were spread-eagled and his flying jacket was open to reveal a white vest decorated with the outline of a slinky nude. He was at ease with the camera and had given the photographer a slow wink.

Another shot: young men in a dice game. They were in full flying gear and one of them held aloft a fistful of money as he blew for luck on the dice in the open palm of his other hand. He wore a baseball cap back to front.

I had reached the American section of the photographs and it was a cultural crossing point, an expansive spread of high spirits.

Other young men arm wrestled, spun girls in the jitterbug, were jaunty even as they climbed at night, laden with parachutes and Mae West life vests, into an aircraft, and gave the thumbs-up sign, blew kisses and winked and generally behaved like gladiators who chewed gum.

The photographs were highly professional and had obviously been taken by someone—the artist whose initials were A. M.?—with a creative sense of composition. They were finely focused and pin-pointed the small details that would not have been seen in amateur snapshots—the dots on the dice, the defined sinews of the arm wrestlers, the black seams on the silk stockings of the jitterbugging girls.

And the S-shaped scar at the side of the mouth of one of those young men.

He was there, suddenly, in the beam of my flashlight. His face was

full on and the scar was like a tiny clasp that fastened his face into a
slight, but not unpleasing, lopsidedness.

I moved the flashlight forward until its beam circled his face
tightly and I held it there for some moments, as if in a clinical probe.
That's how I felt—clinical. Forensic. An analytical examiner of the
evidence. And, prima facie, the evidence was that this was the same
young man in the portrait—*and* the same young man I had encoun-
tered on the runway.

I moved the flashlight back, for a fuller view, and saw that the
photograph was one of a block of about a dozen, grouped closely
together. Above the photographs a caption was written on a strip of
cardboard: Miss Scarlett's Boys. (I noted the two t's.) Below those
photographs, apparently the same faces were ranged in a bigger and
longer shot against the silver fuselage of an aircraft. He headed that
lineup, and stood at the nose, more or less directly under a pin-up
illustration. The pin-up was clearly visible and identified in swaggering script as Miss Scarlett. I moved my torch in closer. Miss Scarlett
was represented, in the main, by an elaborate picture hat and long
legs. The legs emerged from the slits of a billowing gown and the
enveloping brim of the hat swept all the way down to the waist in an
intermingling of ribbons and tresses in which the only evidence of a
face was a nose which peek-a-booed beyond the hat's brim.

Madge. No doubt I remembered the homespun name he had
mentioned on the runway that night because it contrasted so with
that flamboyant figure painted on the side of the aircraft: wasn't
Madge the Scarlett O'Hara *manqué,* wannabe, he had spoken of? I
mused on these lines for a moment or two, perhaps because I needed
a pause from the overall implications of the photograph. Then I drew
the beam back from the pin-up so I had the overall view again.

His ship. His crew. His girl. About the first general thing they
taught me in law studies at Oxford—the law was my original choice
of career—was to simplify facts by marshalling them as tightly as possible and that's what I did now as a means of asserting my intellectual
self and repudiating a tiresome little instinct that *something* had happened to me. I wanted to sniff, to be scathing, to be lightly amused.

Instead, I found myself aware of his quiet presence and the way, in spite of his youth, he was somehow, and in the best sense, patriarchal as he *presided* in that group shot. He was fully uniformed, including his cap. The others wore their uniforms incompletely—some had on sweaters in place of jackets and several were wearing baseball caps. From a lifetime away, they all grinned.

Each man had written his first name above his head. "Johnny . . ." I moved the beam in close. It was a mature hand, though not without flourish; the loop of the "y" ran as a line under the preceding letters. I looked at the rest of the names. Harry, Don, Rick, Dante, Mo and all the others. They were signatories to a self-evident pack of brotherhood that was underwritten by that honor-roll of grins.

I "borrowed" that photograph that night. In fact, those grins are displayed on my desk now, here in Beverly Hills. Why that one and not the other? I really don't know; perhaps his signature gave it an extra personal dimension for me. All I can say for sure is that the impulse to take it was as sudden and sharp as the tug by which I dislodged it free from its thumbtacks. In a peculiar way, I felt that photograph *belonged* to me.

Still, it's theft. Though on the credit side of my character, at breakfast the next morning I completed my duty to Colonel Crinkle by telling him I had been to see his room. I made a point of joining him as he stood in line at the buffet and, suitably casual, mentioned my visit. He was reserved and awkward to begin with, but as I chatted on about what I had seen, including the portrait and the photographs, he warmed up.

"I have plans for that room, my dear," he said.

"Really?" We were seated by then.

"Oh, yes." He raised his glass of orange juice as if in a toast. "I mean to make a detailed inventory of what's there. After that, I'll identify the American boys who were based here, no problem there, and then I'll set out to relate those bits and pieces upstairs to individual lives in the cause of, well, completeness. So many unanswered questions. Who, for example, was sent that Miss Seattle sash and how important was that young lady to his life? There's no clue to his identity. Who, something else you talked about, got that cable from Reno that ended a relationship? Again, no clue. That room, my dear, *abounds* in questions. And now that I've found that room I've just got to dig out the fuller facts behind its story. No purpose in it other than the sheer indulgence of my *need* to know the full story. My researcher's instinct. My—my obsession. Don't deny it. It's what being a historian is all about. As Plato said, knowledge is . . . ."

He was his old boring self again, at least for the time being. He wasn't irritating me, though. I felt well rested. When I went to bed the night before I had fallen asleep almost immediately. And deeply.

My final conscious thought after switching off the bedside light was of all those black-and-white photographs and I had an impression of them merging into a chessboard—a board on which a game had reached an unwinnable stalemate. I had only one move, I decided, and that was to be sensible and reject henceforth any fanciful notions about the paranormal.

The image of that intractable chessboard stayed with me over the next couple of weeks or so, and I used it to shore up the draughts of pointless questions. I did, though, now and then feel a certain irrational loneliness, as if—well, as if I'd called a wrong number long distance, found myself talking to a total stranger with whom I had an immediate rapport, then gotten disconnected and had no means of getting back to him.

Silly.

There were some nights when, on the pretext I needed exercise, I actually considered walking on the runway.

Silly.

A few times I thought of returning to the room, ostensibly to return the photograph.

Silly.

By such rebuke I conditioned myself to my *little* experience—I was scaling it down in my mind—and in due course I became quite sure that it was worth no more than a shrug and that somewhere there had to be a perfectly commonplace and logical explanation. Finally, I thought of him hardly at all, that absurdly named Johnny.

Then one night in the library of the house I looked up from the book I was reading and he was sitting in the chair opposite to the one I was in. No more than four or five feet away from me.

Five

I USED TO SPEND HOURS IN THE LIBRARY. IT WAS DIRECTLY across from the great hall, but its walls must have been stout for the soundproofing was good. Up in my room, on the other hand, the carousing from downstairs thumped in a muffled way that was almost as bad as the real thing. Often, then, following my stint of post-dinner socializing, I would go to the library and read until I judged the night's rowdiness was running down.

It was no hardship. The resident housekeeper kept a log fire going in the big gray stone hearth, to protect the books from dampness, and I would sit to one side of it in a brown leather armchair.

I was reading that night *The Great Gatsby*. I had discovered it on an earlier visit, part of the serendipity of the library, which though on the surface seemed to be dedicated to such tomes as *The Polo Player's Companion* and *Kipling—Poet of Empire* yielded, on examination, true works of literature. I had found there, and read, Virginia Woolf, Chekov, Swift and, a particular find, a French edition of the poems of Paul Verlaine.

And now *The Great Gatsby*. I had read it before, many times and

always slowly, for though I have always dismissed the social significance attributed to its theme I have never disputed that novel's style,
which to me is wholly feminine in the best sense and the prose
equivalent to the finest Irish lace.

So, under a standing lamp with a lemon shade that showed a
horse and hounds hunting scene, I settled down that night to return
to Gatsby's fiefdom of the Long Island Sound and his blue lawns. I
don't know what made me raise my head. Perhaps it was the branch
of a tree scraping the diamond-patterned windowpanes, which
I faced, or the slight displacement of a log on the fire. Anyway, I
looked up.

And he was there.

And this time I did react. I felt a frisson of—No, that won't do, not
if I'm to be honest with myself. Bring on the goosebumps, because
they were there; bring on the chill of surprise compounded by my
knowing that the library, as always, had been empty when I arrived
and, absorbed though I was in my book, I almost certainly would
have heard him entering. And, a front against shock, bring on also my
decision—on the instant, it was my only resort—that it was a hoax
and my only way of dealing with it right then was to show I wasn't
one little bit put out.

Negligently, then, I placed my book, face-up at the page I had
been reading, on my lap, and simply stared at him. A superior who's-
been-a-naughty-boy stare. A challenge: I was determined that the
first words would be his and my response to whatever he had to say
would be scathing. He, for his part, continued to smile.

The standoff, for that's what it was for me, lasted some moments,
then faltered when my book slid off my lap. I'm not sure whether
this simply happened or if I contrived it. Whatever, I had to lower
my gaze to pick up the book from the floor and when I looked up,
the book in my hands, and into the uncomplicated giving of his slow
smile I promptly remembered that passage in *The Great Gatsby* in
which Gatsby is described as having an "extraordinary gift for hope,
a romantic readiness such as I have never found in any other person
and which it is not likely I shall ever find again."

I ticked myself off for totally uncharacteristic susceptibility. His was a trickster's smile, part of his game. Like the scar.

Only the scar seemed so real. It showed, clearly enough, in the fixed powdery light of the standing lamp behind his chair and in the streaking firelight—a deep fissuring that tightened the surrounding skin and gave the side of his mouth an inflection. All the better to smile with, I thought. For, I reminded myself, I wasn't deceived. My pose said so. I had my head inclined to the side, my hand on my chin, my forefinger extended to my cheek. The cool observer.

In that way, I looked him over. That large chair, designed for fat and gouty old Englishmen who needed to spread themselves, heightened his slight build and his slimness. He was in uniform, but bareheaded. He had fair hair, almost blond, and cut short with a parting on the left side. Nothing special about him, I decided. Except for the scar. Very well, then, his smile too. And, placed across the book which he held open at the lower part of his chest, the total beauty of his hands.

At the moment, those hands softly fingerprinted in my mind the identity and the persona of another man I had known. Woody. He, too, had beautiful hands. He was beautiful in all respects, not least in an utter modesty about his astonishing good looks. He had a matching physique and so he was entitled to swagger, but he didn't.

Woody and I were fellow law students at Oxford. He was American. I knew his fiancée, a wildlife photographer, and, half-jokingly, she asked me to "stand guard" over him while she was away on a long assignment in Africa. Woody and I became close friends. We attended the May Ball together, went on picnics, took trips to London, played a lot of tennis.

And breaking a pact with myself that I would never get seriously involved with a man (a contract with a generous sub-clause for affairs) I fell in love with him. Hopelessly as they say. Hopelessly, too, because Woody stayed faithful to his wildlife photographer.

Overall, then, it was a frustrating and painful relationship; it took me a long time to get over it. Eventually, I came to realize that it had been a privilege just to know him and that those hands I had longed to feel on my body—even his touch on my elbow as we crossed a road aroused that wider desire—were incapable of betrayal. He was that kind of a man.

I risk making him seem dull, a prude. He wasn't. He was, in his quiet way, the most joyful person I had ever known. He was witty and, above all, wise—a preternatural wisdom (after all, he was in his twenties) that was part of his idealism. He was studying law as an entree into politics, though I used to think that his looks—the almost caricatured rectitude of his jaw offsett by a boyish romp of flaxen curls—were all he needed to win votes.

Beyond that, I always thought he had a curiously out-of-date face. I was girlish then, literally, but it seemed to me that his face had nothing to do with a high-profile career in the making and instead answered to some vaguely distant era of heroics in which self-serving was subordinate to self-sacrifice. It was a face from that kind of the past, a face that didn't fit into the present, though a face, one hoped, that might have a place in the future. But that was my freshman year and I was giddy on lofty thoughts and first love.

That Christmas, Woody went back to the States on a short vacation and died in a skiing accident in Colorado.

There was a memorial service for him in the college chapel in Oxford, but for me the real tribute came all those years later in the library of that old house in Yorkshire when I yielded my gaze to the hands of that other American . . .

When I visualize it now that opening scene in the library has the shadowy look of an old foreign movie—foreign, perhaps, because at first his words didn't add up to any meaning for me. But at least I got my way and he was the first to speak.

"Say, I heard from Adelle today."

From his book he drew out, then held up, an envelope which he must have been using as a page marker.

"She says they're having an early spring in Atlanta. Georgia in the spring—it's so unbelievably lovely. All those peach trees in bloom.

They're just everywhere. As you'll see for yourself when the war's over. Adelle sends her love to you. As ever."

That was my cue to initiate my plan of cutting him down, and I let it go. "You're—you're incorrigible." I shook my head, unable to resist a genuine amusement at his audaciousness, this act of affecting to treat me as someone who was part of his life.

He replaced the envelope, closed the book. "I'm gonna take your advice and move the rest of my books in here. Did I tell you my roof has sprung another leak?" He leant sideways, fitted the book in the shelf at a place at the level of his shoulders.

He turned back to me, smiled. "That's enough reading for now. Though every time I read *Wuthering Heights* I discover something new and profound. Mrs. Mitchell sure was right—that book has so many layers, so many meanings and insights. To think that Emily Brontë was just a girl when she wrote that exposition into the human soul and its needs and pains and—Sorry. You've heard all this before. And"—his smile broadened—"you'll hear it again, only it'll have real authority when you hear it from her lips, when you meet up with Mrs. Mitchell in Atlanta. You two are gonna get on just dandy, especially now I've sent her your Haworth sketches. I figure they must have got there by now, don't you?"

"Incorrigible," I repeated, and realized I was more than merely amused and that I felt oddly comfortable with him and was prepared for a little while to put up with his nonsense . . . and, as it turned out, his knowledge of Proust, Ibsen, Tolstoy, George Eliot, Jane Austen et al.

I can't quite recall how we came to be discussing literature in general—I suppose the starting point could have been when I felt I had to disabuse him of his notion that *Wuthering Heights* was an unflawed masterpiece—though I do remember thinking at one stage how refreshing it was to talk of things that had nothing to do with production schedules and budgets and deadlines and all the other career imperatives that had filled my life for years, and I was mindful for a fleeting moment of informal sessions at Oxford, late at night like this one, nights with Woody and our friends. Woody, typically, would sit in a corner of the common room and, it was a gift from his wildlife photographer, play an Aztec Indian flute in a range of tremolos and throbbings that echoed a culture's profound wisdom, in contrast to the intellectual skitterings I competed in with the others. It was fun, though.

Likewise, though on a different level, that night in the library evolved as talk at its most pleasurable—and in that I included the sound of this man who called himself Johnny.

With odd exceptions, like Woody, I have always thought of Americans as having milkshake voices—a bit too insincerely sweet for my liking, flavored and frothed and sometimes slurped, according to the various states. But this Johnny's voice had its own vintage: a soft clarity unadulterated by cynicism and self. A wisdom. An overtone of Woody . . . Or, on the moment I allowed for the possibility, was this simply what I *wanted* to hear?

What I did hear that night, unexpected and strident, was the Andrews Sisters. They burst through the door of the library as they led a conga line. Maxine, Patty and Laverne: three little WAC soldiers coordinating a maneuver that, following its established route, would sweep through every level of the house. The conga was a spontaneous, and frequent, result of the hell-raising in the great hall. I had been drafted into a few of those lines, a reluctant conscript doing her bit in a raging choreography that after a circuit of the library—the first, and obvious, port of call—would climb the staircase and slam into the other main chambers of the house, breaking the occasional vase and, that night, shattering our literary tête-à-tête.

At the moment of impact, as it were, we were discussing the role of women in classical poetry. We had gotten onto that because he had advanced the opinion, which I promptly rejected on the grounds her output was so scant, that Emily Brontë rated as a major poet. As an example of a lasting poet I was quoting a few lines from Edna St. Vincent Millay's "Renascence" when the conga onslaught struck.

They were blowing noisemakers, pulling the strings on those

hand-held things that pop and send out showers of colored streamers and, something new, some of them were wearing inflated yellow Mae West life vests and waving Stars and Stripes placards proclaiming HAPPY 1943! It was as if a distant New Year's Eve celebration had broken loose from its moorings in time and washed into that solemn room, swamping the leather-bound tomes.

And then they were gone, swirling up the staircase, receding into echo. They were gone and I was on my own: the chair opposite mine was empty.

I looked around me. He wasn't there. But, of course, he had joined the conga line, had responded to one of the many out-stretched hands, which I had resisted, and linked up to the merriment. He would be back. That was what I wanted to believe, though I knew my hope was as thin as the strips of paper streamers left behind on the carpet.

I stayed in the chair and waited. I waited until the conga line, in bits and pieces now, shunted back to the great hall. I waited longer, until I heard voices saying good nights and the sounds of doors opening and closing across the house. I waited until the only sound was the shuffling of what remained of the fire.

I got up, crossed to the chair he had occupied and sat in it. At eye level, I looked at the titles in the bookshelf alongside me. I found it in seconds, the black-bound copy of *Wuthering Heights* he had placed there. I removed it, opened it where the tip of the envelope showed and pulled out the letter.

It was addressed to Captain Johnny Dean Pepperton at the base in Yorkshire. Two green postage stamps showed the head and shoulders of President Roosevelt and the frank mark across them read Atlanta, GA, and though I couldn't make out the month and day the year was enclosed in the circle like a relic: 1943. The envelope had been opened in a straight slit across the top and I pulled from it three sheets of blue notepaper.

I noted the date on the first page: March 3, 1943. The greeting: *Dearest Johnny.* The opening sentence: *I am writing this in the den and looking out on the peach tree which is in full bloom already . . .*

I honestly meant to leave it at that, no more than the confirmation that there had been such a letter, its authenticity substantiated by the time-faded coppery look of the ink and the way the once neat creases of the pages had become smudge shadings.

In the event, I read on, snooped in that little parlor of the past, and even felt oddly at home there, though maybe I was justifying my intrusion, among the knick-knacks of small talk—the Bundles for Britain committee, the high school reunion, the new butter rationing regulations—conveyed in a decorous, though not fussy, script. The writer said she was a little anxious at not hearing from him for all these weeks, though no doubt, as always, his letters would arrive in a batch; she blamed the censor for these delays. Madge had been back home last week, briefly, and Mrs. Mitchell continued to be impatient with her on account of the way she had launched herself as Scarlett O'Hara. But Madge was Madge and she had the money to do these crazy things and she was never going to mend her ways, was she? Meantime, the writer went on, she was glad he had met Alice over there in England—"Madge was never right for you"—and she looked forward to meeting her one day in Atlanta when the war was over.

Do give my love to Alice. I feel I know her by now. You are always in my thoughts. Your loving sister, Adelle.

Alice? I remembered the initials A. M. on the portrait. Was A. M. Alice? I pondered this, though vaguely, as I carefully re-folded the letter, put it in the envelope and returned it to the book. I examined the book itself for a moment or two, attracted by the hand-tooled leather of its binding. I glanced at the frontispiece, saw that it had been published in New York in 1850 and was a first edition of this imprint. On the opposite page an inscription had been written in a firm hand: *To Johnny. A bright new star waiting to be discovered—the world needs your glow! Margaret Mitchell. Atlanta. Christmas 1938.*

Presumably, this was the Mrs. Mitchell he had spoken of earlier in the evening. Now she had a first name, Margaret. Margaret Mitchell. I knew, I suppose everyone who has ever read a book does, that Margaret Mitchell wrote *Gone with the Wind* and that Atlanta was its great set piece. Was it coincidence, I wondered, or was the woman who had autographed *Wuthering Heights* the author of one of the biggest bestsellers in history? Could be. For was it not so—for a moment my mental locution reflected the tutorials I had taken in cross-examination at Oxford—that the writer of the letter I had just read had said that Mrs. Mitchell was peeved because a girl called Madge was assuming the name of Scarlett O'Hara?

"Ladies and Gentlemen of the Jury . . ." I tried to be whimsical in my thinking. Failed.

I closed the book and replaced it in the gap on the crowded shelf where, I was sure, it had reposed in obscurity for years, out of sight of anyone planning a hoax.

And at that moment I accepted as absolute certainty—part instinct, part evidence—that I had wandered into a complexity beyond the accepted laws of cause and effect.

Six

TIME WARPS ARE THE DAISY CHAINS OF SCIENCE FICTION—
another genre I scorn—and they're not for me. Einstein *is*. Einstein
with his "eyes of a child and giant mind" (that's how that professor of
physics described him) and his love of such simplicities as clockwork
toys and his observation, jotted on the back of a newspaper as he
waited for a train at Basel station in Switzerland, that *"Time is a fascinating train set, full of mysterious shuntings and detours and unscheduled
arrivals on parallel tracks of past and present. Time has no timetable."*

Somehow that explains everything that happened to me. And certainly in the four or five weeks after that night in the library, those
few weeks in which I truly came to know Johnny, there was no
timetable: he was simply, and haphazardly, *there*.

I regret that I didn't keep a diary, but then, other than notations
for appointments, I've never been a diary-keeping person.

What surprises me now, now that I am finally examining what
happened in as balanced a way as I can, is my total acquiescence. I,
this superior and knowing self, accepted the situation as a given, suspended all questioning. Could it have been the illness which later

felled me in London was even then hovering, an incipient exhaustion blunting my perception? Perhaps, though I doubt it. I should like to believe, most self-servingly I agree, that I had reached some kind of informed intellectual decision based on a sensed existentialism which required no explication. Or was it—let's get to the full nitty-gritty of cliche and probably the truth—that I was in love and unthinking and simply glad he was there and I was in no mood to reflect beyond that imperative and that the moment—this seems to be turning into a festival of cliches—was all that counted? Who knows? I don't. *I do not know.* It's as simple and as convoluted as that. But it all seemed to integrate so naturally in my life that questions were needless.

They're there now of course, and unanswerable, though I do keep wondering how, before I *actually* went there at the end of those four or five weeks, I knew Haworth only too well—knew it as a regular visitor there with him—and, crucially, knew his particular route up the moors. *How?*

Again I plead "don't know". I need to be honest about that, and about my feelings for Haworth.

I do not propose to add any decorous prose stitchings to the tapestry image of Haworth and its three-little-maids literary shrine standing as the home of the Brontë sisters, personifications of genteelness and purveyors of all that is turbulent in the human heart.

That's the standard blurb and the implication is that Haworth is beguilingly rustic in a rugged kind of a way, with Heathcliff brooding romantically on the skyline.

The reality, as far as I am concerned, is that Haworth is, or was, brute and gaunt and committed to the virtually non-stop definition of a cliche—windswept moors. The wind from the moors that inspired *Wuthering Heights* has a repertoire that includes blasts, howlings, moans and mean little sideswipes.

Johnny, I'm sure, viewed the wind as appropriate atmospherics. He loved the village high above the Calder valley. He loved the moors and their ruins of old farmhouses. He loved the gray-walled eighteenth-century parsonage where the Brontë sisters lived, with its scratchy inner sense of quill pens devoted to the creation of *epic* literature conveyed now in the unfocused rustlings and tiny spasms of any old house.

Above all, he loved Emily Brontë.

He bowed to her, or seemed to, every time we entered the parsonage. No, I'm exaggerating. What he actually did was incline his head to a gilt-framed painting of the Brontë sisters which hung on the wall (I remember the dull red wallpaper and its blotches of dampness) at eye level immediately beyond the front door. That painting was impossible to avoid. It was done, incidentally, by Branwell Brontë, the sisters' only, and younger, brother. Branwell was a debauchee, addicted to laudanum and alcohol and the sexual pursuit of village youths, though I mention this simply because his painting was a study in chasteness. The three literary lionesses of the day were conveyed as frumps, long-nosed and with mouths set on uncompromising respectability. Anne Brontë was on the left, Charlotte Brontë on the right, and Emily Brontë was between them and the more dominant, as though using *Wuthering Heights* as her own high ground.

Otherwise it was a dull painting, flat and without interpretation. A number of times, though, after his usual potterings around the parsonage as he took notes and made sketches, I found him standing in front of the painting with the absorption of a pilgrim beholding the Brontë holy grail. And when he did that I was reminded irresistibly of Woody when we visited galleries, a reminder so poignant that all resentment I felt over that homage to Emily Brontë was erased.

Excactly like Woody when he was held by a picture, Johnny would swing back slightly on his heels and hold his hands at the middle of his back, the left palm upward and the fingers of the right hand tapping the palm as though in silent applause.

Very well, this has gotten to be a commonplace mannerism—perhaps even an accepted minor protocol of art appreciation—but to my highly subjective eyes it was a link. In those days Woody was so much on my mind that it seems to me now—though I cringe at such sentimentality—that subconsciously I may have been, well, transferring him to Johnny. Not in looks, of course, but in values, attitudes, in an openness to discovery and the cosmic spaces of life in which there also was room for the serendipitous spirit of the beachcomber.

One afternoon, for example, he came down the stairs grinning as he held up a trophy of his pottering. It was a kite, diamond-shaped, and, dust had mouldered into layers of grease on its waxed paper, patently old enough to have been a relic of the Brontë childhood. Johnny said he had found it in a broken glass-fronted museum case in a cupboard.

He took it outside to his jeep where he said he had a bottle of paint spirits, and there I watched as painstakingly, using a rag, he removed the grime, restored that kite to a vibrant cobalt blue on one side and a pure yellow on the other. Its tail, of horsehair, was braided with multi-colored ribbons, and these, too, he cleaned. The string of the kite was frayed and it shredded as he worked, so he replaced it with a ball of twine. Woody, I thought, would have given exactly the same devotion to that kite, seeing in a child's simple toy the symbolism of sky and purity.

On the way back to the house to return the kite, Johnny paused in the graveyard. Jackdaws shuffled, hard-eyed as sentries, between the weary headstones. He raised the kite above his head. "I figure," he said, "that after all these years indoors it deserves the sky."

And he launched it. The wind, as though affronted by that impudent little waistcoat of blue and yellow, hurled it in a bleak cloak sweep toward the trees at the edge of the graveyard and for a moment—I remember suddenly my small gasp—I thought the kite was going to be wrecked. It rose, though, as Johnny played out more twine. Cheating the wind, the kite swept across to the square tower of the church. From there it took off, soared like a cheerleader challenging the dirge of the fundamentalist hymns that had issued from that church for more than two centuries. That kite was spiritual in the best sense, its own *Amazing Grace*. And I was glad when Johnny turned to me as though seeking my assent and, upon my nod, deliberately let go of the twine and granted the kite the full freedom of the sky.

It was what Woody would have done.

Woody. Always Woody. Or it was until that afternoon Johnny and I climbed up to High or Top Withens and the derelict Elizabethan farmhouse where, in *Wuthering Heights,* Heathcliffe lived.

Johnny wanted to do some sketches. The wind didn't encourage callers, and he crouched in the remains of a fireplace for meager shelter as he balanced his pad on his knee.

I, exasperated, decided to defy the wind. In gaps in its roaring, lulls when even the wind seemed exhausted, I could hear the sounds of a waterfall. Johnny had told me there were several waterfalls up there, three or four miles from the parsonage. Listening, I seemed to establish a direction for the waterfall, directly across a tract of the moor enclosed by wire fencing. There was a wooden gate in the fence and I opened it, ignoring a sign bearing a skull and crossbones and the words KEEP OUT—DANGER. The warning was crudely lettered and drawn and I decided it lacked authority.

I was about a hundred yards across, stumbling on clumps of heather and bracken, when I heard shouts. The wind had picked up by then and though I couldn't make out any words I sensed their urgency. I turned, looked back at Top Withens and saw Johnny. He had his hands raised, his palms pushing forward, obviously motioning for me to stay absolutely still. I tetched, but obeyed. He picked up a stave, it turned out to be a handle of a pick axe, and ran to the gate. Once inside the fence, he moved slowly, testing the thickets with the stave, pausing often to raise his hands toward me in that gesture to stay still.

When he reached me I began to remonstrate and his answer was to extend the stave four or five feet in front of us, a line I almost certainly would have followed, and tap it on the earth. There was a terrible swift and gnashing crash and the stave splintered. He motioned me forward, pointed to where the lower part of the stave was shredded between the serrated iron jaws of a mantrap. Above the wind, I heard the sweet dapple of the waterfall.

There were scores of mantraps up there, hidden in the heather and the bracken, oiled and primed to strike devastatingly under the slightest pressure. Once used against poachers, the traps had been rounded up from farms in the valley by the local militia, the Home Guard. Such amateur soldiers were a national setup in the war and they tended to an eccentricity in which they were ragtag in dress and gung-ho in spirit. The Haworth Home Guard, bespeaking the dark mood of the village, used the mantraps as an assault training course to test the mettle of new recruits. Half a dozen men had been crippled for life and one boy of seventeen had bled to death as he was carried down from the moor.

Johnny gave me this background as we made our cautious return, he used what was left of the stave to probe the undergrowth, to High Withens. When he said the traps clamped on flesh and bone with the force of hundreds of pounds I said something like, "So the wind does have teeth." And then I remembered the mashed stave in the mantrap I had very nearly stepped on and I gave up my airy small talk shrugging and began to shiver violently.

He took off his jacket and placed it round my shoulders, even though I was well dressed against the cold. Then he took my hand and gently urged me forward in those few moments I was almost unable to move. And I was glad, immeasurably glad, that it was Johnny who was up there with me. Given the choice, I would have wanted no one else. Not even Woody.

It was as a result of my terror, and terror it was, that I saw Johnny in his own right. It seems to me that, on the level of wishful thinking, my hearkening to my memories of Woody was severed by the steel teeth of that mantrap.

I escaped the mantrap, but I went on to be clamped by another kind of snare—by which I mean a recurring dream I have to this day. That dream has nothing to do with my experience at High Withens, though when it strikes it cripples me emotionally. And a couple of weeks ago that dream very nearly claimed my life.

What happened was that here in unlikely Beverly Hills, where both the security and the dress codes are so discreetly pervasive they seem to amount to a cordon against such down-and-outs as bad dreams, my dream lurched back. Afterwards, I got up, tried to read, tried to watch television, but lacking accustomed surroundings—I'm not used to living in a Spanish-style hacienda—I wasn't able to cope with my agitation. I decided on a drive in the cool night air.

The traffic was slight, it was about two A.M., and I may have speeded; I was, after all, on the run from a dream. After a while, I was out of town and climbing a canyon road somewhere. A sharp bend came up and I failed to take it. The car slammed into the iron rail at the side of the road and the airbag whooshed, enfolded my head and shoulders like a white-fronted nurse.

The car was still and quiet now, it must have stalled, and for a time I was content to pillow my face and head in the airbag's folds. Was I, I wondered, injured? It didn't seem to matter, though; as the first phase of shock wore off first aid came in the form of a drifting recall of a conversation I'd had with a dear friend in London who had urged me to write about the dream, and everything else that happened in Yorkshire, as a means of therapy through confrontation.

Slowly, I sat up. I felt myself for injuries. None, apparently. I got out of the car to check the damage. The bonnet was mangled and the nearside front wheel had mounted the roadside rail. As I was returning to the car, a police patrol cruiser drew up. The officers stated the obvious—that I'd been very lucky. My car, they said, had very nearly gone over a sheer drop of three hundred feet.

One of them, clearly drawing a conclusion from the fact that I was wearing no more than a night-dress and a thin sweater tied at my shoulders, said—and his words teamed up with the advice of my friend in London—"Get yourself a life, lady."

And that's what I'm setting out to do in these sessions at the laptop.

At its simplest, it's a need to put down everything that happened. But though I produce a daily quota of words I am frustrated by the knowledge that I have allowed the fuller text of memory to become a palimpsest overwritten by the scripts that have interceded in my life since Yorkshire and which, I saw to it, kept me overwhelmingly busy.

I am hoping that what is missing, what I allowed to go astray in those fourteen-hour days I was putting in, will, with time and effort, show through. In this I am encouraged by what I remember with relative ease, which I have already described.

Right now I am remembering further treks up to the moors—the three or four times I was with him when, carried in his parachute pack, he hauled stones for the little wall he was building.

It's of a kind known as dry-stone walls. They're called that because no cement is used; flattish stones are placed one on top of the other in such a way that a natural weld is formed, one with apertures or "draughtings", whose strategic placement dissipates the force of the strongest gales. He learnt the craft from farm hands in the village close to the base and properly built, as his was, those ramshackle-seeming walls last for centuries.

His wall was way up on the moors but on exact line to the parsonage; he took a compass bearing to be sure. It was his tribute to Emily Brontë. Only four or five feet long and about two feet high, it was somehow a paperweight of his persona—the expression of a generous, if pointless, chivalry, the very rooting of an idealistically romantic spirit which needed the posterity of that enduring physical link.

"We'll come visit it after the war." I've only just now remembered those words and his familiar assumption that we were close enough to have a future together. What he said is no more than a minor card in the shuffling pack of memory, though it's worth playing.

Finally, there was the occasion of our gala visit to the wall, when he put the last stone in place. What followed was a little ceremony of consecration. First, he removed his identity dog tags from his neck, placed them at the precise center of the wall, in a "draughting", a tiny cave of time.

Then—he said the ancient Romans used to do something similar—he took out a leather pouch of American coins. Dollars. Half dollars. Quarters. Dimes. Nickels. He had been accumulating them for months.

And now, handful after handful, he showered a wrecked winter's sky with his silver fireworks, his affirmation of life and its grander possibilities. (I was right about the Gatsby in him.)

I have another memory of that wall. It was the day I went there on my own. The day, at breakfast, Phil Cowell rose to his feet in the great hall, an uncorked bottle of champagne in his hand, and announced the movie had been aborted. "The bastards called me last night and pulled the plug . . ." He swigged from the bottle. When he looked up his face streamed tears. "But we had fun, didn't we? Here's to your future, kiddos—a future flying bright flags."

Future? Bright flags? I saw only wreckage as I wandered the set. The bulldozers had already moved in. Outside the Stage Door Canteen the goddesses of the day—pin-ups of Dorothy Lamour, Betty Grable, Rita Hayworth—were in the gutters made by the bulldozers' tracks.

I went to my car and drove to Haworth, for I knew I was never going to see Johnny again.

I had no trouble finding the route to his wall. I even knew the exact point at which to skirt the concealed bog on the moors. As ever, the wind blew like a feudal landlord warning off trespassers.

It was an early afternoon in late April. The horizon showed a faint blue, like a trial swatch of spring. But over Haworth the clouds had the gray, packed and seamed look of old marble as though the hellfire and brimstone sermons of the Reverend Patrick Brontë had petrified into this hard slab of sky. The sisters' father was preaching well into his eighties, four- and five-hour tirades, his voice pitched—I had read somewhere—against the wind.

I thought about the old man as the merest point of focus, a means of getting me up on those moors, and I thought also of his three daughters and their words, words written in secret in the parsonage in thin daylight and at night by the stumps of tallow candles they hoarded unknown to their miserly father; words which were an accompaniment to the threnody of the wind, and never more so than in Wuthering Heights.

And then I was at Johnny's wall and I had gotten there without thinking about him, which was my intention. I recognized the wall immediately, for he had created a mound effect at its top.

Only the wall had aged, had settled into the earth, become a small but venerable part of the topography. Outcroppings of heather sent tendrils, like withered legal binding on ancient title deeds, across stones blotched by lichen.

I crouched down, out of the worst of the wind now, and my fingers probed in the apertures between the stones—the "draughtings"—at about the point where I had seen him place his dog tags.

The wind shrieked and I was calm.

For some minutes, my fingers scrabbled in and out of the apertures. And then my fingertips felt something that seemed to move slightly to the touch. I extended my hand as far as I could, grazing the skin on my knuckles and my wrist. There was a bleakly ludicrous moment when I thought my hand was stuck and I had a vision of being trapped there forever. Inside the wall, though, my fingers had some leverage and now they closed on the object they had touched and I pulled my hand free.

I opened my hand, and saw the dog tags.

Time had marked them with a gray-green encrustation, obliterating words and numbers. Demonstrably, though, they were dog tags—three metal rectangles strung on a corroded necklace.

I stayed calm. No surprise, no sense of vindication. Quite without emotion, I wrapped the dog tags in a handkerchief and put them in my pocket.

Then I faced the outraged wind and made my way downhill across the moor.

That night, at the farewell party in the great hall, I got drunk.

The ensuing hangover seemed to stretch over the next two or three weeks or so, a bleary but nonstop round of "striking" the production—long sessions with accountants, most of them Japanese, overseeing the logistics of flying the cast back to America, arguing with agents who called incessantly from the States to threaten litigation over their clients' broken contracts, temporizing with sundry creditors, including the wine merchant who had kept the cellars stocked up.

Phil Cowell called it the IOU Alamo and said I had been the hero of the hour. All I had to do was give him the chance to regroup and he would be fetching me out to the West Coast to work on his next production. Trust me, sweetie.

Eventually, I was back home in my flat in Holland Park. And ill. Simple exhaustion, I reasoned. After a day or two I was running a high temperature. Then I started having the dream.

It flaps in my mind like fragments of grainy black-and-white film on an out of control projector, and it has gone on to tear inwardly at the poise I honed during my reading of law at Oxford and consolidated in my career as a producer of investigative television documentaries. That poise is a crucial part of my professionalism and I can no longer have it jeopardized, especially now that I am in movies. And especially since, as my accident proved, that dream is deadly.

It starts with the sound of the wind, muted at first, mere creakings, like a befuddled old man shuffling in a small and cluttered room. Gradually, the sound rises to thumps and bangings and an uncontrolled rage.

And then it is a gray and cold daylight and I am filming on my own on the moors above Haworth.

Only the wind has blown away the script I have been working on and I am left wondering if those lost pages have any reference to a vintage military jeep that is bumping, apparently on cue, across the brow of the moors.

I make out a white American star on the side of the jeep which is driverless.

The jeep stops six or seven hundred yards away, directly ahead of me. The passengers climb out. Two of them. Shoulder to shoulder, they make their way toward me. I cup my hands across my forehead, against the wind, and see they are women. The camera is rolling as the two move from long-shot to medium close-up. I check the viewfinder and note, in its concentrated focused square, that they have on period clothes.

The small woman, she is very thin and not much more than five foot tall, is wearing a black Victorian bonnet, its rim enclosing the whole of her face, and a black skirt down to her ankles. She moves in short, stiff steps.

The other woman, much taller, *flows* in her movements, which seem to be the very coordinant of the spectacular picture hat she is wearing. And then the scene switches briefly to color—the harsh tones of early Technicolor. The hat—how is she keeping it on in this wind?—is cream-colored and its sweeping brim dips over the upper part of her face. Her lilac crinoline gown is slit to reveal her long legs. Her white gloves reach up to her elbows. It's the hat that holds me, though—its audaciousness, the flare of its red ribbon which romps with the sheened brown ringlets of her hair. The women's faces fill the viewfinder now. In black and white. Their eyes are malevolent.

And I see they are Emily Brontë and Scarlett O'Hara. Their faces are lacerated, layered in dried blood.

"Cut!" I cry. Repeatedly. *"Cut, cut, cut . . ."* But the wind, that Haworth wind, smashes my cry back into my mouth, down into the recesses of my larynx, until I am breathless, strangling on my words.

I wake up then. Gasping. Usually it is the middle of the night.

And that's it. Not just the lethal wind, but also Emily Brontë *and* Scarlett O'Hara. How very . . . *droll*. I've tried that cool, raised eyebrow approach. I've tried indifference and stoicism and yoga and once, I confess, a brand of herbal tea which, taken at bedtime, guaranteed dreamless nights.

Nothing works.

Like a feral cat, that dream stalks me silently. It can lie low for weeks, lulling me into thinking it has gone, and then it pounces, clawing my sleep. Howling. The dark spirit of the wind from the moors seems incarnate in that dream, and that abstract is the core of my terror.

Though in the first days of my dream's then—virtually nonstop repetition, back in Holland Park, I told myself that I was merely . . . *run-down*. I selected the term with due care, a poised hostess of my symptoms who would never entertain that vagrant condition known as a nervous breakdown. No little woman I!

Thus I tried to deceive myself. I unplugged the phone, let the mail pile up, and kept the curtains permanently drawn as I did my best to resist sleep in order to avoid the dream. For how long? Ten days? Two weeks? I can't be sure. In the silences between the dream, I grieved for Johnny; I knew, though in an unfocused way, that he had to be long dead.

One night the doorbell rang. I ignored it. It kept ringing. I pressed a pillow over my head. The ringing persisted. In the end, I went to the door. Andy, my agent, was there.

"I've been trying to reach you on the phone for days. Good God, woman, you look awful."

I told him that night, eventually, the full story. I told him all about Johnny. And all about the dream.

Andy is a middle-aged Scot who parts his wispy graying hair in the middle and wears knitted ties. He is discreetly gay and spends three evenings a week working for the Samaritans. I regard him as my closest woman friend. Which is why he is the only person to whom I confided my experience; to the professor at Cambridge I told the events in general terms, leaving out the dream.

Andy heard me without interruption, one of his virtues, and when I was through he took a slow sip of his Scotch and said, "That dream's got horns and it's got to be sent on its way as fast as its cloven feet will carry it. And there's only one way to do that—*write* it out of your life. *Face* up to it. In fact, confront and write about everything that swept in on you back there. The therapy alone—"

"Therapy?" I was provoked. "If you're suggesting I'm unbal-
anced or—"

"I'm not. Not at all. But you *are* a wee bit distraught and you've
lost weight. That apart, you've had an interesting—a *very* interesting—experience and it deserves to be written about. That way you'll
have organized your thoughts. You'll have points of reference in
place of all this . . . discordance. You might even have a book."

"Oh, goody," I snapped, "a cozy ghost story!"

"I rather fancy it could be a story that intelligent women of all ages
and backgrounds would read and consider with an open mind.
Maybe some men too. The more intuitive ones. Write it."

And finally, after two years, that's what I'm doing.

If it swats for good the tyranny of my dreams then the effort will
have been worthwhile, but there are other imperatives which drive me
on, though I'm at a loss right now to say exactly what they are except
to hazard a musing—no more than that—that the dream is integral in
a way I intuit, but do not understand, to the whole situation: it's as
though the dream is an expression of a particular disquiet in my spirit
and only by this attempt have I any prospect of closure and inner ease.

At its simplest, it's a need to put down everything that happened,
to fill as best as I can an incompleteness, and perhaps end up with a
dossier instead of a grab-bag. I see now the value of having a *personal*
structure if only as, well, a keepsake (and once I'd have scorned such
a sentiment).

With persistence, my overall memory may unblock, just as
strength returned to me in London—though that was Andy's doing.
He arranged for a catering service to deliver a light but nourishing
lunch every day. Most evenings, over my protests, he came over and
prepared dinner. After a while, he coaxed me out to quietly cheerful
ethnic restaurants, Greek and Indian and Thai. He took me rowing
one sunny afternoon on the lake in Regent's Park. We spent several
weekends in Brighton, where he has a small flat overlooking the sea.
He was never fussy.

Over a period of four or five weeks the dream gradually dissipated
(a deceptive lull). I regained most of the weight I had lost. One

evening as we strolled along the Thames Embankment—we had been to an Arts Council reception in the Palace of Westminster—I said I thought he should find me some work.

"Grand," he said. "Your old television station would be delighted to—"

"Not television. Films." I had switched mediums and saw no reason to backtrack; that's how much stronger I felt.

Two months later I signed as producer for a low-budget joint venture Anglo-Italian picture. It was brought in ahead of schedule and recovered half of its costs within a month of release. The same company hired me almost immediately for a two-picture deal—one in Rome, the other in Florence—and though the budgets were not impressive the attraction was that I was director and producer of both. The Rome picture went to video with disconcerting promptness, but the Florence one is set for top awards at Cannes.

So I have worked steadfastly for more than two years now, expanding my career and, in the process—and more than somewhat deliberately—contracting the past.

Apart, that is, from the dream, that chimera of wraiths and the wind from the Haworth moors.

But at least I'm ready to deal with it now, ready also to seek to restore the past, and Johnny, to my memory in the cause of proximate order and sequence—and, yes, the complicated business of being in love. In the pauses that have drifted over me in my sessions at the laptop—more pauses than words—I have come to realize that my feelings for him haven't changed. All I did was subsume them in work. Lord forbid, I am not lovesick per se! Passion has been replaced by nostalgia, and with that has come a need to know more about him, a need both emotional and intellectual. Lately that need has become inexplicably pressing, driven—as though I am responding simultaneously to elegy *and* SOS. That could be the influence of my dream.

What matters immediately is that I have practical means to expand my knowledge of Johnny and that tomorrow I am leaving Beverly Hills for the wider expanses of this country as I set out to swat my dream and rehabilitate my memory.

Ostensibly, the trip I begin tomorrow is a working one. It's a look-see of possible locations and general on-the-spot research for the movie that has brought me here. I angled for this travelling assignment and took full advantage of my status as an old friend of the director—Phil Cowell.

He meant it when he said back in Yorkshire that he would make it up to me, though no doubt the notices for my Italian picture were a factor. He now calls me his "piccolo protégé". I can live with that, especially since my name comes right after his in the production hierarchy.

With entitled flourish, then, I signed the contract and I had no idea at the time that it would complement a scrap of paper I have in my wallet.

During a fleeting trip I made to Yorkshire about a year ago I came by that scrap of paper . . .

The trip was unplanned, the consequence of a totally unforeseen gap in my work schedule. I had nothing to do suddenly and so on a whim I went to Yorkshire.

It rained all day. As I gazed at it through the streaming windows of my car, the old house with its growth-like clusters of gargoyles struck me as having the blurred black-gray look of an X-ray picture swarming with evidence of terminal decline.

I decided I had wasted my time in returning, though the day picked up somewhat when I met, in the village, an old woman called Bessy who had personal memories of Johnny and his crew. Bessy, and the unremarkable circumstances that led me to her, may rate a fuller passage at a further stage. I'll see. At the time, however, she was no more than a source of anecdotes I was quite interested to hear—though equally the teller of tall tales when she said that Johnny's fate was a mystery, that he had simply vanished one afternoon, to the lasting consternation of his crew.

I didn't tell her—there was no point, and besides she had gin on her breath—that I knew precisely what had happened to him.

As part of my regime of discipline in London when Andy was being so solicitous about my health I wrote to the Bureau of War Records in Washington with a formal enquiry. I got a terse reply, a computer flick back to the past: Captain Johnny Dean Pepperton, US Eighth Air Force, was killed in action during the course of a mission to Düsseldorf on the night of May 1, 1944. May Day, I remember thinking. The start of spring, the renewal of life. My musing was without sentimentality; on the contrary, I felt a twist of irony. *May Day!*

Overall, though, the notification didn't daunt me—I had already come to terms with his death—and, in fact, to have that statistical pinpointing was a relief.

And now it proved that Bessy was rambling when she hinted that Johnny had been "done for" as a result of the "bad blood" on the part of the RAF on the base toward "the Yanks".

Let her have her story, I thought. What mattered was that she had known Johnny and over the years had kept in touch with his crew and they with her.

Three were left, she said, and she exchanged Christmas cards with them, and—her gin-blurred eyes beamed on the notion—why didn't she let me have their names and addresses? I demurred, politely. She insisted and copied the list out slowly, a pencil wobbling between her swollen fingers.

Humoring her, I made a show of tucking the list in a zippered flap in my wallet. In my mind, Johnny, too, had been tucked away and, that day-trip to Yorkshire notwithstanding, for me the sprawl of the past had been edited down to those sparse words saying he had been killed on May 1, 1944. There was something healing in that finality, even though my dream persisted. So I suppose I had no real intention of keeping that old woman's list. Though I did. They were the names of his crewmates, after all. His buddies, his—I see no point in making excuses. I kept the list.

We are at the very early pre-planning stages of the movie, which means lots of conferences and coffee and shows of creative contem-

plation as we gaze at empty yellow scratch pads. The working title is
Millennium Man and the story is about an American exile who has
spent virtually the whole of his life abroad and now returns to
explore a twenty-first-century America in a used car. When I first
arrived here, Phil Cowell said that at a later date it might be useful for
me to take off and scout possible locations and "generally empathize
and bond" with the country. Last week I reminded him of that idea
and said I could be ready to leave within a few days.

He thought about this, his hands in a praying posture at his lips;
he's settled down since Yorkshire and has even shaved off his beard.
"Why not?" he said at last. In particular, he wants me to go to Texas,
which he anticipates as a starting point of the movie. After that, I
have carte blanche.

"The US of A is all yours for the next couple of months," he said.
"Follow your nose, your instinct—as I figure it, a hunch is better
than an itinerary."

Actually, I have an itinerary—that scrap of paper with the names
of the three crew members. They'll be worth looking up, at least
that. I have made this commitment, and I need to get out for a while
from Beverly Hills, where retrospection is as profound as who was at
last night's premiere or at last night's most fashionable cocktail party.

I have remembered all that I can in this superficial milieu and if I
have any prospects at all of plotting a route to my occluded past I
sense it may be in the real America with perhaps—who knows?—a
directional nod from at least one, or maybe all three, of those old
men who flew with Johnny.

And so, on this eve of departure, I have a feeling of auspiciousness.
All the more so in that tomorrow, I am flying to San Francisco. One
Harry J. Korda lives there. He was Johnny's copilot in England in the
war and I have the word of that old woman in Yorkshire that he and
Johnny were as close as brothers.

San Francisco

Seven

AS THE PLANE CIRCLED SAN FRANCISCO WAITING ITS TURN TO land, the captain came on and said the temperature down below was a "chirpy" nineteen degrees centigrade, clouds were scattered and the morning mist over the bay was dispersing rapidly. The routine announcement released an exultance in me: *Weather*, I thought. Good, honest, everyday weather. They don't seem to have that in Beverly Hills. What they have there is a sort of chic, a Gucci climate, designed for the exact requirements of the hour—the early morning jog, the afternoon's golf, the poolside cocktail session—and giving off, especially after dark, its own exclusive boutiquey smell of subtly perfumed waxed packaging. The smog and the other air impurities of Los Angeles don't encroach on Beverley Hills. Or they didn't while I was there.

I endured that perfect sheen for nine weeks and I'm tempted to think the reason my dream ripped through it that night was because Beverly Hills and Haworth are, in their different ways, at the polar edges of unreality: one sybaritic, the other stark. Did my sleeping mind put those two constituents together and, aided by a vague feeling of foreboding I had known for several days, did they fuse into the virulence of my dream? That's no more than a passing thought.

What is much more to the point is that immediately after arriving in San Francisco I knew how right I had been to leave Beverly Hills for a while. I stepped into a robust morning that was charged with real color and forms—the first thing I noticed was the creamy spilt-milk streaking of the clouds—and a hearty air that was a good six or seven degrees cooler than the pink and chartreuse dawn that was simpering over Beverly Hills when I left for the airport.

I was dressed for the transition between southern and northern California: a brown tweed jacket over a cashmere polo-neck sweater, beige slacks, flat brown loafers. And I was dressed to make a sensible impression when I turned up at 35 Grove Street, which was where Harry Korda lived. What I had not, could not, plan was my approach to him; that would depend on the man, his temperament, his memory. It could be that he was a geriatric with vacant eyes; I had to be prepared for that possibility. Why, I wondered suddenly, had I not phoned him in advance? Because, I suppose, I wanted this to be spontaneous and all the more cheerfully revealing for that unplanned informality.

And so I was optimistic when I got into the yellow cab outside the terminal building. The driver spent some time looking up Grove Street on a map before we set off. "Got it," he said finally. "It's down by the bay."

Down by the bay . . . Those words raised little sails of expectation in me and no doubt this was why, contrary to the smooth serenading of Tony Bennett on the subject of its charms, San Francisco shaped up for me during the early stages of that cab ride as a sea shanty of a town.

I saw gulls on Mission Street—great white gulls whose sweeping wingspans scripted the spirit of the sea—and scenes of the bay would swing into sight as we breasted the crests of hilly streets. In one of those views I glimpsed a four-masted schooner. At that moment we were in a street of multi-tiered Victorian timbered houses whose fronts tottered splendidly to the sky like square rigging. I wanted this to be Grove Street and, I risked a full tot of heady wishful thinking, I wanted Harry Korda to be a man of nautical aspect, blue-eyed and rubicund, who would have no trouble charting an anecdotal course to the Yorkshire of half a century ago.

The cab carried on.

The rich crop of streets thinned into an urban stubble of shack-like houses and, here and there, large stricken buildings that might have been gutted warehouses. It was as if the cab had driven through the curtain backdrop of San Francisco and into a bleak backstage. The bay was still there, and for some time we had been running par-allel to it, but the shoreline jutted industrial sheds and car-wreck dumps and an oil refinery. The cab made a sharp left turn, climbed a hill, then turned right and stopped at the top of a street that descended steeply.

"Grove Street," the driver said. "What number did y' say?"

I got out at number thirty-five, which was about halfway down. As the driver hauled my luggage from the trunk, I looked around me. This wasn't a street to shop on for a cameo of memory, though no doubt a gun could be bought from the bar and grill, whose grimy clapboard façade featured a neon sign in the shape of a pink cocktail. A vagrant, a man wearing a gray floppy hat, was unconscious against the wall of the bar, his legs spread out in front of him; his right shoe was missing. The street was almost as derelict as he was: single- and two- and three-storey buildings crammed together so that, under the spindlage of TV aerials on the rooftops, they looked like old clothes slung from bent wire hangers in a rotting wardrobe.

Number thirty-five was a three-floor redbrick and as I stood out-side I momentarily regretted letting my cab go. I was angry with myself for sentimentalizing this visit, for persuading myself that this old World War II pilot might be a *character*, living a comfortable life. I looked at the vagrant—the bar was only a few yards down the street—and wondered if the man I had come to meet would be a deadbeat. A rummy, the Americans call them. To encounter such a person, someone shuffling and mumbling, would be no less than betrayal. For a moment or two I actually considered whether number thirty-five was worth playing in this roulette of old men's memories and if it would not be better just to hedge my bets and trust that the next survivor of Johnny's crew would be a sounder prospect.

Then I realized that in such a street, my luggage at my feet, I was vulnerable—though the only person I could see was the vagrant—so I climbed the four stone steps of number thirty-five with a false air of purpose. Set at the side of the door was a faded brass-edged plate listing the names of the occupants and I was surprised to see that the building had a commercial role. A bail bondsman, a notary public and a chiropractor shared the first floor. The second floor was taken by Oriental Jade Imports Inc., Bayside Coffee Supplies and West Coast Investigations. And up on the third floor, a business card slotted behind the Plexiglas gave the information, was Korda Aviation Services Inc. (Harry J. Korda, President). So far from being the lost cause I had feared, Harry Korda, even at his age, was an entrepreneur and, notwithstanding the address, he became blue-chip stock for me. I pressed the entry button next to his listing. No reply. I pressed again, longer this time. The door rasped as the lock was released. I went inside.

Packing cases were stacked in the hallway and a narrow uncarpeted staircase led to the upper floors. There was no elevator. I was halfway up, negotiating my suitcases in the tight space—I wasn't willing to leave them downstairs—when I paused for a breather. As I stood there, I opened my shoulder bag and took out the photograph, the one I filched in Yorkshire, of Johnny and his crew. Harry Korda stood next to Johnny, as if befitting their closeness. His name—"Harry K"—was written above his head. On the flight to San Francisco, I had looked again at the picture of this man and speculated on what changes the years could have made to him. Now, on the stairs, I made a final check. Even an elderly stoop, I decided, could not have diminished seriously the lank frame that soared, almost joke-like, above Johnny and everyone else. He had huge shoulders and a squarish face. No, he couldn't have changed all that much, not in substance. I replaced the photograph and continued up the stairs.

Korda Aviation Services Inc. was announced in black letters on the frosted glass upper part of a door. I knocked, got no reply, so I opened the door and, trundling my suitcases, went in.

I entered a small reception area divided by a wooden counter behind which a squat old man was lining up a shot on a miniature pool table. He frowned at me, held up an admonishing finger to show that his concentration was sacrosanct. I waited as he crouched across the table. The tongue-like flickerings of the cue as he maneuvered to strike, his leathery sharp-eyed face and the dark green velveteen waistcoat he wore over a gray shirt that was open at the neck and exposed a mass of wattles put me in mind of an elderly lizard. He struck; the balls scattered. He straightened up. He couldn't have been more than five six in height. He wasn't Harry Korda, that was for sure.

"Beats aerobics," he said, looking at the balls and not at me.

"I'm quite sure it does."

"That a Limey accent?" Still without looking at me, he was replacing the cue in a wall rack next to which was a gray metal filing cabinet. On top of the cabinet was a black manual typewriter.

"I'm English, yes."

"So what's your business here?" A seeming flick and a slither and, in spite of his age and a paunch, he was directly behind the counter and facing me with his swampy little eyes and his croaky voice. He had hair, dirty gray, in his nostrils and his ears, but none on his scaly head.

"I'm here to see Harry Korda," I said.

"You're too late, girly."

"Oh?"

"Harry's gone."

"Gone? Gone where?"

"Wild blue yonder gone. Deep freeze gone. Couple o' days ago."

"Dead?"

For a moment he stared at me. Then he cackled.

"Alaska gone. *Al-aska*. We got a steady contract there. Thank God. Twice a year. Anchorage, Nome, Fairbanks—that's our run. Harry dead!" He cackled again.

I smiled, politely.

"Whadaya want with Harry?" He wasn't amused anymore and his eyes twitched in suspicion.

"You could call it—research."

"I could call it snoopin'."

"I assure you I—"

"Y' come in here with a dolled-up accent, but how do I know you're not IRS, FAA, DEA AO—"

"Whatever those initials mean, I'm *not*."

"Plenty o'others y' could be."

"All I am is someone hoping to have a personal chat with Mr. Korda and it has nothing to do with snooping."

"Prove it." He folded his arms, made his challenge implacable.

I can see now that the way I was dressed—I suppose I did look official—had made him suspicious. I hesitated. Then I opened my bag and, the only means I had of justifying my visit, took out the photograph.

I put it on the counter.

He unfolded his arms grudgingly, picked up the photograph, squinting as he held it close to his eyes. He examined it for some moments before, slowly, shaking his head, he returned it to the counter.

"Jeez," he said. "Jeez, was I ever that young?"

"You?"

The tip of his forefinger fell on a skinny young man leaning against the fuselage. A young man with curly hair, his hands, thumbs extended, gripping the lapels of his jacket, his head cocked to one side to give emphasis to an impudent grin that told the world to go to hell.

"Me," he said.

"You flew with Johnny?"

The saurian eyes narrowed. "How come you know about Johnny?"

"I—I just do." I'm not quite sure whether I was unprepared for the question or whether my fumbled reply was a deliberate helpless-little-woman act. Whatever, it seemed to disarm him. He shrugged.

"I was ground crew. Chief mechanic. And all the knocks that B17 took, it was a twenty-four-hour job. We gave that old lady more plastic surgery than Gloria Swanson ever had. Boy, that airplane had class."

"Like Johnny," I said, chancing a prompt.

"Yeah."

"How well did you know him?"

"Well enough. But it was Harry who knew him best. Him and Johnny, they were . . ." He broke off, and the lizard eyes scuttled across my face. "You're here about Johnny, that it?"

"Yes."

He gazed down at the photograph, peered hard at the past. "God knows if there aren't plenty of unanswered questions about Johnny," he said softly.

"What do you mean?"

"Uh?" He looked up in a vague way that suggested his words had been private. Then he smiled. A wide, genuine smile that showed, if only for a moment, he hadn't quite lost touch with that young man who had stood at the fuselage of that B17 all those years ago. "I usually take my coffee break round about now. Care to join me, girly?"

He took his coffee black and with bourbon; four brimming shot glasses were put down next to his cup in an accustomed way by a waitress in the bar down the street which, though dark, seemed free of the villainy I had ascribed to it earlier. We sat in a corner booth and looked at each other across a table lit by an imitation electric candle in a pink globe.

"So who the hell are ya?" he said, though not unpleasantly.

I gave him a card, which included the logo of the studio. He held the card to the table light and as he peered he fumbled his own card out of his waistcoat pocket and passed it to me: he, I read, was Tony Donovan, general manager, Korda Aviation Services Inc.

He settled back in his chair. "You makin' a movie about Johnny, or sumpin'?"

"No, my interest is in—well, I suppose you could call it flashbacks about him."

"Flashbacks." He poured a shot of bourbon into his coffee, picked up a spoon. "Flashbacks," he said again and seemed to stir the word slowly in the coffee for a while. "What happened to Johnny, I'd call it four-flushin'." He had his head down.

"What?"

"Uh?" He looked up in the same vague way as he had in the office: an old man's uncomprehending look. I reminded myself to make allowances for his age.

"What I'm doing," I said, "is without harm or embarrassment to anyone. I'd like you to believe that."

He scooped a handful of peanuts from a bowl, chewed slowly, then began picking his teeth with the edge of my card; throughout, his eyes were fixed on me. He leant forward, winked his vote of confidence in me.

"I believe ya," he said. "Though Harry's the guy for the, uh, flashbacks. *Strictly* Harry. I'll put a word in for ya when he gets back."

"When will that be?"

"It's a three-week contract, but it could end up longer dependin' on what extra work he can pick up. Also, he likes Alaska. Wilderness freak, y'know? He just sits at the wheel o' that Dakota and forgets time and the cost of fuel—great flier, lousy businessman."

"Isn't he a bit old to be flying?"

He winked again. A full, slow, knowing, lizard wink. "He passes his twice-a-year physical and he's got clout with some guy at the FAA. So he flies on, which is more than can be said for the business."

Korda Aviation, I learned—and we were in that bar for at least an hour—had been in a bumpy way for years. Harry Korda had started the company as a crop dusting operation after the war. He got married and bought the building on Grove Street, then a not unfashionable address. His wife, a newly qualified certified public accountant, brought direction to the business and extended it into freight. A midtown office was opened. Twenty years ago, she had died from cancer. Without her, Harry Korda slumped and so did the company.

The midtown office closed. Even Grove Street began its inexorable mouldering. He now rented space there to business tenants, most of whom were not reliable payers, and lived himself in a single room at the back of the office.

Harry Korda. Luckless and loner. He wasn't the most encouraging prospect for me. To change the subject for a while and to show a formal politeness, I asked Tony Donovan about his own life.

"I've just mooched along," he said. "Took my old man's advice. He said the secret of livin' was never to be surprised. On the whole, it works. Not many times in my life have I been seriously surprised, girly. Once or twice maybe. Like"—he raised his cup and finished off his coffee—"like the way Johnny bought it."

"It happened to lots of young men," I said.

"Yeah? What did?" He was on his feet, ready to leave, waving away the money I was trying to put on the table.

"Killed in action."

"If that's what y' wanna believe . . ." He was slithering away expertly and swiftly to the door.

"What do you mean—if that's what I want to believe?" He was on the street when I caught up with him, standing under the bar's plastic awning.

"Uh?" His blank old man's look, his eyes blinking and swiveling as they adjusted to the light.

"What you said back there about Johnny."

"Uh?" His flurry of words in the dark undergrowth of the bar seemed to mean nothing to him now and I wrote them off, put them down to his age and the ramblings of the old, like Bessy in Yorkshire.

I went back to the office with him to pick up my luggage and call a cab.

When the cab arrived he insisted on carrying my cases down to the street. Once I was inside the cab he thrust his face inside the window. "I like ya, girly. Don't like many folks, especially Limeys, but *you* I like. So I'll do my best with Harry, okay? So keep in touch, okay?"

"Fine."

"What I can't guarantee is how Harry'll take it. He don't like to talk about the war and in particular he don't like to talk about Mr. Smith."

"Mr. Smith?"

"Uh?" The old blankness, but only for a moment. "Oh, that was a name we had for Johnny. There was this movie—Jimmy Stewart movie—called *Mr. Smith Goes to Washington*. About this quiet, regular guy who gets himself elected and cleans up the act in DC."

And that was when I leaned forward and kissed him on his bald and mottled head.

I spent much of the rest of the day in San Francisco riding the cable cars. And at night another kind of excursion came my way when, in the dining room of the hotel where I was staying, the resident pianist transported me first-class back to Yorkshire via the Chattanooga Choo Choo.

The pianist, I think, must have taken pity on me and asked for my request because he mistook my pensiveness and the fact that I was the only solitary diner for unhappiness. In truth I'd had, and so unexpectedly, a lovely time on the cable cars. Though utterly out of character for me—I'm bemused still by the way I felt—I responded to the charm and, above all, the simplicity of my transportation up and down the hilly streets; for the first time in ages I was totally relaxed.

I did other things too. I went to the Golden Gate Bridge and Fisherman's Wharf. But, like a child drawn to a funfair, I made my way back to the cable cars and their slow climb and heady drops and their exuberance of sparks and, for me, a sense of easy solitude. Once or twice I felt I ought to be shamefaced about such unsophisticated pleasure, but I reminded myself that this was my day off before I carried on to Texas and though it was too bad that I had missed Harry

Korda, nonetheless I had made contact and I had every right to enjoy these hours in this novel and unguarded fashion.

And so in the roll and sway of the cable cars I threaded my various colored beads of happiness and felt the strongest link to him. To Johnny. For this surely was his kind of city. It was hope and light and space and all this I seemed to see and feel through his eyes, his values.

The exhilaration left me feeling pleasantly tired and instead of going on, as planned, to a Hungarian restaurant I'd read about I decided to have dinner at the hotel. I was shown to a window seat in the dining room and I gazed out at the city in its evening dress of lights, a finery that soared without strutting. One of the skyscrapers was in the shape of a pyramid, a white beacon at its apex—a beacon that pulsed on and off, as if signaling the spirit of San Francisco. Thus my musings—I forgot the grubby parts I saw earlier—and they were set to music by the young man at the piano.

He played well. Ballads, blues, some of the shorter classics, notably Chopin. Once or twice we exchanged smiles, he in his elegant isolation at the white grand piano, I in mine, at the table for one in the window alcove. A waiter came across and said the pianist wanted to know if I had a request. I hesitated, at a loss for a moment. Then— "You might ask him if he knows 'Chattanooga Choo Choo.'"

He did. He smiled, gave me a discreet thumbs-up. He made the number special. He began by skirting it, a series of riffs that echoed the sound of an oncoming train. A train approaching from far away, the American night and old Europe behind it. A train crossing from a distant era to the here-and-now and making its long haul for a solitary passenger: me.

The pianist announced its arrival with a plangent note, followed by a pause, then a thrust of allegro, then with all the bravura of "All aboard!" we were off and traveling and, in my mind, the Andrews Sisters were jiving and snapping their thumbs . . .

Pardon me, boy,
Is that the Chattanooga Choo Choo?
Track twenty-nine. . . .

So it was that I was railroaded back to Yorkshire. And Johnny.

You'll leave the Pennsylvania Station
'bout a quarter to four,
Read a magazine
And then you're in Baltimore
Dinner in the diner
Nothin' could be finer
Than to have your ham and eggs in Carolina
When you hear the whistle blowin'
Eight to the bar
Then you know that Tennessee is not very far. . . .

I knew the words by heart and I had faith that this simple timetable of hope and vision and the need to move on always to a shimmering future had once existed in this society because I had seen these virtues in his eyes and heard them in his voice.

And doesn't that sound just too sentimental? It's true, though. Just as it was true that the Chattanooga Choo Choo swept me along the track of time I had all but allowed to stall in my mind—namely the day after the night in the library.

It didn't come back all at once. It formed, triggered by the tune, in the arbitrary way of memory. After the pianist had switched to other numbers, the fragmented and wispy italics of that day gradually became the bold print of total recall in a near-enough complete page of the past.

The morning of that day I was working with the second unit—that was a memory that didn't have to be unearthed—on a small but tricky scene in which an actor sat astride a five-hundred-pound bomb and built a tower of playing cards on its surface. The page of script I had to go on said he was a flier who had been an architect in civilian life and this careful assembly of the cards expressed (way too

cutely, I thought) his ambivalence over his vocation to build and cre-
ate and, his present role, to destroy. As they will, though, the cards
kept tumbling before they reached the requisite height.

A floodlight bulb popped—the cards collapsed. A breeze came
from somewhere—the cards collapsed. The actor moved fractionally—the cards collapsed. So it went on, take after take. Normally, I
would have been impatient, but that day my attention was totally
focused on that scene and away from my own house of cards and
what had taken place in the library. Rigidly, I had closed my mind
on that; it seemed like the only sensible thing to do. I made the decision as I left the library and climbed upstairs to bed and on the
strength of it I slept well, slipped into a vacuum in which no questions were asked. And now, with equal resolve, I was narrowing my
concentration to the specifics of getting the shot right, leaving no
room for personal shadings. Finally the tower was built, the scene
completed. Only a few ancillary shots, mainly close-ups of the actor's
hands, remained, and though I lingered needlessly for a while there
was no reason for me to stay on the set.

I left the hangar where the scene had been shot and set off for the
administration trailer to confirm with the production coordinator the
arrangements for the next day's shooting. I knew exactly what that
schedule was and indeed what it was going to be for the next few
days; I was out, however, to keep as busy as possible to check and re-
check and take notes where none were needed. Tunnel vision
seemed like a good pro-tem idea. I saw no other option.

But I didn't get as far as the trailer. I was climbing the small grassy
rise leading to the service road between the house and the airfield
when I heard the toot of a horn. I looked round and saw a stationary
jeep on the road, some yards to my left.

Johnny was at the wheel.

He reversed to where I was standing. He smiled at me, his right
hand looped casually across the wheel. It was the first time I had seen
him in daylight and I was struck by how young he looked, with only
the scar at the side of his mouth testifying to the possibility of a wider

experience of life. That was my initial reaction and it didn't develop into rebuke, skepticism or interrogation, such as what did he think he had been up to in the library last night. I knew no exasperation, no surprise. It must have been at that moment that I came to final terms with whatever was unfolding in my life.

"I'm going to Haworth," he said.

"Have a nice day," I said, and added—I don't know, but it may have been a feeble attempt to put him in his place—"to quote the standard insincerity of your country."

He made no reply. Smiling, he simply leant across and opened the passenger door. And I got in. Unhesitatingly. It seemed a perfectly natural thing to do.

The weather had improved a little—it was warmer than it had been and there may even have been some blue to the sky, though I can't be sure—and he was wearing a brown nylon windbreaker, the Eighth Air Force insignia above the breast pocket. He had on his cap. He had pulled out a tartan rug from the backseat and tucked it round my shoulders. And I was happy.

That happiness continued until we got to Haworth, until he switched off the ignition. Almost immediately, I began to feel edgy.

I didn't like Haworth. There was no prior prejudice on my part; the place simply oppressed me. I didn't like the cramped and winding steep streets, their rounded cobblestones like clenched fists. (Some of the worst Luddite riots took place there.) I didn't like its snaking rows of blackened little terraced houses with the layers of gray slates on their roofs evoking a sudden, and irrational, memory of the collective gaze of an armed militia that had pressed in silent menace around me as, back in my television days, I tried to interview a rebel leader in a remote Baltic republic whose name I have long forgotten. I didn't like the moors that rose, high and barren, above the village. And more than anything else, I didn't like that blowhard cliche of Haworth—the perpetual wind from the moors, a permanent sound effect for the sundry torments of the Brontë sisters.

Of all places, we ended up that day in the graveyard. The wind, in suitable lost souls' mode, harried the tombstones, with creaking branches of trees and spirallings of dead leaves part of the stale repertoire. He, meanwhile, did some sketching, sometimes standing, sometimes down on his knees. I stood, for some protection, under an oak in which crows flapped and rasped their claw-sounding curses on the edge of the wind. I wince over such melodramatic words, but that's just how it was.

Finally he came up to me, smiling and flipping through the pages of his sketch book. "Emily's burial place," he said. "I thought I'd give it another try. It's amateur stuff compared to your work, but at least I don't give up."

My work? I was tempted to challenge him. I settled instead for, "Are we leaving now?" We were.

I was always glad to leave Haworth, but never more so than on that first visit. The moment he turned the keys in the ignition of the jeep I began to feel better: it was as if happiness had a simple on and off switch.

That professor of physics at Cambridge mentioned to me time's "boomerang factor"—a swirl of sheer molecular energy with a tendency (nothing spectral, pure science, he insisted) to swing back to its beginnings, when it was time present, and re-group in its original form. It was as simple as that, he said.

Remembering that day in the jeep, however, I seem to see my own simplification: time was a spinning top, a humming arc of color in which I felt the glow of my happiness as we climbed hilly roads and descended into curled villages.

This has just occurred to me, but perhaps that's why I was so happy riding the cable cars; maybe, without conscious awareness, I was reliving the essence of that day. So, inspired by memories, I decided I had a fine excuse for lingering a few extra days in San Francisco— my research for the movie. I met with someone at the mayor's office, I searched out several media people, but beyond that, I was a diligent idler. A couple of mornings, rising early, I huddled in an outcrop overlooking the bay and watched the dense mist unfold over the Golden Gate Bridge and layer away in sun-gilded papery sheets like gift wrapping on a gorgeous present. I dawdled in little parks and cracked peanuts and fortune cookies (*Simplicity is Luxury*, one motto assured me) and fed them to the pigeons. I had doughnuts and coffee from Spruce street-corner kiosks that, true to the cosmopolitan ethos of the city, had *Have a Nice Day!* printed in dozens of languages on frontages flanked by battered green buckets of fresh flowers (a free buttonhole for every customer). For no reason other than a celebrant's gesture, I bought a box of Rainbow Firecrackers. I waved a Stars and Stripes flag, handed to me by a fellow spectator, as a brass band headed a parade of a local charity organization and thumped democracy down the elitist length of Nob Hill. Thus my mooching, my mood of quiet happiness.

And then I saw, on my last full day in San Francisco, the young man who reminded me of Johnny.

I was giving myself a farewell trip on a cable car when I noticed him. He was sitting on one of the seats that ran longways at the front of the car and I, six or seven seats away and from an aisle position, was able to see him fairly clearly. Same slight build, same cut and color of hair, same line of features.

He was wearing chinos and a light brown windbreaker, the lapels raised to his ears because this was a typically cool San Francisco day and the windows were open.

He was reading a book, and casually—I was no more than routinely interested in him at that moment—I craned my head in order to read the title. It was *Selected Poems of Robert Frost*. A twig snapped on the blocked trail of my memory and I recalled Johnny reciting one of Frost's best-known lines to me: ". . . *But I have promises to keep, and miles to go before I sleep* . . ."

So? Frost, after all, is universal. But the way that young man was reading was Johnny's way: the book held almost at eye level, the eyes dreamy in concentration, the index finger tracing the lines as if every word had to be *felt* as well as read. It was how Johnny used to read poetry: slowly, raptly, tactually.

And, I was watching him intently now, those hands—Johnny's hands! In their physical beauty, in their symbolizing of the very grasp of the force and generosity of idealism—Johnny's hands.

Wishful thinking? I cautioned myself so. I decided, or tried to, that here was a pleasantly nondescript young man reading a book of poetry on a cable car and that on a basis of tenuous attributes I was being quite trite and silly about him.

He closed his book. He looked up and smiled directly at me.

And it was Johnny's smile.

It was the smile I saw for the first time that night in the library in Yorkshire—a warm and uncompromising smile, such as one gives a much loved old friend, a smile untainted by politesse or on-the-make motives.

I trust I smiled back. I can't be sure. I was both flustered and elated. I leant forward, peered, wondering, a momentary giddiness, if it was there—the S-shaped scar at the side of the mouth. But, as I have said, the lapels of his jacket were raised and the lower part of his face partly concealed.

The cable car halted at one of its stops, at the crest of a hill. He got up and left. Should I follow him? I actually half rose. Too late. A bell clanged and the doors closed and I didn't even glimpse him as the car dipped sharply down the hill and I set out on my own descent of self-admonition and discipline on the lines of for-God's-sake-pull-yourself-together-woman.

I tried to ignore a dissenting and totally authorative second opinion, one cued to the context of what had just happened—the voice of that professor, that Einstein disciple, as we took afternoon tea in his study at Cambridge.

As well as its larger aspects, time has its little parlor tricks. Its—how shall I put it—Jack in the boxes. Someone long dead can pop up. Now you see him; now you don't.

It's late. I ought to be packing for my flight to Texas in the morning. Instead of which, here in the hotel room, I've been layering my
laptop with my experiences of San Francisco.

And now I'm back to pondering the professor's Jack-in-the-box
analogy. Rationally, I want to believe that it was a Johnny look-alike
I saw on the cable car. Emotionally . . . damn it, emotionally I want
to believe that it *was* Johnny.

Texas

Eight

SAN FRANCISCO STAYS IN MY MIND AS A SORT OF SLOW WALTZ—
sweep of piano music, sway of cable car—that *may* have skirted the
corridors of time. (Though that's a musing I keep for just before I fall
asleep.) As for Houston and Dallas—barn dance!

A stomping of Texan identity. A bobbing of Stetsons. A show-off
flash of buckles and spurs on alligator-hide cowboy boots. Male
cities. And you'd better believe it, little lady.

No doubt I am being unfair, in that my San Francisco reverie was
far too recent for me to come to terms with the rawhide energy of
the Lone Star State.

I was treated well by the business chiefs, civic leaders, journalists
and academics I interviewed in the cause of movie research. Most of
them were men and some of them insisted on squiring me socially.
Accordingly, I experienced the standard gallantry of the corsage pre-
sentation and the attendant ceremony of having an orchid fixed to
me, so that I felt duly pinned, cataloged and showcased as a species of
chauvinistic Texan male attention—the little lady.

I wanted to think that such condescensions were mainly why I disliked Texas. Not so. I came to realize that Johnny, in the sense of his values and his expansiveness of spirit, had no place there. And so during much of my ten-day visit I was wretchedly lonely.

Against my will, my intellect nagging at me to see the incident as the virtual mirage of an errant mood, I kept remembering the encounter with the young man on the cable car in San Francisco.

And that obviously was why I reacted as I did in a Dallas art gallery one afternoon.

I was there as a fill-in between an appointment I had with a local historian and also because in the morning newspaper I'd read a snippet about the gallery's NASA-sponsored exhibition of abstract art entitled *Time: Dimensions, Concepts, Enigmas*. It was no more than a piquant little coincidence, I'm not pretending otherwise, that an exhibition reflecting the generalities of my own preoccupations was on show. I decided it was worth a short visit.

It was a beautiful gallery, spacious and delicately chandeliered— beyond its swagger, Texas knows how to curtsy to culture—but, while I was there, sparsely attended. And so, as I walked down the central corridor, I noted, a turn of my head in passing, the sole occupant of one of the smaller rooms. A young man.

Well, I took him to be young: his back was to me as he stood before a huge canvas that took up about the whole of the room's far wall. He was slim and not very tall. Even in my glimpse of him, these details stood out because of the size of the painting.

I moved on, but I had taken no more than two or three steps before I paused and looked back to the entrance of the room. In that young man I sensed something familiar, and not merely the physical aspects I had seen so fleetingly just now: an altogether deeper outline of his identity and persona moved, strongly but without specifics, in my mind. Hesitating, I tried to distract myself by taking an interest in the sculpted frieze of Botticelli angels in the arch of the room's door.

Then—an impulse, an instinct, a yearning—I went into the room.

It was empty.

Given the fact that only a few moments had passed since I had seen him and that I had kept my eyes on the door, there was no way he could have left unseen by me, so he must have left by another door. The only other door—and, ostensibly browsing, I did a thorough search—was at the end of the room, on the right and parallel with the huge painting. Only that door was locked from the inside by two large bolts, at the top and the bottom.

It must have been—I flicked the cliche nervously, as one would a cigarette lighter—a trick of the light I had experienced. Yes, of course. The lighting was diffused, shadowed, presumably to give additional tonal touches and heighten the mystery of the exhibition's theme. Easy, then, to imagine a person in that room; after all, my own career had taught me about the artfulness of lighting effects.

I'm not sure I convinced myself, though. Otherwise why would I feel this need—quite pressing in its own small way—to record what I saw or (the rationalist in me) what I *thought* I saw in the gallery that day. Why?

To the tangible, though: that huge painting at the end of the room. In both execution and concept, it was epic—vividly colored geometric swirls integrated, in the softest tints, with interlocking prisms. Initially, I regarded that painting, called *Time Trail,* as a means of asserting my intellectual self after my trick-of-the-light-fancyings. Finally, it fascinated me, perhaps partly because its cosmic exposition was so powerful that my ephemeral sighting of a young man may not, after all, have been so remarkable.

The grayness I was driving through was total. The road I was on, the barren landscape on either side, the horizon—everything gray and flat. I tried to scale it all down to a schoolroom slate on which I could chalk the ABC of my thoughts, do my little sums of reasoning. (Simplify, simplify, as the philosopher—Emerson, I think—advocated as a first approach to complexities.)

And that was my precise idea, an idea validated—or so I persuaded myself—by a small circle at the exact center of the painting I saw in Dallas. That circle was the lynchpin of the painting—a core of order, an absolute in the middle of the metaphysical chaos. That was what I needed—a nexus of order, of absoluteness—for in succumbing to such sustained loneliness in Texas I had exposed an uncharacteristic lack of discipline which had to be corrected in case it got out of control. I needed to assemble the *real* facts, and they were plentiful, pertaining to Johnny and Yorkshire, and duly file them in sequence, in my mind and onto my laptop, and use them as a counterweight against the larger confusion. As in the small circle in the painting. I suppose this sounds pretentious, pat, convenient; perhaps it is. All that I can say was that it seemed like a good idea and I recognized that its execution demanded solitude. Hence, two days after my visit to that gallery in Texas, I hired a car and set off across the Texas hinterland.

In that gray wilderness, sunless but clammy, I found myself confused by the map references that were supposed to get me to New Orleans eventually, and though my memory bearings were clear in generalities—I needed to delineate two events, one in London, the other in Cambridge—I somehow couldn't focus in on them.

I was trying too hard, tensing up, and, contrary to my resolves, two or three hours out of Dallas my thoughts digressed to my last day in San Francisco and the trip on the cable car and the young man who looked like Johnny. I remembered, possibly a response to the flatness of the terrain I was now driving through, the downhill swoop of the cable car after he got off. And then, in its capricious way, a distant memory cut in and I was recalling another day, another country, another vehicle. Johnny's jeep.

It was late afternoon and we were driving up a steep hill. There was a sunset behind us and it filled the rearview mirror like a palette. Johnny was talking about Madge, the girl back home. He was saying she had taken to making scolding calls to him from army bases in the States. Even senior rank officers, he said, needed official clearance for overseas calls and had to put up with long delays. But Madge simply stamped her foot and got a priority connection. He smiled, shook his head, said he guessed Madge truly thought she was Miss Scarlett.

We reached the top of the hill, looked down on a lake on one side and woodland on the other. It was a pretty view, until it all started to tilt—until the lake and the woods seemed to lurch from side to side. I was aware of speed, a mad speed, and of Johnny's hands spinning the steering wheel and his foot hammering repeatedly on the brake pedal as the jeep hurtled down the narrow hill.

"Hang on tight!" he said. I thought, curiously dispassionate, I'm going to die. "Hang on tight!" he repeated.

I remembered the jeep gradually slowing down. Johnny, it turned out, had somehow maneuvered the nearside front and rear wheels into the verges of the ditch at the side of the road so that the rutted grass acted as a brake. Finally, the jeep slewed gently enough into the ditch and stopped.

He made sure I was all right, then got out and inspected the jeep. He returned and dug around in the back for a canister and said he would be able to fix what had gone wrong. It was the brake fluid, he said. The mechanism, he added, looked as though it had been tampered with: it wasn't the first time it had happened, he said, and it had been remiss of him not to run a check before we set out. Then he said something along the lines of, "I guess I don't have to tell you it's their idea of a joke."

"It's my idea of attempted murder," I said.

And that was it, a further strange piece of stained glass added to the window of memory. I carried on trying to enlarge my view, in that gray Texan landscape, of what was factual and bona fide, the purpose of that particular journey. Nothing came. I was aware of the events, but I was inhibited, my mind refusing to lock into the starting points that would grant me the narrative sequence I needed to unfold crucial provenance.

In my frustration, I turned on the radio. Static. It was as if the harsh grayness I was passing through had a sound. I worked through the whole band of the radio. More static. More gray sound. *Though not quite* . . . What I heard now was drizzle, a slow and mean rain. I had broken through and made my connection with a particular episode of the past.

I thought of the rainy afternoon in London when I called in at the public laboratory to pick up the dog tags; I had handed them in for analysis a week earlier, paid my fee, and now I had received a post-card saying that the tests had been done and the "item" was ready for collection.

By then I had been back from Yorkshire some weeks and, thanks to Andy's ministrations, I was fairly well restored. I think I may have persuaded myself that, as someone who was no longer psychologi-cally messed up, I could now afford the purely rational gesture of having the dog tags analyzed. I saw it, or wanted to see it, as a neutral enquiry, one that merited little more than a shrug of curiosity.

I duly presented my postcard at the laboratory where it was glanced at grudgingly by a frizzy-haired and unsmiling fattish woman with cracked red varnish on her bitten-down fingernails; I notice women's hands too. She picked up the postcard from the counter and shuffled off to the back somewhere.

The laboratory had white tile walls and a tinny smell, like an empty saucepan burning on a low flame.

When the woman returned she had a brown envelope in one hand and in the other she jiggled the dog tags casually and I was sud-denly, and unreasonably, outraged that such a woman should be han-dling them so indifferently. And I knew then that, my recovery and my cultivated nonchalance notwithstanding, the dog tags *did* matter to me. Profoundly.

Now she shook the dog tags in front of my face. "This the piece you handed in?"

"Yes." I wanted to protest at her insensitivity, but how could I frame it—really, she'd done nothing wrong—without sounding merely petulant?

"Then you'll need to sign a 'goods received in acceptable order' slip," she said, reaching for a pad.

"I wish to see the person who carried out the analysis," I said. It was my way of getting back at her.

"What?" She frowned. Good. "It's all in the report." A squalid fingernail tapped the brown envelope.

"And," I smiled sweetly, "I'm quite sure the report is the jargon equivalent of glorious Technicolor, added to which I'm not at all sure the *goods* are in acceptable order. They're—they're badly chipped. Therefore I am invoking my statutory rights as a consumer to see the individual responsible."

She glared at me. I smiled at her. Point scored. "Wait!" she snapped. She waddled off again, taking the dog tags with her. I waited at the counter for about twenty minutes and though I knew I had overreacted I didn't regret my little stand.

She returned with a stooped middle-aged man in a white laboratory coat. He had thinning black hair and a long nose that twitched as he put the dog tags on the counter and faced me. "What's all this about then?" he demanded. "Chipped? I had to make some incisions for analysis. Take scrapings. It's not treasure trove you sent in, you know, not a priceless Roman artifact or—"

"I know," I said. "It's just that I always make a point of going right to the top in complex personal matters."

"Oh." He blinked, lost his defensiveness. He was mine. "All this is, I'm afraid, is an old military ID necklace. World War Two. American issue."

"Really?"

I didn't mean it as a pat on the head, but he beamed, saluted himself with the little snap by which his hands tugged at the sides of his lapels. "It was simply a question of identifying the alloy batch of the metal and the Americans in those days were using a particular strain of titanium in dog tags and so, with the computer, I was able to trace the product back through the formulary records to the point of origin."

He picked up the dog tags, cupped them in his hand, looked down on them and, as though he were a palmist, said, "These were found in West Yorkshire where they had been buried, though above ground level, for many years."

"Why—yes," I said, disarmed.

Another beam. A bingo beam.

"All in a day's work, you know. I can pinpoint the area because there are traces of limestone, a kind peculiar to West Yorkshire, in the lichen encrusted on the metal. And I know they were above ground because of the nature of the lichen."

"I found them in a wall on a moor," I said.

"Where"—the next best thing to hugging himself, he folded his arms across his chest—"they had lain for something like half a century."

"How can you be so precise?"

"The spectrometer. It measured the reflected density of the accreted lichen. A bit like counting the rings on a tree trunk to find the age of a tree."

"I see," I said, curiously polite. "Thank you. Now all I have to do is clean them up somehow."

"And we can do that for you as well." All Sir Galahad now, he raised the folding edge of the counter in a cloak sweep motion and, with a nod, asked me to follow him. We went to a back room where he invited me to sit on a stool at a steel bench while he crossed to a refrigerator from which he took out a jar containing a cobalt-blue liquid. He placed the jar on the bench, unscrewed the lid and dropped the dog tags inside. "Just give it a minute," he said, drawing on a pair of latex gloves.

After a few seconds, flecks of matter floated up, and soon the liquid swirled, rather like those transparent spheres that simulate snowstorms.

Then it intensified, and there was something cosmic about that frenzy of particles. My reaction, I suppose, could have been influenced by a lingering debility, but I seemed to see in microcosm a distillation of the very essence of time; it was as though Shakespeare's sound and fury fizzed and frothed in that laboratory jar, mocking conceits that beget grudges—I thought, fleetingly, of my snooty manner with the receptionist—and wars, and by which we hold our lives precious and significant, even unique. But we all end up as dust and, gazing at what was happening in the jar, I seemed to perceive that only a few lives are charged by the true and enduring glow of the life force.

The liquid went still, a brown-green deposit on its surface. He dipped a pair of tongs into the jar, removed the dog tags and put them on the bench. And suddenly I felt nothing as I gazed at those three gray rectangles of metal strung on a bracelet; it was as if I had breathed in a stray whiff of anesthetic in the laboratory and had become numb.

"A final rub-down," he said, and began to pass a swab across them. Bending to the task, he rubbed vigorously, as if he were doing a small household chore, and it struck me that he lived on his own and, for no good reason, I felt sorry for him. "Ah," he said. "Ah, I'm starting to get what could be a serial number. And a blood type, or I think that's what it is."

"May I try?" I said, and I swear I thought I was offering the woman's touch to this sad bachelor, divorcé or widower of my fancyings.

"If you like." He took a fresh swab out of his pocket, handed it to me. "Watch your fingers, though, because there could be acid spots left on the surface."

I rubbed briskly on the discs and it was like scraping away at one of those scratch cards that promise the possibility of a fortune. Indeed, I got the big prize. The letters "erton" showed up at first; then "Pepp" and I had the whole word: Pepperton. I continued rubbing, removing the final traces of sediment. Finally, I had: Pepperton, J. D. Captain. US Eighth Air Force.

I felt exhausted suddenly, as though I had completed an immense labor. My friend in the white coat glanced over my shoulder at the dog tags. "Wonder who he was," he said.

"I wonder," I said. Wearily.

No elation. Not even a small sense of triumph. Just weariness.

No false steps, no fluffed lines: that memory passed through my mind like a well-rehearsed play. There was a second act, a finale, a tricky exposition of the entrances and exits of time's metaphysics. I tapped the steering wheel a couple of times—the paced way actors knock on wood to counter stage fright—and faced up to Act II.

The day I picked up the dog tags from the laboratory I phoned the physics professor and asked if he could spare a little time to see me. His pleasure, he said. Tomorrow, I suggested? Fine, he said.

Two or three years earlier I had used him in a documentary that, tied to an outbreak of crop circles and UFO sightings near Stonehenge, purported to be an incisive examination of such phenomena. One of the researchers had put forward his name—I'd never heard of him—on the grounds that a Nobel Prize–winning physicist would add gravitas to the usual assemblage of hippies, farmworkers, village constables and clerics who come with the extraterrestrial turf. Though well into his seventies, she said, he was respected as one of the world's boldest thinkers in the field of scientific metaphysics.

I was in a pub not far from the laboratory when the professor resurfaced in my mind. I don't like pubs. I find them a summation of everything that's insular and cramped and crafty about English life, and it was a measure of my bewilderment that day that I went into this one because I felt in need of a brandy. It had a long bar that stretched, just like much of England itself, from, at one end, olde worlde kitsch (hundreds of Toby jugs displayed on shelves) to, at the other end, public relations slickness (Warhol and Hockney prints). It was lunchtime and the place was crowded, mainly with young businessmen who brayed general nonsense. As I opened my purse to pay for my drink I saw Johnny's dog tags among the loose change and was almost tearful.

I picked up the dog tags. They weighed nothing. And as my hand closed on them I felt that somehow—*somehow*—they lacked the substance of *fuller* information. I had the precisely revealed fact of them so why this desperate need to seek further evidence of . . . of what?

But, of course, it was the sheer open-endedness of the issue, the nature of the enigma, that had seized me in this imperative to try to achieve a totality of explanation. The *fact* of the dog tags wasn't enough; I needed the *truth*. But how? And from whom?

I opened my hand, moved my thumb slowly across the dog tags and remembered—vaguely, but with growing shadings of significance—the professor. It was something he said on that otherwise silly documentary about UFOs, something whose specifics I couldn't quite recall but in which I now sensed the possibility of relevance.

I took a taxi to the television station where I used to work and asked if they would rerun the documentary for me. In the viewing room I sat through the usual twaddle about crop circles and huge flaring discs in the sky from which disembodied voices spoke a mysterious language down columns of light.

And then the professor appeared, filmed against the background of Stonehenge: a smiling, squeaky-voiced, tiny man, but broad-shouldered in what he had to say.

"Crop circles and twirling flying saucers are the geometry of simpletons and add up to society's ten-second attention span. Thus the vast and profound concept of time is trivialized. Little green men—pah! What about visitors from the past? Time's dimensions are such that the past can, and sometimes does, interlock with the present. The past, in short, is capable of reforming on the basis of a perfectly valid Einsteinian-based hypothesis of random matter and energy regrouping. It's really quite simple and happens without the aid of crop circles and flying saucers."

And—*cut*. Two days of filming the professor for twenty seconds or so of air time. That's television. In this case it was the ruling of the head of documentaries who, against my strongest objections, said the program needed to come down in favor of UFOs and crop circles, and, besides, the professor's squeaky voice didn't "play" well. The professor took no objection to the truncation and replied to my standard note of apology with a suggestion for a series, tilted to a populist angle, on metaphysics. I did, in fact, craft out a scenario for such a

project, but it was no more than a gesture against the head of documentaries and I wasn't surprised when it was vetoed on the grounds
that it had no ratings potential.

When I called the professor after watching the rerun of the documentary he seemed to assume there may have been a revival of interest in his idea and I didn't disabuse him; I'm more than capable of
dissemblance. Also, my weariness hadn't lifted.

I took a train to Cambridge, a slow mid-morning train whose aimless
halts trailed my doubts: was this, I kept wondering, such a good idea
after all? My repeated response was to chide myself for my lack of
challenge and to remind myself that there was *some* prospect that at
the very least he might have a theory about what I was going to tell
him. I had, and I tried to be firm about it, nothing to lose. What I
had lost, and I was self-pityingly aware of that, was the elation that
was my due after seeing Johnny's name on the dog tags: I felt
cheated. And, as I have said, weary.

Still, I scrounged up a smile for the professor. My independent
woman smile. My dissembler smile.

He lived on his own in a Georgian cottage on the river and when
I arrived he was in the garden, at a lathe and chiselling wood for a
rowing boat he was making. As we shook hands, I saw there were
wood shavings, curled like miniature scrolls, in his swept-back silver
hair whose uneven ends seemed to flicker, as if in some perpetual
physics exposition.

We puttered about in the garden for a while. He showed me his
beehives and the papayas he was trying to grow under glass. In his
gray corduroy trousers and old blue cardigan he looked like any simple old rustic, except that in his tool shed—there as a private joke
and, I'm sure, his refusal to give ego the chance of any house room—
was his Nobel trophy. Finally, as casually as I could, I came to the
point of my visit: I said a woman I knew well, a former colleague,
had experienced something that might just fall within the sphere of
his research.

"Time?" he said.

"Yes."

"A bit chilly suddenly, don't you think? Should we go inside?" We went to his study, which was a fairly ordinary room except for a huge window, overlooking the garden and the river, in the form of a perfect parabolic curve. I said no, thank you, to his offer of a sherry and once we had settled in—I on a chintz sofa and he in a bamboo frame chair upholstered in a greenish batik print—he said, smiling, "So. Your friend."

"Francoise," I said.

"French?"

"Algerian." The embellishment was spontaneous and the shift in geography seemed to broaden the base of my credibility. "She works in films and it was during her last picture, set in Yorkshire of all places, that she had this . . . this experience."

"Tell me about it."

I did. And smoothly, in spite of my weariness. In the cause of detachment and convenience, I assumed my television presenter mode, allocated myself no more than five minutes—a *lot* of air time—and, briskly and in sequence, told more or less the whole story. He listened closely, though expressionlessly, and didn't inter- rupt once. I rolled into my "wrap-up." I estimated I had about ten seconds to run of my five minutes, and made my tone suitably half amused, and half indulgent.

". . . then, when she had the dog tags analyzed at the laboratory, when she saw his name on them, she says she knew, beyond any pos- sibility of doubt, that what she had experienced was, well, some kind of reality."

"Um." He nodded vaguely a couple of times, but otherwise didn't move for a few moments. "Your friend, this, er, Frances."

"Fran*coise*." Was it a test? But I saw no guile in his uncomplicated blue gaze.

"Francoise. Of course." He flicked a wood shaving that had strayed from his hair onto his forehead; a low forehead, almost pri- mal. "Francoise—how old is she?"

"Mid thirties."

"Um. Not menopausal, then. As to her emotional state generally, is she, would you say, stable—or as stable as one can be in this lunatic age?"

"Totally."

"And what about her worldly intelligence?"

"Honors graduate. The Sorbonne."

"Proves nothing, really. There are Fellows of this university who can read the Dead Sea scrolls but can't cope with a telephone directory."

"She's the most worldly-wise person I know."

"Um." He brought the tips of his forefingers to his nose and looked down. His feet, even given his smallness, were miniatures. He had on brown brogues and though the shoes were caked in mud from the garden, the laces were tied in little looping bows that matched them perfectly, like mathematical square roots, as if he had worked out a calculus while tying them.

"And you did say"—he continued to look down—"that she had taken every step to ensure that this wasn't a hoax of some kind?"

"Absolutely."

He looked up and straight at me. "I would have to meet Francoise, of course, though as an interim judgment I would hazard that she may—*may*—have experienced the displacement of bat time."

"Bat time?" I echoed, both the question and my vulnerability as I felt my bright faked confidence flaking and smudging like overdone cosmetics.

He chuckled, a flutey sound after the high pitch of his voice. "I like to think of it as my very own, um, buzz word," he said, "though I've given up hope of claiming authorship. You see, I believed I had launched the concept of bat time at a congress I addressed at the Smithsonian in Washington a few years back. But since then papers have crept into the learned journals here and there in which various experts have ascribed the theory of bat time to themselves. Where's the harm, though? It's a little yo-yo for them to spin and it makes a change from time's arrow, which I am sure you know is a stock phrase of this branch of physics, though that arrow can, in theory, move backwards and indeed has metamorphosed, though it depends on one's school of thought, into time's boomerang, which is time sweeping in arcs but faithful to its starting point. What it all comes down to is quite simple, of course, namely what was implicit in Einstein's cherished wish to ride a beam of light. For as the young grand guru himself, Professor Stephen Hawking, has conceded, time travel is indeed possible on the premise that if one goes faster than light one can go back in time. It's there, demonstrated in Einstein's general theory of relativity. And at the University of Sussex, and shame on Cambridge, they're working actively on the concept of the 'exotic matter,' that's what it's known as, which will literally fuel time travel and make it a doddle. But I've wandered from bat time and I do apologize."

That was the general tone of his talk during most of my visit and though I hadn't brought a tape recorder and was not taking notes that squeaky voice runs through my mind like a cassette tape and I think I've done justice to him in my paraphrasing. I think, too, I've conveyed something of my confusion.

Eventually, after several other digressions, he got back to the specifics of "bat time," which he said was a periphery of time itself, though an important one.

"At its simplest," he said, "bat time is a maverick force of molecular energy which hasn't settled into the past. It hangs about, as it were, inchoate, and sometimes it swarms—hence bat time—and assumes total fidelity of original form rather like a film that has reposed in a camera for many years and can still, provided the chemicals are intact, be developed into a picture. As to the cause of swarming, it could be a physical disturbance. Such was so in the case of Francoise, didn't you say?"

"Yes." I had told him, of course, about the re-creation of the World War II airfield.

"Quite. So, in consequence, there was a swarming of bat time and she was its receptor. In theory. Invariably there's only one contemporary individual involved in these cases. The point is, we have total cause and effect for her experience. A scientific explanation."

"Even though she met a—" I hesitated. Then said it, slipped it on its way with a too-hasty supercilious smile. "A ghost?"

It was the worst thing I could have said. He frowned. "Hate that damned word! *Hate* it! It's cheap, counterfeit and insulting. In the literal sense, there's no such thing as a ghost. I'm talking about the *past,* you understand, and its *scientific* manifestations, not—not ghosts!"

"Of course," I said, placatingly, but by then he was leaning forward, his hands so tight on the sides of the bamboo chair that it squeaked along with his voice as he launched into a passionate little polemic.

"The past isn't a remote and abstract speck behind us; the past is the next room. Only the door's locked and we—society—can't be bothered to look for the key. And why? Because we're too busy watching television. Oh, we take live pictures from the other side of the world and from outer space itself for granted, but let it be suggested that an inherently similar energy field as the one which makes television possible is transmitting the past into the present, not as an image but as a virtually three-dimensional reality, then society, in its sophisticated wisdom, sneers. This friend of yours, this Francoise, could have strayed into a part of the past—and that's how it happens; people simply meander off course—and though there is absolute scientific provenance for her experience her story would be sneered at, though there would be a sizeable degree of credibility for her were she to say she'd had an encounter involving a UFO. What a paradoxical age we live in! An age of marvels taken for granted, an age of natural phenomena rejected by the prevailing philistine mind which has no inclination to savor fuller experiences—speaking of which, would you care for Darjeeling tea and Fig Newtons?"

Over tea, he went on to talk about those he had met who had experienced "bat time."

"Interestingly, all of them women," he said, which seemed like a plus for Andy's intuition when he urged me to write an account for women of all ages and backgrounds.

- "I'm not saying categorically that men do not experience such episodes"—carefully and with what seemed like scientific precision he dunked a Fig Newton in his tea—"and it could well be that male pride gets in the way of not owning up.

"Women, on the other hand, are not nearly so—what's the word—uptight. They actually seek me out, some of them, in a spirit of genuine, albeit bewildered, enquiry. Others I hear about anecdotally and get in touch with. Over the years I've assembled a fair dossier of case histories; I've thought of making them the subject of a book." He dunked another Fig Newton. "Such fascinating stories deserve the widest possible audience, wouldn't you say?"

"As long as they're true," I said, trying to be properly skeptical.

"Oh, I've verified them." He smiled. "Of course, I would say that, wouldn't I? As part of my fail-safe, however, I stick to a criteria in which those I interview at length—and fewer than a third of the women I see reach that stage—need to be extremely intelligent, emotionally stable and senior figures within their professions. This isn't intellectual snobbery; it's sheer pragmatism. I mean, a housewife or a secretary, say, may have a high IQ but their accounts of their experiences are going to be potentially debunkable on the grounds that they are filling humdrum lives with fantasy. Life is unfair. But there it is. More tea?"

As he poured, from an exquisite silver teapot with a line of elephants carved on the handle, I glanced out of the window and saw that hot air balloons were rising from a field on the other side of the river. I could see figures, some of them waving scarves, in the balloons' baskets.

"The students are practicing for an international festival of hot air ballooning in Austria," he said. "If you like, I can row you across and we can take a closer look."

I said I would rather stay there and hear about "bat time," and I'm not sure whether I was humoring him or whether, the way I was feeling, the prospect of a row across the river was altogether too much, and he wondered if I would be interested in his two most recent case studies. I nodded and put on an intelligent "yes, please" look.

He told me first about a Scandinavian woman, a partner in an international consortium of architects. With her colleagues and others, she was visiting a derelict building in London's dockland as part of a site-finding tour for the European headquarters of a global computer company. Intrigued by the brass Oriental mouldings and insets of a large teak door, she let the rest of the party go on while she photographed the features. This done, she opened the door, found herself in a long and crowded hospital ward where nurses in long gray gowns and white starched collars and hats bustled between iron beds occupied by men. They were haggard, these men, and shivered under coarse brown blankets supplemented, here and there, by what appeared to be military greatcoats. At intervals, at the foot of the beds, there were monkeys in raised wire cages. She walked the length of the ward and back again. When she left, she sought out the rest of the party, took them back to where she had just been, easily recognizable by the distinctive door, and opened that door onto a bare spread of rotting floorboards and gutted windows. A thorough search of every floor showed no evidence of her "ward". The building, unoccupied for years, was a dangerous ruin, though her subsequent enquiries showed that it had been built as a military hospital for soldiers who had contracted cholera in the Crimean War. An idiosyncrasy of that hospital was its use of monkeys as a diversion, a primitive therapy, for the men. And the door itself dated back to the Ottoman Empire and was a souvenir of the Crimean War.

His second story—and he moved straight into it without inviting comment on the first one—involved a noted woman economist, a departmental head at the World Bank. She had taken a summer let at a house in a remote part of Cornwall, a county she was visiting for the first time, in order to finish a paper she was writing on Third World GNP projections. One extremely hot afternoon she was sitting at her computer at her desk overlooking the garden, fans blowing on either side of her, when she heard a dull explosion and saw smoke rising from a small flat-topped hill, less than quarter of a mile away.

She went to the hill, and looked down on a scene of carnage in the cove below. Bodies were sprawled at varying distances, obviously hurled by the explosion. She scrambled her way down and saw that children were among the victims. There was nothing she could do immediately, so she raced back to the house and telephoned the emergency services. A patrolling Coast Guard helicopter was in the vicinity and was diverted to the spot. And found no evidence of disaster. Not there or anywhere else in the region; it did a complete sweep. Meantime, ambulances had arrived and a hospital had been put on standby. The police were furious. They breathalyzed her, and though the reading was negative they threatened charges of public mischief.

She, for her part, abandoned her GNP statistics for some days and concentrated on local sources of history, particularly the parish records. She discovered that the hill from where she had seen the smoke rise marked the site of an old tin mine and that there had indeed been a terrible explosion there—on a June day in 1886. Seventeen were killed, four of them "scratters," the name for children who were used in the mine because their size enabled them to move through small openings impassable to men.

The cause of the explosion was "bleeding," or melting, dynamite in an uncovered box outside the mine shaft on the hottest day locally in living memory, with the temperature peaking at 96.1 degrees Fahrenheit at three P.M., only a few minutes before the tragedy. And not only was it about three when she heard the explosion, but the temperature at that hour—it was mentioned casually on the regional weather report on that night's television—reached 96.1 degrees, equalling the record that went back to a day in 1886.

Listening to him as he described these events I realized, my own experience notwithstanding, that I wanted to be bored or privately

and superciliously amused—anything that would have asserted my
accustomed self. It was perverse of me: he had told me more than I
had expected to hear and now I was seeking to reject it. When he
asked me, then, dunking away with a Fig Newton, what I thought
about the women's experiences, I shrugged and said, a bit petulantly,
"Offhand, illusions seen through an alcoholic haze."

He nodded. "Reasonable point. The architect had a glass of wine
with lunch, three hours before she entered the building. As for the
economist, she was, as I have mentioned, breathalyzed by the police
and no trace of alcohol was found. I too, in my way, breathalyzed
them—I am always thorough in my questioning—and having talked
to them extensively and assessed their background and temperaments
I can attest to their total sobriety in all respects. They were not publicity seekers, nor neurotics. They had nothing to gain from what
happened to them—indeed, given their high professional status, they
had potentially much to lose."

"What if"—I played, though without much flourish, my last logic
card—"what if they had stumbled into an artificial re-enactment, the
shooting of a film or television scene?"

"Precisely," he said. "Indeed, they hoped that such would be the
case. But their every enquiry in this respect proved fruitless. Mind
you, your mention of film sets posits an appealing analogy. The past,
in bat-time context, is, well, suspended scenery. Random chunks of
time waiting in the wings, waiting for the center stage cue."

And that's when I conceded to myself that he was unassailably
right, this erudite little man who dunked Fig Newtons and plunged
his prodigious intellect into the black hole of his research.

But though he had my confidence, I continued to feel drained. I
took a sip of tea. It had gone cold, scummy. I sat there, trying not to
look faded, chipping in as required with a bright smile and a knowing nod as the afternoon went in and he orchestrated time in the
form of the swirling curves he executed with a black felt-tip pen on
a flip chart as he explained—"it's really quite simple"—the theory of
time bands and the "interplay of the fourth dimension" and the

"boomerang curve" and quantum mechanics and molecular electronics, Brownian motion and the potential inherent in combining electromagnetism with gravitation principles.

The room became increasingly claustrophobic with his learning. And then, through the sweep of that parabolic window, I saw three balloons—one red, the other yellow, the third blue—rising in exact formation from the other side of the river, drifting upward against the translucent emerald sheen that characterizes the late afternoon skies of the Cambridge fens.

The yellow balloon, in the middle, rose slightly above the level and equidistant horizontal line of the red and the blue balloons and the resultant triangle was a moment's perfect symmetry, somehow emblematic of the professor's fantastic spins and equations and propositional calculi, floating illustrations of the beauty and the remote trophies of pure scientific reasoning.

And in that dusky green instant I knew order. Understanding. Ease. Euphoria soared in on me and I was free of the ballast that had clamped on me so inexplicably in the laboratory.

That mood, that epiphany in which I accepted without reservation that there were things beyond my ratiocination, saw me all the way back to London. In my flat, I decided to celebrate with a glass of wine. As I was opening the bottle, I flicked on, out of habit, my answering machine. Andy's voice came on, talking of the Italian film deal he was negotiating for me: was I, he wondered, up to flying out to Rome the next day to meet the backers? A couple of days, no more, he said; the sunshine might do me good.

That night as I packed I realized that my earlier mood, the airy feeling that had sustained me from Cambridge to London, had gone—seemingly whisked away on the little gust of reality that had come with my decision to make that short trip to Italy.

In fact, I stayed on there. Initially, for nearly six months. I surprised even myself with my capacity for work. It didn't occur to me, not then, that my industry was also a way of evading questions to which, rationally, there were no answers. This pattern of behavior

extended across two years. I was making movies and promoting a
sort of personal amnesia, putting the past into the narrowest frame, an
ever-diminishing focus.

Though, of course, there was my recurring dream, the past as a
bleak whirlpool—which was why in Texas I set out on that bid to
establish a lifebelt of sorts in the form of that circle of order at the hub
of the vortex in all of its forms.

There it all is, then. And if I am dithering over whether I have
achieved my circle or only a pinhole (though even that must be useful) it could be because I am somewhat tired. It was a long journey
across that gray expanse of Texas and four or five times I got hopelessly lost, which made me feel silly and little-womanish and added to
my emotional strain. Also, the green screen of my laptop—in its
mustering of words, as busy as a parade ground—flickers at the back
of my eyes.

I have done that work in a small motel, not far from the border.
The motel is in an isolated setting and unpretentious, which suits me.
I have been here for two days. Apart from work, I want to rest up as
much as I can for my hoped-for meeting in New Orleans with the
second man on Bessy's list—a Dante Centofanti (delightful name!).
He was Johnny's radio man in Yorkshire.

My first night here, after the opening slog at the laptop, I decided
to ease my tension with a drink and I came round to the tiny bar
adjoining the reception desk. I was joined by a lank youngish man
from Houston who turned out to be a bible salesman. I resigned
myself to a short session of boredom, but instead of religion he talked
civics; he said, a modest aside, he had graduated summa cum laude in
that subject. Possibly because I am English, he extended his theme—
not a monologue, a give and take in which he wanted to hear what I
had to say—into America's lost opportunity as a world leader on a
grander scale of aspiration.

"Do you know what Abraham Lincoln said?" He had brown,
thoughtful eyes. "He said, 'America is the last best hope of the world.'

And what has that last best hope turned into? The couch potato and the sound bite."

Recklessly, I agree, but as I was onto my third drink by then, I decided that in spite of the total lack of physical resemblance he had overtones of Johnny. I was restored. No longer tired.

But then my bible salesman had to call up a bottle of bourbon and proceed to get drunk very quickly. I left him slumped over the bar and muttering to himself. My tiredness returned.

That night I had an odd little dream. From a phone booth high on the moors in Haworth I was calling the police in Houston. Above the wind and the distant connection, I was reporting Johnny as a missing person.

My last night here. I am sitting on the porch and remembering, a fortuitous postscript to this journal, a Chinese proverb Johnny used to quote: *Every man in his lifetime ought to fight a war, plant a tree, and write a book.* As I think of these words the moths around the porch light spiral in vertical columns, like hieroglyphics, and I feel a small translation has been added to my understanding of his life. Johnny fought his war and, if an enduring wall in Yorkshire counts, planted his tree. As for his book . . . perhaps, in a way, I am writing it.

And in New Orleans, and I'll be there tomorrow, maybe former Master Sergeant Dante Centofanti will have a page or two to add.

New Orleans

Nine

IN THE EARLY DAWN OF MAY 20, 1944, JOHNNY'S B17 SPUTTERED
across the North Sea toward the English coast on two engines, while
onboard Dante Centofanti's twenty-first birthday celebrations
throbbed on full power.

"Champagne? I swear we had a crate of it! Champagne and Maine
oysters—where the dickens did they get Maine oysters from?—and a
tub of my favorite ice cream, butter almond, which they'd kept cold
in thermos flasks. And then Johnny made his way back to toot
'Happy Birthday' on the sax. There he is, see?"

The old man showed me the monochrome photograph taken in
the aircraft. He and Johnny, half-crouching in a confined space
between struts, were at each side of a large white square on which
stenciled words proclaimed, YOU MADE IT DANTE—21 TODAY! At the
foot of the improvised birthday card, in almost equally large letters,
was the date: MAY 20, 1944. Johnny, smiling, raised the saxophone in
his right hand above his head in a gesture of triumph.

I thought: I didn't know he played the saxophone. I thought: I've
learnt something useful about him, a little added dimension of his

being. I thought: I knew he played the piano (that knowledge was there suddenly, unbidden); his sister had taught him.

That was the careful lineup of my reaction, and it seems to me now that I planned it that way to put off, even if only for a few moments, the implication, which I spotted almost immediately, of that photograph: that Johnny had not died in a raid on Düsseldorf on the night of May 1, 1944, as I had been officially informed.

I was vaguely discomfited by this for May first had settled in my mind as an anniversary, the only one I had for him—I never knew the date of his birth—and though I wanted to believe there had been a simple clerical error in my notification, I was also primed by something Dante Centofanti had hinted at a little earlier for a greater complication.

And so it turned out to be.

Johnny's death, I was to discover, was not a clean-cut killed-in-action affair, but something foul and needless and coldly premeditated.

And now everything has changed and this indulgent little pilgrimage of mine has become a—a cause. A possessed investigation into a crime that took place half a century ago. Very intense, I know, but that's what I feel.

That's why, by the light of the reading lamp, I sit stiffly at the desk in my hotel room. I have no idea how late, or how relatively early, it is, for I have taken off my watch, tucked it away, so I should not know, to the hour and the minute, the way time has been streaming unused into this unforeseen vortex in my life. I am smoking cigarettes. I take a couple of puffs, stub out, light up another one. It's the first time I've smoked since I stopped in my second year at Oxford and I resumed—I went down to the hotel kiosk and bought a carton—because I thought it might break the block that for so long had me staring helplessly at the green and empty flicker of my laptop screen. And though I am writing now, and though perhaps I made a reasonable start, I am conscious of emotions as unsteadying as that shove of Dante Centofanti's as he rocked my particular boat.

"The Germans didn't get Johnny, young lady. No way. . . ."

If only he hadn't spoken throughout with such quiet and total conviction. If only I could dismiss him as a delusional old man. I can't. I saw the intelligence and the integrity in his eyes as he described the events preceding Johnny's fate and the subsequent cover-up and I found him utterly credible.

My impulse is to shove it all down on the laptop here and now, an affidavit from a prominent banker, which Dante Centofanti is, or was until he retired. But such directness is beyond me at the moment and I see stiltedness and confusion resulting and a disservice to him and to myself. And, most of all, to Johnny.

It seems to me that I need to sidestep for the time being—it's the only way of dealing with my present impotence—and place our meeting in due sequence of my stay here in New Orleans. I'm not going to be able to sleep, not after what he had to say, so I might as well use the time as constructively as I can and lead up to that meeting and trust that this approach will bring form and due context and order to what I was told. Yes, I do believe that makes sense. So—

I arrived here six days ago and checked into this smallish hotel in the French Quarter, largely because its lilac-painted frontage and its terra-cotta roof tiles and its hanging baskets of anemones reminded me of a place I used to stay, during spring vacations in my student days, in Provence.

I have a balcony with curved and latticed green railings and my first day I took the phone out there, lounging on the recliner, and called the phone company operator and inquired about a number for Dante Centofanti, whose name wasn't in the city directory.

The operator, after noting his address, asked me to repeat his name. "Dante Centofanti?" she echoed. "Honey, if he ain't in the regular listin's we'll try the Yellow Pages under *Eye*-talian opera singers and if he ain't there we'll scale downa note or two and try pizza parlors!" And she laughed, a gorgeous, sassy yuk-yuk-yuk, an intoxicating eye-rolling mirth. Her laugh gusted New Orleans' billing as The Big Easy and it seemed I was listening to the very spirit of the city. When she came back on the line with the out-of-town number she was still in fine humor. "I got your man, honey. Dante Centofanti! I reckon a gal could dine out on that name,' specially if she was eatin' spaghetti." Another round of yuk-yuk-yuk and she was gone. In the days that followed I was to develop an odd little nostalgia for that laugh, a minor sense of loss: for New Orleans is not a happy city.

That day I knew none of this and I was smiling over the operator's response as I called Dante Centofanti's number. A woman answered in the tottering tones of those to whom old age is a high-wire act. I asked to speak to Mr. Centofanti and she gasped. Then she shrieked at me. "You dirty tramp! He's my husband and he's also a married man!"

Almost immediately, he came on the line. "And henpecked too," he said, reassuringly sane and amiable. "Please excuse Martha. She's a little, uh, sensitive today."

Briefly, I told him I had gotten his name from someone called Bessy in Yorkshire: perhaps he remembered her?

"My memory for names isn't what it was, but there's always plenty of room in it for Bessy. How the heck is she?"

Bessy was just fine, I said, and I went on to answer a few more of his old soldier questions—sundry things such as was the beer still served warm over there?—before I moved to my point. I said I was an academic researching aspects of the war and, one of my case studies, I was interested in what he could tell me about the man who was his captain in Yorkshire.

"Johnny?"

"Captain Pepperton, yes."

"Make it Johnny. He wasn't one for rank. Though if it came to a choice of saluting him or any of the presidents we've had for the last forty years I'd tweak my fingers for Johnny."

"He sounds special."

"He was. But how come you lit on him?"

"Apart from Bessy, random choice. The book is going to be called—"

"There's gonna be a book?"

His voice tugged interest and I remembered a nun at my old convent school saying of me that I was so glib I could make a fortune selling encyclopedias.

"I hope so, yes. Its working title, at the Oxford University Press, is *The Unknown Soldiers* and it's meant as a series of essays that will give depth and meaning to a cross-section of otherwise unrecorded lives."

That nun was right, of course. I *can* be glib. But how else could I have explained my enquiry to him? He said he would be happy to talk to me, but wondered if I could delay my visit for a few days. "It's Martha, my wife. She's, uh, sick. She's just back from one of her residential stays at the physio clinic and she's gonna be kind of unsettled for a while. How about next Wednesday?"

I agreed to that, and he asked me where I was staying and said he would send his "buggy" round to pick me up.

Meantime, I got on with my salaried business of researching New Orleans.

Sweet Georgia Brown, aka my telephone operator, welcomed me to this vaunted birthplace of jazz, but in the days that followed I heard no overtones of her laughter. No one seemed even to smile, not genuinely, at any rate. New Orleans had its mouth set on the fact of its economic bankruptcy, its notorious corruption—at the social affairs department at Xavier University I was told it is the most corrupt city in the United States—and, certainly at the time of writing, an out-of-control murder count that thrives on what is thought to be the worst drug racketeering in the nation.

The French Quarter is pretty and well-tended, but it's like a water lily in a swamp. Wander a little way beyond its quaint bistros and its jazz clubs with their pastel-striped awnings and shaded fountain-splashed courtyards and before long used syringes in the gutter are the local color as the numerous crack houses take over.

A veteran social worker, a grandmother with a particular knowledge of the street gangs, spent a day driving me around their territo-

ries. Whenever we stopped, she kept the engine going and her foot
permanently poised above the accelerator pedal in case we had to get
out fast. In no way was she highly strung; she was simply streetwise.

"These kids are the worst kind of hopheads and they could open
up on us with anything from automatic fire to mortars just for the
hell of it," she said. "After college, I did a stint in the Peace Corps,
mainly in the Gaza Strip, and I felt a whole lot safer there than I do
here. New Orleans is one sprawlin' war zone. But then, which big
city isn't? There was a cover on *Time* not so long ago. Picture of a
dope-crazed kid carrying a gun. The headline said, 'America the
Violent.' No kidding. It's war."

I think now of Johnny and his war and, in the limits of that context,
of the 20,000 American fliers who died on missions flown from English bases. *Yanks.* Fairly recently, more or less since I committed
myself to the task of remembering Johnny, I have at odd moments
pondered the changed semantics of the word Yanks and the way, in
the war, it must have achieved consonance with Knights. For surely
they blazed banners, those Yanks, as they garlanded gray England
with nylon stockings and Hershey bars and the gloss of Glenn Miller
and went on to prove to a class-bound country that men could
chomp cheap cigars and chew gum without compromising the fun-
damentals of chivalry. Of course, there had to be rotters and cowards
aplenty in their numbers, but at least among that 20,000 of the US
Eighth Air Force in England who never made it back home there
self-evidently had to be a nucleus of idealism, no matter how naive,
and its attendant disciplines of courage and selflessness.

Today the noun Yank is little used, is almost archaic. It's as though
not a generation but a whole race had died out. I have the feeling
that a relatively swift evolution has sharpened selfishness, blunted
simplicity and debased values in these United States. And though this
impromptu moralizing tone surprises me somewhat (detached observation is more my style), I've got to say that no matter what went
wrong with the old America, I cannot imagine it would have coun-

tenanced some of the sights I saw that day in my tour of the ghettos of New Orleans.

After five crowded days and nights here—among other things, I remember pools of urine in the corridors of juvenile detention centers and droplets of newly applied cologne on the pink forehead of a civic dignitary who talked to me in his office during the course of his weekly session with his cosmetician—it was time to keep my appointment with Dante Centofanti. I was ready for the let-up.

The "buggy" he said he would send for me turned out to be a limousine, with a chauffeur in a light blue uniform. The early stages of the journey, about forty miles, were across an industrial swathe of petro-chemical plants and aerospace factories, and then the land lolled into farms and sugar plantations. We went through little townships that were pigtail neat and braided with doting architecture that seemed to share the same parentage: places with white-framed churches with blue-faced clocks and, along with boutiques and European delicatessens, a marked abundance of gilt-lettered antique emporia with names like The Gladstone Bag and Aunt Agnes' Will.

In one of these communities we turned left at the main traffic light, and drove along a lane of cyprus trees and then turned right through electronically controlled gates to climb a long, curving drive edged on each side by poplars. The car stopped in front of a four-storey house with a tiered pagoda-style roof and walls of irregularly formed stonework. On its own in acres of meadows and woods, the house might have been a country club. It was, by token of his description of his car, Dante Centofanti's "shack."

He was over by an outdoor swimming pool. The chauffeur pointed him out to me; he was pushing a small girl on a swing. Or I thought it was a small girl. I saw the doll she clutched. He waved to me, stopped the swing, took his companion's hand, and the two came forward, she dragging behind him the way children do when reluctant to meet a stranger. As he coaxed her, looking down and smiling in the manner of a loving grandfather, I took in that he was of medium height—about five ten, I guessed—and a little plump. He was wearing loafers, beige slacks and a brown shirt open at the neck. He was almost bald on top. What I *truly* noticed about him as he drew nearer, what was inescapable, was the splendor of his moustache, which positively streamed and looped across the whole of his round and ruddy face like a silvered copperplate signature of his fancy name.

"Dante Centofanti," he said, extending his hand. "And this is"— he extricated the small figure that had tucked itself away at the back of his legs—"this is Martha, my wife." She had her thumb in her mouth and her doll squeezed under her arm, that tiny and bent old woman. A blue ribbon flared in her scraggy gray hair, which was worn in the front in a fringe. She squinted at me through bloodshot eyes, slowly removed her thumb, snarled, "You leave my poppa alone!"

"Dementia." He smiled, ruefully. "She'll take to you. I know I have."

And I had taken to him. I liked the way money hadn't made him arrogant. Though why, I wondered, did such an inherently modest man—and even in those first few minutes I could tell he was that— wear a grandee's moustache? The answer came to me later and it was on the lines that his moustache affirmed his dated values of candor and square dealing.

As we entered the house I had a warm anticipation, notwithstanding Martha and the affluence, of small talk about Johnny and his place in a surer and simpler America, two generations removed from the squalor and crime I had seen in New Orleans.

But then Dante Centofanti had to go and tell me of his theory, indeed his absolute conviction, that Johnny had been the victim of a murder plotted in village England.

It's unfair, of course, but I keep thinking of Martha as a twisted omen of the way the day warped. In fact, I really didn't see so much of her. After my arrival, she came into the lounge with us, decided to be polite to me and recited a few lines of "London Bridge Is Falling Down" before consenting to be taken out on the lawn by a woman servant. Another servant (there was no shortage of help) brought in coffee, and, when I asked, Dante Centofanti said he had no objection to my using a tape recorder.

At first, for about an hour, he dealt in simple reminiscence, which was exactly what I sought: little daubs of remembrance, stray pigments to fill the gaps in my picture of Johnny. The spools on the tape recorder turn now as I replay the tape and mix the words into colors and textures. Johnny, I learnt, had cultivated a small garden on the base and had grown American staples, corn cobs and sweet potatoes and pumpkins, in those days unknown vegetables in England. He had taken an interest in cricket, had schooled his crew in the basics of the game and, properly kitted in "whites", they played regularly on the village green against a team of locals. He had tried, and failed, to introduce baseball to the Yorkshiremen. He had a Jack Russell terrier, a gift from the local poacher.

"Cute little mutt. Stays in my mind because my father used to breed Jack Russells. He won prizes. Johnny's dog was no prizewinner, it had bandy legs, but it sure had a fancy name. He'd called it, uh—Ah, me and names! My blind spot. What I do remember is that he'd called it after this baddy in a book he was, uh, kinda into."

"Heathcliff?" It was worth a shot, though until then I hadn't known, or didn't remember, he had a dog.

"Yeah! that's it. The little dog's name was—How'd you know?"

"I—Bessy must have told me."

"Heathcliff. Sure! Isn't it just amazing that all these years that dog's name has been lying in my memory like—like a buried bone? I guess the title of the book is up there in the darkness as well."

"*Wuthering Heights,*" I said.

"Wuthering—!" In his delight, he slapped his knee with his hand. "Bessy told you that as well, huh?"

"It's a—a classic."

"Guess so. For my sins, I've never really been a literary reader. *Reader's Digest* and *the Wall Street Journal,* that's my level. Still, I do remember, now you've got me going, that Johnny was kinda fired up about that book. *Wuthering Heights*—it's a village, right?"

"Not exactly."

"Oh. 'Cos there was this village he was always takin' off to on account, as I think I remember, it had a connection with the book."

"That would be Haworth."

"Haworth!" Another slap on the knee. "Exactly! You gotta excuse me, young lady, but this was a long time ago and for me it's a bit like coming out of a tunnel. But now my eyes are adjusting to the light and I remember we used to rib him that the way he was always there, he must have had a girlfriend stashed away in, uh, Haworth."

"Perhaps he did. Emily Brontë." I smiled archly. He smiled back, but in a slightly nonplussed way. It was obvious he knew nothing of Emily Brontë, so I switched the interview to what he, as a banker, could give his full attention and probity to: a character reference.

"What made Johnny so special?" I asked.

"He—Well, I'll come right out and say it. He was one of those once-in-a-lifetime persons, literally that, whose example guides you for the rest of your days."

Down in print, it seems fulsome, a Rotary Club eulogy, but in direct speech—there in that sweeping lounge which enclosed its version of the American Dream in everything from jade Oriental statuary to original masterpieces of art on the pale yellow walls—the spontaneity and the sincerity were real.

I went on, very much the formal academic researcher. "Could you give me a specific?"

"His—his strength. He wasn't a big guy, five nine maybe, but he had the *inner* strength of . . . of a legion."

"In what way?"

"In the way he *carried* us. His crew. In—I guess in his faith."

"Religion?"

"Not—not per se. I never knew whether he was Episcopalian, Jewish, Catholic or—I mean, there was nothing, uh, preachy about Johnny, but he—he spread the word. And that word was hope and it was courage and it was loyalty and—Look, young lady, I don't want to make a testimonial dinner outta this, but he had these things and that's why he was such a helluva pilot."

"A hot shot?"

"A *quiet* hot shot."

A pause. Then an affectionate chortle. "Young lady, the number of times he brought that B17 back when it was no more than an airborne junkyard. Tail section all but shot away, hydraulics gone, two and even three engines down. Whatever mess we were in, Johnny always got us back. *Always.*"

Another pause. A long one. A pause of thirty-one seconds: I timed it in an earlier replay. In hindsight, I recognize that pause as a countdown. Words he had been repressing for years—ultimately devastating words—were petitioning him, and sitting there, both hands clasped round a coffee mug, he was pondering a decision to go all the way to the front line of memory.

It could have been that the formality of interview, the mute but judgmental presence of the tape recorder on the glass-topped coffee table in front of him, had acted as catharsis. I don't know. But toward the end of that pause he looked at me with a candor in which his eyes—large, brown, Italian eyes—were solemn, indeed almost stricken. When he spoke, his words, until then fairly measured and at times halting, were rapid, as if he had reckoned that if he hesitated the seal on the long silence would stay unbroken.

"After all Johnny went through, he didn't deserve to buy it the way he did. Okay, your number's up, that's it, that's war. Hard luck. A guy dies in action and it's rough, but you can understand it, accept it philosophically. If Johnny had to go, that's the way it should have been."

"But he did—he did die in action." My voice on the tape sounds smugly sure, a there-there voice, a patronizing your-memory-isn't-quite-what-it-was voice.

"The Germans didn't get Johnny, young lady. No way."

Those words—he had brought his hands together and the tips of his forefingers were placed at the point of his chin—were slow and considered. Verdict words. And I continued to challenge them.

"But surely you know he died on a mission to Düsseldorf on May the first, 1944." He shook his head in slow dismissiveness. Hadn't Tony Donovan, back in San Francisco, seemed to imply a similar skepticism? And Bessy in Yorkshire—what exactly had she said? At the moment, I couldn't summon up the details. It wasn't important. Old people had faulty memories and I had the facts. I smiled and corrected him.

"I have my information officially, in black and white," I said.

"And I also have something in black and white, young lady. If you'll excuse me, I'll go fetch it."

Smiling, he rose from the white leather horseshoe-shaped sofa we were sharing, he on one side, I on the other.

As he left the room I noticed for the first time that he had a slight limp in his right leg. Outside, on the lawn, I could hear Martha chanting "Ring o' Roses" and those crayon marks of childhood were blurred by her croaky old woman's voice. Sometimes, he had told me, she imagined herself to be a seven-year-old—that day she was wearing white ankle socks and a cotton dress printed with teddy bears holding balloons—and sometimes she thought she was his bride of three or four months and would accuse him of affairs. No wonder, I thought, the poor man was confused and had made that mistake about Johnny; the limp was both in his leg and in his memory.

Reasonably satisfied with this explanation, I got up and went to look at his paintings. Though he professed ignorance of literature, he knew the value of art, if only its monetary worth: there was work there by Vermeer, Corot, Miró, Ben Nicholson, Edward Hopper and René Magritte, among others. I estimated that at least $20 million hung on these walls. I reflected, browsing among the collection, on what he had mentioned of his career; he had retired as president of the investment counselling division of one of the major banks in Louisiana. He presided still, on those walls, in the form of a company portrait in which, gray-suited, he sat behind a mahogany desk, a furled Stars and Stripes flag to the side, and projected rectitude— positively flourished it in that moustache of his. I was looking at that portrait when he returned, carrying what seemed to be a photograph album.

"Someone at the office called that my Gilbert and Sullivan look, though I don't know what part they had in mind," he said, putting the album on the table in front of the sofa.

"The Lord High Admiral—the moustache alone grants you that rank," I said. He chuckled. I crossed to the sofa, sat down. He tapped the cover of the album, which had the dulled red of old sealing wax. "I have a photograph here, but before I show it to you it might help round out the kind of person Johnny was if I told you a little about the state I was in before my twenty-first birthday," he said.

"Of course." No harm in humoring him.

"No one forgets their twenty-first birthday, right?"

"I suppose not."

"You don't. And as I approached mine, young lady, I was in a bad way. We'd been going through a rough time, you see. The flak, the night fighters. I—I started to crack up. I became fixated on this idea, it was a regular obsession, that I was gonna die on my birthday. Kept having this dream. I'm back home and I'm blowing out the candles on this big white-iced cake. Swell. Only the flames on the cake blow toward me and I'm on fire and that white cake is the arc of a searchlight and we're dropping down that beam and we're blazing and—"

"How awful." Heard now, my words sound like mere politeness; in fact, remembering my own recurring dream, I felt some empathy.

"It was Johnny who pulled me through. Just as he did with two or three other guys when they were going nuts. He talked to me, listened to me, sometimes three and four in the morning. He showed me the meaning of—of commitment. Okay, so I'm the big-shot banker, but without Johnny—Point is, I was drinking, popping uppers—you could get them even back then—and I could have ended up as a medical discharge. Vets' hospital. Psychiatric treatment. The bank, I joined them from high school, wouldn't have taken me back with that kind of history, and they'd have found out. Thorough people. So the reason I'm sitting here today in this big house—two sons Harvard-trained lawyers, a daughter who's a top-flight surgeon—is because one guy saw me through, turned me round. Only he said, typically, I did it myself."

"I'm sure you did."

"Oh, I never stopped being scared. But maybe I picked up the handy knack, Johnny's doing, of grace under fire."

Grace under fire yet! Beneath my interviewer's set smile I flinched and decided I could do without this commemoration by cliche. I have since pondered that momentary spasm and wondered if I was bracing myself for the unexpected, checking the handrails of cynicism so that I should have a full grip of self-possession to deal with whatever Dante Centofanti was leading up to. He, meantime, continued with his account of the events surrounding his birthday.

"The night before I'm gonna be twenty-one, after eleven days of stand-down would you believe it, we're on a mission. Stuttgart. No trouble in remembering that! I was sure this was fate. Good-bye, life. I wrote letters to my folks and Martha—we're childhood sweethearts—saying I love them and I'm sorry I'm not gonna be seeing them again. I spent most of the rest of the day in chapel. Finally, we're in the air and it's midnight—I've been checking the time to make sure that at least I know something of my birthday—and the Germans are giving me a twenty-one-gun salute from ground batteries. A full thirty minutes of this and the outer starboard engine takes a hit. But we carry on to the target. We drop our bombs and we're limping home on three engines when a Fokker Wolfe rakes us and its cannon shells knock out a port engine and a chunk of the wing.

"We shake the Fokker Wolfe and we're bumpin' through clouds and I'm still sure we're never gonna make it. Only at the same time I'm calm. I figure that since I'm gonna die nothing else can shock me and then, jeez, there's this almighty pop behind me and I'm jumpin' up in sheer terror . . . and it's one of the guys, crept up on me with a bottle of champagne he's just opened next to my ear."

He laughed. A great tears-in-his-eyes, head-shaking laugh. And the tape, in isolation, seems to distill that sound and to present it as a vintage toast to his young manhood, his coming-of-age. "Young lady, the party I had. The party! Here, see for yourself."

He opened the album, took out a photograph and handed it to me. It was an A4 print, glossily clear, with its only technical flaw a blurred star-like effect on the horn of the saxophone where the flash-bulb had been reflected.

I held the photograph at a measured mid-distance from my eyes, determined not to compromise my role as the impersonal inter-viewer, and I looked at Johnny and took in the uncalculated heroics of his dress: his goggles shoved up to his forehead, his oxygen mask clipped to his left shoulder with its unplugged tube hanging across his Mae West life jacket. I considered, carefully, his young smile and the way it seemed to be given wisdom by the random heraldry of the scar at the side of his mouth. My eyes went to the saxophone, held aloft, fanfaring the moment.

And all the time I had noticed the date and chosen to ignore it, and continued to do so as I gave my gaze to the Dante Centofanti of May 20, 1944: chubby, with slightly pouted cheeks, thick dark hair and even then, though far from maturity, his moustache. He looked very drunk, very happy.

A lifetime on and he was still under the influence of that celebra-tion as he recited the facts of the champagne, the oysters, the ice cream, the birthday toot on the sax.

"The whole thing was Johnny's idea. Johnny's *inspiration*!"

I continued to examine the photograph, paused now over the scrawled signatures and messages from the rest of the crew on the huge makeshift card.

"Is that, or isn't it, the perfect photograph?" he said.

"Perfect." I handed it back to him. Hesitated. "Only—well, there's a lack of focus in it as far as I'm concerned. According to my information Captain Pepperton—Johnny—was killed on May the first. Whereas, as the photograph shows, your twenty-first birth-day—"

"Was on May twenty. I figured an intelligent young lady like yourself would spot the, uh, discrepancy."

"There must have been a—a mix-up."

"Cover-up." He said it with quiet emphasis. A banker's decision. He looked at me levelly and the remembered twenty-first birthday had gone from his eyes.

"What?" I said.

"I feel like a stiff drink," he said. "How about you, young lady?"

"Gin and tonic."

I watched him as, over at the bar at the end of the lounge, he poured a whisky for himself. He paused, considered the amount in the glass, then added to it liberally, though I felt he wasn't a serious drinker.

He brought the drinks across, sat down, raised his glass. "To Johnny," he said. "And to the cause he served in life—the truth. I figure it's finally time I made up for my own shortfalls in that respect. I have a story to tell you, young lady. A—a shocking story."

Ten

STUPIDLY, I LIGHT YET ANOTHER CIGARETTE, BUT HERE IN THE
hotel room I am aware of deadlier fumes—the disturbed, dust of the
past. On one level that odor is as stale as the cliche that was said of the
GIs in England in the war, "Overpaid, oversexed and over here,"
and on another it is the acrid burn of the homicidal instincts of a tiny
coterie of the upper class who used that same phrase as a writ to justify a calculated and sustained bid to destroy Johnny and his crew.

"They did their damndest to get us blown out of the sky, young
lady," Dante Centofanti said.

"They" were a few of the young heroes of Bomber Command,
and one in particular, patricians who had learnt the art of ruthlessness
and winning at all costs at some of the top public schools in the land.

"These guys are kids, same as we are, and in the war life is *really*
cheap. I mean, when you're dropping bombs wholesale on cities I
guess the taking of life in other ways could seem to be of no great
account. All part of the killing game. Just another blood sport."

I have switched off the tape for the time being and in the silence I reflect on a group of very young Englishmen in Yorkshire who showed what breeding can do in the refinement of lethal intent.

I muse on the nature of evil and on my own self-righteousness. What right have I to adopt a superior moral attitude to New Orleans, or to any American city, when all that time ago in the village England of Mrs. Minniver a malevolence worthy of the Dark Ages was taking place?

For Johnny and his crew were systematically targeted by a group led by a man who—but I need Dante Centofanti's words for this. I'll switch on the tape, find the place . . .

". . . the kingpin in this setup was a young squadron leader and he had one of those hereditary titles. The duke of—of—damn, the name's gone for the moment. Ask me to quote anything to do with figures, like the Dow Jones average, no problem. But these last few years, me and names—oh, man! It'll come to me as I talk, his title. Had a Scottish sound to it. Darndest thing is I can see his face clearly. Straight yellow hair, combed flat. Very pale blue eyes. Slim. Could *seem* charming, but at other times . . . I remember he was riding his horse on the base one day—the horse was part of his image, you understand—and it threw him at a hedge. He got so mad he took out his twin-bore and shot that horse. Pedigree animal, perfectly sound, and he—we called him the duke of Dillinger, *that* I do remember, on account that this sounded a bit like his actual title—I'll not rest until I remember what that was—and also on account that he was as cold-blooded as John Dillinger, the American gangster. Your age, I don't expect you'll have heard of Dillinger."

I told him I had and I remember thinking, trying to be wanly amused, that it was a mite hard to picture a ducal Dillinger at work in wartime Yorkshire. I'm not sure, to be honest, whether I was keeping an open mind or whether, privately, I wanted to discredit his words as ramblings.

I persuaded myself that my attitude was one of healthy skepticism. But his story built to a strength and a logic underwritten by the quiet certitude of his banker's voice. He explained, and made perfectly credible (I came to acknowledge that) the genesis of a resentment that festered into a sociopathy, a killing mood, licensed by vested pride in the British Empire. And the brute force historically man-dated to maintain that sovereignty had its full expressions at the base in Yorkshire where the plumed helmet of colonial supremacy was dangerously tweaked. For the Americans lived in the manor house and the senior RAF officers had to rough it in run-down farm labor-ers' cottages on the estate.

"We were the Yanks—the bloody upstart Yanks—and *we* were the lords of the manor!" he said.

"So you can understand that this wasn't exactly a hunky-dory setup with the RAF guys, especially the upper-crusters. It was lousy planning, strictly zero psychology, by someone at the top and our understanding was that this was Eisenhower himself, since we were a special unit. Did I mention that we were a special unit?"

"No. But I knew about it."

"Yeah? Anyway, apparently Eisenhower insisted on our privileged treatment as a way of asserting himself with Churchill—they were supposed to hate each other—whose idea, it seems, it was that we should fly with the RAF. The manor house was requisitioned for us, then, and the RAF fellas, who are living on basic rations, were only too aware that our bill of fare included steaks and fruit and anything else that passed for the fat of the land. Also"—he chuckled for a moment—"also, we had a butler.

"Okay, so the guy's down on the manifest as the maintenance man, but he'd spent all his life in that house as butler and he's not inclined to switch his frock coat and his striped waistcoat and his starched collar—he loved that get-up—and we, come on, we're kids, didn't encourage him to change his ways. We gotta kick from him opening the door for us in his finery and, you betcha, we put on the dog.

"Only we were put in our place—namely all alone in an empty sky that could, and often did, fill up with German night fighters. And that *didn't* happen by chance. The duke and his buddies made sure we lost our way. Time after time. We were the upstarts in the manor house and they meant to foreclose on us. And did they mean business!"

"I see," I said, and I put down those words carefully, a small patch of neutrality, my move to stand aside from the warring expanse of his memory and the possibility of faulty recall and the bias of an old grudge. I kept reminding myself that I had to be sure—notwithstanding that he had shown me the birthday photograph of Johnny, with all its implications, I *had* to be sure. In the end, of course, I was, and now I wish I had been able to write him off as an unreliable witness, in which case I would not be sitting here, my eyes scorching on cigarette smoke and the steady circuit of the tape mocking my turmoil.

Right now the tape is picking up the shrill tones of Martha on the lawn as she chides her doll. Through the window I saw her wagging her finger at it—"You're a bad, bad, bad, bad girl"—and overlaying this is Dante Centofanti's slow voice, at times infuriatingly slow, as he explained how the duke was able to direct the virulence against the Americans.

"He flew the lead ship, a Lancaster, ruled the roost when the squadron was airborne. He ran his airplane like an exclusive club. Okay, so he was the only title onboard, but there was another guy, his navigator, I think, whose family owned just about half of some African colony, another one who—talk about cronyism! He'd hand-picked that crew so that they were all strictly huntin', shootin' and fishin' types and that's another reason why we were their quarry—one big silver sittin' duck that was repeatedly deserted by the rest of the squadron and left to the mercy of the German night fighters.

"But maybe I'm getting ahead of myself. So that you'll understand the background, the intensity of the whole business, I guess I'd better tell you about the visitin' ballet company and the, uh, the rape scene that wasn't on the program."

"Sounds fascinating," I said, and my facile response, and I cringe now when I hear it again, was part of my bid to be balanced.

"Fascinating?" He shook his head, but smiled. "I'm not sure that's the word. The duke's sister, now, *she* was fascinating. Young lady, I never was a hot-blooded man, but she was the second or third sexiest woman I've ever seen. She was his twin, only there was no resemblance. I mean, she was dark and sultry and he—point is, she ran this ballet company that toured military bases and brought culture to the lives of the, uh, gallant boys—so long as they were officers. No kiddin'. The British military, they had this officers only rule. Guess they figured the enlisted guys couldn't handle tutus and leotards.

"Anyway, the duke fixed for the ballet company to visit the base and London told us that the dancers and the musicians, and there were lotsa them, would be put up at the house. So we moved out of our rooms and bunked all together in the billiard room on the ground floor. Night of the performance we took ourselves off to what we called the Stage Door Canteen (it was no more than an extended Quonset hut) to watch *our* version of the ballet: a Tarzan movie. That sticks in my mind, y'know, the fact that it was a Tarzan movie. Strange, huh? Johnny came along too; as an officer, he could have gone to the ballet, but he figured his place was with us."

He paused, took a sip of his drink, and just then Martha, in the garden, pressed her doll to the window and moved its arm in a waving motion. He waved back. I did too, though perfunctorily, and maybe she sensed this because she glared, turned the doll toward me and viciously punched its rubber face. She lurched out of sight, cackling. He shrugged and half-smiled in his embarrassment.

"You'll have to excuse Martha," he said.

"Of course."

"Where was I?"

"At a Tarzan movie."

"Ah yeah, Tarzan. Only the real hollerin' came later. Dead of night later. First of all, though, when we got back to the house we found the ballet company and the officers and some big-wigs from

the village are having an after-the-show party. The duke's sister spotted us and insisted we have a drink. She was wearing this red outfit
that was just about see-through—though Buddy swore he never
meant her any harm."

"Buddy?"

"Buddy Falzoni. Italian, like me. Though that's not the reason his
name stays even in *my* mind. He was nineteen years old. Our ball
turret gunner. Kid from hicksville—Kentucky or someplace like that.
On a hunch vote, I'd say Buddy was innocent."

"Of what?"

"Rape. The duke's sister."

Those words were spoken very quietly and now he stared ahead in
a vacant way, apparently oblivious of me and Martha. She was at the
window again, her eyes rolling, her nose pressed flat against a pane as
she solicited attention. I felt a sudden impatience with both of them,
like, I remember thinking, an uncharitable visitor to an old folks'
institution—a context which suited me at the moment since it
brought perspective to this absurd notion of his that there had been a
plot to "get" the crew of the B17. He was an old man. He wandered.
It was his due. Martha, furious at being ignored, banged her forehead
against the glass. He started slightly, as if coming out of a short nap.
He turned, blew her a kiss. She grinned wetly, shambled out of sight.

"All she needs is kindness," he said. "Someone, I don't remember
who, once said that old age is a shipwreck. I'll go along with that, but
not with the view, all too common today, that its more acute victims
are flotsam."

"Indeed," I said, and abandoned my fleeting and expedient theory
about the possibility of his own latent senility.

He picked up his glass, but put it down before it touched his lips.
"I, uh, seem to have strayed from the point of Buddy Fanzoli and the
duke's sister. Though maybe you're finding it all kinda tedious."

"By no means," I said, though frankly I was allowing for a long
and pointless story with, the rape notwithstanding, no climax. I was
wrong. The tape turns on an account that ought to have been part of
a broader scale of evidence in a World War II courtroom . . .

•   •   •

"To rejoin the ballet company party, then, in a manner of speaking, and it went on way into the night. We got pretty tanked up, ready to swear allegiance to jolly old England. Finally, they're playing 'Auld Lang Syne' and the party's over and we're staggering off to the billiard room and our cots and mattresses. Sack time.

"Seems that we hadn't been asleep more than a few minutes—though who can tell?—when there's this unholy din that has nothing to do with sustained snoring. I mean bangs and yells and—the door to the billiard room bursts open and someone puts the light on and it's Buddy who's crashed in and he hasn't a stitch on and there are all these scratches down his face and he's trying to say something about wanting to go to the john.

"Now what you've got to understand is there's no john on the ground floor, which is where the billiard room is, so the guy has made his way to the first floor, which is where his regular room is, and that room just happens to be a couple down from the one that's been allocated to the duke's sister.

"Buddy never denies going into her room, but he insists it was an honest mistake in the darkness. He says all he did was accidentally trip over her bed. She says rape. Screams it. Gouges it across his face with her fingernails."

He looked at me, clearly expecting a reaction. I nodded. One of those staple nods used on television in which, in a jump cut, the interviewer is shown registering unspoken intelligent attention and, where appropriate, human concern. Behind my nod, though, I wrote off the relevance of the rape; I had signed on for his grand memory tour and I would simply have to put up with his more pointless stops en route.

"Buddy's put under close arrest and court martial papers are prepared," he resumed. "Those days, in the military, rape was a capital offence. There was a place in England where the Americans had built their own gallows. It was known as the rape rope and a whole slew of GIs over there took that, uh, swing. So Buddy's in a sweat. Three days later, however—just three days—word comes through that the duke's sister has decided not to press charges on the grounds that they'd both been drinking and she's misunderstood the situation. So Buddy's released. It didn't take much to figure that some top-level pressure had been brought to bear. Whatever, it's bad news for Buddy."

"Bad news? Why?"

He was silent for some moments. I can see him now, that decent old man in that room of priceless art, his own hapless figure in the landscape of the past; I see his finger making a slow circuit of the rim of his whisky glass, as if tracing the line of memory.

"The, uh, wreaths started arriving," he said finally.

"First one was found propped against the front door by the butler the morning after Buddy was let out. Regular funeral wreath. A black sash across it. And pinned to the sash a white card with Buddy's name on it. Nothing else. Just his name.

"After that, a wreath was found at the door every morning for, oh, ten or eleven days. We, uh, got used to it. Laughed it off. We figured from the start it was the duke's doing and, sure enough, early one morning the butler looks out of the window and sees the duke's batman sneakin' up and leaving a wreath. He knew how to make life hard for us in the sky, as I've explained, but his war of nerves at ground level . . . kids' stuff. That's our thinking.

"One night Buddy takes off to the village to meet a local girl he's datin'. He didn't turn up for breakfast and we figured they'd spent the night together; it had happened plenty of times before. What does turn up, however, is the wreath, same as usual, except that this time there's a big X scrawled across his name. So? What's the big deal? That's our attitude, until—"

He broke off, cleared his throat, and I listen now to that dry rattle on the tape.

"—until, uh, Buddy's body was found later that day. Hanging from a tree in the woods at the back of the house. It was the poacher found him, the guy who gave Johnny the little dog. Buddy's a big guy, two hundred pounds at least, and it took four or five of us to get him down."

"Suicide?" I expressed the immediate inference.

"Uh?" He blinked. "Yeah. Suicide. Or that's what the official report said. Only it, uh, it overlooked a couple of, uh—details. Like the blow to the back of his head. Like the fact that a wreath, identical to the ones that had been left at the house, had been put round his neck. And no matter how hard Johnny tried, he couldn't get that report revised. In London a kid lieutenant heard him out—the generals were too busy—and said Buddy had been brooding over his arrest and incarceration and, get this, that he had a long record of clinical depression. Come on! This is a farm boy who's off-balance only in the way he can never hit the right notes when he's singin' his head off in the shower. That report, that *detailed* probe, was rushed out in under a week."

"Fuck you," Martha piped, unseen, from the lawn, her voice for once pitched to something like childish innocence. Apparently pleased with the sound, she went on to loop it onto a verbal paper chain. "Fuck you . . . fuck you . . . fuck you . . ." On and on. Softly, like a birdcall. Then she stopped.

"Damage limitation," he said, and at first I thought he was talking about Martha's condition for he had paused, uncomfortable, during her short recitation. But it turned out that he was back with the case of Buddy Fanzoli.

"That's what they call it nowadays—damage limitation. Right? I guess the generals figured that a suicide was acceptable, just about, but a murder—no way! Our tiny part in the war had been dreamed up by Churchill and Eisenhower and their brainchild had to be upheld as a credit to its *noble* begetters!"

Abruptly, he downed the rest of his whisky, pulled his lips sharply on the taste, and I had an impulse to exploit the vulnerability of the moment and ask the only question that now mattered to me—what had happened to Johnny? But I held back, sensed quite strongly that he had imposed a tacit protocol in which he would get to this crux in his own time. Or am I making excuses and could it have been, as with the birthday photograph, that I was

putting off hearing that truth? Or perhaps wanting to avoid it altogether?

He shook the ice cubes in his glass as though they were dice and
ventured a modest gamble. "I'm gonna break the habit of years—
doctor's orders, y'know—and risk another blast. How about you,
young lady?"

I declined.

In fact, I've had nothing but coffee since then. Lots of coffee, sent up
by room service, in an effort to keep my head as clear as possible as I
transcribe these tapes. All the same, I am suddenly tired. The layers of
cigarette smoke sculpt seductive sleep. But I must finish the full
account before morning, when I check out of this hotel and leave
New Orleans. I *must*.

This urgency is every bit as real as the police sirens I hear, muted
but still frantic, as they streak across the crime-sprayed New Orleans
night. I, too, have this sense of responding to an emergency, this
sense of deadline. I'm professionally conditioned to deadlines,
though this one matters more to me than all those that have gone
before in the promotion of my career: this one is an imperative of
personal truth, a truth which can't be delayed for a night's rest, and
it could be that for the first time in my self-centered life I am being
selfless.

Back to the tape then and my attempts to assemble his words into
a fairly cohesive narrative. He said so much and I dither still over
parts I have excluded as needless. Though what absolutely must go
down now is his detailing of the means used to desert the B17 over
enemy territory. At the time of telling I was exercising due caution
over what he had to say, making allowances for exaggeration. I no
longer doubt his veracity in any respects—his recounting of the
hanging marked my conversion—and now I'll press the reverse button and locate the words that describe how the B17 was systematically left stranded . . .

•   •   •

"We were pretty well okay on the outward leg of a mission, and that's because we had the safety of numbers. Somewhere over the North Sea or the Dutch coast our squadron would rendezvous with the rest of the strike force, which could be as many as two hundred airplanes from other bases. Those ships would press on into Germany in a solid wave. Convoy principle. Good insurance.

"Once a target was reached and then bombed, though, there'd be plenty of disarray, as maybe you can imagine—and the main thing was to get the hell outa there fast and so the individual squadrons more or less looked after themselves as they headed for home.

"And that's when we'd hit big trouble. I'm the radio man and I'd find that all the frequencies, which worked perfectly well on the way out, were either totally jammed or faulty. What you've gotta understand is that the frequencies were controlled by the lead ship. Now with the radio jammed we had no means of checking our place within the rest of the squadron, which could just drift away from us—and it just about always did. With the radio transmitting but faulty the situation really wasn't any better because there'd be garbled messages, buried in static, from the lead ship, in which the best you could do was salvage bits and pieces about changes in map coordinates and altitude headings for the home run. That's all—bits and pieces. Nothing definite.

"The information that's coming in from England about concentrations of night fighters—information passed on by other airplanes—never reaches us and, I swear, the changed map references we do pick up from the lead ship are meant to divert us to just where those fighters are lurking.

"Somehow we, by which I mean Johnny and the navigator (I'm just the messenger boy), have to decide what's best to do in, uh, Operation Orphan—and no kiddin', young lady, that's the name the duke has assigned to his little wheeze. Operation Orphan!

"That designation is very much an open secret on the base and he wants us to know all about it because he knows there's not a damn thing we can prove other than we got lost, which is par for our course. Some course! It has more traps and hazards than . . . forgive the mixed metaphor, but he's stacking the cards against us and those cards showed the swastikas of Fokker Wolfes. We're just what those German pilots are waiting for, a nice big B17 that's strayed from the rest of the flock. Now this isn't something that just happens now and then. It's regular. A pattern. It goes on month after month—it's why I was cracking up before my twenty-first birthday."

My next step has to be to press fast-forward on the recorder so that this passage dovetails with what he said at a later stage.

"Darndest thing, young lady, but after what happened to Buddy the duke changed—became Mr. Nice Guy. For a while. I mean, we flew some missions in quick succession and for the very first time we met with no problems. No malfunctioning radio, no getting lost. Talk about noblesse oblige, he even had us placed in the middle of the squadron—the safest spot—which means we have extra protection. Hey, this was great. This was R and R. We actually were landing without firing distress flares. There's a catch, though—the duke is out to cut a deal."

He paused, looked at me, waiting for my prompt. "A deal?" I said.

"A deal to lay off. Johnny, you see, has realized he's getting nowhere with London in seeking the reopening of Buddy Fanzoli's case and so he's, uh, *elevated* his campaign. And what the duke is saying, by example, is that if Johnny stays his hand, life's gonna be a lot safer for us."

"Perhaps," I said, and my point reflected my own selfish pragmatism, "perhaps it wasn't such a bad deal."

"Sure." He nodded. "And I guess that's why Johnny put it to the vote. He asked us one night, this was during the duke's friendly period, if we approved of his trying to get justice for Buddy. We all knew what he meant, of course—he meant did we want to stay in the duke's, uh, grace and favor, by dumping Buddy. He got a full show of hands. Okay, so some of those hands didn't exactly shoot up—including, I'm ashamed to say, mine—but in the end, it was

unanimous. He thanked us for our backing and said he would continue to try to set up a meeting with the senator."

"Senator?"

"Yeah, Senator, uh—uh—darn, the name's gone. He was a big
shot on one of the defense committees in Washington. I have a
notion Johnny knew him in a friend-of-a-friend kind of way. Anyway, this senator's a noted criminal lawyer and a champion of the
underdog, and, in fact, I tried to get in touch with him myself after
the war, only to find he's died a few months before. Point is, this
senator's planning a trip to London as part of a fact-finding congres-
sional delegation. All this is in the *Stars and Stripes* because the senator, maybe he's bucking for re-election, wants to check on the
morale of GIs in England and he's asking, through the newspaper, for
servicemen with worthwhile grievances to contact his secretary,
who's there ahead of him, at the US embassy in London. He's after
headlines, of course, though he has a genuine enough reputation.

"And Johnny—going above the heads of the generals—has put in
his request for a meeting, the result of which are phone calls to him,
Johnny, from the embassy. These calls are to the house, but they're
routed through the base switchboard and so you can be sure that
word got around as to what he was up to. And I have no doubt that
our friend, the duke, came to have a swift appreciation of just how
much a liability Johnny was. We *all* were, come to that.

"Heck, in the case of Buddy Fanzoli's murder we're a planeload of
witnesses and it would solve a lot of problems if we were to be shot
down. So, once it becomes apparent Johnny's not playing ball, the
deal's off. We're back to the rough rides again. The jammed radio.
The useless map coordinates. The night fighters. The—"

"But—what happened to Johnny?" I breached the unwritten rule
of the interviewer, and impatiently at that.

He flicked his moustache with the back of his finger and, for just a
moment, dressed me down with a look in which I saw the full
authority of his banker's gaze: it was as though I had spoken out of
turn in the boardroom.

"I *am* getting there, young lady. My approach may seem fuddy-duddy to you, but my fiscal instincts—checks and balances—call for the full assemblage of details in the cause of appreciation of overall dimensions."

"Quite," I said, pointedly.

He twinkled a no-hard-feelings, grandfatherly smile at me and went on, in what appeared to be a total non-sequitur, to talk about the four or five times the B17 landed at bases other than its own.

"Nothing special about that," he said. "You can't make it home, you put down where you can. But, you know, beyond death and taxes, there's one other sure thing about life—and that's irony. The irony, or the start of it, in what I'm reaching now is that on this occasion we were flying home in one piece. We didn't have so much as a scratch. Okay, so the radio's out, but that's for the perfectly legitimate reason there's an electrical storm raging over England. In the past we've always picked up transmission once we were out of range of the lead ship and we've used the radio to get a fix on our home base. We can't do that this time on account of the storm. And this time, because of the usual detours we've taken, we're good and lost and, because we've taken on less fuel on account of an extra-large bomb load—that happened from time to time—we're running acutely short of gas. When we sighted the coast we had eleven minutes of flying time left. The navigator did some rough and ready calculations and figured we might just be within reach of an airfield on the map. We were. In fact, we spotted that field because it was billowing flames—turned out it had taken a pounding from German bombers a couple hours before and the flames were from burning airplanes and vehicles. Now, and here's where the irony starts to bite, when we flopped down on that base for no more than a fuel stop our undercarriage smacks into a bomb crater. No serious damage, but we're disabled. Okay, so you're wondering what the point of this story is, right?"

"Frankly, yes."

He took a slow sip of his drink. "The abstract point is irony." He put his glass carefully on the table and looked at me. "The specific point is that our mission that night was to Düsseldorf and the date we were over the target was May first, 1944."

"But that was the night—"

"Sure. The night Johnny was supposed to have bought it. I bought it that night as well. Officially. We all did."

"I don't under—"

"You will."

Martha's face leered at the window, her fingers clawing her cheeks—distending her mouth, pulling down her eye sockets. He strummed his fingers playfully at that horror mask and she ran off. He turned back to me, began to explain what happened on May 1, 1944. And afterwards . . .

"As you might imagine after what they'd been through in the air raid, we were the last thing that base wanted to see. Still, what happens when a stray turns up is that the host base, it's their responsibility, puts through a displacement report to the home base—condition of aircraft, state of crew, that kind of thing. We filled in all the necessary forms for this process; we'd been through it all before.

"Only this night, understandably, they'd got plenty of other things on their mind and the displacement report is put to one side and, we discover later—and this is where the irony becomes consolidated—never sent.

"We're at that base only a day and a half while we patch up the ship. It's minor damage so, since the ground crew there is busy salvaging its own wrecks, we fix it ourselves. All the time we're assuming that standard procedure has been followed and our base knows where we are.

"It doesn't, of course, and when we don't show after twelve hours our base, more standard procedure, reports us as a no-show to the Eighth Air Force. Cables go out to our next of kin breaking the bad news that we're missing. Then we turn up and our base has to get back to the Eighth to unscramble the situation.

"Now the Eighth, or that section that deals with us, is distinctly put out on account that it's lost face by having to file a report to Eisenhower and Churchill, who probably don't give a damn anyway, that we've bought it and the experiment has suffered a setback.

"It doesn't matter that we're back and in one piece; the Eighth is very snotty and is trying to say that it was our responsibility to get in touch with our base as soon as we landed at the other field. Johnny, in fact, is hauled right off to London to be torn off a strip. The petulance of generals, huh?

"And if you ask me this is why, as a form of punishment and as a lesson not to be bad boys again, there's a delay of five or six weeks before the cables go out to our folks letting them know we're okay. Or it could be, the war's at full pitch and plenty of guys are dying every day, that the bureau of records in London, overstretched as it's bound to be, has given us low priority on account that we're no longer casualties. Then again, it could have been a regular old snafu, of which in the war there are more than there are snakes in the jungle. Who knows? Still, it's hard on our folks, that long wait for the news we're safe."

"Letters," I said, making a point of being the disinterested interviewer. "The crew must have been writing home during that time. Surely the families would have known from their letters, the dates on them, that they were all right."

"There was no airmail in those days, young lady. Our letters went to the base censor. Delay. Then they went to the central censor. More delay. Then they were dumped in a port warehouse. Further delay. And there's still the voyage Stateside to come. My letters home take eight, nine weeks. There's a war on and it's the slow boat to China for personal mail—and also for that cable saying we'd got back safely from Düsseldorf after all. All the waiting and wondering, some trauma for the folks back home." He paused. "And that trauma didn't end for Johnny's next of kin, his sister, because she got a cable that was totally different from the one received by the families of the rest of the crew."

"Oh?" That's all: *oh.* My monosyllable is so slight that, on the tape, I cannot discern any reaction behind it. Nor do I remember any.

He turned his head to look out of the window and seemed to be gazing at a Stars and Stripes flag draped from a long white pole on the lawn.

"The follow-up cable to Johnny's sister is notification that he was killed in action while on a mission to Düsseldorf on the night of May first, 1944."

"But that—it simply doesn't add up."

"It does, young lady." He kept his eyes on the flag. "It adds up to, uh . . . *expediency.* It adds up to the happenstance that Johnny, like the rest of us, was already down on the record as being missing on a mission to Düsseldorf and that the cables saying we were safely back hadn't yet gone out. Which played nicely into the hands of the, uh, powers that be. The generals. All they had to do was make sure that any letters he had written from May first onward didn't turn up, and that had to be a simple matter of mail intercept."

"You have me lost," I said.

He turned to me, smiled. "I guess I do at that." He crossed his legs, folded his hands across his knee. "Let me try to, uh, *audit* the situation. Step by step. Okay?"

"Fine."

He nodded. "Let's open the agenda with that crusading senator I mentioned—Johnny had firmed up an appointment with him. For May twenty-seventh; I told you, anything to do with figures I remember. I have no doubt the duke was aware of this. Just as I have no doubt that he and his cohorts were responsible for what happened to Johnny on the twenty-third of May."

"And"—I hesitated, remembering his reproof over my earlier directness, though it could have been (I can't be sure) that I didn't want to know the events of May 23. "And what did happen?"

His hands gestured outward a couple of times, as though making a space in the clutter of memory for what he had to say. "I don't know the, uh, *particulars* of what happened. That's conjecture. As to working up to some kind of a conclusion, the starting point's gotta be what I *saw* that day. What we all saw."

"Which was what?" I put the question crisply, impersonally: or so I thought.

"We all saw Johnny driving out of the base in his jeep on one of his regular jaunts to, uh—*that* village."

"Haworth."

"Haworth. Sure." He uncrossed his legs and also seemed to switch moods. For suddenly he digressed. "He took me there a couple of times, you know. Up on the moors. Windiest damn place I've ever been in except for a trip I made once to—"

"So"—I cut in; this was no time to wander off track—"he set off for Haworth. And?"

"And . . . and Alice was with him in the jeep."

"Alice?"

"I guess her name stays with me because my mother was called Alice and so were all the firstborn daughters in her family in a line going back five generations. Tradition, huh?"

I tensed on this irrelevancy, then promptly proved that I, too, could be prone to the superfluous: I indulged a personal curiosity.

"Who was she, this—this Alice?"

"Johnny's girl," he said. He put his head a little to the side. "You know, you're kinda like her. I'm not sure whether it's your looks or your manner. Maybe both. Anyway, she had something to do with—with art. Yeah, I remember now, she'd sketch us after we came back from missions. I think she stayed on the base. That's right—it's coming back to me—she had quarters at the back of the house in what used to be a stable block."

Johnny and Alice. I tried for a private moment to mock the commonplace sound of that pairing. And then, briskly, I resumed the interviewing mode: a poised, noncommittal look of expectancy as I waited for his next words.

"I'll never forget the sight of that jeep leaving the base, you know," he said. "Never." He tugged at his earlobe, smiled. "Johnny called that jeep The Old Lady on account—this is me and figures again—it had near a hundred thousand miles on the clock when it was assigned to him. He drove her very sedately, The Old Lady."

Rambling old man! It didn't occur to me, not then, that he was skirting the past, easing his way back. All I knew was my snap of impatience.

"With respect, Mr. Centofanti, I don't think a slow-moving jeep is taking us very far," I said, though I was careful to smile.

He turned to me and there was no rancor in those brown eyes.

"And with equal respect, young lady, I think you're exceeding the speed of due chronology. I want to do my best, really I do, to give the pattern of that morning and its subsequent events. Part of that pattern is what I was talking about a few moments ago—irony. Because that morning seemed so perfect, weatherwise and in other ways, that everything stood out with extra clarity. Which is why I have such clear recall of Johnny and Alice in the jeep—yes, and right down to the fact that they had the little dog with them. That morning it seemed like nothing bad could ever happen again. *Irony*. Now I'm telling this like an old man, I realize that, but I'm not a dribbling old man—not yet—and I would ask you to bear with me while I tell the story *my* way. Or, and this isn't a rhetorical question, is that asking too much?"

"Of course not," I said. And thereafter, realizing it was futile to try to hurry him along, and also chastened, I reverted to being the complaisant interviewer. Listening to what he had to say I saw the scene of that morning as Johnny drove out of the base, where already the trolleys were lined up to stock the B17 with five-hundred-pound bombs: for it was due to fly a mission that night.

Only Johnny never returned from his jaunt to Haworth.

Eleven

THAT MORNING—MAY 23, 1944—JOHNNY'S CREW WAS PLAYING
baseball on the house lawn. Spring wore a medal that day: the sun
shone and the blossoms on the trees were sudden and radiant and the
young men from the other side of the Atlantic rejoiced in their vital-
ity. I have Dante Centofanti's banker's word for it . . .

"Spring had been late in coming and then—yowser!—it was
there. Gee, the sky was so blue, the sun so warm, and, hey, that blossom. We'd gone through months of drizzle and fog and, what with
that and what we're putting up with on the missions, we've been
about as cheerful as patients in a psychiatrist's waiting room. Then
along bounces this perfect day and—and we knew hope. Every one
of us. No one said so. Young guys don't—or they didn't, not my
generation—articulate their feelings. But I'll tell you this—we played
an inspired game of baseball that day. And why? Because that day
touched the very life force in us."

And Johnny died that day.

Though as I listen again to his words on the tape I fail to find any
tone of irony behind Dante Centofanti's spring pastorale. Surely,

however, he had to be temporizing. Still, what I hear at this moment on the tape is the sound of his chortling.

"Hey, this will tickle you. Half-time and the butler strides across the lawn all done up in his frock coat, as if he's an emissary of Winston Churchill. He likes us on account we keep him stocked up with booze, and this day he has a pitcher of iced lemonade on a silver tray. He has on his white gloves, very pukka, and we had an all-American thirst for that lemonade. And then we're back playin'. Hard and fast and yet somehow in slow motion, or that's how I remember it. It was as if we had to hang onto our youth, make the day last, make it worth a thousand days of being young. I guess that sounds crazy, huh? But it's as if we had to cram the whole of our youth into that day because, in spite of the hope we felt—and, young lady, suddenly we were in blithe spirits—we also figure that we could be running out of days. We knew that we were due to fly that night—Cologne, as it turned out—but that didn't matter. What mattered was the—the immediate. The moment. What mattered was our limbs, full and responsive, our eyes bright and—

"We hear this peep-peep. We look round. It's Johnny driving by in his jeep. Johnny and Alice. The two of them give us a wave. They wave like they haven't gotta care in the world. Two kids out to make the most of that gorgeous day. Irony. Yes, sir, irony . . ."

The tape runs silently now, making a slight shushing sound, like faraway surf. I'm familiar with this pause, have timed it at a little under a minute, and know that this surf sound bespeaks Dante Centofani mustering the strength to enter the dark water of memory.

"As I think I mentioned to you, there's a whole unbroken string of Alices in my family. My uh, my grandmother, another Alice, was the first woman gold assayer in the Yukon and her nickname was . . ."

For a moment or two he paddles aimlessly in such family history, then faces the water head-on. ". . . In between Johnny and Alice was Johnny's little dog. It all looked so, so complete. And that was the last we ever saw of them."

He looked directly at me, perhaps expecting an expression of dis-

may. But I stayed behind my uninvolved interviewer's front. I nodded, I think. Left it at that. Waited.

"Tell the truth, Johnny ought not to have gone off base, not when
a mission had been called. But the day had got to him too. We knew
that from the letter he'd been writing to his sister."

"Letter?"

"We, er, found it on his desk in his room. A half-written letter.
Blue notepaper. His fountain pen lying diagonally across the page.
The top of the pen hadn't been replaced and the ink had left a blot.
I'm not claiming a sudden feat of memory; it's just that—well, these
details are filed permanently in my mind in a little pigeonhole the
years haven't managed to close. You see, when I saw that letter, after
I read it, I knew, *we* knew, that something bad had happened to him.
It was late by then, you see, and—and I even remember the last
words in his letter; they're in that pigeonhole as well. Not word for
word, of course, but he had written that it was such a glorious morning he was going to take himself off to—to—"

"Haworth," I said.

"Yeah. Haworth. Anyway, he wrote, he always wrote to his sister
before a mission—say, isn't memory the darndest thing? I mean, how
is it I've just now remembered he always wrote to his sister before a
mission? Mystery, huh? I, uh, digress. Sorry. What he went on to
write was that he'd finish the letter later in the afternoon when he
got back from, uh—"

"Haworth."

"Check. Only it was late, way after midnight, when we went to
his room as a group and found that unfinished letter. We went there
and nosed around the way we did because we were worried about
him. I mean, this is a guy who is totally reliable, a guy we trust more
than anyone else. Why hasn't he phoned? Why hasn't he found some
way of getting in touch? Why?"

Because he was dead. Because on that perfect spring day something corrupt moved and claimed him. And, presumably, Alice. And,
I take it, even his Jack Russell terrier, Heathcliff.

I am taking a short break from the tape; I can remember enough from what I have already heard to summarize some of the later events of that day and of that night.

After the baseball game, the crew dispersed. Some of them crossed to the armament trolleys and amused themselves by chalking slogans— sentiments like "A Slam from Uncle Sam!"—on the bombs that were meant to be dropped over Germany in the night. Others went to the Stage Door Canteen to play records and shoot pool. Two or three, so hot was the day, stripped off and showered at a standpipe outside a hangar.

When they all met up again it was in the house, in the great hall, for the early dinner that was customary before a mission. They were a little surprised, though no more than that, by the time the butler, that devotee of ritual, sounded the gong in the corridor and Johnny had yet to appear; it wasn't like him not to be established at the head of the table in what the crew jokingly called "Poppa's chair." They held dinner for him for a while and then one of them went to his room to remind him he was late. He wasn't there. Someone else checked Alice's quarters and she was absent too. The crew wise-cracked that the two of them had gotten cozy in a haystack and, as they started dinner, settled for the reasonable explanation that the jeep had broken down—a flat, a snapped axle, the radiator over-heated in the sudden warmth. He would turn up at any moment. That was their conviction, but two hours later it had drifted into wishful thinking, into the fidgety rustle of magazine pages turning and the sotto pulses of small talk around the table, and the drone of a phonograph playing low somewhere in the room. Dante Centofanti remembered those sounds, another plus for his memory, and he remembered also that now no one wondered aloud why Johnny had not been in touch. Instead, and it was a virtual rota, a man would get up, leave altogether too casually and return a few minutes later and shrug slightly to signal that Johnny had not returned to his room unseen.

Meantime, the moist spring night was budding with short bursts of aircraft engines as ground crews carried out final pre-operation checks: the briefing had been called for 7:45.

About twenty minutes before this time, they went to their rooms to put on their flying suits. I need the tape again, to fast-forward it until I reach the place where I am asking a question.

"By then, of course, by the time of the briefing, you'd reported him missing?"

"No."

"But—but why ever not?"

"Because, young lady, that would have been to turn him in. Operationally we were under the overall charge of the RAF and for a guy to absent himself from the base before a raid . . . That was a court martial offense. Okay, it probably wouldn't have gotten anywhere, but Johnny had enough on his mind without that kind of hassle. We had our own private exit at the house and he'd slipped out and—and, well, we kept tight-lipped about it."

"But there could have been enquiries, checks, a search."

"We—we did what we thought was right at the time. Maybe it was bad judgment, I honestly don't know, but there was no faulting our loyalty to Johnny. Besides, a guy who'd come through all those missions over Germany, what real harm could come to him when he takes a spin on the peaceful country roads of Yorkshire? That was our thinking. We were too young, I guess, to consider the treacheries of fate, irony, call it what you will. He would come through—that was his record, his style. And we took that hope to the briefing room. He would be there, waiting for us. He would have gone there early to discuss tactical matters with the briefing officer—he'd done this a couple of times before—and that would be why he'd missed dinner. Only . . . only he wasn't there."

As the tape turns, its silver spool head reminds me of an electronic worry bead and I have an impression of Dante Centofanti shuffling his words from hand to hand. At the time, I felt impatient and made little or no allowance for his age and the effort of looking back so squarely on the past. I hear again on the tape, for example, that in the briefing room, a barn, the sounds and the smells, particularly the smell, are of young men with "problems with acute wind"; his banker's decorum restrained him from using the basic term.

"You see these old movies and it's all heroism at the briefings, close-ups of Gregory Peck and the muscles moving in his face. Well, believe me, young lady, what *moves* with these guys is their bowels! They're young and they're healthy and they're scared and they've not long eaten and you can smell their fear, literally. The British are the worst offenders on account that there's so many baked beans in their diet!"

His joke, his nervous joke, and the tape relays my dutiful laugh, my little dab of lacquer on the ragged edge of my suppressed exasperation at his slowness. Finally, he is reaching the point, recalling that because the briefing was, as always, crowded and intense, no one on the RAF side seemed to have noticed Johnny's absence.

"We're tucked in at the back of the barn, our usual place, and while we're still hoping, even then, that Johnny's gonna turn up we're also figuring that if he's a no-show we can maybe get away with having the mission flown by our copilot. This is a lanky kid from the West Coast. A redhead. Guy by the name of Harry, uh— Aw, gee, me and names. Harry—Harry—"

"Korda." I was goaded into my reply.

"Harry *Korda*—That's right! How'd you—?"

"I'm hoping to meet him."

"He's still alive then?"

"Yes. He runs a small aviation charter company out of San Francisco."

"Son of a gun! Son of a—You'll let him know that you've met me, uh?"

"Yes." Tersely.

"You'll give him my best and tell him if he's ever down New Orleans way he's to—?"

"Yes. *Perhaps* we could get back to—"

"Sure. Only I guess Harry's the man for the whole story. Bottom line–wise."

"Really?"

"Harry's gotta know just about everything. Only, the shock—he's buttoned up about it. Or he was, last time I got in touch with him. Closed as a clam. Still, that was just after the war and my bet now is that he'll want to cooperate with you. But for the time being you're stuck with me and while I can snap out facts and figures—the banker in me—in other respects I, uh, dawdle. To be honest, this whole business is—it's painful as hell. And it's a pain I should have dealt with years ago instead of settling down to make my pile. I—I feel I've betrayed Johnny."

"No, of course, you—"

"And that's why I'm talking to you, young lady. Putting the record straight. As long as it's down *somewhere*." A sudden pleading was in his voice, in his eyes, in the way his hands balled together. Then he relaxed. "But let's get back to the briefing, huh?"

"Let's."

"We're, uh, halfway through and by now we know that the target is Cologne and there's gonna be scattered cloud cover, some of it cirro-cumulus. Crazy that I can remember details like that, while in other respects . . . Still, what the heck. We're halfway through the briefing when this other RAF officer inches onto the platform and whispers something in the ear of the base commanding officer, who's one of the brass behind the desk. He gets up and leaves, the CO, and a few minutes later he's back and looking distinctly white about the gills. He pauses at the desk to take a sip of water and it spills—that is *so* clear in my mind all of a sudden—but he doesn't bother about this and crosses straight to the briefing officer who's at the map and pointing out ack-ack placements, and has a whispered word with him. The briefing officer sits down abruptly and the CO, who's an old guy, voice like James Mason—James Mason yet! How come I can remember the sound of his voice when—Sorry. The CO faces everybody and says he has an announcement to make. Which is that

the American crew has to return to their quarters immediately. All
except for Lieutenant Harry—Harry—"

"Korda."

"Yeah. And Harry's to report to the CO's office. So the rest of us
went back to the house. We figured that the RAF had discovered
that Johnny was AWOL and they were demanding an explanation
from Harry. At the same time, why interrupt a briefing for that? So
we moved on to our second theory, which is that the jeep had
crashed and Johnny's hurt and—Harry would know."

"We, uh, while we're waiting for Harry, we try to concentrate on
a game of poker. We hear the Lancasters take off for Cologne. Three,
four hours go by. We're strictly going through the motions of poker
when someone finally says why don't we take a full gander at
Johnny's room. Just to make sure everything's in order. It was—it
was something to do. And that's how we came across the letter to his
sister, the letter saying he'd gone off to, uh—that village."

"*Haworth.*" I enunciated my reply, resenting my role as hand-
maiden to his memory.

"Yeah. And everything else in his room pointed to a guy who'd
ducked out for no more than a couple of hours. His flying suit was
there. His personal papers. His paybook. His wallet. Everything. All
of which gave the lie to the story they tried to foist on us later that
he'd been posted to special duties. And what made that lie a whopper
was when we came across the mascot he always wore when he was
flying. *Always . . .*"

Johnny's mascot: a silver squirrel seated at a typewriter. (A memo
of memory reminded me.) I had seen him wearing it. I was prepared,
then, for Dante Centofanti's next words.

"It's no bigger than a dime, this mascot, and it's a pin in the shape
of a squirrel that's typing and I guess I remember it so well because
whenever we landed Johnny would say it was the squirrel that had
seen us safely home. Cute, that squirrel. It was given to Johnny by
the author of *Gone with the Wind.*"

"Margaret Mitchell."

"Sure. Even I know that. They both came from Atlanta, you see, and Johnny, when he was a kid, worked for her around the house—did the gardening, I think—and she gave him this squirrel pin and he treasured it. Always wore it in the same spot—the lapel of his flying jacket. Right-hand side."

Actually, above the breast pocket. Left-hand side. And he wasn't, or not so far as I knew, Margaret Mitchell's gardener; he was the newsboy who delivered the *Atlanta Constitution* to her home every day. That's how their friendship started. She saw the promise of the writer in Johnny and told him to always store up experience, hence the squirrel at the typewriter. She also, among other names on a reading list she drew up for him, recommended the works of the Brontës, particularly Emily, as paradigms of prose. Now I'm digressing, filling in while, on the tape, Dante Centofanti's words trail the slow return of the crew from Johnny's room and the resuming of the poker game . . .

"We should have been making sack time, but who can sleep? We're all keyed up, wondering what Harry—and what was taking him so long?—was going to tell us when he got back. We just huddle round that table, drink some, pretend we're playing poker. And after a while no one is saying a word. All you can hear—it's like I was there now—is the slap of the cards on the table and the hooting of the owls in the wood.

"And then that silence is broken by the sound of the Lancasters returning from Cologne, which has got to mean it's four, four-thirty in the morning. Those planes sweep right in over that old house, rattling the windows and everything else that's loose.

"They're still coming in when—when Harry turns up.

"He's there. In the doorway. And he looks terrible. Like he's aged, like—or this is how it seemed at the moment—he's been away twenty years instead of just overnight. We rush up to him and it's only then we see he's not alone. Behind him there's a clutch of RAF guys, including the CO. There's also a civilian policeman—he has on one of those pointed hats, you know?—and a guy in plain clothes.

"It's a crazy kind of a scene, all the more so in that as we come up some of those other guys are trying to bundle Harry out. I guess they'd expected us to be in the sack and so they're shoving us back as they move into the hall and toward the front door. We're clamoring out to Harry, what the hell happened, Harry, and they're giving him, and us, the bum's rush.

"We're still keeping this up when, and God knows where they came from, a couple of big MPs are there and, I swear, one of them has a Sten gun trained on us and he pulls the safety lock back and— *click.* That sound, the release of the safety lock, freezes everyone for a split second and then it was Harry turned to us and told us the worst. He didn't say a word. Just shook his head and gave (it was very specific) the thumbs-down sign. And then they bundle him outta the house and these two MPs are standing at the closed door, facing us, one with the Sten gun, and it begins to sink in—Johnny's a goner."

On the tape now, my voice has an unyielding sound, as if programmed to robotic efficiency. "So there had been an accident?"

"We, uh, bought that. Kind of. Or at least made a down payment. We were all in. Confused. I guess it suited us, when we sacked down, to figure that the jeep had crashed. It was only after we'd slept on it that—I mean, why all the mystery? Why wouldn't they let us talk to Harry? Why the MPs with the Sten gun? And why the lock on the door to Johnny's room the next morning?"

"Lock?"

"A heavy metal bar running the width of the door and a padlock on it. Accident? They were going to a lot of trouble for an accident. And—and then the wreath turned up."

"Wreath?" How fatuous my repetition sounds.

"Butler brought it in at breakfast. Just as he'd brought in the ones for Buddy Fanzoli. Same kind of wreath. Same kind of card. Same handwriting. Only this time Johnny's name was on the card. And, same as with Buddy, a large X had been written across it."

"Surely—surely not." The tape relays the inflection in my voice, but nothing of the inner protest under my cool interviewer's mien.

"Surely *yes,* young lady. We, uh—the pressure we're under—I guess we rioted. We rush out of the house with that wreath. A couple of guys have baseball bats with them, and while that isn't part of the overall plan, it's the mood we're in. We make our way, half-running, to the CO's office with our proof, the wreath, that Johnny had been—that it was no accident.

"We're nearly at the office when we're intercepted by these MPs. The baseball bats fly and out of the corner of my eye I see at least two MPs down on the ground with blood streaming across their faces.

"Then we're in with the CO, we just crashed in, and we're hollerin' that we want justice for Johnny and this guy's half-standing behind his desk and he's saying, in that James Mason voice, he'll take our wreath, there's good chaps. And we say like hell he will, this is our evidence. Only his request is backed up by MPs who've come in behind and they've got guns. Now that he has the wreath he's saying that sending it was no more than a prank—in bad taste, yes, but a prank. He'll take steps to see that the offenders are disciplined. Big deal! As for us, we're to be court-martialled for mutiny. He's very crisp now. We say we're talking murder and know who did it. He says we're talking rubbish and that Johnny has been posted to special operational duties. We say we'll not even begin to believe that until we've heard it from the lips of our copilot, and, we demand to know, where is Harry? He tells us that's none of our business and orders us out and we're herded back to the house in handcuffs and under armed escort."

I forego the tape for a while. I know the script, after all, and I can visualize the scene as that bedraggled group of young Americans, prisoners in the land they had been fighting for, were marched back to the house. As they shuffled past the RAF transport compound, horns were hooted in derision and they saw that Johnny's jeep was parked there, recognized it immediately by his stencilled name across the bonnet. The jeep showed no sign of having been in an accident. An MP stood guard over it.

They were not court-martialled. Instead, one at a time over the next couple of days, they were transferred to embarkation points. A man would be told he had a few minutes to pack and then a bus, a car or a truck would be waiting for him. In Dante Centofanti's case he was taken, a solitary passenger in the back of an enclosed truck, to

Oxfordshire. The next day he was aboard a cargo flight bound for the South Pacific.

Dante Centofanti called it Operation Cover Up, and of course he was absolutely right. London, he said, clearly decided it couldn't risk a scandal of this magnitude getting out and separated the crew and scattered its members to remote bases across the world. To places like Australia, the Aleutians, Africa, Burma, Greenland. He learnt of this diaspora only after the war.

Harry Korda, he said, had the shortest journey—he was posted to London and the headquarters of the Eighth Air Force. He guessed, in view of what Harry Korda must have known, that the generals felt they needed to keep a close eye on him.

Early in 1945, after contracting chronic malaria, Dante Centofanti got a medical discharge. He returned to New Orleans and his old job as a junior teller in the bank. Back to the tape . . .

". . . there I was taking in and handing out money and all the time I'm thinking of my IOU to Johnny. It's down to him that I'm back home in a safe and steady job—and feeling lousy. I tell myself I'm still weak after the malaria, and while that's true I'm also using it as an excuse not to do anything about Johnny. But where do I start? How? And wouldn't it be better—oh, the insidious way this keeps sneaking up on me—just to let the past be the past and make the most of my fresh start? The war's over for me, after all. Yeah, and for Johnny. *Everything's* over for Johnny.

"The upshot is that this one night I call Johnny's sister in Atlanta. There were no other Peppertons in the book, so she was easy to trace. I had no idea of what I was gonna say to her. It was a—a gesture call. Though I also wanted to find out what she'd been told about him.

"Gee, she's so thrilled to hear from one of the crew. She says Johnny's told her all about me, about my moustache and—then she becomes emotional. She starts talking fast. Her nerves. And before I can say anything much she's saying, her words even more rushed, that she's glad I was able to bail out over Düsseldorf that night. My reaction is—it's *uh*? Something like that. Her words are even faster now, like she's trying to outrun the pain, and she says that when she got the telegram saying Johnny was missing she had the strongest feeling he was alive and that this carried her through until she got the message confirming that he had been killed on the night of May first.

"Bingo! It all comes into place for me. The way they'd fixed that cover-up. He's reported missing to start with, just like we all were, and so all they gotta do is fill this vacuum, like it was a grave, with the news that he's dead. Very neat. Very nasty. I'm—I'm kinda stunned.

"Meanwhile, she's saying she's proud, but not surprised, that Johnny stayed at the controls of the ship to keep it as steady as possible while the rest of the crew bailed out. No kiddin', this is what she's been told. And—and who am I to disabuse her? Where's the point? Better to leave the poor woman alone with the consolation of the lies that have been fed to her. That's what I'm thinking and I guess I would have left things at that if she hadn't gone on to say something else."

He paused. A tight-lipped, stiff pause, given extra expression by the way he now sat rigidly straight, his hands on his lap locked together at the fingers.

"What she goes on to say is to mention a letter she received from Johnny's superior officer praising Johnny's courage and skill as a pilot and what a privilege it was to have flown with him in the same squadron. This letter, she says, is all the more special because the writer is a man of the aristocracy. And it's only then that I realize she's talking about the duke!

"Okay, so no doubt it's a pro-forma, the kind of letter that goes out automatically when a guy buys it, but I still feel as if a knife's twisting in my guts and all I want to do is get off the phone. When we finally hang up she's sobbing—she still thinks I bailed out—and I'm . . . I'm trembling. I tell myself it's leftover malaria in my system, though I know it's another kind of—of fever."

He looked down, slowly opened his knotted hands, unflexed his fingers. I heard a knuckle crack. He looked up, at me. "I reckon whoever said the first casualty of war is the truth had a point," he said.

I nodded. Neutrally. But though I wanted to be the remote bystander I knew, at heart, that I was in the thick of his rough house of memories. On the lawn I could see Martha, quiet now, her doll on her lap and sitting cross-legged while the woman servant, in a folding chair, read to her from a picture book. Dante Centofanti carried on with his account.

"I try to leave it at that, the phone call. I tell myself Johnny's sister's been through enough so why add to her grief? But—call it my banker's instinct—it seems to me a whole big moral account is in the red and in the end it seems to me that nailing the truth about Johnny matters more than his sister's feelings.

"I start by writing to the War Department in Washington saying I'm enquiring about the whereabouts of an old buddy I served with in Yorkshire. Back comes the standard notification of his death in action on a mission to Düsseldorf. Now, if only to show I'm not paranoid, I'm not accusing Washington of conspiracy; that cover-up took place in London and Washington is simply relaying what it was told. I need that piece of paper they sent me, however, as evidence of the lie that has been perpetrated.

"Then I start lobbying congressmen—which is how I came to discover that the senator Johnny had fixed up to see is dead—and they think I'm a crank. Everyone does. Hold on, though. Sure! There was a time when a big New York magazine approached me with questions about Johnny. Yeah, one of the crew came to see me for the magazine. Guy by the name of—it's gone. Memory! Anyway, it doesn't matter none because I guess the magazine interest fizzled.

"But it's such a long time ago and in so many respects it's all mixed up in my mind. All I knew was that I wasn't gonna give up. Okay, so I'm not getting anywhere on my own, but I figure that once the rest of the crew return, or those that are coming back—I know of at least two who are dead—then it could be that some of us could get together and press Johnny's case as a group. What I also figure is the possibility that Johnny's a back number to them by now.

Was I wrong! These guys, I tracked most of 'em down through the vets' organizations, have been fighting Johnny's corner when they were in uniform. They've been doing the same as me, writing letters and—and getting nowhere. Letters to congressmen, newspapers, even to the president himself. No replies. Because they were letters to the censor. One guy in Burma, kid who was at law school before he was drafted, had prepared a regular legal submission to every member of the Supreme Court and set out to beat the censor by trying to smuggle it out through a Red Cross nurse who was heading back to the States. He was found out and put on court martial, but was told the charge would be dropped if he promised not to attempt such a thing again. He refused. Took his punishment. It's things like this that testify to the spirit of that crew and the way we were gung-ho for justice."

He paused for a moment, glanced across at the flag on the lawn. "Only as things turned out, I, uh, flunked the gung-ho test," he said quietly.

"I don't believe that for a moment," I said.

"Young lady, I—I copped out."

He looked at me fleetingly, almost in panic, then gazed over at his company portrait, shaking his head, as though finding fault with that detailed study of his uprightness. He turned back to me, sighed.

"All I can say," he said, "it's thin extenuation, I know, but all I can say is that I wasn't finding it easy to make ends meet. I had a GI mortgage on a tract house, but thirty-five dollars a week (I was on minimum scale) wasn't easy to manage on. Also, Martha was pregnant with our first child and on account that my father had been laid off at the defense plant I was doing what I could to help out there and my mother, God bless her, was running up hefty hospital bills because she was chronically sick. These were my domestic preoccupations that afternoon I was summoned upstairs to see the president of the bank."

Outside, unseen by us, Martha shrieked. "I'll piss where I wanna piss, ya bitch! I'll piss in ya face if I wanna!"

He seemed not to hear this as, deeply preoccupied, he moved his hand back and forward across his chin. When he spoke, and he was silent for a while, he avoided my eyes.

"There are managers in the bank who've never even been in the president's office," he said, "and yet he wants to see *me,* just about the lowliest member of the staff. He tells me he's heard a lot of good things about my work and he's thinking of promoting me to floor supervisor, which is a bit like being told I've won the Irish sweepstake.

"Just one snag, son, he says. What's that, sir? He looks at me over the top of his glasses and says I have to make up my mind whether I want to be a banker or a crusader. And I knew right off that the campaign *was* working, that it had gotten somebody worried and that the president of the bank had been asked to, uh, intervene. Oh, I *knew*!

"That was my cue to speak out as a fearless American, to quote on a theme of liberty and justice for all. Only, and there was nothing wrong with my memory in those days, I . . . I, uh, forgot my lines.

"Like a good banker, I closed the vaults on . . . on Johnny. As time passed and my career moved on, which it did fairly steadily— not leaps and bounds exactly, but a firm upward curve—it seemed easier and easier to secure those vaults. War was war and terrible things happened and there was no percentage in brooding. None. And then the time came when Martha and I moved into St. Charles Avenue in New Orleans, and even today there's no better address in the city, and—*wham*—another set of bolts had slammed fast."

But they had a time lock, those vaults, and that day, half a century on, it had activated and spilled the drafty past on a scale Dante Centofanti had never anticipated. He admitted this to me in the closing moments of our meeting, when our talk had become general and I had put my tape recorder away.

"Young lady," he said, as I got up to leave, "I didn't for a moment countenance going as far as I did. I figured on a few general anecdotes about Johnny and I'd leave it at that. Only once I got rolling, I, uh—and I'm glad I did. I feel I've finally balanced my books. I'm only sorry I still can't remember the duke's title." I said it wasn't important. Johnny's story, he wanted to know, *would* be published, wouldn't it? Yes, I said, and sincerely wished this to be so, wanted that banker to have made a wise investment.

In front of the house, in the soft late afternoon, Martha hobbled up to us in what she may have imagined was a skip. She carried a bunch of wildflowers. She hesitated, suddenly shy, then took a ribbon from her hair and tied the flowers with it. As I bent to take them she put her arms round my shoulders and whispered in my ear, ever so gently, our own sweet little secret—that I was a fucking slut.

As the car exited the drive and headed toward New Orleans I experienced a curious sense of dispossession—as though back there in the house in impersonal attendance with my tape recorder I had pressed the stop button on my emotions, leaving me cut off now from reaction of any kind.

What I knew was a kind of calm numbness and I persuaded myself that it was no more than my usual insouciance. Until, that is, when we were about twenty minutes into the journey, I leant forward suddenly and asked the driver to stop at the next pay phone.

We pulled up at a drugstore in a suburban street. It was about five P.M. The door of the old-fashioned phone booth in the store closed on me like a confessional and I owned up to feelings—to agitation and a certain indeterminate anger—that merited the contempt of my accustomed self. I scoured for quarters in my bag and fumbled out my address book; I justified my urgency on the grounds that if I waited to make the call from my hotel room, the offices of Korda Aviation probably would be closed for the day. That explanation, however, didn't cover a restlessness that demanded immediate results. In calling San Francisco I was counting on both Harry Korda's return from Alaska and the passage of half a century having changed his unwillingness to talk about Johnny: I *had* to know exactly what happened to him.

Tony Donovan, the general manager, answered the phone and recognized my voice at once.

"Hey, Limey lady! Where the hell are ya?"

New Orleans, I said, and was Harry Korda back from Alaska?

"Nope."

I told myself it didn't matter. It *did*. "But he's been away for nearly a month."

"Sure. We got lucky. Pulled an extra contract. I've talked to him on the phone. Mentioned ya. I'll remind him again when he turns up."

"And when will that be?"

"Next week, week after. Who the hell knows?"

"I can't wait that long."

"What's the big hurry, girly?"

"I've just been talking to another member of the crew, Tony. A man called Dante Cento—"

"Dante Centofanti?"

"You remember him?"

"Hey, who could forget a name like that? That name was built around his whiskers. He still got the whiskers?"

"Yes, he—Tony, there were things he told me about what happened to Johnny. You were over there in Yorkshire and you must know the story. You *must*. Tony . . . are you still there, Tony?"

The line from San Francisco seemed to hold a depth of silence and the extra quarters I shoved into the phone to firm the connection clinked like an anchor chain.

"Tony?"

"Yeah. I'm still here. I was—I was thinkin', that's all. And the answer is *no way. Listen,* girly, I like ya and I don't mind actin' the go-between for you and Harry. But nothin' more. Call me anytime to check on his movements; don't—repeat, *do not*—call me to check on the past. That's strictly Harry's business. Okay? Whatever's to be said comes from his lips. And that's *final.* Okay?"

Okay, I said. I hung up, stood there in the booth and tried to convince myself that it was idiotic to feel so let down and frustrated. I wondered, vaguely, what now?

The phone discharged my surplus quarters—and my memory hit an arbitrary jackpot. Colonel Crinkle! I remembered, as the coins rattled, the way he used to play, with such consistent success, the one-armed bandit in the great hall. Colonel Bob Crinkle, our technical advisor back in Yorkshire, our resident bore and know-all, the man who had told me he planned to research the artifacts of the house and, through them, trace the identities and the stories of those young Americans.

As much as Harry Korda, perhaps more so given his professional thoroughness, he would know the truth about Johnny and, in his preening way, would be only too happy to pass on the proof of his astuteness. For obvious reasons, I had forgotten all about him until that moment in the phone booth. Now he mattered to me. Crucially.

On the drive back to New Orleans—I thought his number might be among my things at the hotel—I recalled our last meeting. That was the final farewell party (we had three) following the collapse of the movie. Everyone had exchanged addresses and numbers, of course, and he gave me his card. If ever I chanced to be in Arizona I was to be sure to look him up, he said.

It was a mutually awkward moment—brutally, I had denounced him as a bore and our relationship had never been quite the same— but now there he was, presenting his card and showing he had no ill feeling. I was touched and drunk and I kissed him. And promptly forgot him.

In my hotel room I dug out my attaché case and searched through the row of pouches, inside the lid, containing the accumulation of cards I judged useful—my sole criterion in relationships—or potentially so. And his wasn't among them. I was quite prepared to press my search for him through every phone book in Arizona, though it struck me I might be able to shorten that task by calling a journalist, who had helped me in my movie research, on the *New Orleans Times-Picayune*. I phoned the paper and she called back a few minutes later with his number, which she had gotten from his listing in the yearbook of the American Society of Historical Authors. I called him at once.

"You'll never guess who this is . . ." My archness was calculated.

He said he was thrilled to hear from me and when I said I was flying to Arizona the next day—my sense of urgency hadn't modified—to do some research on Phil Cowell's latest movie he gave the assurance bona fides by insisting I be his houseguest. "I'm always here, my dear. All you've got to do is turn up. Any time. But the sooner the better and the longer the better." I jotted down the details he gave of the routes I should take to reach his home.

As soon as I hung up I called the front desk and asked to be booked on a flight to Phoenix (he lived about two hundred miles west of there) the next day. They rang back and said there was space on the 11 A.M. flight. I told them to make the reservation.

From room service I ordered a chicken sandwich and coffee and then I turned to the task of replaying the tapes, listening to Dante Centofanti's words from beginning to end. I did this several times, making notes on what needed to be in direct quotes, what could be summarized and what could be left out altogether. This, of course, was a normal editing process. What I was also trying to edit was my mood. I had to trim back, as far as I could, on personal exclamatories and parentheses in order to make sure that the strength of the text was in the starkness of the facts relayed by Dante Centofanti.

Whatever its shortcomings, the job is finished. It stands, in its own way, as a matter of record. And that's what I set out to achieve, resolving that I literally could not rest until the account was down in its totality.

I have worked all through the evening and night, worked, once I got over my initial inhibitions, at a pace I have never managed before.

And now dawn shifts in the sky.

A few minutes ago I got up and opened the windows to let out the cigarette smoke and, with it, the vapors of the past. I lingered on the balcony for a moment or two and the innocence of first light misted the city so that buildings were blurred and hope was in focus: the daily second chance we so routinely ignore. I surprise myself with

such reflections, remind myself they are the result of sleep depriva-
tion. Even so, here and there outside closed jazz clubs and bars,
vagrant neon signs, strays from last night's carousing, struck me as
paint flecks on a canvas as yet untouched by the splatter of headlines
telling me of new violence, in this city and across the world.
Ephemerally, in that indigo dawn, renaissance hovered over New
Orleans, and though even now I am rationalizing on what a sudden
intake of oxygen can do to a tired mind after a long slog in a smoke-
congested room I know I did not imagine the sound I heard as I
stood in the sweet air of the balcony. It was a wisp of sound in otherwise total silence, but it had a rhythm, a resonance, a grace note. It
may have been a winch on a riverboat on the nearby Mississippi, or a
transistor radio somewhere, or even, if only to prove I am ever open
to reality, some early risen hotel maid using a vacuum cleaner. I
strained to identify that sound. But it was so distant, and yet so definite . . . like Johnny playing the sax on another dawn as his B17
limped across the North Sea toward the shoreline of England.

Arizona

Twelve

GOD, I WAS SUCH A BITCH ABOUT THE BRONTËS! I AM REMINDED of this, and the way I nagged Johnny, because the woman next to me on this flight to Phoenix is quarrelling with her male companion, in the aisle seat. It's one of those everyday whispered disputes that can be much more virulent than a brawl.

After staying up all night, trying to put Dante Centofanti's story in order, I had planned to sleep on the plane. But whenever I began to nod off, the grievances of this stranger alongside me prodded my drowsiness with the impact of her fingernails as they rapped on the plastic tray, open in front of her, in periodic summation of her argument: "You're wrong, wrong, wrong!"

These are the only words of hers I can make out. They emerge from the indecipherable verbal drone by which she, her head close to his in a series of aggressive nods, imagines she is keeping her rancor discreet. And then, out of this buzzing, she flares as identifiable Queen Bee as those scarlet nails sting on the tray and she enunciates that he's "wrong, wrong, wrong!"

Effectively, that's what I kept saying to Johnny on the subject of the Brontës.

Frankly, I'd rather have forgotten all that, but those unyielding red nails seemed to have strummed my discordancies into some kind of shape.

I seek to assure myself that I couldn't possibly have reached the declamatory scale of the woman in the next seat. She's about my age. Gray-suited. Short dark hair. Snub nose. And, of course, those long red nails. (I've *never* used nail varnish.) I see that she is wearing a wedding ring, and while this doesn't prove she's married to her companion there's a certain wretched intimacy between them. For his sake, I hope she isn't his wife. Not that I'm sympathetic to him per se. He has brownish hair and a small mouth and a generally smudged presence, like a hastily taken snapshot. He doesn't answer back. Not a word.

Neither did Johnny. But his was the silence of independence (it was, wasn't it?) and perhaps even wry amusement (though I own up to the possibility of wishful thinking now in this respect) when I got on with my Brontë baiting.

"You're wrong, wrong, wrong!" There she goes again, the scarlet flamenco of her nails drumming on the tray. I would have moved, but the plane's full; an earlier flight to Tucson was cancelled and its passengers took every spare seat on this one. My only resort, once I realized that my prospects of sleep were gone, was to ignore the standard announcement of the cabin crew requesting that personal computers not be used in flight—I've found they rarely enforce it—and haul out my laptop. It was better than simply sitting there and I was sure I was bound to have some supplementary notes and general observations to add to what Dante Centofanti told me. I didn't, or none that I could think of then. Or now.

So it seems I'm stuck with my nagging of Johnny and though I'm by no means wholehearted in writing about this I do so in the knowledge that if my account is to be an honest one I must acknowledge my own failings—and the fact (the sheer gaucherie of it makes me squirm) that I was jealous of Emily Brontë. *There*. It's down. Out

∴

in the open. Wasn't so bad, was it? Yes, it was! I seem to have repu-
diated my intellect and all the other poised attributes I take as read in
my life. But then, regardless of what that professor said about the
unfathomable geometry of time and the way the past can slot into the
present, didn't I do precisely that when, out of some ineffable
instinct, I went along with that whole episode in Yorkshire? Right
now, however, it's all too confusing for my tired mind. What is clear
is my nagging. Not with the stridency of "you're wrong, wrong,
wrong!"—I am due that concession at least—but with an insistence
which, though it was meant to be subtle, seems to grant me a certain
sorority with my shrewish neighbor in the next seat.

Didn't I, for example, set out to sabotage his pleasure in the movie of
Wuthering Heights? I have no trouble remembering that. We were in
Haworth and making our way up the main street, cobblestoned and
steep and as dark and twisted as old rope—a trek for anyone, but a
natural thoroughfare for the wind. Johnny had seen the movie, with
Laurence Olivier as Heathcliff and Merle Oberon as Cathy, in the
Stage Door Canteen the night before. He was enthusing about the
screen fidelity to the original story and the way the landscape was so
authentic in its desolation. To which I maliciously pointed out that
Wuthering Heights—windswept moors and stricken farm buildings—
had been shot on a back lot in Ventura, a few miles beyond Hollywood, during a heat wave in the early 1940s.

They used, I said, an old western set, the standard fixture of that
lot. (I spoke with authority, a movie buff who had been president of
the film society at Oxford.) The papier-mâché outcroppings were in
place, I said, and the cardboard prairie backgrounds simply had to be
toned here and there and—hey presto, *Wuthering Heights*. I imagine I
smiled brightly, subsuming my nagging—the fact that he was wrong,
wrong, wrong—as small talk. Similarly, I said, the Wild West street
with its sheriff's office and the saloon was adapted to a rural community in Yorkshire (amazing what dark varnish can do I pointed out).
As for the wind machines (no doubt another bright smile)—well,

since Olivier had complained of a teensy cold on his chest, they pumped out hot air scented with eucalyptus. Oh, and *such* tantrums on the set, I assured him as the wind seethed and we pushed on to the top of the village. Filming was halted because one day Olivier retired to his caravan between scenes and found that wardrobe had neglected to lay on the silk robe he was accustomed to and had left a cotton one instead. So in a regular Heathcliff fury he had stormed off the picture and was away for nearly two weeks. Merle Oberon, meanwhile—sweet, tragic Cathy—was sulking because Olivier had ended their affair and was playing the field with three or four leading ladies and at least one leading man and in consequence she came out in a rash which she blamed on the white tissues they were using in the snow scenes. They switched to cotton wool and when this didn't work they substituted goose down and, when the rash endured, they resorted to vanilla ice cream flakes. No luck there either. Finally, I said—all droll amusement, of course—they had to cut down the number of snow scenes.

That rancid popcorn of long-ago Hollywood lore sours in my mouth now, but it illustrates the tenuous extremes I was prepared to go to in my trashing of anything to do with the Brontës and Haworth. I was careful, though, not to single out Emily. I dealt with the sisters as a group. Called them, in Americanization, his Bronte Babes, said that under their shawls and bonnets and demure expressions they were a little chorus line of calculating hoofers, never out of step in the promotion of their self-interest. (Actually, I believe this to be so, though that's a weak excuse.)

Fair enough, I would say—and how many times did I state this case?—that in order to overcome the prejudice against women writers in nineteenth-century England they peddled their books under male pseudonyms, but wasn't this shrewdness at odds with a femininity so rarefied (and here I was quoting from biographies) that on their trips to London they fluttered and seemed in actual peril of swooning when they were introduced to men? "They were strategic swooners, your Bronte Babes, measuring their stumbles, even as they reached for the smelling salts, so they would be cushioned gracefully by the most well-heeled publisher to hand . . ." I seem to hear my voice now, somehow above my head, as though it were an in-flight announcement.

On a wider scale, I remember my voice in other tones—I remember my happiness and the sound of my laughter—but since I am presently considering the nagging me I am forced to confine myself to that register and the crafty variants I brought to it.

Let Johnny remark on the sensibilities of the Brontës and my inclination was for round-eyed parody. Mercy, and indeed, they were sensitive, good sir (that was the general tenor of my response), which presumably explained why their delicate gazes stayed steadfastly away from the working life of Haworth. I found such an approach was handy for reiterating that in those days of the industrial revolution Haworth was crammed with families who worked the new mechanized looms at the textile mills and sanitation in the village consisted of one communal water closet. Children as young as six and seven, I would remind him, were working ten- and twelve-hour shifts and dying of typhoid, dysentery, diphtheria and tuberculosis as well as that good old standby of Merry England—malnutrition.

A few bowls of soup from the hands of the Bronte Babes may not have come amiss, I would say, but of course they were so terribly, terribly busy penning their bestsellers—Emily with her saga of the tragic Cathy and Heathcliff, Charlotte with her epic of love-finally-triumphant between the patient governess and the tormented Mr. Rochester in *Jane Eyre,* Anne with her tale of the abused wife in *The Tenant of Wildfell Hall.* With such plots to develop they could hardly be expected to find time for the local suffering. Now could they? A sweet, sweet summing-up smile, my version of "You're wrong, wrong, wrong!"

But to what effect? For he never made any reply to my arguments. Did he hear them? Suddenly, I find myself facing an awkward possibility I may have tried to sidestep before, did he *literally* hear anything I said—that young man who, put at its simplest, wasn't *there*? And were his words to me words he had once said to someone else—to the Alice mentioned by Dante Centofanti—long ago, words which

were now part of that replay of time? I could do with some elucida-
tion from my erudite professor friend in Cambridge in this respect,
but in the absence of that all I can say is that he was *real* to me. Real
enough to be nagged!

That little observation puts me back on a solid everyday note and
I remember now challenging his conviction that the sisters' father,
the Reverend Patrick Brontë, was a fighter for justice. How often
did I remind him that the Reverend Brontë was no crusader, but a
brute tyrant? (Which he was.) How often did I point out that his reputation as a social reformer was part of the Brontë bunkum in which
the bewhiskered cleric widower emerged as loving paterfamilias, a
man left to grieve alone after the untimely deaths of his daughters?
How often did I explain that their early deaths—Emily, at thirty, of a
chest ailment, Anne, only five months later and at twenty-nine, of
consumption, Charlotte, also of consumption, at thirty-eight—and
the longevity of their father (he made it to eighty-five) had given rise
to a sludge of populist sentiment that had buried the truth about the
Brontës?

"And that the truth had a lot, if not everything, to do with the sins
of the father . . ." My preachy, bitchy words sift back to me. Though
with them comes a bonus—a sudden and hitherto totally buried
recall of one late afternoon in the Reverend Brontë's study in the
parsonage at Howarth. It has formed in a seeming instant, and I must
set it down.

Johnny knew someone connected with the church, a sexton or a
churchwarden, and had unhindered access to the parsonage. This day
he wanted to check certain entries in the parish records.

I stood impatiently by the door and he sat in a stiff-backed horsehair chair at a circular three-legged table while he turned the pages of
a ledger bound in brown leather. The room was small and shadowy
and smelled of all the tallow candles that must have spluttered there
in counterpoint to the old man's mutterings. The walls, I remember,

were hung with glass cases of stuffed birds and animals. A shriek owl. A hawk. A raven. A clutch of bats strung on wire so their wingspread could be seen. A fox. A badger. A hare in its winter coat. That room closed in on me like a trap.

Johnny glanced up from the ledger and remarked that the Reverend Brontë's handwriting was perfectly formed. I think I remember my exact reply.

"Which was more than could be said for the man—he was a moral hunchback." I felt the cold more than usual that day and I wasn't in the mood to mask my tension. I went on to litanize the abuses committed by the Reverend Brontë—this may have been when I used my "sins of the father" line—and took my main reading from the eminent Victorian biographer, Mrs. Gaskell. (I have, of course, the standard English Lit. knowledge of the Brontës.)

I mentioned his rages: the time he took scissors to his wife's best dress and slashed it to shreds even as she lay desperately ill, in bed; the time he gathered up his children's party clothes and hurled them on the fire as the work of the devil; the time he rampaged and sawed up all the furniture. He ruled, I pointed out, that children should be indifferent to the pleasures of eating and dress and so while he dined on his own and well—he had a particular fondness for roast pork—the children subsisted on a vegetarian diet, mainly of boiled potatoes.

And those sharp bangs that resonated through the parsonage on Sundays? Why, I said, they were dear papa as he fired his pistols randomly, one in each hand, from the windows as he reminded recalcitrant parishioners who had fallen behind in church attendance that his wrath was deadlier than God's.

No doubt I had recited much of this before, but that room licensed repetition, and more, so I brought in the modern feminist literati—in particular I remembered a starkly white-faced Canadian woman poet who had lectured at Oxford—who held that Reverend Brontë had committed incest with his daughters and, worse, that they in their competitiveness had submitted willingly, though Anne, it was said, had finally fled the parsonage on this account and gone to live elsewhere. I rather doubted, I said to Johnny, that he would find all that in the parish records.

And I smirked. I remember it quite distinctly now, that smirk—the nag, neatly packaged as cool amusement, the implication, carefully layered in the sins of the father, that Emily Brontë, assiduously un-named by me, could not have been the pure, if troubled, pilgrim of the moors.

Johnny closed the ledger. He smiled, suggested it was time we left. He showed no sign, to my further annoyance, that he had been won over by my measured reasoning: I acknowledged then neither jealousy nor nagging.

I do now, of course, and with a certain relief; a feeling that I have brought a little cohesion to the disorder of the past. And disorder abounds. As I sit here on this aircraft, my laptop on the plastic tray in front of me, I have a sense—I put it down to drowsiness—that I am facing an old-fashioned rolltop desk with its various drawers and interstices spilling with all kinds of bits and pieces of memory. Still, haven't I just now done some useful filing in the precise cataloging of my jealousy and nagging?

I am rather taken by that cozy notion of a rolltop desk and I reassure myself that squared away in its central cabinet is the now-documented opinion of that Nobel laureate physicist in Cambridge that the events of Yorkshire were an "out of time" experience, a perfectly valid scientific phenomenon—inherently, I suppose, no more remarkable than the fact that at present I am travelling six miles above the earth at a speed of six hundred miles an hour while on a television screen in the back of the seat facing me a picture relays the live broadcast of a quiz show.

A quiz show! How we trivialize. It seems to me that perhaps only the simplest minds and the most learned ones—an aborigine in Australia with his faith rooted in the Dream Time and a professor in Cambridge who is time's votary in terms of recherché propositional

calculi—share a common cosmic ground and a oneness in the funda-
mentals of a mystery and a truth.

And, after that pseudo-philosophizing, what now? The young
woman next to me has toned down the berating of her companion,
and it's ages since her voice, and her fingers, rapped out that he's
wrong, wrong, wrong. If I wished, I could sleep, but suddenly I'm
quite happy to drift, the pulses of words on the laptop screen proof
that my personal electronics are in order as my drowsiness eases me
into automatic pilot.

Lullingly, then, it occurs to me that having made due acknowledgment of my jealousy and nagging I am entitled to recall the
happy times. They must be there, nestled in the crannies of that
notional rolltop desk, a whole scattered alphabet of memory . . . *A, b,
c, d, e, f, g, h, I gotta gal in Kalamazoo.* Of course! The night Johnny
taught me to jitterbug!

Was it in his room? I'm not sure. It must have been his room for we
were alone and I see—suddenly I appreciate Dante Centofanti's
mused wonderment about memory and, as the professor said, the
Jack-in-the-box way it springs its surprises—the little wind-up
phonograph on which the old record wobbled at the edges as it spun.

A, b, c, d, e, f, g, h, I gotta gal in Kalamazoo! I didn't know he could
dance; it seemed at variance with his bookishness, his avocation as a
Brontë acolyte. I am, on the grounds that it's coquettish, no more
than a token dancer. Oh, but that night I danced! He slid me under
his legs, brought me back up, twirled me. That dance, that jitterbug,
was a choreography of his idealism, his belief in joy in all its manifestations. I didn't want that song to end. How did they go, the rest of
the words?

*Don't wanna boast but I know she's the toast of Kalamazoo-zoo-zoo-
zoo . . .*

Frolicsome, simple, innocent words. And oddly stirring. Streamers
fluttering around the scroll penned by the Founding Fathers and

underwriting that there was a warranty to that first gleamingly genuine product of the New World—a vouched-for "Life, liberty, justice and the pursuit of happiness."

That's what Johnny and I were doing as we jitterbugged that
night: we were pursuing happiness, American-style.

And in that spirit we kissed. Briefly, innocently on his part. The
kiss happened as he swooped me up from the floor to the level of
his shoulders. It wasn't just a peck he gave me on my lips, but—
reluctantly, I have to be honest—it wasn't passionate either, wasn't a
let's-sit-this-one-out sexual invitation. It was a warm kiss, a fun kiss.
Part of the jitterbug. We carried on with our dancing. . . .

> *I raise a toast to my*
> *beautiful rose in*
> *Kalamazoo . . .*

Whatever America's ills in those days, the jitterbug was mightier
than the goose step and the bright smiles of hope surely had to have
outshone the hard leer of the nation's crooks and cynical oppor-
tunists.

And then it all wound down—the McCarthy witch hunts, Viet-
nam, the assassinations of the Kennedy brothers and of Martin Luther
King, the disgraced Nixon—just as the record of "I Gotta Gal in
Kalamazoo" wound down that night. Elegy, I venture, has all kinds
of lyrics.

I wish anew that I had kept a diary of that time in Yorkshire. Only I
didn't, and all I have is a scrabble of recollections, some of them clear,
most of them vague, others stowaways still in the holds of memory.
It's a bit like having a collection of old newspaper clippings—some
easy to read, others smudged and others broken in mid-sentence and
carried over to another page that isn't there. (I have no idea of what
happened after we jitterbugged.)

But there's one "clipping" that's going to be complete in every

detail, its own docket of indictment—by which I mean the pinpointing of the place and the manner of Johnny's death and, above all, the
naming of the guilty party, or parties.

This long after the event there's not the remotest chance of official
enquiry, but I'll settle for justice in the form of that standard courtroom phrase, "Let the record show . . ." And it will. The plane banks
slightly and as a flitting of sunshine moves down the wing and into
the cabin I see the outline of my face, like an imprimatur of my
resolve, on the laptop screen. The further words I am going to be
putting down there in the near future will suffice for me and will
amount to my own private prosecution in which I am on my way to
see my star witness. Call Colonel Bob Crinkle, who, properly
coaxed, will tell the truth, the whole truth and nothing but the
truth—conditional, of course, that his cleverness and tenacity as a
researcher are duly noted. I smile. Confident of my case, I am now
going to take a nap in the hour or so before touch-down in Phoenix.

Thirteen

FOR A HISTORIAN, COLONEL CRINKLE LIVES IN THE MOST FUTUR-
istic of houses. Totally remote, it is built on two rectangular levels,
the upper part streaking out beyond the ground floor. The walls are
of mirrored glass and the general effect is of a surreal ice cube in the
surrounding desert.

In the clear Arizona air, air so pure that nothing ever rusts, I spotted the house when I was miles away. As I drove nearer, I appreciated the aesthetics of the design: simple yet bold, the lines in
symmetry with the mesas in the distance. The integrity of the house
to the landscape was absolute, its own oath of honesty, and I knew a
renewal of my certainty that Colonel Crinkle would know the total
truth about Johnny.

This close to justice, or the written version that would serve as its
surrogate, I felt near-euphoric. That mood had been building in the
five or so hours it had a taken me to cross the desert from Phoenix—
a city I left immediately, so urgent was my need to talk to Colonel
Crinkle.

I hired a car at the airport and soon, following the colonel's instructions, I was in the desert.

I drove at speed at first, then slowed, awed by the size and the shapes of the rock formations in that reddish terrain.

Sometimes they sheared to wild and spiky heights and were the color of mahogany and silver birch, as though they were the drift-wood of the desert, and sometimes they were squared and multi-layered, like ancient documents, the birth certificates of time itself.

I was absorbed in all of this when it came to me that the butler's name was Beresford. The bell-pull of memory tugged randomly and there, as clearly as if a visiting card had been brought to me on a salver, was the unsolicited, and, so it seemed then, quite useless infor-mation identifying the butler who ministered to Johnny and his crew.

Until that moment, I was never aware of knowing that name; in fact, all I consciously knew of the butler was what Dante Centofanti had told me. Now, however, I was remembering that Johnny used to praise Beresford's conscientiousness in keeping a good fire going in his damp room.

My memory rekindled on that and I saw the wicker box of logs by the side of the fireplace and, in its surrounds of blue tiles decorated with coat of arms motifs, motives, the bright little crest of the fire itself.

And as I crossed that awesome red desert the flicker of humble firelight brought back a view of Johnny's room.

A smallish room, a timbered roof and whitewashed walls, some-where toward the back of the house. There was a desk, plain except for a surface of tooled green leather on which was a black portable typewriter and, next to it, in an oval stand-up frame, a photograph of his sister. She was a few years older than Johnny and her brown hair was parted in the middle. Her eyes were thoughtful and slightly anxious.

In the far corner of the room, a bookcase. Somewhere else, I wasn't sure where, two clothes lockers of unsheened olive-green metal, military looking. The wind-up phonograph to whose music

we had jitterbugged was on top of a brown cabinet. On the floor, on
a grayish scatter rug, was a cushioned dog basket, though I couldn't
remember ever seeing Heathcliff, the Jack Russell terrier. There
were two or three chairs. Ordinary chairs. And a camp bed, always
impeccably made up.

Thus my inventory, and I wasn't at all surprised by my recall; for
the sheer expansiveness and primal depth of that the desert sanc-
tioned time's dimensions and made my episode in Yorkshire seem
like a mere paper clip.

Now that paper clip has been prized and yielded sheafs of memory
as page after page of the past started to fall into place in my
unblocked mind. They centered entirely, those memories, on his
room, which was where I was happiest, which was where the door
closed on Haworth and its draughts.

So far as I know, though hidden memory may yet surprise me, we
never made use of his bed, but the room was full of our intimacy, our
mutual understanding. I seemed to spend so many nights there, in
the easygoing nodding of the firelight, though there couldn't have
been that many. For the first time in my life I was a good listener,
anxious to hear all about him.

What he had to say about himself was indirect, allusive, as though
he had said it all before to me (or to Alice?). I was happy enough to
listen, to gather up stray conversational references and form them
into a whole.

And so I came to know that his mother died when he was three
and that his father was a lawyer whose persistent defense of the
deprived, white and black, meant not only that he died poor, but also
virtually bankrupt. (Hearkening back to what Dante Centofanti said,
was it through his father's legal connections that Johnny had set out
to reach that liberal senator in Washington?)

Johnny was sixteen at the time of his father's sudden death from a
heart seizure. His sister, Adelle—there were just the two of them—
was nineteen and in her first year at Georgia State; she had hoped to
become a doctor, but now she had to leave college and take a job as
a stenographer to keep up the one-level family home in Atlanta.

Johnny, in high school, contributed to the household through part-time jobs, one of which was delivering the *Atlanta Constitution* newspaper. And that's how he came to meet Margaret Mitchell.

I like that story—and he was fond of repeating it—for its clean lines of simplicity and its convolutions of chance: of the period, it was very American. Johnny delivered the papers, they were rolled and tied, from his bike, throwing them at the doors as he rode by. One day a woman appeared on her porch and called for him. She stood there, a file of typescript in her hand, as he walked up her drive.

"She said she had enough of cannon shell going through her mind without taking a salvo at her front door and in the future would I be good enough to *bring* her the paper?"

I think I may have remembered his very words. He didn't know then that she was writing *Gone with the Wind,* just as she had no idea that her ten years of slog on that book would bring her the Pulitzer Prize and international celebrity. He kept his promise to deliver the paper sedately and in time—it began in one summer morning when she offered him a glass of iced mint tea—they became friends.

Eventually, and shyly, he told her of his ambitions to write and, perhaps, to paint. He showed her examples of what he had written and thereafter they met once a week for mint tea—on the porch in summer, in the parlor in winter—while she took her mind off the American Civil War to discuss the strategies of prose in, and he quoted her approvingly, the "constant battle royal" for the reader's attention. (A bit arch, that phrase, but this was the Deep South of the 1930s.)

I am not one of the millions of women who have read *Gone with the Wind*—in my supercilious way I pre-judge it as a mere best-seller—but I have always admired the heroic independence of spirit by which Margaret Mitchell dedicated ten years of her life to the project. So I was interested in everything he had to say about her.

He talked also of *his* Miss Scarlett, the pin-up painted on the B17. The Miss Scarlett who in reality was called Madge. Madge Slattery. That homespun name contrasted so strongly with the flamboyant figure on the nose of the aircraft that I had no trouble remembering it as I drove across the desert. I came to know a fair bit about her. Rich Madge. Spoiled Madge. Willful Madge. Hence her ridiculous groupie-like affinity (she actually liked to dress the part) with Scarlett O'Hara.

Stupid girl. That, though, was the extent of my resentment. She was no more than a froth to me. I mention her now only because of something curious he said one night, or curious as far as I was concerned.

He was talking, as he had at least several times before, of his decision to end his relationship with Madge and to replace the Miss Scarlett insignia with that of Moonmaiden. I think I was listening to him in a half amused way—the notion of my likeness on the side of a bomber surely entitled me to that—and then, and this, too, he'd gone over before, he was describing her resistance after he had written and told her of his intentions. Troubled, he looked across at me that night and said, with a pleading that I can only describe as heartfelt, "Just how can I convince her, Alice?"

"*Alice?*" I paused, a little put out at being addressed by a name that wasn't mine, which is Amanda. "And just who might Alice be?"

It was something like that, said as a would-be flippancy. But he appeared not to hear me. And there on the Arizona desert I remembered his anxious preoccupation and seemed to hear his voice as clearly as if it had been played on my tape recorder.

"I had to be fair and square and tell her the truth about us, didn't I? Didn't I, Alice?" Again! "How can I find the right words to convince her we're through?"

My recollection of my reply was preserved in the pique I felt.

"Do it by the book. Tell your Miss Scarlett that frankly, my dear, you don't give a damn!"

My memory ran out on that rejoinder. A snap stop, like a break in a reel of film. Alice? Dante Centofanti's minnow streaks of information vis-à-vis that name darted in my mind—as well as mentioning that she was Johnny's girl hadn't he also said she looked like me?—but I let them go.

Instead, I thought for a while on a more general theme of memory and that way its flitting odd shapes somehow fused with the towering configurations all around me on the desert.

Then I started to muse on the nature of chance and how a day trip I took back to Yorkshire had led eventually to so many other directions. I pondered the events of that day—no problems with memory there—and since they account for my presence here in Arizona they must be noted.

It was a Monday. I had flown in from Italy on Saturday, returning to England briefly after nearly six months away, and spent what was left of the weekend with my agent, Andy, at his flat in Brighton. From Brighton I drove to Heathrow, fairly early in the morning, to meet the Italian distributors of the movie I had recently completed. They were due in on a Rome flight and were coming across to discuss the movie's final publicity details, prior to its English premiere in London. But in the arrivals hall a notice said all flights from Italy had been cancelled and a resumption of the service wasn't expected for at least twenty-four hours.

Driving out of the airport, I wondered what to do with the vacuum of an unplanned free day. I headed north. To Yorkshire.

I didn't think of *why* I was going; I simply went. And ended up sitting dismally in the car and gazing at the house through rain-torn windows. In that distorted view, the house dripped its blackness like old tarpaulin and it seemed impossible that once it had been streaked by the Andrews Sisters jiving to "Chattanooga Choo Choo."

There was a rapping on the side window. I turned and faced furious blue eyes. I opened the window. An old woman was there. "We're not open to the public!" she declaimed. She wore a tattered yellow raincoat, its hood tied tightly at her chin, and muddy green waders. But aristocracy was in her voice, a falsetto that belonged to the high staircase of life. She was in her late seventies, maybe older.

I explained that I'd stayed in the house when it was leased to a film company and, happening to be in the neighborhood, I thought it would be nice to make a return visit. "For old time's sake," I said.

She hesitated; then her eyes shaded from outrage to mere inconvenience. "In that case, I suppose you'd better come in for a moment." She squelched off, carrying a blue plastic bucket full of wild mushrooms. I followed her.

Lady Dorothy, that was her name, and she stressed the Lady, took me to a narrow kitchen where she motioned me to sit on a bench running the length of a pine table. She made coffee. Out of her raincoat she was a little less formidable, a frail old woman in a print frock, though her face, long and gaunt, was its own lineament of lineage. Her white hair was bunned severely at the back. She put a mug of coffee in front of me, took hers to the top of the table, where she sat in a rocking chair.

"So, do you like my house?"

I nodded.

"Lived here since I was born," she said. She hefted up the blue plastic bucket from her feet, emptied the mushrooms on the table and began de-stalking them. "Always restless when I'm away from the place, which was why I was none too happy when I had to upsticks for you film people."

"I hope there were some compensations," I said, for I knew exactly how much the lease had cost and had protested to Phil Cowell at its excessiveness.

"Enough for a little holiday," she said. "Went on a cruise. Glad to get back. Too many foreigners. Of course there had been foreigners here too, hadn't there? Americans. Your film chappies. Left the place in a shocking mess. Daddy used to say all Americans should be castrated."

She seemed to be doing something like that as she de-stalked the mushrooms.

Sliding my interest under the surface of small talk, I asked, "Wasn't the house also taken over by Americans in the war?"

She looked up. "Fancy you knowing that." Carefully, she removed a sliver of mushroom skin from her thumb, as though

unpeeling a minor layer of history. "It was requisitioned for a bomber
crew. We were turfed out, there were seven of us then, and relo-
cated—first time I had heard that word—to a cottage on the estate.
Daddy was enraged. Even the butler was requisitioned. Actually, I
found one or two of those Americans to be quite . . . civilized."

I picked up a mushroom that had strayed my way. And asked,
very casually, if she remembered anything in particular about them.

"What?" Her voice reared, in unaccountable affront.

I smiled, the polite guest. A name, I said. A face. A—I decided
against specifying the S-shaped scar—a *characteristic.*

"I don't do games! Feats of memory! I have no truck with any
transient Tom, Dick or Harry!" Her words were shrill and her eyes
splintered on rage. I was utterly taken aback. She blinked for a
moment, put her head down and, rapidly now, resumed her de-
stalking.

"If you're so interested in those wartime Americans, though I
can't for the life of me imagine why you should be"—she didn't look
up but her voice was steadier—"then I suppose the person you
should talk to is our local GI bride." And she snickered, a hard, dry
sound.

"Really?" My reply was no more than a formality; after her
strange outburst of a moment or so ago I decided she was part of the
decay of the house and I had a sudden desire to be out of that place.

She snickered again as, snapping away at the mushrooms, she
pressed on me a withered truffle of ancient scandal in the form of a
story of a local woman who had given birth to an illegitimate child
fathered by one of the Americans—a woman who still lived in the
village and actually flew the Stars and Stripes in her front garden. I
must have passed the house, she said; it was on the main road con-
necting the village to the highway.

"We call her our GI bride. Our blight!" She glanced up for an
instant and her eyes brimmed malice. I felt for my car keys in my
pocket. "A bad lot from the start," she went on. "Wasn't a man,
young or old, safe from her. And I include the clergy. Even today,
even in old age, she flaunts her whoredom in the flying of that

damned flag. The parish council has asked her repeatedly to take it down or at least not to fly it on St. George's Day. But it's her—her floozy flag. Her way of continuing to defy the standards of the village. That flag went up in the war and there it stays to this day—a slut's landmark! Slut! Slut! Slut!"

Her voice spiralled to a near-shriek on this repeated denunciation and I stood up hastily, jingled my car keys as though calling for order and announced, with a shattering lack of originality, that I had remembered another appointment.

As we shook hands I felt the slime of wild mushrooms on her fingers, as if the spite of long-ago gossip had become its own fungus.

I drove quickly down the drive and cursed the folly of my trip, which had yielded one madwoman and an incessant rain that showed no sign of easing. At the curve of the drive, I glanced in the rearview mirror for a final look at the house and its dark and drenched swab of turrets and eaves. And, again, I resorted to my earlier question—why had I gone back?

Oh, say can you see . . . My ironic reflection as I spotted Old Glory on the fringes of the village just as I was estimating that even in the rain I could, if I drove fast enough, make London in little more than two hours. I wasn't aware of looking out for the flag, but there it was, a soaked shred of America in front of a solitary cottage. And I stopped.

I had no intention initially of doing much more than that; this was just a pause. GI bride, for goodness' sake!

Bless the bride, as it turned out—bless Elizabeth (Bessy) Mogdon-avitch, Bessy Thwaites as she was, who had taken, by deed poll, the name of her common-law American husband. All of this, and more, awaited me inside the cottage, though as I walked up the path and past the dripping flag I was convincing myself that on a day that had gone so badly wrong I was making no more than the most perfunctory of calls simply to prove to myself that my natural tenacity hadn't been soaked by the weather and everything else. Why, I might even find a little sardonic amusement.

The old woman who answered my knock was small and plump with a round face like a hand-painted doll—twin spots of cheerful blue for eyes, bright red for her cheeks and lips. A blonde rinse intermingled with the scalloped cut of her white hair. Barbie Doll grown old, I thought. I said I was writing a magazine article about the war and the influence of Americans on village England and these phony credentials granted me immediate admission by my beaming hostess who never once asked how I came to know of her.

"Tha's come t' reet place, lass." Her Yorkshire accent, rooted in flat vowels, was as knobbly as a cabbage stump, but even at the age of seventy-five—she was as frank about that as she was about everything else—her femininity was palpable. She wore a pinkish dress, down to her ankles, and a long double string of bright green glass beads. She might have been dressed for a downmarket cocktail party, though her taste was for her homemade gin, taken neat, and she promptly produced a bottle. As we dunked tumblers—and after my session at the house with Lady Dorothy I was ready for a real drink—she said, "The Yanks, God bless 'em. And especially Tony."

"Tony?"

"Me 'usband, luv. If not in law, in spirit. That's 'im over there, on't top o' telly."

I looked across at the television and saw a framed head-and-shoulders photograph of a grinning young man with a huge chin and crimped black hair. Master Sergeant Anthony Mogdonavitch, tail gunner, US Eighth Air Force. I got the details later. Meantime, Bessy was remembering her wedding. (I am doing my best to recall both her words and her dialect.)

"I were all in white. I showed t'village, I did. They could blacken me name all they liked, but I were in *white*. Oh, and t'ceremony . . . It were luvly. Book o' Common Prayer, tha knows. Wilt thou, Elizabeth Thwaites, tek this man, Anthony Mogdonavitch, to be . . . ? I've kept 'is name ever since, by deed poll, even though it weren't a proper service. Not lawful, tha knows. Would tha like t'see t'pictures, luv?"

And of course I had to say yes. While she went off somewhere to fetch the pictures I wondered what she meant about the service not being lawful. Though I wasn't really interested. I would flick through the old pictures, then tell her I had to be on my way. She was a muddled old woman—I glanced at the large tumbler of gin she had poured for herself—and clearly not competent to answer any questions I might have had for her. Still, she meant well and her gin was excellent and for the moment I was content enough to sit there, on a chintz two-seater sofa, and, faintly amused, note further evidence of her confusion in the extraordinary disarray in the little living room—brown paper parcels, a cardboard box full of china dogs, a collection of brass kettles tied at the handles with a polka dot headscarf and, grouped closely together on the table, seven or eight old alarm clocks, the kind with twin bells on top. The clocks, stopped, showed different times.

She came back with her wedding album, settled it on her lap as she sat next to me on the sofa. "Tha mun excuse t'mess in 'ere," she said, "but I'm 'avin' me once-a-year turn-out for t'village fete. I've told 'em they can tek anything—except me memories." Chuckling, she opened the album.

I said she was a beautiful bride, and meant it. She was dark in those days, her hair worn down to her waist. A slim girl, she stood at the side of her big-chinned American, in civilian life a fireman in Atlantic City, and there was confetti in their hair as they posed over a blacksmith's anvil.

"Alice took t'pictures," she said.

"Alice?"

"Johnny's girlfriend. Johnny were t'captain. Tha reminds me a bit o' Alice, luv. In looks."

"I do?"

She nodded, turned the pages, and the photos became less formal; the groom held her across his shoulders in a professional fireman's lift; they squirted champagne at one another; wickedly she raised the skirts of her wedding dress thigh-high.

Then there were scenes of the reception, including one in which she danced with her young man. No, he was altogether slimmer than

Master Sergeant Mogdonavitch. Smaller. And he held his head at a certain angle, as though giving total attention to something she had just said to him. Apart from a line of upper profile, I couldn't make out the face.

"This man you're dancing with," I said.

She peered for a moment. "Johnny," she said. "That were Johnny. He had a way o' . . . o' listening."

There were other shots of him as we made our way through the album. Full-faced ones, some of them, and though he was there in detail, smiling and chatting, none defined him as well as the one, his face unseen, where he danced with Bessy: the camera had plucked a moment and produced an encompassing study of his grace. Alice's work, I took it. Though I didn't see anyone in those pictures, and there were a number of women in them, who remotely resembled me. Perhaps I didn't look hard enough; perhaps I didn't want to see Alice. I've no idea.

Finally, Bessy closed the album, rested her hands flat and evenly on its cover, as if carrying out the concluding rite in a private and familiar liturgy. I got round to asking her—for having seen the photographs I was that bit more interested now—why she said her marriage hadn't been lawful. For a moment or two she worked her wedding ring backward and forward with the thumb and forefinger of her right hand.

"The base commander, he were RAF but he 'ad the say, wouldn't gi' 'is permission," she said. "I were pregnant, d'y'see, and 'e knew it. There were them in t'village as saw to that. I mean, I were t'local bad girl, 'specially after that business wi' t'curate . . ."

And she went on to tell me that story, not in any way in self-pity but as part of her simple honesty.

The curate had been a noted county cricketer who had also played for England and so he was prized by the village, coveted by families with daughters of marriageable age (and Lady Dorothy, it occurs to me, could well have been one of the candidates).

He was in charge of the church choir, to which Bessy belonged. After choir practice he always insisted on her staying behind to help

him clear up, and always made a point of locking the door. She submitted to him out of a child's fear that he would set the "demons of
hell" on her if she did not, or if she told anyone. One night after
choir practice the village constable found her trembling and sobbing
in the street. He, neither a great church-goer nor (a greater heresy in
Yorkshire) a great cricket fan, made a report. The subsequent investigation led to the curate wading out into the river one night and
drowning. And figuratively, it was the ducking stool for Bessy, as the
village ostracized her; she was taunted at school, abused in the street
by old women.

Then the Americans swaggered in and with no good name to lose,
she "dropped me drawers" for Master Sergeant Mogdonavitch, her
Tony, with his lavish gifts of nylons and Hershey bars.

She got pregnant and Tony, delighted, filed a routine application
to marry. Her father, when she confessed her pregnancy to him,
threw her out of the family home with a flourish that boosted his
standing in the village, where he was a clock repairer.

Tony rented the cottage for her, the same one she lived in now.
There she nibbled on Hershey bars, a nonstop pregnancy craving,
and tasted the tang and the space of Atlantic City, which was where
she would be headed for one day as a GI bride. But the CO stood in
the way.

"Johnny, t'captain, signed t'papers but the CO wouldn't 'ave no
truck wi'em. So Johnny took it up wi' the American Air Force in
London. But they hummed and hawed and—time were gettin' on. I
were showin'. One day I were reet depressed, full o' tears, and Tony
said we'd just go ahead and 'ave a make-believe weddin'. A fill-in,'e
said, till Johnny got things sorted out.

"It were a grand idea. Cheered me up no end. I made me own
dress from parachute silk and come the big day the blacksmith's
forge—he'd been paid off in cigarettes and Hershey bars—were all
done out in ribbons and flowers and Johnny, right and fittin' as captain, took the service, and, oh, he made a lovely job o' it. I were the
'appiest bride in England."

Not for long. Six weeks later, as the B17 crossed the coast of Holland, a fighter swooped at its tail and a burst of cannon shell hit with such devastating accuracy that what remained of Master Sergeant Mogdonavitch was sucked into the night sky over the North Sea.

Johnny called in at the cottage to break the news to her, in the very room we were in. I looked around and my gaze settled on the old and stopped alarm clocks, time dead on their stricken faces.

"He said I were family and the crew would alus look after us," she said. "Me and t'baby."

And they did. Appointing themselves as godparents, they bought the cottage for her and her child, which turned out to be a boy. The cost, in those days, could have amounted to no more than a couple of months of their combined pay, but it was still an extraordinary generosity—that real estate transaction was Bessy's Declaration of Independence and, her Tony apart, I could understand why all those years she had kept the Stars and Stripes flying in her front garden.

"We lacked for nowt, me and the bairn," she said. "Even after the war, aye and long after, they kept in touch. The letters, the dollars when they could afford them. *And* the Hershey bars! They were a reet grand lot, Johnny's crew, and the pity were that he weren't there to see how they stood by me ower t'years. Only he . . . disappeared."

She looked at me, befuddled. "Disappeared," she repeated and swallowed her sigh in a swig of gin; I had said no to another drink and she was on to her second or third and determined to talk about the disappearance.

"Seems like the last his lads saw of him were one morning when he set off in his jeep. Never came back. Or that's what they said in their letters to me. This were after t'war, tha knows, and they were back in't' States. What happened after Johnny disappeared is they were all posted 'ere, there and . . . Sudden like. As for Johnny—well, there were bad blood on the part of the RAF to the Yanks. Very bad blood. So God alone knows what happened to 'im. God alone knows."

She was rambling, sloshing about in gin, and I saw no point in telling her that Johnny had been killed on a raid to Düsseldorf. It was time to be going, though I stayed a little longer when she switched back to the topic of the crew's loyalty and how they had never reneged over the years to "see to" her. And that, I decided, though I owned up to bias, was a tribute to Johnny. Now only three of them were left. Would I, she wondered, like their names and addresses. I said, getting to my feet, that I didn't want to trouble her.

"No trouble, luv." Slowly, tediously and pointlessly—or that's how it seemed to me at the time, for it was long before Phil Cowell asked me to go to the States—she copied her list for me and, because I liked her, I reciprocated by folding the scrap of paper carefully and putting it in my wallet.

Just before I left, she showed me a photograph of her son, a chartered accountant in Leeds. Like his father, his chin was a slab, but he was no chip off the old block. Indeed, he was the complete English gentleman as, top-hatted, he posed solemnly outside Buckingham Palace after his investiture with the OBE by the queen.

"Prim little bugger, isn't he?" Bessy said.

Privately, I agreed, though to be diplomatic I asked what his name was. "His middle name's Tony, after his dad," she said. "As for his first name, I wanted summat as 'ud *say* it for the Yanks. Vicar were a bit flummoxed at t'christenin', but 'e agreed. And so that baby were baptised Hershey Anthony Mogdonavitch—Hershey after t'chocolate bar!" She winked and chortled—and I do believe her hilarious originality could have been why I hung onto her list of the crew's survivors.

Recalling that moment as I drove across the Arizona desert, I laughed out loud. Hershey Mogdonavitch OBE! How audacious. How in keeping with the spirit of the young Americans, the last of the Yanks, who surged into England in the early forties and showed, to what I imagined must have been a generally grateful female population, that though they were newcomers to war they were old hands at conquests.

Poor Bessy. A stranded GI bride. But through her I had made it to Arizona and now I was going to find out the truth about Johnny's fate by way of the testimony of a wartime historian.

And, as it turned out, I wasn't at all wrong in my hunch that Colonel Crinkle had all the answers.

I just hadn't counted on him being a hostile witness.

Fourteen

THIS LAPTOP OF MINE IS A MASTERWORK OF SOPHISTICATION, though I seem to be using it as a pack mule as I pile it with words—and whether they are the lopsided load of memory or the stuffed pouches of my opinions on America, I am finding I literally cannot rest until those words have been put into place, strapped down.

I tell myself that the sensible course would be the taking of selective notes for due reflection in a study, but that counsel is overruled by the growing imperative to write the narrative as I go along. No delays.

Which is why, late at night, as it was after my meeting with Dante Centofanti, I sit here in this room in Arizona and work when I should be sleeping. I've spent the last few hours writing up what I thought and felt as I crossed the desert to meet Colonel Crinkle. And now, the chronology established, for the sequel to that trek—the dismaying denouement to our reunion, the stiff rage in which he regarded me as the enemy.

The irony is that it all began so harmoniously and, in the light of the subsequent confusion and rancor, I need to go back to that beginning—my arrival at his fantastic house of glass and Colonel Crinkle holding out his arms in welcome and then hugging me. "My dear! I hope you've come for a *real* stay and that you won't be taking off after just a day or two."

His bright tan was the color of a blood orange and, in spite of his jeans and open-necked plaid shirt, he looked somehow baronial as those glass walls mirrored the sky and the clouds like a drifting mural that reaffirmed this house's kinship with the broader nobility of the earth.

He lives here on his own (his wife died some years ago) with Mopa, a Navajo Indian woman, his housekeeper. Mopa took me to my room, on the second level of the house. It's an unpretentious room—a bed, a wardrobe, a straw chair—but it is extravagant in its views, through those sheer glass windows, of the desert. I looked out and watched the late afternoon light deepen the colors of the canyons in the distance. Mopa, in the next room, was running a bath for me.

The bath was sunken and the water, piped up from an underground stream, flowed from between a little raised pile of rocks in which tiny desert flowers, blue and yellow, grew in mossy fringes. Anywhere else and this would have been affectation; here, it belonged, was part of a natural affirmation. After my long drive, the water was cool and perfect, and my only reservation was that Mopa stayed in the bathroom, by the door, a beige towel draped over her folded arms. I smiled at her a couple of times but she stayed expressionless, that squat and barefooted Indian woman, her hair, black shading to white, worn long and straight.

After I got out and towelled myself dry she indicated, by signs, that I should lie facedown on a nearby low table and I saw I was in for a massage. I was happy to go along with what seemed to be a custom of the house.

There was a strip of mirror, level with my eyes, fixed to the end of the table and I watched her idly as her fingers tapped my back. Then her hands began to move in circular sweeps in the center of my spine and up to my shoulder blades. I glanced at her face in the mirror. A round face, quite unlined, almost the face of a girl, her dark and slant eyes like mahogany eaves under the narrow ridge of her forehead. Her face stayed set and silent, but her hands were their own fluency in the murmur of relaxation they were creating within me.

After a few minutes she paused and put her hands into the large satchel-like pocket at the front of her brown dress, made from thin canvas material. From the pocket, I watched in the mirror, she drew out a handful of twigs. She passed them experimentally between her stubby fingers; some she rejected and put back in her pocket, others she snapped in several places and then started to lay them across my shoulders.

"What are you doing?" She ignored my question, ferreted out more twigs and repeated the process of examination, rejection, snapping and the placing of twigs on my shoulders. Now she took from her pocket something small and round, a mottled white in color. "Egg," she said. It was the first time I had heard her speak; until then, I had thought she might be mute. "Rattlesnake egg."

For a moment, she held the egg between finger and thumb. Her pressure tightened and I heard the tiny crack of the shell and saw the gobbet of glowing white fluid, like a spilling of candle grease on my shoulder. I flinched, somehow anticipating a burn, but what I experienced was a permeating icy glow.

And then she was pummelling my shoulders and the upper part of my back with her knuckles and I was aware of a rush of fragrances. Juniper. Pine. Honeysuckle. I could feel the twigs, but no pain.

"Demons," she said. "You have demons."

I nodded in drowsy agreement. Who didn't have demons? The desire to sleep was strong. I had the impression that what moved on my back was a mulch of my worst memories—Haworth and the wind and my dream and the curtained silence of my flat in London in those weeks of my illness—and that these were being drawn from me, made harmless.

"A wind hunts you. The demons fly in that wind . . ."

Her voice was far off, a thin but clear echo. I gasped as a sluice of cold water struck me and washed away those words as the mere marks of a surface dream. Fully awake now, I saw she was ladling the water from a stone urn. She placed a towel across my back. "Finished," she said, and left.

On the floor, I saw some of the twigs she had used. They were thinner than matchsticks and only two or three inches long. They had a shaggy bark, like brown and white cotton strands. Their most common feature, though, was serrations of tiny sharp thorns. Craning, I examined my shoulder in the mirror, expecting to find scratches. There were none. Local culture, I decided, briskly amused.

Later, as we sipped pre-dinner tequilas on the veranda, I mentioned to Colonel Crinkle that Mopa's massage had left me feeling invigorated. He smiled. "She has the touch." Her father, he added, had been renowned as a tribal medicine man and she had inherited his skills. Even today Navajos would arrive unannounced, often from hundreds of miles away, and though there had been no prior messages she would be waiting for them with a tray of freshly made-up nostrums that could be anything from a powder wrapped in dried lizard skin to a sprig of eagle feathers dipped in the blood of a coyote. "Darned thing is they work, and not just for her people." He went on to recall guests of his who had been treated by her, most recently a former Surgeon General who had come down with a severe toothache. "This guy was roaring with pain. She told him to put this flat pebble on his tongue. He was so desperate that in the end he did just that—and it *worked*. The pain stopped, almost instantaneously. Now at your age, my dear, it's only natural that you're skeptical, but take the word of this old-timer that some mysteries in this life are way beyond our understanding. Way beyond."

I nodded, reflected that I knew a thing or two about mysteries myself. I looked up at the stars. Such stars! In England we are starved of stars, cheated by a climate that imposes a near-permanent cloud cover. But there on the desert in Arizona it was as if the Big Bang that had created the Grand Canyon had shattered a vast and

empyrean mass of crystal and sent its fragments and shards to hang for
all of eternity, glorious and frozen in the night sky, shimmering on so
many unknown echoes.

I asked him about his house. He said it had been designed by his
wife, who had been an architect in Phoenix.

"She sprang it on me," he said. "We were in a restaurant one
night. I had only just returned from Europe and was still in uniform,
and she said, I remember her words exactly, 'Honey, the war's over,
so let there be light!' And she unfurled, there on the table, the blueprint of this all-glass house she had been working on in private. Very
next day we were out in the desert, scouting for sites—the house, she
said, needed space—and we filed for this one here, which was our
first step in going for broke."

He filled our drinks from the pitcher on the table and I mused on
the American Dream, circa 1945, surely a vintage year for master
builders. Johnny's generation. Some with his values. All that hope, all
that promise flowing down the gangplanks of the returning troopships and into that nation whose vast tracts were wide open for aspiration and freedom. I remembered the Andrews Sisters, back in
Yorkshire, singing "Don't Fence Me In" and making it sound, or it
suited me to think so now, like an anthem to the American spirit.
"Oh give me land, lots of land, under starry skies above . . ." At least the
colonel and his wife had achieved their starry skies.

"Helen only ever wanted to do one thing and that was architecture . . ." He carried on with the story. During the war, newly graduated, she went to work for a practice that was handling military
contracts; her job was to design portable prefabricated hospitals and
field morgues. As an antidote, her vote of confidence in the future,
she began drawing plans for the house, this dynamic of light, airiness
and vision.

After the war, the man whose job she had been filling came back
from the army and she was let go. The colonel, meantime, was back
in his old teaching post in the history department of the university
and supplementing his income with articles about World War II, dis-
sections of campaigns and strategies. Some of his material was syndi-

cated, and this led to the offer of his first book. Even so, the rewards were not great. Still, it all helped.

"Every dime we had—every dime we didn't have, come to that—went into this house," he said. "We discovered we couldn't have children, so the house was our—our baby. Friends said we were crazy to live so far out. Well, we did, and it was as simple as that. We built this house bit by bit, taking the material out on a hired truck, workmen, too, when we could afford them. My father died, left me some money. Not a lot, but I secured a couple of loans on it. Even persuaded a publisher to cough up an advance for a three-book deal to be completed in eighteen months, with a hefty penalty clause in the contract if I failed to deliver. By the time we finished building, we were wallowing in debt, but, as you can see, we were rich in stars." He laughed softly.

That laugh stays with me because it contrasted so markedly with his subsequent fury and his identification as that most uncompromising of right-wingers—a military reactionary. Still, I am sure that in building that house he and his wife had more than mere property in mind. I believe they were moved by an ideal: a resolve, in the aftermath of war, to add something enhancing to life.

They were American veterans in the most elegiac sense. Class of '45. And once there had been so many of them. I wondered how Johnny would have fared if he had survived. Johnny as an old man: what might he have achieved in his life? I thought about his youth and the rare quality of his quiet commitment and decided—in retrospect I should like to find it maudlin and, of course, it is, but I can find no good reason to cancel it out—that his eternal flame was in the stars. With that came a nudge of depression, a downdraft on the thermals that had buoyed me up all day. Then Colonel Crinkle started asking me questions about Phil Cowell's latest movie and, in answering him, I pulled out of that trough.

He listened politely. "Sounds interesting," he said. "Mind you, I think the picture Phil was shooting back in Yorkshire would have been something special. He had lousy luck on that one, uh?"

I said the lousy luck was of Phil Cowell's making and that he had bankrupted the movie with his wastefulness and self-indulgence. Colonel Crinkle shook his head. "You've got it wrong, my dear. The Arabs folded up their tents on that picture because their aerospace deal here in the States fell through." He paused. "Or maybe you didn't know about that?"

No, I said, I didn't. He smiled, and as he raised his glass to his lips the tip of his tongue did a swift little circling of the salt-encrusted rim as though savoring his accustomed role as the purveyor of inside information.

The Arab backers of the movie, he said, had been fronting for a Middle East consortium that wanted to buy into sizeable chunks of the US military aerospace industry which had been hit by defense spending curbs. The movie was to have been a "sweetener" in this process, an Arab-financed tribute to American heroism. But a Senate committee became alarmed at the size and implications of the deal; they saw the Arab world setting up a virtual command post in the United States, and, discreetly, made sure it did not succeed. "In the overall scheme of Arab monies involved the picture was no more than a date pit to be spat out," he said.

None of that had been mentioned in the gossip of the set; I wondered if even Phil Cowell had known. "Are you sure of all this?" I asked.

He leant back, pleased with himself. "When it comes to facts, my dear, I am the most voracious and pertinacious of individuals. Facts are my cause and, yes, my folly. I have literally crates of facts about World War Two, material I will never use but which I *need*—facts are my addiction and I'm totally hooked on them." A giggle teetered out of him; he was a bit tipsy, as he had been so often in Yorkshire.

Now was the time to ask about Johnny, but Mopa appeared and said dinner was ready.

And, of course, it wasn't difficult—no more than a few opening wide-eyed questions—to get him to expand on the role of that B17 at the RAF base in Yorkshire. As Mopa served the first course, a crayfish soup garnished with tiny red peppers, he talked of how Churchill and Eisenhower, late one night over brandies, had discussed the feasibility of a B17 flying with the RAF. "Churchill was all for it, but Ike, he was ever cautious, needed some persuading . . ." I had heard it all before, but I accepted it as a necessary preliminary and wasn't at all impatient.

On the contrary, that room, with its sense of endless space, soothed me. Even what was most tangible there, the heavy oak table at which we sat and the uncarpeted flagstone floor, seemed minor details in an infinity. Toward the rear of the room, unseen from our cove of candlelight, a fountain splashed softly and in its ripple his voice sounded like words from a remote shore.

". . . that B17 performed magnificently. The *Miss Scarlett* she was called. Though later her name was changed to *Moonmaiden*. Quite an apt name, considering she flew only night missions."

"What about her crew?"

My question, listening to it now, sounds measured and appropriately artless, in spite of the influence of tequila. "Typical American boys of the period. They chewed gum, played the field, were lonely for their girlfriends and families back home. Ordinary Joes. I got to know them quite well. Vicariously, you understand."

"Ah, yes. I remember you saying you were going to research the memorabilia of that room in the house, link up what was there with the identities of the crew."

"And I did." He preened, modestly.

"That must have been quite a task."

"Um? No, it—"

He broke off as Mopa brought in the main course, steak with a side salad of pickled cactus pears and herbs. He refilled our glasses.

"Another toast," I said. "This time to your ingenuity in tracing the crew."

"Oh, it was no big deal, my dear. Contacts in, uh, high places, you know. In no time at all I had full access to the records. It was as easy as that. So I don't rate a toast."

"Then how about one to the crew of the B17?"

"I'll sure drink to that. Yes, I'll drink to those ordinary American boys whose kind you don't see anymore. Or at least I don't. I see kids who are bored and sullen and frequently violent. But I remember—okay, this is old man's talk—but I remember the vibrancy of that generation. It was as if they had an—an inner light. An innocence. And with that vibrancy and that innocence there came a natural, well, heroism. As for those boys on that B17, they were superheroes, the way they flew more than twice the span of the normal operational tour. Everyone looked up to them. Everyone."

"Except . . . the RAF." Replayed, my voice is level, conversational.

"Um?" He was adding French mustard to the side of his plate.

"The RAF—the RAF on the base—had no time for those Americans."

I felt a vague sense of recklessness, as if I had jumped a stop light, but his reply was equable.

"A bit of resentment, no doubt. Jealousy. Rivalry."

"And murder."

I said it quietly, making it sound like small talk, at that moment when he was making the first cut into his steak. The steak was done rare and as the blood seeped out he gazed down at the plate as though my decorously expressed accusation had opened an old wound.

He kept his eyes lowered for a moment or two, though when he looked up at me he was smiling. "What was that you said, my dear?"

"I apologize for introducing such a note of melodrama to your dinner table, Colonel, but what I said was murder."

"Now why would you say that?" He tilted his head at an amused angle, which irked me; I was being patronized.

But I tried to maintain a polite tone in my reply, though it was stupid of me—I blame the tequila—to be as direct as I was at that stage.

"I say that, Colonel, because two members of the crew of that B17 died in circumstances that pointed overwhelmingly to the culpability of a group of RAF officers, and one in particular. One man's death was made to seem like suicide. The other man—he was the captain—simply disappeared one morning. *Permanently.* The last time he was seen he was with a young woman. So we could be looking at three victims."

"Who"—he was about to transfer the first bit of steak to his mouth, then changed his mind, simply held the fork upright, his elbow on the table. "Who told you that, my dear?"

My dear! Old provocation flared, but I kept my words steady. "A surviving member of the crew."

"Some old war rummy with an addled brain." He was smiling still, but somewhat rigidly.

"No, Colonel, a former banker of considerable standing and rectitude. After all these years, he wants to set the record straight."

"And you—what do you want to set straight?"

"Justice."

"Justice as in what?"

"As in—war crimes."

"I—I can't believe I'm hearing this."

"Loud and clear, Colonel. I've other members of the crew to interview and—"

"How did you get their names?"

"That's—that's my business."

A weak, defensive reply. But then in the last few moments the whole tenor of the occasion had tilted. He wasn't even smiling now. Just sitting there, tautly upright, holding that stupid fork as though it were a pikestaff and he was the idiotic guardian of the past I was trying to unearth. Oh, but he *knew*! At least I'd proved that. What crushed me was his failure to openly corroborate what had happened; I'd been so confident of his cooperation. Daunted and nonplussed, I looked down and saw (at first it seemed inconsequential) that his name was worked in the gold leaf on the rim of my plate: Colonel and Mrs. Robert Crinkle, United States Air Force. Then it occurred to me that a man who had his name on his crockery had to be treated like fine china. I changed my approach. I looked up at him. Smiled.

"I fear I have upset you, Colonel. I had no intention of doing that and I apologize most sincerely."

He lowered his fork, as though in ceremonial truce. "It was a—a spasm, that's all. An old man's spasm. Guy gets to my age, I guess he's entitled to a little spasm." He worked up a smile on this feeble whimsy. His fork went to his mouth and he started to chew.

I cut into my steak. Carefully. "I simply assumed, you see, that since you were happy to talk about the B17—"

"That was some ship."

"Quite. And I thought that you, knowing everything about it—"

"*Her.* To fliers of my generation, any airplane has the female gender. Some are just dames, of course. Others are bitches—no shortage of bitches." Did he glance at me pointedly then? "And some are ladies."

"Which takes us back to *Miss Scarlett,* I suppose."

"Latterly *Moonmaiden.*"

"You and your facts!" I smiled. Big, sunny, open smile. I can do it, when necessary. "Anyway, as I was saying—this is such a delicious steak, by the way—I assumed you'd be willing to tell me the whole story. I was wrong, and we'll leave it at that of course, but simply to get *my* explanation out of the way, I thought you would be willing to talk because, well, the crew of that B17 were your countrymen, after all. But you have your reasons for staying silent and I have absolutely no doubt that they are good ones."

He looked at me, dabbed at his mouth with his napkin. "Has it not occurred to you—I'm talking generally, you understand—that some parts of the past are better left undisturbed, that some bones are better left unpicked?"

"But you're a historian, Colonel."

"Which doesn't make me a scavenger, my dear. I unearth, that's true. That's my profession and my nature. It's also my nature to respect what is told to me in confidence. It's the military man in me."

"Of course." I opened more petals of the English rose smile I had cultivated when I was in television—the Venus flytrap, one of my producers used to call it. "But you did tell me about the aborted Arab deal, and presumably that's just as secret."

"Yes. I, uh—I allow myself leeway. Besides, that was just a business affair. Skulduggery, yes, but no violence."

"So you're admitting there *was* violence in Yorkshire?"

He tensed. A little pull at the side of his mouth. "I—I didn't say that."

"Not in so many words."

He took a sip of wine, then leant toward me. "What's your—your *agenda*, my dear? I mean, no offense, you talk blithely about crime and justice, but after all this time what's the point? What *is* the point? Even if you were able to prove anything, who's going to believe you? More important, who's going to *want* to believe you, my dear?"

He was smiling, but I sensed a sneer and that's why I replied as I did. That and the tequila and my disappointment at his lack of cooperation and—that old standby of justification—his calling me "my dear".

"Millions," I said. "On both sides of the Atlantic. What happened in Yorkshire is a natural for a television documentary. A script outline is in the hands of my agent right now and both the BBC and NBC are showing interest. I'll have my war crimes tribunal, Colonel, in the shape of that most open of forums—television."

Bluff. Angry, stupid bluff. I could have persuaded him, but I overstepped and I hear that now in the snapped precision of my voice.

"So it's muckraking?" He was back to sitting upright, at attention, his napkin clenched in his right hand.

"That, Colonel, is the standard political response to anyone who seeks the truth."

"Truth? You talk about *truth* and yet you deceived me into believing that your visit was one of friendship and all the time you were out to—to use me."

"For the best reason in the world. To expose a cover-up going all the way back to 1944. I honestly felt, I was *sure,* that you would want to help me. I assure you, I came here in good faith."

He looked at me coldly. A military gaze that was totally cut off from the sprightly little man who had greeted me so warmly on my arrival. He court-martialled me with his eyes.

"Forgive my directness, but I have no confidence in your veracity. I care for your country in the sense of its history and traditions, but I have a declining respect for its people. You have done nothing to reverse that judgment."

I couldn't decide, and still can't, whether it was a stuffy little speech or oddly dignified. Slowly, he rose, and I remembered the way he had done just that back in Yorkshire, in the control tower that day when he was wearing his track suit. Now, once again, he looked down on me, and suddenly it seemed that the seeming infinity of space in that room had been sucked away: there were just his eyes, boxed in between the thin flames of the two candles.

"I must advise you strongly not to proceed with this course. I must point out also that I retain and use my military rank and I have a total commitment to the duties of office and my obligations, and honor, to uphold the good name of my country in all respects. And now I wish you good night."

He flung down his napkin and stalked out of the room. Now that, I thought, *was* a stuffy little speech and a stuffy little exit. I sat there for a while and sulked, then brooded. Mopa arrived to clear away, was expressionless at the sight of the uneaten food and returned with coffee. I had two or three cups, black, wished I had a cigarette, then went up to my room.

And here I am, tapping away. It's almost dawn and after their brilliant text of the night the stars are fading rapidly and look like Braille marks and I suppose I draw on that image because last night I was stumbling and then blind in my handling of the colonel. Hubris. I was too assertive, too eager. And I'd had too many tequilas.

I'll try again at breakfast, with greater tact this time. He, too, I am fairly sure, will have slept off his tantrum. And that's what I'm going to do now. Stretch out on the bed and have a couple of hours' sleep.

I am writing this on the afternoon flight from Phoenix to Chicago.

Chicago will come in handy for my movie research, but, more to the point, Lou Eggenberg lives there. Formerly Sergeant Eggenberg, a waist gunner, so Bessy told me, on the B17: I am hoping he will be able to draw some kind of a bead between Dante Centofanti's evidence and Colonel Crinkle's silence.

For he didn't show for breakfast. I was up before seven, anticipating he would be an early riser. I lingered at the breakfast table, eating nothing but drinking numerous cups of coffee.

Finally, I went up to my room to fetch a book. And outside my room I found my luggage, all packed and neatly assembled: my two suitcases, my briefcase, my laptop in its strapped container.

"Colonel's orders," Mopa said. I turned. She was standing a few feet behind me. She showed no expression.

I said I wanted to see him. She shook her head fractionally. "Colonel's orders," she repeated. She came forward, picked up the cases and began to move downstairs with them; I accepted that my eviction was absolute.

Outside, she waited at the car until I was in the front seat. I turned the ignition switch. She had been watching me impassively until then. But now her hand stretched out and her fingers gripped the top rim of the door.

"You—be careful," she said.

"I'm a good driver," I said.

"Other things. Other *winds*. Be careful."

Other winds? I seemed to see a stirring of foreboding in her flat gaze.

"What do you mean, Mopa?"

She blinked, moved back from the car. "Have a nice day," she said. Expressionlessly.

Chicago

Fifteen

THE FBI AND THE MAFIA CALLED ON ME AT MY HOTEL IN Chicago this evening. Jointly. Or that's how it seemed. Though I must admit that the events of recent hours may have left my objectivity impaired.

Still, the fact of my visitors is evidence enough that Colonel Crinkle has done his duty, as he sees it, and reported me to the authorities. Apparently I could be deported for investigating Johnny's death. The FBI man said as much, though politely. The other man, the one who certainly *looked* Mafioso, stared at me bleakly, as if reflecting on a less formal solution.

Oh, it's all too ridiculous! The Mafia, for God's sake! I'm exaggerating; I've *got* to be. I'm simply a little strung out from lack of sleep, the long drive back across the desert to Phoenix and an extremely uncomfortable flight from there to Chicago.

That noted, however, what cannot be diminished is that an attempt was made here to warn me off.

It took place as I sat in the coffee shop, only a few minutes after I checked into the hotel. The plane had flown through thunderstorms

and air pockets virtually all the way to Chicago and this, in the aftermath of my turbulence at Colonel Crinkle's house, had left me with
one of my rare headaches. I decided, even before going up to my
room, to resort to that English cure-all—a nice hot cup of tea.

Only that wasn't so easy to come by. The waitress, when I made
my request, did a very American thing and went into a recital of the
various teas on offer. Just tea, I said, somewhere between Assam
(broad leaf or green) and Paraguay (herbal and strawberry-flavored).
She returned with a glass of iced tea. I said I wanted regular tea, dark
and hot, and that I didn't mind slumming it with any old tea bag.

Her next attempt was tea with slices of lemon floating in it, which
I've never been able to take. I'm afraid, a reminder of how unpleasantly English I can be, I snapped at her: surely, I said, a simple cup of
tea wasn't beyond even *her* comprehension. She was very young and
Asian, Vietnamese perhaps, and, I would guess, newly arrived and
unaccustomed to Western boorishness. Her eyes widened and her
lower lip trembled.

Waiting for that elusive tea, I tried to justify my behaviour. I was
tired, crushed after my failure with Colonel Crinkle, I had been
bumped about in the air to the extent my head ached and, in any
case, she was *just* a waitress. But my arrogant self failed me and I
remained aware of the startled hurt in her young eyes.

So when this middle-aged black man hovered at my booth,
smiled, then asked if he might join me for a few moments to "discuss
a little problem," I assumed he was hotel management, there in a pla-
catory role after what I feared had been the waitress's tears in the
kitchen. He *seemed* hotel managerial: a plump man in a gray pinstripe
suit with a waistcoat.

As he settled down on the other side of the booth I said right away
that the fault was mine entirely.

"Fault?" he said.

"With the waitress."

"Waitress?"

"You *are* with the hotel?"

His smile broadened, a sweet smile that creased his eyes. He put on a pair of half-moon glasses and appeared more than ever like the senior executive in charge of customer relations. "No, ma'am, I'm with another, uh, establishment," he said.

He flipped a silver badge out of the top pocket of his waistcoat and I read the words Federal Bureau of Investigation. I thought instantly of Colonel Crinkle. He replaced the badge.

"You mentioned a little problem," I said.

"Nothing we can't work out," he said, and went on, in the same easygoing tone, to ask me if this was my first visit to Chicago. I nodded. "It's a city like no other," he said.

And at that moment the other man turned up. He was fiftyish, tall and just about skeletally thin, gray-complexioned and with a bald head and an almost comically elongated face that curved into a half-moon chin. Like Mr. Punch, I remember thinking, and I have tried to hang onto that image ever since. Only Mr. Punch never wore a patently designer suit of some sheened black material. Unannounced, the newcomer sat down next to the FBI agent, who promptly tetched and remonstrated with him. "Will *you* get the hell outa here?"

The man said nothing, simply stared at me. His eyes were dark and the foggy grayness of his face gave them a swampy look. I stared back at him.

"And have you got a badge too?" I said.

"I got this," he said. Limply, he held up his left hand, the palm open toward me. In the center of his palm was a tattoo of a black rose.

"Family," he said, and the inflection might have been poised on the point of a knife. "Family as in crest. As in heirloom. Priceless. A passport that gets me through *any* doors. *Anywhere."* His voice, I remember thinking, ought to have been a rasp, only it was soft and somehow feminine with a lisp cuddled into it. He edged his palm a little closer to me.

"Such a pretty rose," I said. "I might have one done myself—next time I'm in a flea market."

He closed his hand, placed it outstretched on the table, possibly so that I would see the thick gold ring on his index finger—a ring

whose oval opalescent setting enclosed another black rose. Ridiculous man! I glanced at his half-moon, Mr. Punch chin, resolved that
my response to him should be coolly knockabout, though it was my
head that was taking the pounding. The waitress came with the tea.

She avoided my contrite smile, looked at my companions to see if
they wanted to order. The FBI man shook his head. She left. I made
a little show of adding milk and sugar to my tea. I took a nonchalant
sip.

"So," I said, all poised with the teacup in my hand, "are you two
a regular duo?"

"No way, ma'am!" the FBI man said. He glanced at Mr. Punch,
shrugged exasperation. "I guess he followed me here. Mr. Hanson's a
private investigator."

Hanson. I would have expected something rather more Italianate.

"For private read exclusive," Mr. Punch said. "For exclusive read
very important clients."

"I'm sure the lady's impressed," the FBI man said. "Now why
don't you move your ass?"

"I wish you'd both do just that," I said, "but not before you've
explained the nature of your business with me."

The FBI man did the talking after a pause in which he gave Mr.
Punch a sizing-up look, as though trying to determine how advisable
it was to say anything in his presence. Or was that just an act? Were
they really there as a team? After all, he knew his name. He said, the
FBI man, that information had been laid—he actually used that
phrase—that my purpose in coming to Chicago was to make contact
with an individual with a view to creating a situation that could be
prejudicial to the best interests of the United States.

The way he intoned it, I felt I had taken delivery of a writ. I
smiled, trusted I looked properly amused. "And who *laid* this information?"

"I have no idea, ma'am. Even if I did, I wouldn't be at liberty to
divulge the source. I'm just the messenger, a field agent doing his
job."

"I'm a messenger as well, only *I* come to the point," said Mr.

Punch. And he leant slightly toward me to make it. "Back off." He had a small mouth, the upper lip full and delicately heart-shaped at the middle; on a girl, such a mouth might have looked dainty, on him it was sinister. "This is no birthday party, so make sure your candles don't get blown out." He made a blowing motion with those cherub lips and I smelled his breath freshener. Mint. "Back off, uh? Completely. And make a start by not looking up Lou Eggenberg."

He knew the name of Johnny's crewman. I was discomfited. My headache throbbed.

"Land of the free, gentlemen?" I said, regretting that I couldn't think of a stronger irony.

"We don't do badly," the FBI man said, "just so long as you follow the rules."

"And if I don't?"

He fitted in a sigh between his smile. "You're in this country as an alien on a temporary work visa. It may—*may*—be deemed necessary to review that status. My advice, ma'am, is to stay on the sidewalk and avoid any awkward turnings."

"That way you don't end up *lost* in an alley," said Mr. Punch.

"My friend here is a regular good ole boy at heart," the FBI man said, back to smiling broadly again. He stood up, tapped Mr. Punch on the shoulder. Mr. Punch rose, grudgingly.

"I hope you enjoy your stay in Chicago, ma'am," the FBI man said, extending his hand. "Thank you for your time." Mr. Punch said nothing, simply stared at me. But at the coffee shop exit he did raise his hand, palm forward, in a mock wave—the left hand, the one tattooed with the rose.

Up in my room, I sat on the edge of the bed and reasoned things out. Colonel Crinkle must have made a phone call. Obviously, he had given my car registration number to someone. I had been spotted when I reached Phoenix, perhaps even before then. Maybe I had been followed as I drove across the desert and there could be no doubt that I had been watched at the airport and my reservation on

the Chicago flight noted. A simple computer rundown of the survivors of Johnny's crew would have come up with the information
that Lou Eggenberg lived there. Hence my encounter with the FBI
and—was Mr. Punch really Mafia? *Family.*

I remembered how he had stressed the word and then paused, letting it hang like a framed diploma. And then the black rose; hadn't I
once read somewhere, or heard, that this was a symbol that had orig-
inated in Sicily? Come on! He was Mr. Punch, strutting on his tinpot
stage, and I, tired and headachy, had overreacted.

That made sense. But there was a heckler in my little hall of reasoning, and I realized why. Mr. Punch's hands. Not so much the
black rose, that was trite thug showmanship, but the way his fingers
were short and thick and blunt at the tips and the way his thumbs
were splayed and brutally knuckled. I'm never wrong about hands—
never—and I accepted now that he was totally ruthless.

I recalled Mopa telling me to be careful.

But what possible reason could have justified the approach of
those two men? Why should the authorities and others, those "very
important" people Mr. Punch claimed to represent, be interested in
what was, leaving aside my personal feelings, an obscure episode of
World War II?

I decided (it was the only explanation) that Colonel Crinkle must
have exaggerated when he made his phone call. Old soldiers could be
chronically paranoid. Clearly, he had presented me as some sort of
conspirator threatening the American way. Maybe, I tried for a light
note, they thought I was plotting a repeat of the Great Chicago Fire
of 1871.

Satisfied, at least for the moment, that Colonel Crinkle had mis-
represented me and ignoring the fact that this didn't quite account
for Mr. Punch's role, I wondered what to do next. Dinner and an
early night made sense, but first I would phone Lou Eggenberg. His
name and address checked out in the directory. I called him.

"Yeah?" The voice was old but not croaky.

"Mr. Eggenberg?"

"Himself and no other."

"You don't know me, but—"

"I figure you're the English doll they told me not to talk to."

"They?"

"Couple o' guys."

"Was one black and one—"

"Both white. Young. Jerks. Dropped by this afternoon. I told 'em to get the hell out. I do as I please."

"Does that mean you're willing to see me?"

"Ya got nice legs?"

"Reasonable."

"I'm willin' to see ya."

"When? I'm free right now."

He wasn't. It was his poker night, he said. Tomorrow he was going to a funeral. "Irishman. Used to be a big-time ward boss, so I guess I'm looking at a whole day's wake. Couple of days to get over the hangover, which takes us to Friday. Friday any use for ya?"

We agreed on a time, in the morning, and I got round to telling him the reason for my visit, or rather I repeated the academic research story I had used on Dante Centofanti.

"That so?" From his tone, I don't think he believed me, though he was amiable.

"Till Friday, then," I said.

"Yeah. Tomorrow and tomorrow and tomorrow. Shakespeare. That's so any jerks who're listening in to this call can say we used a code."

I decided I was going to like him, though after I hung up I had other things on my mind, namely the extraordinary measures that were being taken to scare me off: not only had I had visitors, but so had he.

I tried not to dwell on that though and from my briefcase I took out the group photograph of Johnny and his crew, their names written in ink above their heads. I wanted to check my impression of Louis Eggenberg over the phone with the young man in the photograph.

"Lou E." There he was. Skinny. A little less than medium height. Spiky hair. Spiky face. Spiky grin—and a wink to go with it. But then they were all grinning. A collective good cheer which expressed their youth and, I wanted to believe, their confidence in the person who was bringing them through. I looked at Johnny and noted, as I have before, that his grin wasn't part of the group impudence. A grin it was, though, the slow, indulgent grin of the older man—and he looked both mature and youthful—who was proud of his boys.

Owning up to sheer sentimentality, I felt the day owed me some compensation, I took the photograph over to the writing table and propped it against the stand of the reading light. Then I pulled up my laptop and began to set down the day's events.

And that's what I've been doing ever since. I've been working slowly, for I still have that headache, and, I must beware of this tendency, I haven't eaten. But the day is down . . .

Just a moment ago I looked again at that photograph. Age has imposed its sepia on the print, but something blazes out of those young American faces. Courage. Loyalty. Hope. And all distilled in their grins.

I suppose I draw a certain comfort from those grins tonight because, though I hate to admit it, I continue to feel unsettled by Mr. Punch and what his hands said about him. Even if I never see him again he has a place in my life—he is, I have to concede in all honesty, the only man who has left me feeling a personal sense of real threat.

Still, I slept well that first night in Chicago, felled by the exhaustion of all that has happened in recent hours. But as soon as I opened my eyes Mr. Punch was on my mind—a certain smudging of those hands in my gathering consciousness, a fingerprinting of phobia.

I told myself I was being as stupid as a schoolgirl and on the strength of this exasperation I got out of bed briskly, ordered breakfast from room service, showered and dressed.

And then, like an actress in a bad movie, I was peering out of the window, trying to see if Mr. Punch had positioned himself on the other side of the street for a strategic overview of the hotel's movements.

Idiot! At this scared-little-woman rate I'd soon be shrieking at the sight of a spider . . . I was caustic in my self-condemnation.

After breakfast, which I made a point of eating leisurely, I settled down with the phone and the task of arranging a schedule for the day. It was, as always, easy—mention a movie project and Americans are endearingly anxious to cooperate—and its organizing tucked away the wisps of my earlier fears and left me feeling my usual confident self again. Even the most self-sufficient of us, I reflected, was entitled to a little lapse.

A couple of hours later, with plenty of time before my first appointment I was out on the street (a stroll seemed like a good idea) and back with my fear of Mr. Punch.

It began with a small spasm of vulnerability and worked up to a conviction that he was there, among the crowds, stalking me, his hands twitching to the alertness of his purpose. It seemed that my stern talking-to, back in the hotel, had been a stand-in for a fear I couldn't rationalize, but which was nonetheless real. Despising my weakness, I kept looking back. Would-be casually, of course, but searchingly.

And I suppose that's when I started to become aware, peripherally at first, of the sheer individual bulkiness of Chicagoans and the fact that in this respect this is the most physical city in the United States. In this land of polarities these citizens stand out, overall, not because they're particularly fat or tall but because they're barrel-chested, *compact*. Virtually to a man—even, I think, to a woman.

I remembered—anything to keep my mind off Mr. Punch—a video shown on the plane in one of the few quiet periods of that bumpy flight. The video was a Chamber of Commerce booster, a welcome-to-our-city kind of thing, and among its boasts was that Chicago was the meat-packing capital of the world and its citizens ate nearly three times as much meat as anyone else and that this showed, a national statistic no less, in the breadth of their chests.

And it does. It occurred to me that, business-suited or not, these distinctly chunky Chicagoans ought to be wearing hard hats and that among them Mr. Punch, all skin and bones in his designer suit—I felt the first easing of tension—would stand out like a fancy pants on a construction site.

That imagery, born out of the SOS of my apprehension, broadened in my mind like a chunky Chicago life vest and I saw him in proportion, saw him as no more than a bogey man who had said boo at a time when I was spent and susceptible: all I had been doing was carrying last night's anxieties, the outcome of understandable fatigue and strain, around with me.

My fear of Mr. Punch was over—*just like that!*—and, I was sure, over permanently, its puniness (and *his*) exposed by all this human avoirdupois on the streets. Positively skittish in my relief at the recovery of my full independence, I gave my wrist a mock slap, my acknowledgment that I had indeed been a "silly girl."

I walked for about another half hour, absolutely no temptation to look back now, and then I took a cab to Lake Michigan, which fronts the city and affords the best panorama of the skyline. It was a warm day, sunny, but the breezes from the lake were sharp and chopped, as though doing their sparring bit to prove that everything about Chicago is pugilistic, sinewy. I thought of Chicago's greatest native poet, Carl Sandburg, and what he had to say about the place. "Here is a tall bold slugger set vivid against the little soft cities." The skyscrapers, seen from this distance, *were* sluggers, blunt heavyweights that eschewed fripperies.

Frankly, I felt a feminist duty to be contemptuous of Chicago, with its swaggering male proclamation as "the city of broad shoulders" and its opportunistic slogan of "Where's mine?"

And yet, and here's the paradox, over the next couple of days I came to *see* Johnny in this city, as someone who could have belonged here as both writer and reformer.

There's a particular adrenaline to Chicago—a sort of merger

between the breezes from Lake Michigan and the blarney of its original Irish kingmakers. Chicago is a blowhard with an eye for refinement, for class. And that's why Johnny would have belonged here. Its literary native sons—among them Sandburg, Hemingway, Nelson Algren, Saul Bellow and Upton Sinclair—are more numerous than in any other city and, more than anywhere else, it continues to draw, and nurture, writers and artists in general from across the land.

And though Chicago's cemeteries have more tombstones bearing the names of gangsters—four hundred mown down during Prohibition alone—than anywhere else, it also created the skyscraper and has outstripped New York by having three of the five world's tallest buildings. Frank Lloyd Wright, the architect, built his renowned Home and Studio on Chicago Avenue and was a seminal force in the development of the city's skyline, which on closer examination turns out to have more aesthetics than are apparent in that view from the shoreline.

Towering too are the Chicago Symphony Orchestra, the city's robust and innovating theaters that make Broadway seem like a bit player and, in its total of Nobel Prize laureates, the world leadership of the University of Chicago.

Beyond the facts, though, what I *sensed,* and initially resisted, about Chicago was that in spite of what is appalling and crooked in its background, it is truly a city of the possible.

And though I for one would never want to live in Chicago, I am stimulated by its vigor, which is why, at about midnight, I am not at all weary. I see Lou Eggenberg tomorrow, and I wanted these words down before then. I have found them easy to write and I contrast the energy of my present mood with my first night here and the influence of Mr. Punch. That all seems so distant and I find it difficult to recognize the person I was then, tired and stressed and headachy.

As for Mr. Punch, he's evaporated. I haven't seen him again nor felt remotely nervous about him; it's as though, on the street that morning, those chunky Chicagoans moving with their shoulders elbowed him out of my sight and out of my consciousness. I have, though cursorily, asked several high-ranking policemen if they knew of a man called Hanson who might be a private detective and who might have links with organized crime, and none of them did; nor, more tellingly, did they recognize his distinctive description. Mr. Punch was a cheap frightener, a comic strip charlatan, and, accordingly—and here's a Chicago-minted word—I zapped him!

I savor that little moment, but I think Chicago must bring out the triumphalist in everyone. Chicago's original collateral was cheek and it has never stopped flipping the wild coin of chance. Though some bets have failed and plenty have been dirty fouls, the overall record is an impressive one.

It took cheek, along with positively biblical inspiration and theatrical timing—in the first year of the twentieth century—to make the Chicago river run *backward* to halt the flow of sewage into Lake Michigan. And it took cheek to stage the World's Fair right in the middle of the Great Depression.

Chicago continues to spin its coin, but for all its concomitant conniving winks it never fails to give the full nod to talent. It could be that Chicago recognizes that talent itself, even in the most self-effacing, is a form of cheek.

And cheek is Chicago's raison d'etre, which is why it stands out, swaggers, in a nation where, from what I read in the newspapers and see on television, suspicion, hostility, insularity and selfishness are the norm.

England, on a miniature scale, is the same. But then England has never recovered from losing an empire. America, it increasingly seems to me, and especially in the grinning perspective of that group shot of Johnny's crew, has lost by default an even greater global possession—the sovereignty of plain old-fashioned Yankee cheek to charm, cheer and inspire the rest of the world.

About ten minutes ago I was revising these words—rewriting a sentence here and there, making one or two factual corrections—when the phone rang.

Preoccupied, I didn't answer immediately. When I did, the caller, a man, wanted to know if I was interested in life insurance.

"Do you know how late it is?" I protested, though my gaze was on a split infinitive I had spotted on the laptop screen.

"It's never too late for life insurance," I was told and got the usual rapid spiel of "guaranteed protection" and the like.

This wasn't cheek, I thought; this was a sleazy little deal in which, even in a hotel of this standing, a salesman had obtained a guest list from a desk clerk and was working his way through it.

"*Not* interested," I said, interrupting him, and I was on the point of hanging up when I caught his next words.

"How about astrology?"

"Excuse me?" A thin amusement eased into my perfunctory impatience.

"Predictions. There's a sure-fire personal service on offer. Take your stars for tomorrow. The forecast is that it would be wise for ya to back out of a *certain* appointment—do that, and you won't need to bother with life insurance."

Click. He hung up. As the line buzzed on the dead connection the voice rolled retrospectively in my mind: the soft tones, the lisp.

I replaced the phone. I crossed to the door and put the security chain in place. I decided, folding my arms across my chest, that the air conditioning was on too high.

And standing there, feeling the cold, I owned up to the fact that I hadn't, after all, zapped Mr. Punch.

Sixteen

SO. IT WASN'T PART OF MY PLAN, BUT HERE I AM ON A TRAIN that's set to travel the near one thousand miles from Chicago to New York—and I am trusting the trip will also haul me out of my latest writing block.

For yesterday I saw Lou Eggenberg and what he had to say was so complex, so revealing and, in the end, so harrowing that after I had played through the tapes and made editing notes in the hotel last night I had no idea of how or where I could make a start. I was as stymied as I had been following my meeting with Dante Centofanti.

This time, though, I didn't resort to cigarettes; instead, wide awake in my frustration—I'm accustomed to writing swiftly and decisively—I ended up looking at late-night television. I had no interest in what was showing until a group of old men in blazers and straw boaters appeared on the screen in a lineup against a locomotive. As the loco whistle peeped, they tipped their hats and began to harmonize (what else?) "Chattanooga Choo Choo."

The news item concerned a Barbershop Quartet train charter that, the very next morning, was taking hundreds of singers from Chicago and Illinois to the finals of a contest in New York. "Come join us as we journey to bring a smile to old Broadway," one of the singers said in his role as pitch man. "We still gotta little space, but hurry. It's a pricey ride, sure, but it's for charity and the singin's gonna be real sweet. The number to call for reservations is . . ."

I called that number. Immediately. And the result is that I now repose in my very own brown leather and chrome booth—it's the most expensive space, but it's for charity and it's on expenses—on this long and silver train, my surrogate "Chattanooga Choo Choo."

I tell myself, and it's the truth, that in any case New York had to be part of my movie research and that this unexpected ride there will give me the variety and the solid stretch of time to relax my mind and deal with my writer's block.

I also want to believe that it's an unashamedly sentimental journey for me—though, I might as well face that truth, it's basically a flight from Mr. Punch.

He hasn't been in touch again, but that call the night before last unsettled me profoundly and when the phone rang the next morning, bringing me out of an edgy sleep, I tensed. It was only my wake-up call.

From the club car, which is only a carriage length from where I am sitting, I hear a barbershop quartet: *The bells are ringin' for me and my gal, the birds are singin' for . . .*

And away from this foolish innocence of love and birdsong I hear suddenly, in my mind, the words of Lou Eggenberg. "The duke [he said "dook"] did it. He bumped off Johnny. He owned up to it—yeah, and with pride. The duke of Dillingbrae."

Dillingbrae. The name Dante Centofanti couldn't remember. Actually, Lou Eggenberg said—and he proved to know his subject well—he was a phony duke, for there was no legal provenance for the title. Generations back the family had simply set up its own dukedom, with a crest and a line of succession, based on the arrogance of wealth and social rank (a claimed distant kinship with the British Royal Family).

". . . be that as it may, as far as we were concerned he was the duke and that day, after the war, we tracked him down, Pete and me, we tell him we're gonna hang another title on him and this time a *real* one—murderer. And he says, his very words, 'Oh, jolly good.' And the guy means it! He figures he's untouchable and you can see that in his eyes. Those pale blue eyes. Psycho's eyes.''

A moment or two ago, just about the time the train was pulling out of the station in Chicago, I searched out those particular words on the tape, though now I've switched it off. There's so much more to be put down before that climax, and so much more to follow on. Little wonder I was bewildered and stuck last night, and though my mind is easier now I still need to tune up my approach to all that he told me, to aim for the right note—which is what the singers are doing in the club car. Right now falsettos are warbling that *Casey would dance with the strawberry blonde while the band played on* . . .

All of the singers on this train are old—since I can't yet focus on my subject I might as well reach for words that are readily to hand— but youth pipes in their voices and parades in their dress: bow ties, candy-stripe blazers and, above all, those jauntily worn straw boaters whose hatbands proclaim the names of the singers' towns and cities. I think just about the whole of the Midwest must be represented here.

There are wives along too and some of them are vocalists as well and known as Jillettes. This much I learned when, shortly after I boarded the train, I was swept along to a pre-journey reception in the club car which, in anticipation of sustained festivities, is three club cars linked together.

I was given a huge cocktail called a Barbershop Bounce—brandy, bourbon and bitters in a long glass shaped and colored like a barber's pole—followed by two or three cups of a potent punch. I reflected, admittedly from a narrow and alcohol-tinged angle, on the capacity for living of elderly Americans. In England old age is a drizzle; here, or at any rate in that club car, it's a fountain.

A huge generalization, I agree, but one impossible to resist in a club car where ordinary men and women who would be classified as geriatrics in most societies were showing that they were old hands at the life force. They are Johnny's generation—which *doesn't* mean they are, or were, paragons. Like everyone else, they will have their histories of their cowardice, cruelties and betrayals. But they are the products, now the waning survivors, of what once was, *had* to be, a *broader* America.

If that sounds like undiluted nostalgia, it isn't. I acknowledge the gross tyrannies and injustices of this nation's past and, those barbershop singers notwithstanding, I am suspicious also of all the tacky furniture—the cracker-barrel stove in the general store on Main Street, the swinging porch chairs in the twilight—by which Hollywood has upholstered the image of a folksy nation at ease with itself. But America genuinely had something the rest of the world didn't have. A spirit. A nerve. A dash. Perhaps if I trawl back through the tapes and let Lou Eggenberg be my spokesman in this respect . . .

"I can remember when we were proud to be Americans—*proud*. Guys signed up to join the Lincoln Brigade to go fight fascism in the Spanish Civil War just because they *were* Americans. Now they enlist in the Neighbourhood Watch. Y' give up smoking today and you've paid all your dues to the higher cause of morality and idealism. Me, I preferred America when the spittoons were full and it had some vital juices in its belly and in its heart. We were two-fisted then. Sure, this country was awash with corruption, but there was a matchin' high tide of ordinary Joes who were willin' to bruise their knuckles for the next guy if they thought he was gettin' a bum deal. We were *Americans* then."

And in those feisty words I feel my writing block breaking up. . . .

Lou Eggenberg rides his convictions, and he has many, from a wheelchair, though this doesn't cramp his general mobility and—I remember various dartings and whirlings—seems almost to enhance the quicksilver of his spirit. He stays in my mind as an elderly sprite. A streetwise sprite, though his side-of-the-mouth locution can also deliver fluency in French, Italian and Latin. He's a sprite who knows how to make a pass too.

And I very nearly stood him up. As with Harry Korda in San

Francisco, it was where he lived that discouraged me, that derelict tenement on the South Side. "This is the address you gave me, lady, but y'sure this is where you wanna be?" the cabdriver said after we had stopped.

"I suppose so," I said. "I'd like to sit here for just a minute." He shrugged. I looked out of the rear window and waited for the car I was sure must have been following us to turn the corner into the street. There were a number of cars parked there, between the spilling garbage cans, but they had the rusted look of fixtures. I watched for two or three minutes, but no car appeared. Had Mr. Punch given up? Of course he had! He was all breath and no teeth.

On this forced note of reassurance, I got out of the cab, paid off the driver, and he, still solicitous, stayed as I climbed the short flight of steps to the tenement entrance. The door lurched on buckled hinges and was hard to open and as I pushed against it only my fears moved: what if Mr. Punch was waiting for me, his foul hands flexing, behind the door?

The door gave. I entered a lobby where damp green and peeling walls showed through streakings of graffiti by the light of a single ceiling bulb in an iron grille. No Mr. Punch. No anyone. The only evidence of occupancy was a gag-inducing stench of urine. Only a vagrant could live here and I didn't want an old man stumbling in the rags of memory as he tried to locate Johnny in his mind; I forgot at the moment, and perhaps conveniently, that Lou Eggenberg had been lucid on the phone.

I went back to the door, but the cab had gone. If it had been there, I think I would have taken it, would have ceded seeming capitulation to Mr. Punch—and had that been an option in my mind right from the start?

I decided not to think about that. Instead I took the elevator, where the smell of urine was even more concentrated, to the twenty-first floor. On the way up I granted, though grimly, Lou Eggenberg a sense of humor when, on the phone and in the course of amplifying details of his address, he said he lived "a la penthouse."

But even that caprice didn't prepare me for the man who answered the door to my knock and thrust out his exuberance in the welcome spread of his arms. "As I live and die, a cutie pie! So I once wrote greetin' cards for a livin'. My post-Hemingway period. Come in; come in—I'm not gonna eat ya. I'm just lickin' my chops, is all."

He spun his wheelchair round and I followed him down a short passage into a fairly large room that looked like an unkempt bookstore. Crammed shelves rose to the ceiling on all four sides and he removed three or four volumes from a bright yellow easy chair so I could take a seat.

"The penthouse," he said, gesturing around at the shelves. "Guaranteed views of ancient Rome, Greece, Versailles, Babylonia, not to mention your legs. Dancer's legs. Very sexy ankles. I'll go get us some coffee."

A pirouette of the wheelchair, and he was off, streaking to a kitchenette behind a bookcase.

Sprite, I thought. The green eyes, the thin face, the tincture of beard at the chin, the snub nose, the blue spotted bandanna tied across the grandly sloping forehead, such hair as he had worn in a small ponytail tied with a rubber band. Sprite. A will o' the wisp in the slums. Renaissance man, too; I glanced down at the books— Proust, Camus, Voltaire—he had taken off my chair and placed on the brown rush-matting carpet. Nearby, a Fedora among the berets, was a paperback collection of Raymond Chandler's Philip Marlowe stories. Books were the main decor of the room, though here and there were art posters of nudes. In a corner, there was a much-pitted archery target and next to it, on a set of racks, a collection of body-building weights.

"So who needs lifestyle when you can live in your own junk-yard?" He was back, bearing a collapsible tray, which he set up between us.

As he poured the coffee, I took out my tape recorder. He glanced up as I flicked the on button. He winked. "Testin', testin'—the lady has sexy legs."

I said he was sleekly packaged himself, and so he was, in an electric blue track suit that stressed his slim build.

"I work at it," he said. "Weights. Bit of archery. Most of all, I juggle."

"Really? What do you juggle with?"

"Clubs. Balls. Anything."

And he scooped a handful of chocolate chip cookies from the plate on the tray and sent them into an arc. He had huge hands, out of proportion with his build, but his fingers were fine, long and delicate.

He continued the juggling, widening the arc, contracting it, tilting it. "Ain't I the show-off, uh? Why, I can play the harmonica and juggle all at the same time, which is what I do at the community center. For the kids. Tough kids. I hold classes. Try to teach 'em they can do more with their hands than inject dope or squeeze triggers. Show these kids a little respect and they respond. Well, some of 'em do. Some of 'em are just way, way gone. Am I borin' you, honey?"

"No," I said, and I think I meant it. He slid the palms of his hands together and the cookies funnelled down on the plate, one after another.

"Bravo," I said.

"A knack." He shrugged. "We all got knacks. I juggle; some people spin stories—you said on the phone you were doin' some kind of *academic* research concernin' Johnny."

He hadn't believed me; he wasn't another Dante Centofanti.

"That's right," I said. "A research project." I looked straight back at him and couldn't remember a time when I had been under more intense scrutiny. His was the gaze, I noticed how sharply green his eyes were, of a jurist, or at any rate a shrewd bartender weighing up a customer who has asked for credit. And then he winked his way back to spritedom. "I trust ya." He hadn't bought my story, I was sure of that, but he had accepted me.

I smiled, started to go into the background that had brought me to his apartment. "Every year you receive a Christmas card from a woman in Yorkshire called Bessy Mogd—"

"Bessy Mogdonavitch, sure. Used to juggle Hershey bars and nylons for her. She was a dish. And then Tony, Tony Mogdonavitch, moved in on my act. They got married. Sort of. Only Tony was—"

"I know. He was killed in a night fighter attack. Bessy told me. I met her not all that long ago and she told me of how Johnny's crew had kept in touch over the years."

"I guess we rate long service awards, uh? How's she doin'?"

"Fine. She, er—she let me have a copy of her Stateside Christmas card list. There are three names left on it. Yours and those of Harry Korda and Dante Centofanti."

"Those jokers still around? Harry Korda was the copilot and Dante Centofanti—what a name, uh?—he was the—"

"The radio man. I've seen him. I'm hoping to catch up with Harry Korda. Meantime, I had a long meeting with Dante Centofanti in New Orleans."

"Yeah? And what did he have to say for himself?"

"He said that he thought Johnny was—that he was murdered."

"He was right. Mind if I smoke?"

"No."

He winked, veered off in his chair to the other side of the room, leaving me to ponder his casual corroboration of murder: I told myself that while Johnny's fate was somehow recent in my perspective, and urgent, he stood a lifetime away from it all. But, as I was to discover, he was far from indifferent.

He returned, unwrapping a large cigar. He lit it, tilted his head, exhaled. "One of my wives," he said, "divorced me on account she couldn't take cigars."

"You've been married more than once?" It was no more than a polite question.

"Five times." His beam seemed to expand this personal statistic into his estimate of a lifetime's achievement. "One thing I couldn't juggle was marriage. In turn, I married a continuity girl in the movies, a would-be opera singer, a waitress . . ."

I heard out his raffish marital litany and sundry attendant anecdotes. I indulged him until he was in the middle of a story about a former wife who, every time they quarrelled, stripped naked, strapped on a piano accordion and played Strauss waltzes. "It was her shrink's idea," he was saying, "and—"

"Do you think we could get back to Johnny?" I said.

"Sure." His green eyes smiled equally through cigar smoke.

"If Johnny was murdered—"

"He *was*." He waved away the smoke with his hand.

"Then that presumably explains why on my first day in Chicago I was approached by an FBI agent and a man who said he was a private detective and strongly advised me to stop asking questions about Johnny."

"So? I had a couple o'visitors myself. Mentioned that to you on the phone."

"Yes, and that proves that—"

"All it proves, honey, is that the official mind loves a secret. Strictly routine. A reflex. Come on, this is World War Two, the way-back-when war, so who gives a crap that Johnny was murdered? What's it matter? But someone gets wise to the fact that you're diggin' around askin' questions and so, matter of form, y' gotta be warned off. Bureaucracy is all it is."

"I think you're oversimplifying bureaucracy."

"Please! There's nothing more baroque than bureaucracy. It has more twists and turns than . . . it just doesn't believe in straight lines. I speak as an expert."

"And what gives you that stature?"

His smile was puckish as he picked up on my slight reproof—his airiness and self-interest had irked me—but he carried on, unruffled.

"My kid brother Herbie, for one. He's seventeen when he's sent to England in the war. He's one of thousands of GIs who mass off the coast of Devon in 1944 for a practice run of the Normandy landings. Only the Germans have been tipped off and they're waiting, just off-shore, under a fog bank. Their torpedo boats move in on those landin' craft. And Herbie is one of 749 American bodies that wash back on the beach."

"That's sad, tragic, but . . ."

"What's also sad and tragic is that the survivors are told if they breathe a word about it they'll be court-martialled. Y'want more sad and tragic? It takes *forty years*—until, you'll forgive the language,

fuckin' 1987—before the authorities on both sides, the Americans
and the British, own up to that foul-up, and then only because a
newspaper is threatenin' an exposé. That's bureaucracy. So what
fuckin' chance does Johnny, one guy, have in the truth stakes? What
fuckin' chance?"

In the last few moments his words had become vehement and
now, for an instant, he shot me a startled look, a seemingly tacit apology for this unforeseen emergence of an old passion. He lowered his
head, appeared to slump. He rolled his cigar between his fingers. The
cigar had gone out.

I had an odd, and totally out-of-character, impulse to reach out
to him physically. I compromised with words. "We can at least try,"
I said.

"Don't you think I've done that?" He didn't look up.

"One more push."

"Y'sound like a midwife."

"I could do with an extra pair of strong hands."

He looked up at me, smiled. He leant back in the wheelchair, re-
lit his cigar, burnt down now to almost a butt. He scratched the end
of his nose.

"What exactly did Dante Centofanti have to say?" he asked.

I told him, as briefly as I could. He nodded.

"Dante Centofanti's singin' the right song, so to speak, but he's
got the words kinda mixed up," he said.

"What does that mean?"

"It means Johnny wasn't killed because of that business with
Buddy Fanzoli and the duke's sister."

"I'm—I'm lost," I said.

"Lemme show y' the way." He stubbed out his cigar in an ashtray.
"It's true," he said, "that after the rough justice handed out to Buddy
Fanzoli the duke was givin' us all the breaks. Those Lancasters, they
were pamperin' us. Shepherds, no less. For a while. The beginnin' of
the end came one night when a young American airman knocked at
the door of the big house, was admitted by the butler and
announced, to everyone's surprise, that he had been posted to our

crew. His name was George. Quiet young guy, anxious to please. Had been a theology student from Mobile, Alabama, and was now evidence of the wrath to come. You wanna ask why?"

"Why?"

"George was black."

I have switched off the tape for a moment; I can get by with a short summary.

The US military was totally segregated in the war and the arrival of that young black airman was supposed to be an experiment in race relations, though Lou Eggenberg was skeptical there. The Eighth Air Force, he pointed out, was taking insupportable losses in its daylight bombing and was desperate for replacement fliers. The B17 and its crew, detached as they were from the American presence in England, was ideal for a litmus test to see if black and white could "take." Each crew member had to fill in a regular report, in the form of answers to a printed questionnaire, on the social aspects of the experiment and, in particular, how George was reacting to combat experience. Back to the tape . . .

". . . George is showin' the whites of his eyes. Just like the rest of us. This is on account that the duke has withdrawn his security blanket and left us naked up there again, ditched hundreds of miles from the Lancasters. A garbled radio message, or no message at all, a faulty map reference—we're at his mercy."

He tapped his finger in his stubbed cigar, as though prodding the wreckage of the past. When he spoke again his words had the tone of an old judgment.

"If you ask me, the duke, honor satisfied and all after what he and his boys did to Buddy Fanzoli, was genuinely prepared to write off the rape of his sister, but damned if he was gonna permit the violation of old Mother England and the Empire. And that's what George stood for. He was the white man's worst fear—the native, the wog, the nigger. That's how the duke and his cohorts saw him. I mean, there was George lordin' it at the big house with the butler dancin' attendance on him, and there was the duke not only piggin' it in a farmhand's cottage but also comin' from a colonial background in which his family had estates all over India and South Africa. When he was drunk, which was most of the time, he'd ride by on his horse and shout about our bloody kaffir. George. Okay, George didn't get a wreath with his name on it, but there was no shortage of burnin' crosses on the lawn of the house. I guess Dante Centofanti didn't mention that, uh?"

"No, he didn't."

"It figures. Memory, I mean. It's selective. Any cop will tell you that. There can be no end of witnesses to a crime, but a week later they've all got a different story. In particulars, that is. People choose a picture and, with the best of intentions, they stick to it. Which is why, all these years on, Dante Centofanti has forgotten things that are clear to me. And aren't I the smartie pants, uh? I remember well because I juggle. It concentrates the mind; psychiatrists use it for people with amnesia. Me, I can look back and see those crosses burnin' on the lawn just like it was Alabama and not England. Oh, those bastards . . ."

For a little while, I've been taking a break looking out of the window. The train has yet to pick up any speed and we are ambling through a series of rural communities. The tape runs on and Lou Eggenberg's comments on the Ku Klux Klan and fascism in general rasp against the butter-pat of voices from the club car: *Yes, sir, that's my baby, sure, sir, don't mean maybe . . .*

I gaze out on a township that looks freshly unwrapped, a gleaming gift of scenery which might almost have been designed especially for this folksy train ride—a white church, a saddler's store fronted by hitching posts, an ice cream parlor, a Buttons 'n' Bows shop. All radiating seemingly fresh paint.

But now I must contemplate another view, a view thousands of miles and many years distant, for the tape has reached the stage where Lou Eggenberg is describing the gala garden party on the lawn of the

hall in Yorkshire and the way it struck out for the propaganda rosette
of racial integration.

"... it was some occasion. You betcha! Big Anglo-American
event. What I remember most vividly, even more than the incident
with the dead fox, which I'll come to, is the maypole. I see that maypole streamin' all those colored ribbons. Alternatin' Union Jacks and
Stars and Stripes ribbons. Very pretty. Very innocent. Round and
round it goes. I guess it's the juggler in me sees it that way. Though
that *merry* swirl has also built up in my mind as the whirlpool that was
part of the treachery that swept Johnny up and did for him . . ."

Seventeen

VILLAGE ENGLAND, AND COMMUNITIES ACROSS A WIDE AREA SUP-
ported the garden party, laid on the maypole, the brass band, the
Morris dancers and the floral display of the Stars and Stripes made by
the Women's Institute and the Mothers' Union. The US Air Force,
for its part, flew in the champagne, the smoked salmon, the lobsters,
the suckling pig, the asparagus tips, the cheesecake, the ice cream.

And the blacks.

"Thirty or so black guys—hey, and some built like prizefighters—
are on the lawn," Lou Eggenberg said. "The weather is only so-so,
but everything else is style.

"The butler, all frock coat and starched shirtfront, is bowin' and
scrapin' among those blacks, toppin' up their champagne.

"And these guys are not one little bit impressed. They don't give a
shit, and it shows. They're arrogant. With cause. They belong to the
Three Hundred and Thirty-second Group, which is for black fliers
only. These guys are the crème de la crème—except for the color of
their skin. Which means they can't go in the same mess as whites or

to the same movie show. Why, they can't even piss alongside a white guy. So they're a mite uppity. Wouldn't you be?"

He shook his head, smiled, gestured folly with the flap of those huge hands.

"Anyway, they're here on the lawn because—leastways this is the official version—the experiment with George has proved such a success. George, by the way, has been with us all of two or three weeks. And they—the all-wise, all-seein', all-cheatin' *they*—have decided that his experience has shown the truly stirrin' possibilites of racial harmony.

"The story is—no one has confirmed it but everyone has heard it, includin' the RAF—that in a matter of weeks two additional B17s are gonna be attached to the base and they're gonna have mixed crews. Accordingly, the black guys that day are on a special trip, pathfinders, so they can go back and tell their buddies about this great new thing called racial tolerance. Yeah? The RAF has boycotted this little soiree: the base commander, for one, regrets he has the flu.

"But a little detail like a cold shoulder isn't gonna get in the way of a great public relations exercise, and in this department the US military cracks propaganda like a monkey shelling peanuts. The good ole Eighth Air Force has brought along a film unit and they're shootin' this newsreel about black and white gettin' along just dandy—and if that went on release my name is George Washington. Still, it's somethin' to have at the ready, a contingency in case they ever have to prove they went out of their way to promote goodwill.

"What the hell, though, the villagers cooperate in all this on account that in those days most ordinary English folk—strictly as opposed to the duke and his kind, you understand—see no threat in blacks: England was all white then and a black man was kinda novel. On top of this, the civilians have been promised a banquet by the advance PR team and they could do with a change from Spam and powdered egg. So the cameras focus on all this harmony and there's no shortage of shots of RAF fliers gettin' on just fine with their black Yank buddies—only these RAF guys are Americans shipped in wearin' RAF uniforms. But why should spoilsport truth get in the way of a good stunt?"

"Quite," I said, with a smiling briskness which was meant to suggest that I was edging away from this crowd scene of his memory, letting him know, politely, that I questioned the relevance of his story.

But either he didn't get my message or he ignored it, for he carried on.

". . . in time, however, the champagne gets to work and these black guys not only are unbendin'; they're grabbin' the ribbons of the maypole and chasin' the skirts of the nubile village maidens in a good ole rustic fertility dance. Round and round. Hop, skip and jump. Hugs and kisses. Clap hands and grab ass, know what I mean? The Morris dancers are callin' out the steps and bangin' on their tambourines and some of the blacks have whipped off their shirts. It's no orgy, understand—boys and gals come out to play is all it is. Just innocent fun.

"Only the duke doesn't see it that way. He's there suddenly, watchin' from the fringes of the lawn. Way he sees it, I figure he's experiencin' the imperialist white man's nightmare—the overrun of virgin England by the black hordes. He's there with three or four of his crew. They're on horseback, they've been out huntin' and they group there like a court, protectors of the realm. Uh!

"Johnny goes across to them and a few of us close ranks behind him, like we sensed there might be trouble. Dante Centofanti didn't mention this?"

"No."

"That's memory for ya. Strictly limited vision.

"Anyway, Johnny invites the duke to join the party, to come on over and have some champagne. Which isn't the best idea in the world because the guy's already been drinkin' hard; his eyes, they're kinda unfocused. What the duke does next is to reach down in his saddlebag and bring out a dead fox. He says, I don't remember the exact words, but he says that what's happenin' on the lawn is an insult to England and that he's holdin' Johnny personally responsible. And then he hauls up the fox by its brush, swings it round his head, yells, and these words I *do* remember, 'Today the fox, tomorrow the nigger's friend.'

"Shakespeare it isn't, but he puts some style into what he does next—which is to swing that fox round his head and then let it go. It whams Johnny across the shoulder. Johnny, not a big guy, sort of staggers back, and the duke and his cronies gallop off."

"It all sounds rather hammish," I said, a deliberately tempered response.

He smiled. "I guess it does at that. Though my experience has been that life, where it counts, is made up of hammish scenes. Or is that because I worked in the movies for a while? Be that as it may, our last sightin' of Johnny, only the day after the business with the duke and the fox, is pure corn-fed ham. I mean, Johnny's in his jeep with his gal—you have more than a passin' resemblance to her, by the way—and they're off for a drive in the country on a day—and here that ham starts sizzlin'—that's springtime with dimples."

The day of the blossom. The day recalled so vividly to me by Dante Centofanti—though, in the main, Lou Eggenberg's lyricizing of that day was on the baseball prowess of the crew's bombardier, one Dwight O'Donnell, who before the war had played a trial season with the New York Giants.

I wonder how Johnny felt that day. Did he, glancing in his rearview mirror, feel menaced when he saw the red sports car behind him? Tracking him. Lou Eggenberg, on the tape, is coming up to the part where that sports car takes shape. He has just described Johnny's peep of the horn as he drove out of the base in the jeep . . .

"We give him a kind of a wave and he slows down like maybe he wants to pass the time of day. But all our attention is on the game because, as I was sayin', Dwight O'Donnell's at bat and when Dwight hits—Wham! It's sheer magic. So Johnny drives on without stoppin'. Dwight, meantime, hits yet another inspired swipe—they're comin'

one after the other—and I guess just about all the crew goes searchin'
for that ball on account, the way Dwight hits, it's our last ball.

"We follow the general direction of Dwight's over-the-hills-and-
far-away ball, which is to the left of the house at a point where the
lawn rises steeply. From here, we can see the RAF gatehouse to the
base; at the house we have our own private entrance, which means
we're not checked. Anyway, we're searchin' for the ball when we
hear this roar and clashin' of gears and the duke's sports car—it's a
low-slung red Bentley—shoots along the base road. It's goin' so fast
that the MP at the gatehouse, who's moved out to make a routine
check, has to fling himself back to avoid bein' killed.

"We make some kinda general comment about the duke being
crazy drunk again—so what else is new?—then we go back to what
matters, which is findin' the ball. But on account of the particular
elevation we can also see the road to the west, which is the one
Johnny is on.

"It's a high, twistin' road to be taken with a lotta caution. We see,
in an incidental kind of way, Johnny's jeep climbin' the road and
then the Bentley comes into view, behind the jeep. Only suddenly
the Bentley is takin' due care, which is strange. The duke yields to no
one on the road, especially us. We're there, as far as the duke is concerned, to be overtaken and side-swiped into a ditch. Johnny's given
orders: whenever we're out drivin' and the duke comes up behind us
we're to pull over. Okay, so it's tuggin' the forelock, but it's stayin'
in one piece. Yet here he is now maintainin' his distance behind the
jeep, makin' no effort to overtake. Strange. Then they go out of
sight, the jeep and the Bentley, and out of our minds. It's something
we've seen out of the corner of our eye, is all.

"Then it's a day and a half later—I'm in a truck on my own and
they're shippin' me out to a ship in Southampton as part of the
cover-up Dante Centofanti told you about—when this little scene
between the jeep and the Bentley does a replay in my mind. I
hadn't thought about it before on account that, like the rest of the
guys, I'm all mixed up by Johnny's disappearance and everything
else that's followed on; all the stuff that Dante Centofanti's men-

tioned to you. Then, in the truck, it comes to me—the duke was on his best behavior that day because he was plottin' murder. He was keepin' his distance behind the jeep because he was stalking Johnny. Waitin' for the right moment. There could be no other possible explanation. Uh?"

He looked at me, his head on one side, his eyes reasoned as he awaited my reply. I went straight back to law school for it. "It's circumstantial and tenuous," I said, though in those stock, cautious words I think it could have been that I wanted to blunt the possibility that his death had been such a brutally schemed affair.

"I see what ya mean," Lou Eggenberg said. "But circumstantial and tenuous go right out of the window in the light of what happened not long after the war."

"And what was that?"

"We, uh, look him up. Two of us. We go right up to the ancestral door in Scotland. Knock knock. Who's there? Friends of Johnny's. Johnny who? Johnny the Yank ya murdered. My dear chaps, do come in. Any friend of Johnny's is an enemy of mine. It was my pleasure to bump him off and it's my pleasure to have you as my guests. So decent of you to take the time to visit. I mean, honest to God, that's more or less how he went on. Psycho."

I sighed. It's there on the tape: a long and pointed sigh.

"What's wrong, honey?" Lou Eggenberg asked.

"I came here for facts—not fancy dress."

"Yeah?" He grinned. "You want more dressin' up? Here goes. It's on account I taught Ernest Hemingway to juggle lemons at the American Bar in the George V Hotel in Paris that I end up makin' that call at the duke's castle in Scotland. And that's a *fact*. You can write me off now and leave, no hard feelings on my part, or you can stay and listen."

I stayed and listened and in the end saw the tangible proof of what he had to say—almost literally a chapter and verse documentation that would have stood up in any court of law as a twin indictment of murder and of the massive cover-up mounted to keep that crime a secret.

•   •   •

A musical interlude while I massage my fingertips—when I'm absorbed, I type hard—and listen to a club car warbling of "Sweet Adeline."

The singing has been going on nonstop. While the tape turned on murder and on conniving in high places I have heard at the back of my mind, in a sort of sonic twilight, distant, tossed lanterns of song as though those barbershop quartets had grouped into search parties and were trying to find a lost America that would respond to "Peg o' My Heart" and "Makin' Whoopee" and "Yes, We Have No Bananas!"

Not a chance, guys, and besides life *never* was a bowl of cherries. I smile, though, for I warm to the spirit (and that admission surprises me!) that keeps faith in a myth.

Or maybe my mellowness is down to the fact that I simply needed a break. Meantime, my fingers are supple again and so I turn back to Lou Eggenberg's story.

After Yorkshire, he was sent to North Africa. In less than a year the transport squadron he joined there was posted to Italy. He was in Rome when the war ended and he decided to take his discharge there. Before the war he had been a copy boy on a newspaper in Ohio and now he figured that a spell in Europe as a journalist might enable him to return home with the stature, licked into shape by his glib tongue, as a foreign correspondent.

"I headed straight for Paris. I could speak French—I studied the basics in high school—and, besides, Paris is where the action's at. More specifically, Paris is where Ernest Hemingway's at and for any expatriate American who's over there looking for any kind of a job to do with words Hemingway in those days is the only point of contact.

"He's as easy to find as a public monument: he's that big pile o' horseshit rooted at the bar at the George V. And there's an admission charge—you gotta buy the great man booze before he deigns to notice you. That takes time, like weeks, and money. I've saved up most of my pay from North Africa—what else can you do when you're stuck in a desert?—but now I'm goin' broke fast and, frankly, I'm on the point of headin' back to the States. Then one day it's my turn. Hemingway condescends to give me the nod and asks if I'm any good at arm wrestling. Please! He's built like a bull and means to use me as a floor show for his other stooges at the bar. I say I can do better than arm wrestle—I can juggle. And I proceed to do that with lemons from a bowl on the bar. Hey, he's impressed!"

I wasn't. I saw no point at all in what he was saying and I only just managed a smile. He tilted his head and winked at me.

"Isn't it the darndest thing," he said, "how your life can pivot on trivia? I mean, if I hadn't juggled those lemons that day I'd have gone back to Ohio and maybe ended up as editor of the *Toledo Blade*. But I juggle lemons in Paris one afternoon and everything changes. It's not just that I get to see the duke in Scotland; it's . . . *everything*. The whole bag o' tricks.

"But to resume the story, and to shorten it, Hemingway decides he wants me to teach him to juggle—I'm the matador of jugglin' as far as he's concerned—which makes me a Grade Two hanger-on in his circle, and, is that guy mean, I'm still buyin' him drinks.

"His payment in kind, however—and I'm givin' him lessons most every day—is to introduce me to one of the editors in the United Press bureau in Paris. Result? I gotta job. What I do is go through the tapes of the other news agencies and also through the whole of the French and Belgian press to see if there's anythin' worth followin' up. I do this for quite a few months. Conscientiously. It beats runnin' copy in Toledo and it's an education in that it enables me to know just about everything that's happenin' in the free world—includin' the fact that the duke is dyin' from injuries received in the war."

"Really?" I was interested now; his story might have a point after all.

"You betcha. And the way it comes about is no big deal. Y'see, there's this tabloid in Paris and it's covertly financed by the OSS, the forerunner of the CIA. It's very heavy on American propaganda which it incorporates cleverly in gossip and tittle-tattle and glossy pictures of celebrities. Which is how I come across this piece on the duchess of Windsor, aka Mrs. Wallis Simpson of Baltimore, who's as popular in France as she's hated in England, where she's persona non grata after all that baloney about the abdication. Only accordin' to this article I'm readin' the duchess has sneaked in a trip to the sceptred isle to visit her favorite godson, a wartime flyin' hero who has only a short time to live. And that hero is the duke, no less; he's named an' all.

"There's a picture of him, just an ordinary head-and-shoulders shot, and the story gives the whereabouts of his castle in Scotland. Now all of this isn't any twist of fate—more like a twist of lemon, considerin' how my jugglin' with Hemingway led me to a job in which, routinely and unremarkably, I come across this particular item.

"Anyway, like a good newspaperman I call the British embassy in Paris and get through to the press attaché with my query about whether the duchess had gotten royal dispensation and made the trip to England. If she had, it would have made a good story to send back to the States.

"The attaché snorts at the whole thing, but says he'll look into it. He calls back with an unequivocal denial about the duchess's trip, which I'd expected, but goes on to confirm that she is the duke's godmother and that he is in a bad way—so sick he couldn't manage an investiture at Buckingham Palace to get a medal—and that he's holed up at the ancestral home in Scotland. He also puts me wise, off the record, to the fact that the dukedom is, as he puts it, *de facto* and not *de jure*, which is a diplomatic and very British way of saying it's phony.

"Now the next stop in all this is London—that is, if you're interested in goin' that far down the line, honey."

I nodded. I sensed a long and tortuous trip, but by now I also sensed truth at the end of it. He winked and got on with his tale . . .

"I'm in London a couple o' weeks later. I go over about once a month on account that Pete Verker, who was our flight engineer, lives there. Like me, Pete hadn't returned to the States. Used to be an auto salesman in Philadelphia and he was drafted just before some, uh, *gentlemen* from the West Coast caught up with him on account o' his gamblin' debts. He figures they might still be waitin'. So he's teamed up with this New Zealander and their racket is sellin' surplus military vehicles and they're doin' swell. But to get to the point, we're in this bar in Piccadilly and it's late and a couple o' very nice hookers are smoochin' us and I mention to Pete, strictly small talk, this development with the duke.

"And Pete says why don't we tootle up to Scotland? Confront the guy before he pops off. And he means that we should start like right now! He says we owe it to Johnny to find the truth. I, uh—I demur. Hey, I say, let's go back to bein' cozy with the gals and the booze before I opened my big mouth. I liked Johnny, don't get me wrong, but I was never all fired up about him, like the other guys. Like Pete.

"I mean, I just don't see any percentage in a long trek to Scotland which is gonna end with a door slammed in our faces. Pete, on the other hand, always plays the long shot. He's a gambler and a salesman and he's so good at these things he's a millionaire by the time he's thirty and dead of a heart seizure before he's forty. But that's another story. What I'm tryin' to say is that Pete knows how to be persuasive which is why, strictly against my will, we leave that sweet bar in Piccadilly and head for Scotland . . ."

For a while, his narrative became picaresque as he described how he and his friend, this Pete Verker, set off in a vehicle built for ruggedness—a Mercedes-Benz staff car, formerly used by the German High Command. The car had bullet holes across its long bonnet, "like the zeros Pete was gonna build into the askin' price on account, or this was gonna be his sales pitch, that this was the getaway car used by the generals after they tried to assassinate Hitler. What a salesman that guy was! What a hustler!"

No doubt that drive began as a drunken escapade. But hangovers must have supervened and still they pressed on to Scotland, halting only for petrol, which they bought with black market coupons for cold sausage sandwiches and tea in enamel jugs at remote transport cafes. A couple of times the car broke down and once it plunged into a ploughed field and had to be towed out by a tractor. It was foggy and cold, for this was mid-winter, and the heater didn't work. But they kept going, all the seven hundred or so miles to the tip of Invernesshire. Escapade had turned into quest, which was in their hearts from the start, though Lou Eggenberg stuck to his story that he had been hustled and that Johnny didn't really matter a damn to him.

That journey took more than sixteen hours. Finally, they were driving in sleet on a single track bordering a frozen loch at the head of which a castle surfaced, "dripping like a U-boat. That was my first impression. Though I was numb with cold and I was tired and hungry. Guess I might have been seein' things. Maybe what really was there was the next best thing to the castle in the Emerald City and that what I was seein', that black mass of wet granite, was my mood. Could be."

He remembered an ancient manservant opening the door to them, a man wearing a leather apron and polishing a silver tray, and then there was an old woman leaning on a stick as she listened to their story; or, rather, she listened to Pete Verker, ever the salesman.

She left them standing in a drafty hall whose walls were an arabesque of stags' antlers. She returned with a woman in the uniform of a military nurse, a red cross on her starched white blouse. To the nurse, Pete Verker repeated his easy spiel: they were wartime buddies calling on a former comrade in arms. At length, the nurse said they could have five minutes, no longer, and took out a fob watch to show they were on countdown. She led them to a room at the top of a flight of stone stairs. Five minutes, she repeated, checking her watch, as she closed the door on them, leaving them alone with the duke. Lou Eggenberg's direct quotes now . . .

"He's propped up on pillows in this big bed, biggest bed I've ever seen. He's holdin' an oxygen mask to his face. Just about all we can see above the mask is his eyes. Those pale blue eyes. And right now they're amused. He's recognized us. Then suddenly he jerks the mask away from his face and there's this snake-bite hiss of oxygen and he's sayin', 'Peekaboo, Yanks!' and we see that most of his face is missin'. Plumb blown away and surgically wired up.

"Next thing he's pattin' the bed, invitin' us to sit down. Had a little accident, he says. He has a lotta trouble speakin' and has to keep usin' the oxygen, but he gets it out that his Lancaster was holed by night fighter cannon shells and crashed in flames in the North Sea. He says that only he and his sparks—that's what the RAF called their radio men—survived. They're in the water for hours. The spark's life jacket is ripped so he's hangin' onto the duke. 'Poor chap,' he says, 'died in my arms.'

"'And speakin' of poor chaps,' Pete says, 'how did Johnny die?'

"The duke clamps on the oxygen mask, like he's hidin' behind it. Only he sees we're not scared. His eyes show he's enjoyin' this. Meantime, I'm fumblin' in my pockets for a pencil and paper because suddenly it seems important that what's said here is written down.

"I say to him, I've got the pencil and pad ready now, that he and his boys strung up Buddy Fanzoli, didn't they? And he nods and smiles and is altogether very pleased with himself.

"'You do the same to Johnny?' Pete says. I'm writin' this down, remember, though clumsily on account my fingers are still numb. He makes no reply, but we can see he's takin' gulps of oxygen and as it turns out he's doin' this to build up a reserve for the proper delivery of his words. *Le mot juste.* Pete repeats his question and the duke whips off his oxygen mask and says, I write it down, 'Hanging is for underlings. Your captain was dispatched with a flair worthy of his rank.' You can see the effort these words have taken, and then he starts to giggle.

"Pete's about to lay one on him, but I grab hold of his arm just in time. I mean, you can't hit a guy with a face as messed up as his, and besides, we need to keep him talkin'. Only he won't stop gigglin'. He's gaspin' for breath and he's gigglin' and in the end I shove the oxygen mask over his face because, and I guess this sounds crazy, he seemed to be usin' all the air in the room and I can actually feel this tight band across my chest."

I think I know how he felt, for suddenly I feel claustrophobic, need *my* breathing space away from that bedroom in that castle in Scotland and the man with the ruined face who murdered Johnny, and I have an impression that I am positively inhaling those sound breezes from the club car as life without complication is celebrated. *Standin' on the corner watchin' all the girls go by* . . . The voices flutter like colored scarves as Lou Eggenberg gnaws on that bleak old bone of memory . . .

". . . I say, I'm out to flatter him, out to make him boast of just how he killed Johnny, so I say I gotta hand it to him, it was pretty clever the way he tried to get our whole crew bumped off all those times he left us on our own at the mercy of the night fighters and he slips out from behind the mask and says, 'I'll take a bow for that, old chap.' And Pete says . . ."

On he goes. On and on. And from the club car a skittering of another song. *When it's apple blossom time in Orange, New Jersey* . . . I have a sudden surreal feeling that I am in two parts of the past, a withered mid-winter Scotland and a lush summery orchard in New Jersey where the fruit is altogether too exotic, too perfumed.

"'How'd you kill him, uh? And his girl. How'd you kill them?' Pete's patience gives way again and he moves in with the direct question. And the duke starts gigglin' again. He's tauntin' us. All part of his sport . . ."

Ain't she sweet, see her walkin' down the street . . . The latest offering from the club car repertoire and abruptly I feel a panicked impatience with these singers. These—liars! These yodelling Yankees in their Happy Valley America—there never was such a place. It was a Tin Pan Alley pastiche, tunes plonked out by cigarette-stained fingers on pianos that were instruments of propaganda in the mass manufacture of the feel-good factor, the American Dream counterfeited on cheap sheet music, and the warbling in the club car isn't that far removed, in delusion and cynicism, from the manic giggling of the man who murdered Johnny and—

Well, now, what brought on that little spume of fury? Tension, I suppose. And I feel better for its release. *Take me out to the ball game* . . . I hear the singers now for what they are, genuine celebrants of a remembered good life, which may or may not have been; it doesn't matter, just so long as they *think* their America had existed. And I return my full attention to the tape.

". . . no matter how we tried, he just wasn't sayin' how Johnny was murdered. He's not gonna give us the satisfaction. Instead he's goin' on, between gasps, about America bein' a scum race, a mixture of niggers, Jews, gypsies and bog Irish and Hitler had the right idea, and we will do him the honor of stayin' for dinner, won't we? I swear! What the hell, we're glad when the nurse comes in and tells us our time's up.

"As she sees us down the stairs and outa the house she tells us he's stayin' alive on willpower and oxygen, in that order, on account that both his lungs were cindered by the blazin' oil he swallowed when he dove repeatedly into the sea to save his crewman. The man's a hero, she says. Sure. And pardon us if we don't salute him."

He went on to describe his return to Paris and the writing there of a long article, a step-by-step indictment of the duke. When it was finished, he showed it to Hemingway.

"His verdict, a week or so later, was that it was lousy with adjectives but that it seemed to have one honest noun at its core—truth.

"He says to leave it with him. I figure I can write it off. But six or seven weeks on and I get a letter from this major magazine, now defunct, in the States saying they've read my piece, which Hemingway had recommended to them, and askin' me to look them up as soon as I can. Come to momma—the big time is beckonin'!"

Two days later he was crossing the Atlantic in a liner—though he was on course to ultimate disaster.

Eighteen

THREE BLASTS RESONATED FROM THE FUNNELS OF THE LINER *Normandy* as she came within sight of the Statue of Liberty and in the far rolling echoes of that sound Lou Eggenberg, quoting the poet Walt Whitman, said he seemed to hear America singing.

"It was first light and I was up on deck and it was like I was listenin' to the very fanfare of democracy. Regular lump-in-the-throat stuff, y'know? I remembered all my old radical convictions. And I remembered Johnny and how America needed his sort in order to get into shape as a true world leader."

He paused in this telling. He smiled. Winked.

"And then I reminded myself to cut the crap and that I was back here for my own kudos. In all honesty, I gotta own up to that. I was a kid and I wanted to make my name. Johnny wasn't my crusade— he was my means to an end."

Whatever his ambiguities, the espouser of justice on one level and the dedicated promoter of his own interests on the other, Lou Eggenberg at least wasn't a hypocrite. He acknowledged Johnny's

virtues but was not prepared to be sentimental about him, and in my
book that made him a clear-eyed and reliable witness.

Meantime, there was no doubt that his name was in the making,
for he was warmly received at the offices of the magazine in New
York.

"They wine and dine me at the Stork Club, no less; okay, so it just
so happens that it's the managing editor's birthday and I'm invited to
the shindig. Still—see what happens when ya juggle lemons for
Hemingway?—they tell me they see this story as making the cover.
What they want me to do, to make it all watertight, is to get sworn
affidavits from the crew testifyin' to the whole business that led to the
murders of Buddy Fanzoli and then Johnny.

"And Alice, I say, bringin' in Johnny's girl, because I figure that a
triple killin' boosts the value of the story. I swear, this is how merce-
nary I am at the time. Sure, they say, and Alice. Only I pick up that
Alice is kinda marginal to them, as is Buddy Fanzoli. What they
really want to go big on is Johnny, which is fair enough, I guess, considerin' he was the captain.

"Anyway, I say, all enthusiastic, I'll round up these guys, no matter how many miles I gotta put in on the bus. No bus, they say. Airplane. They're puttin' me on expenses and it's first class all the way.
This gives ya an idea of their commitment.

"I already have a couple of specific addresses to work on and the
others roll on from there, from leads the first guys I see give me. I
hear, in due course, of the guys who've been killed in action followin' the break-up of our crew in Yorkshire and these include poor
old George, the token black. He was transferred back to the
infantry—he was sent to us as a gunner—and he bought it in Burma.
That's life, that's war and now it's my brilliant career that counts as I
cross and crisscross the country from Seattle to Boston, includin' a
stopover in New Orleans to see Dante Centofanti. I guess he told
you about that."

"No. I think he did mention though that a major magazine was
interested and—"

"At least he remembered that, which says somethin' for a guy with worm holes in his memory. Comes with age. So does meanderin', so I'll get on with my story. I end up with twelve guys precisely, includin' myself and Pete Verker.

"Normally, a B17 has a crew of nine, but in our case it's four or five over that, what with guys doublin' up on account that we're supposed to be studyin' RAF tactics. Anyway, of the twelve names I have, eight are the original crew that flew from day one. The others are guys who didn't do the full run but were with us long enough, like twenty or so missions, to know the score vis-à-vis the duke. Ya follow?"

I nodded. His logistics seemed unimportant.

"These guys," he went on, "just can't do enough for me. All except for one. As for the others, it doesn't matter to 'em that they've signed a piece of paper—I signed it as well—swearin' them to silence about anythin' to do with their time in Yorkshire. It doesn't matter shit to them that in makin' their notarized statements to me they're riskin', at the very least, withdrawal of all their benefits under the GI Bill of Rights—special mortgages, car loans, college grants. What matters to these guys is justice for Johnny and they're puttin' *everything* on the line for this. All except for this one guy, the only no-can-do. I *plead* with this guy. Harry, I say—"

"Harry?"

"Yeah. Harry Korda. Johnny's copilot and closest buddy, I don't think! Twelve guys, one Judas—the numbers kinda work out, uh?"

Quiet words, those. Tellingly quiet: the tape snares a lifetime's bitterness.

"He weasels on about publicity bein' painful for Johnny's sister. I say she's entitled to the truth and that, in the name of justice, we're fightin' her corner as well. Am I comin' on strong and crafty! Only this is Judas and he's craftier. Because it's not long after that I go to Atlanta to look her up for background on Johnny and so forth and she point blank refuses to see me—she's been warned off by Harry Korda who's told her I'm out to spread lies.

"Believe me, when it comes to betrayal and dirty tricks in general this guy's a pro. This is also the guy who's gotta know most of the

answers about Johnny. This is the guy, like Dante Centofanti told
you, who's called out of the briefing that night when Johnny didn't
show and who returned in the middle of the night and gave us the
thumbs-down to show that Johnny was dead.

"And this is the guy—oh, and suddenly that day after the war I'm
face to face with him and this seems very significant—who instead of
bein' packed off someplace where it's too hot or too cold, like the
rest of us were, instead rides out the rest of the war behind a cozy
desk in London.

"In the end, that day, I see he's not gonna yield and I say I trust
he's made a killin' with his twenty pieces of silver and I get the hell
outa there. Judas! Okay, so I'm in it for my own lousy selfishness, but
his kinda sell-out . . . To this day it still stinks to me. A Judas stench!"

He shook his head slowly on this remote perfidy and I thought he
might be going to lapse into an old man's brooding. That's why I
said, in a business-like tone that stood for a shake of his shoulder, "So
what happened next?"

"Uh?" He looked at me and his face was blurred. Then he grinned
and was sharp and sprite-like again.

"I guess that, in order of importance, what happens next is that the
duke dies, but not before he issues a statement, pretty well on the eve
of his death, through his lawyers. The magazine, y'see, has been
makin' enquiries from its London bureau and the result of this is the
written statement that in the matter of the deaths of Buddy Fanzoli
and Johnny he has no comment to make. No denial, you'll note, just
a highly incriminatin' no comment."

"That's no more than inference," I said, back at law school again.

"Okay. But where the inference starts whistlin' Dixie, *and* in
Latin, is when he says, all in that one-paragraph statement, that he
never at any stage bore any ill will against Alicia Marensky."

"Who?"

"Alice. Johnny's girl. She was Russian."

"Really?" I said it briskly, brushing away a moment's fatuous
resentment over simple Alice being mysterious Slavic Alicia.

"Yeah. And the statement says that Alice came to no harm in a situation that could have been construed as a personal *causus belli*."

"Justification of war."

"Sure. Though at the time I didn't know what *causus belli* meant. Had to be explained to me by my editor. I guess that's what got me around to studyin' Latin. Very devious language, uh? No wonder it's the language of the law. Elegant. Crafty. I mean, here's the duke mentionin' *causus belli* and Alice in the same breath, though what he's *really* sayin is that he bumped off Buddy Fanzoli and Johnny. Only he's makin' no comment there—he's winkin', havin' the last laugh—whereas in the case of Alice he comes out with a straight denial and goes to his grave as an English gentleman who wouldn't harm a woman. And if ya believe that—"

"What did they believe at the magazine?"

"They saw this as an extra shorin' up of a story they'd had faith in from the start. Though they still weren't particularly interested in Alice; I guess Russia and all made her seem kinda remote. Or could it be that the Cold War was emergin'? I said we oughta check Alice out—background stuff, maybe try to trace her family in Russia—but they said there wasn't the time because they were thinkin' of runnin' the article as part of the first anniversary of VE day, which was only a few weeks away.

"What really clinches the whole story is when I produce the affidavits of the crew. The editor I'm workin' with—one of those friendly Harvard guys, elbow patches and horn-rimmed glasses—says it doesn't matter all that much that Harry Korda has backed off. We got eleven guys on our side, he says, and that's a whackin' majority. He claps me on the back. They're gonna go with the story, he says. Big. The cover."

"Was it—was it published?" Do I hear now, on the tape, a certain wariness in my voice? I can't be sure.

"It was . . . *printed*."

I look back now and see him pursing his lips on that inflection. He smiled, held up his finger to signal that he had something to do, turned his chair and moved off, though not at a spritely dart this time, to a corner of the room. He rummaged there for a while and came back, still slowly, dusting off a brown folder tied, in a bow, with a white silk scarf bearing the crest of the Eighth Air Force.

He handed the folder to me. "Care to do the honors?"

I tugged at the bow, feeling like a slightly self-conscious guest of honor at an unveiling in which, I tried for brittle minor amusement, a few well-chosen opening remarks might be appropriate.

But when I opened that folder I was quite at a loss for words.

What I saw was a large head-and-shoulders color photograph of Johnny on the cover of a magazine. The collar of his flying jacket was turned up. A shy smile was tucked into the corner of his mouth at the side of the S-shaped scar, which was well visible. He was bareheaded, his hair slightly tousled.

Inset into the edge of that photograph was a much smaller one, that of a grinning young man with wavy dark hair: this turned out to be Buddy Fanzoli.

The cover was patently a proof. The magazine's masthead wasn't in place and a small box at the top of the page had "vacuum cleaner ad?" scrawled across it in red pencil. The date was there, though— June 2, 1946—and, on the right of the page in an oval, the price, 15 cents, and, between the illustration of two eagles rising from smoking eyries, the magazine's corporate message: *Incisive reading for intelligent Americans*. I lingered for a moment over these details, the small print as it were, before I moved to the headline.

It was bannered across the page—THE RAF'S SECRET AMER-ICAN "KILLS"—and continued, vertically and in smaller type, down the right-hand side: HOW THESE TWO YOUNG U.S. FLIERS PAID WITH THEIR LIVES FOR CROSSING EN-GLISH CLASS LINES. *See pages*—the page numbers hadn't made the proof.

Carefully, it was flaking at the edges, I turned over the cover and looked down on a spread of yellowed text under a headline that said,

A PUKKA AND PRIVATE WAR. A sub-heading read, *In 63 missions a US B17 flying from England dodged flak and night fighters, but could not shake off its deadliest enemy—the RAF.*

I glanced at Lou Eggenberg. "If you wanna plough through five pages, be my guest," he said.

Amply documented, largely in the form of the testimony and anecdotes of the crew, the article maintained a pace that at no time resorted to the skid marks of crude exposé: it stated its case with the quiet authority of total certitude. It was all there, comprehensive and interwoven, and it moved, sequence by sequence, to that post-war culmination in which Lou Eggenberg and Pete Verker confronted the duke and he boasted of what he had done.

Alice got only a cursory mention. She was described as a Soviet war artist seconded to the Allies as "a gesture of solidarity" and she wasn't credited as Johnny's girlfriend: she was down as his "companion" the day he disappeared and it was noted that "she also failed to return from what was meant to be that simple drive in the country."

Here and there in the text sundry senior officers—American generals and British air marshalls—had their say and, in their various ways, harrumphed as they decried the whole story as a fabrication and insisted that Johnny had indeed been killed on a mission to Düsseldorf on May 1, 1944. Neatly juxtaposed against one such denial was the photograph of Johnny, the one shown to me in New Orleans, celebrating Dante Centofanti's clearly identified twenty-first birthday on May 20, 1944.

There were other photographs of Johnny and quite a few more—no doubt because of his social standing he was on file at picture agencies—of the duke. He was lank and fair-haired and, like so many patricians, his smile combined both arrogance and standard charm. In only one picture—he smoked a pipe as he stood against the tail fin of his Lancaster—was he in uniform. The rest of the shots illustrated his social life. He raised a glass of champagne at a debutante's ball in Mayfair. Top-hatted, hands in his pockets, one foot mounted negligently on a mounting block, he discussed form with Noel Coward at Ascot. Garlanded, he sat in a racing car and accepted a winner's kiss

from a girl in Monte Carlo. On a tennis court he demonstrated a
serve to the Duke of Windsor. In Jaipur, a shotgun slung from his
bush jacket, he posed as he placed his hand on the head of a dead
tiger strapped to the bonnet of a safari truck.

The pictures were cliches, parodies, and that may have been why
I could find no evidence of homicidal psychosis in his gaze, why I
ended up characterizing him in my mind as a standard playboy, circa
1930s. As such, and to my surprise, I felt no emotion about him, only
a faint boredom; perhaps I had met too many updates of his kind at
Oxford.

I made a written note of the headlines and as I put the proofs back
I got around to making that speech which had crossed my mind as an
awkward flippancy when I tugged at the silk scarf around the folder;
now that I hear it again on the tape it does rather sound like a formal
address, though I meant every word.

"This is brilliant, both as journalism and in the rhetoric and logic
of pure advocacy," I said.

"I was just the legman, honey," Lou Eggenberg said. "The, uh,
corps de ballet back at the magazine did most of the fancy steps."

"They did you proud."

"Yeah. So why'd they jilt me for Betty Grable?"

"I don't understand."

"You will. Just excuse me while I fetch another cigar."

A flourish of cigar smoke, a wink as knowing as an eye patch, and he
was ready to explain that remark about Betty Grable.

"I took a vacation to Bermuda on the strength of what they paid
me—boy, that was some check!—but I made sure I was back for
publication day. In fact, just after midnight I'm at a newsstand in
Times Square waitin' for the magazine to be delivered. It's rainin',
but why should I care? I'm about to be launched as the big-time
journalist. After two, three hours a truck dumps a bale o' the magazine and it's the longest couple of minutes in my life while the guy

who runs the newsstand is cuttin' the twine on that bale. Finally I have the magazine in my hand and—and Betty Grable's on the cover. I look inside—my article isn't there. Just more pictures of Betty Grable winkin' and smirkin' like—like she's sendin' a last-laugh message from the duke."

At the offices of the magazine that morning he was told that the editor who had worked with him was on assignment in Mexico. He insisted on talking to someone. He waited most of the day before he was shown into the office of the deputy managing editor.

"Right from the start this guy's shifty, uncomfortable. He tells me the story was dropped at the last minute for legal reasons. I remind him it was checked by lawyers and cleared for publication. He says y'can never be too careful with libel. I say it's Johnny who's been libelled. Libelled by silence. And it's the rest of the crew that have been libelled, denied their chance to speak out against the murder of their captain. I'm bangin' on the desk now. Literally.

"But this guy keeps goin' on about it just bein' our word, and I say we're a fuckin' jury and that Pete Verker and I are the foremen because we were there when the duke owned up to what he did and now the duke's dead and ya can't libel dead men.

"And that's when this guy sort o' sighs and leans forward and says, 'You're whistlin' against the wind, Lou.' It's the *way* he says it; he's puttin' me wise.

"I ask where that wind's blowin' from. He taps his fingers on the desk for a few moments. 'High places,' he says. 'Very high places.'"

Lou Eggenberg went on a binge and came to on a Greyhound bus. He knew where he was going, though: Hollywood.

"I figure—the gall of the greenhorn kid, uh?—that maybe I could get a studio interested in Johnny's story. I had nothin' to lose. I had the magazine proofs and I had chutzpah. I realized I needed an agent and I got one; it wasn't so hard in those days. I made a few enquiries and I heard of this agent whose son, a naval flier, was killed in the war. So, havin' found this guy's weak spot, I just sat in his waitin' room for days on end jugglin' walnuts—he grew walnuts on his farm in the valley and always had a bowl of them in reception.

"First thing he would see when he got to his office of a mornin' and the last thing he saw at night was me jugglin'. In the end, he has to call me in. He says he doesn't handle circus acts and I say I'm one of the daring young men on the flying trapeze that did sixty-two missions over Germany until it was nobbled by the RAF. Gee, I was a cocky kid! I got him interested, though.

"The result is that we package the story in script form—I learn a lotta useful things from him in that respect—and it starts doin' the rounds. Meantime, he's gettin' me bits and pieces o' work. Scenes in scripts that were shootin' and had to be changed on account that some puff-head actor doesn't like the sound o' the words. I find I gotta flair for this; it's just another form of jugglin'. The pay is good; I can live two, three weeks on what I do, mainly one liners, to a couple a pages of script.

"Then the word comes through—a studio is interested in *my* script. Not one of the big ones. But it's known for its independence and its liberal stand; Orson Welles is one of its backers. We swing into pre-production right away and it emerges they've done a deal to borrow Alan Ladd to play Johnny and though I could think of better choices Ladd has pretty good pull at the box office, and that's where my heart is. A full crew's hired and an old mansion in Santa Barbara is leased as the house in Yorkshire. I'm poppin' bennies so I can stay awake nights to polish the shootin' script to their satisfaction and though I'm a bit pissed off at the changes they want—they wanna play down the black angle and I have to change Alice from a Russian to a Canadian—I go along with it because it means a screen credit for me. Things all round are goin' so well that on the strength of my prospects I get married for the first time, to a continuity girl I've been shackin' up with. Then—wham! The movie's off. No explanation. Not to me.

"Zo, my agent, says this happens all the time. Sure it does. But not when a movie's so far ahead in pre-production and not when it's a small studio that can't afford to take that kinda loss.

"There it is, however. I'm back to doin' bits and pieces again and, since Zo seems to have gone cold on the script, I'm passin' the word about it on my own. I'm mailin' actors, producers, directors. One day Zo calls me in. Good news and bad news, he says. I tell him to give me the marzipan first. He says he thinks he might be able to sign me as a co-writer for a Jimmy Cagney picture—a screen credit at last. Now give me the crud, I say. He shuffles papers on his desk, any excuse to keep his eyes down, and says I'm to stop promotin' the script about Johnny. Why? He won't say, apart from somethin' general about the wanin' public interest in war movies.

"This I won't buy and in the argument that follows I walk out on Zo. There's plenty of other agents. But as I move from one to another I find the work slowin' down. Still, I keep pushin' my script and I'm sure that one day someone's gonna have the guts to take it up; even in Hollywood there's gotta be some good guys.

"Though I should talk—it's not like I'm wearin' a white hat myself. I see that script as the mortgage on the over-the-top house I bought when I got married and on car repayments and restaurant bills and when it comes to the bottom line I don't give a shit about Johnny."

"I do not for one moment believe that." The firmness of my reply surprised me somewhat. "You were young and ambitious and more than a bit self-centered, but above all you were loyal. I—I believe in you."

He winked. "Say, will you marry me? I'll teach you to juggle."

"Just keep balancing the facts."

"Oh, the facts tumble way outa line. Except—except that I'm sure my script has a hex on it when these two process servers turn up and I'm subpoenaed to appear before the House Un-American Activities Committee."

"Didn't that happen to a lot of people?"

"Yeah. But from Hollywood they want strictly the big names, the

ready-made headlines. Me, I'm the literary equivalent to an extra, a
nobody, and yet they're out to blacklist me. I'm called the day
Humphrey Bogart gives his evidence, and chickens out of makin' a
stand. I get the usual openin' question—were you or have you ever
been, dee dah dee dah? Nope. I'm a maverick, not a Communist.
But my questioner is a shitty little guy with rimless glasses and he says
I must know communists in the movies. Sure, I say. He wants me to
name names. No way, I say. Not even initials, he says, smirkin'. It
riles me, that smirk, so I say if he'll pass me a pad I'll give him initials
and maybe we can do a deal. He gives me a pad and I write down
those initials—FU. I get six months for contempt.

"I do three weeks in the slammer and then they tell me I can go.
Free man. Only I'm on bread and water. There's strictly no work for
me back in Hollywood. In no time my marriage is blown and my
house is repossessed and I end up pumpin' gas in Santa Monica."

Everything's comin' up roses . . . From the club car, just now, a rendering of the spirit of the American Dream and, on the tape, the
recital of Lou Eggenberg's hard luck story and its eventual transcen-
dence to that other extreme, the American Tragedy. It's evidence,
linked to what happened to Johnny and the further violence this
engendered, so I'll get on with its telling. Or, rather, I'll let Lou
Eggenberg do this as he recalls what followed on from his stint as a
gas station attendant.

"One day I tank up a vegetable truck and tell the driver he doesn't
have to pay if he'll take me wherever he's headin'. Which turns out
to be Nebraska. I get a job on a paper there. This bein' the bible belt,
they give me the church beat, would ya believe it.

"Still, it's a job and I settle down and do well at it. Now and then,
like once a month, I hop over to Omaha and shoot the breeze in a
bar with guys from the big local Air Force base. I do some showin'
off about what I did in the war and I guess maybe I'm not too discreet
in discussin' the whole bag o' dirty tricks that was unloaded on us in
Yorkshire. What the hell, it makes a good story. Where's the harm?

"I'll tell you where the harm is. It's in two generals comin' to see my editor one afternoon. After they've gone he calls me in and says I'm canned. Through. This is exactly one week after I've put in my first year on the paper and I've been awarded a merit pay raise. The editor, who's a part-time preacher and a regular Joe, says he can't discuss why he's firin' me, but—and here's the giveaway—why don't I avoid a lot of future grief and try the newspaper market in Canada? He offers to give references about how good my work is to a buddy of his in Ontario.

"Why the hell should I go to Canada? My country 'tis of thee, sweet land of liberty—yeah, and as the years go by I start puttin' that tune to bounce time. I get a job on a paper, I settle—twice I get married—then I'm bounced. There's no denyin' the rhythm. No denyin'.

"Finally I'm in Detroit and for the first time I'm workin' for a big city newspaper. I'm into my third year, a record for me, and I figure the paper's been tipped off about me by now but it's so big it isn't bothered. While I'm there I've won three journalism awards. Okay, they're not Pulitzers, but I'm the favorite to be the next city editor. I am so sure that at last I've found security that I get married again. Bride number four. We take out a mortgage and we buy a weekend lakeside cabin.

"And then I'm bounced.

"I go to a bar and get stewed. It's rainin' heavily. I have cause to remember that, the rain. In the end, my wife comes lookin' for me. She'd heard what's happened and she's been searchin' for me in bar after bar and she's wet through. She's an Irish gal but with no temper. She just wants to take me home. She's twenty-four years old and she's pregnant.

"When I see her in the bar, all rained on, I just start bawlin' my eyes out. That leaves me feelin' ashamed and to prove what a tough customer I am I dry my tears and insist on drivin' us home. Ella tries to talk me out of this, but then humors me.

"The rain is heavier than ever and I'm drivin' very carefully . . . or I think I am until I wake up in the hospital. They tell me the car was hit by a freight locomotive on a crossin'. Ella died instantly; she was on the side that took the impact. I say, anything to duck the truth, that my legs hurt. They say I haven't got any legs. Or none to speak of. My left leg was amputated below the knee, my right leg slightly higher up. They say I'm lucky to be alive. Honest to God, they say I'm lucky."

Throughout, he had spoken quietly and without self-pity. Now, head on one side, he considered the tip of his cigar in silence for a few moments.

Then he put the cigar in the side of his mouth and was jaunty again.

"But, what the hell, I'm still on my own two feet. Wanna see me pirouette?" He made his wheelchair spin a couple of times. He winked.

Tough old bird. American eagle, no less—that near-extinct species that dates back to the days when Americans were Yanks.

We talked only a little longer. This-and-that talk about the jobs and escapades that followed his accident—he was a night clerk in a cheap hotel; he composed greeting card verse for an ad agency; he was a croupier in Las Vegas, where he married for the fifth and last time, though his bride walked out on him after only a day—and as I was leaving he looked up at me, solemnly by his standards, and said, "Whatever it is you're doin' about Johnny, try to make sure that you do justice by him. Promise?"

Promise.

It's dark outside. In my concentration I was unaware of the light going and my laptop, which I have on the window ledge while I sit on the edge of my bunk seat and type, has slewed and its screen is refracted by the window and the green pulsing letters seem like fire-flies outside behind the glass. I feel I could stay here with that manu-factured chimera of fireflies, but I am overruled by hunger—I haven't eaten since breakfast—and the knowledge of the nonstop buffet in the club car from where, right now, I hear that once all–American assurance that *Happy days are here again . . .*

I am still wearing the straw boater that was presented to me in the club car; I need all the jauntiness I can muster.

I stayed with the singers until after three A.M., when even they decided they needed sleep. Not before a grand finale, though, in which dozens of them grouped in ranks in front of the long bar and launched into "Yankee Doodle Dandy."

As their voices rose on the opening notes a mock cannon was fired and streamers were shot into the air. And it was through these cascading tendrils and the star-spangled balloons that fell at the same time from the ceiling that I saw a face I seemed to recognize.

He stood, in the open doorway between the carriages, only a few feet away, and stared at me. I brushed streamers and balloons from my line of vision in order to see better, but then the cannon plopped a second time and more streamers spun and when I looked again he was gone.

I might have been prepared to write it off as mistaken identity had it not been that for a moment he had his left hand raised palm up in sardonic greeting and I glimpsed, even though it was just a blur, the black rose tattoo.

New York

Nineteen

THE TRAIN STREAMED INTO NEW YORK ON THE SUNNIEST OF mornings, but I shuffled in a damp fog of personal foreboding.

Hundreds of straw boaters bobbed on that platform of Penn Station and I, one of the first passengers to disembark, loitered ignominiously behind a large ornamental pillar and tried to spot Mr. Punch.

He wasn't there, or not that I could see in that throng, and I wanted to believe he had been a blink-of-the-eye imagining, a spin-off from a Barbershop Bounce (and I'd had a couple of those deadly cocktails at the late-night party in the club car). I knew, though, that he *had* been on the train, that even now he could be watching me from somewhere in that cavernous station.

I waited until the train was quite empty, until the group-singing of "Give My Regards to Broadway" by which my fellow passengers had descended on New York was a scrap of echo from the concourse up above.

And still no sign of Mr. Punch. I ventured out from the shadow of the pillar, looked for a porter. All of them had been taken. A few cleaners, with mops and buckets and disinfectant sprays, wandered here and there, but otherwise the platform was deserted. The train made little shuddering end-of-journey sounds, as though sleeping off its long-haul hangover.

There were no trollies left either, so I picked up my luggage and made for the exit. Normally this would have been no more than an inconvenience, but today it was a trek. I was spent. I hadn't been able to sleep after my sighting of Mr. Punch in the club car.

I have never known a longer night, but though I was furious at this out-of-character reaction my tetchings were overcome by my twitchings. And so when I made up my bunk for sleeping I put the pillows at the window side of the berth; thus positioned, the reading lamp kept on, my gaze was never far away from the door and primed for that filmic cliche—the slow turning of the handle from outside.

I sought to justify my paranoid alertness in this respect on the grounds that the door lock didn't work. This was an old train, shunted out for the barbershop charter, and, the tiniest of details in the way railroads in America are being rundown, I had a useless lock.

I thought of calling the attendant, but it wasn't reasonable to expect a lock to be repaired in the middle of the night. What also wasn't reasonable, I got round to some firm self-counselling, was my idiotic behavior, this classic little-woman syndrome.

But dread can be arbitrary, can be as simple and as immediate as mere fatigue or as complex and remote as the stirring of a buried childhood memory. I wondered, and tried to be jokey about it, if, when I was small, I had been scared by a Punch and Judy show.

I was scared now, though I refused to admit it at the time, when the train lurched on sharp bends and the door handle, along with every other fixture, rattled. Often, too, when speed was cut abruptly as we slowed to pass through stations, the door would burst open and mad white platform lights would slice into my berth and, for this flickering chiaroscuro had the look of old black-and-white film, I would be reminded irresistibly of that scene in *Psycho* where the knife stabs repeatedly by the shrieked glare of the naked bulb.

Since that movie, I found myself thinking at one stage, the crazed knife killer bursting into a room had become a mere walk-on in the crime statistics and the discovery of my body—stabbed, garroted or smothered—would not be all that newsworthy, save for the fact, I was doing my best to be sardonic, that my travelling companions were barbershop quartet singers.

I found myself yearning for their voices and their melodic avowals of the wholesome life, but lacking barbershop quartets I had to settle for my mantra of "silly woman, silly woman" in rhythm to the sound of the wheels on the track.

Silly woman, right from the start, in assuming that in taking the train I was leaving Mr. Punch behind in Chicago. My last-minute booking had given me a sense of getaway. But I was wrong, and now I was as strung out as the whistle of the train in the stark darkness.

After that kind of a night, I suppose I was entitled to feel like a refugee as I hauled my luggage across Penn Station to the taxi stand. I told the driver to take me to the Plaza Hotel; I had made the reservation in Chicago and I knew exactly what I was going to do there: hang up the Do Not Disturb sign and sleep myself back to sense. I had been living at an extreme pace for some time now, skimping on sleep and food—only pretzel sticks and cheese dips were left when I got to the club car—and a few hours of rest and a sensible meal would restore me to my accustomed balanced self. It was as simple as that.

I started that therapy by leaning far back in the cab and closing my eyes for a moment or two—but even as we drew out of the rank my head swung involuntarily and I was peering out of the rear window, looking for Mr. Punch commandeering a cab to follow mine. He wasn't in sight. Throughout the ride, though, I was fidgety.

Outside the Plaza, I lingered on the upper steps, waiting for him to emerge from a cab. Cabs drew up, people got out, but he wasn't one of them. Even so, after I had checked in, I took a corner seat in the lobby and watched the entrance in case he had observed my arrival and had told the driver to stop a little distance away in order that he could walk to the hotel and move in on me with his characteristic stealth. If he had appeared, I would have confronted him. Made a scene, even here in the murmuring lobby of the Plaza.

At least I was angry now—a healthy, bracing anger that suddenly left me feeling in charge and upright—and when I went to my room with its calm russet decor and its spaciousness I appreciated how, in the claustrophobic train berth, I had crouched on a stupid, if understandable, fear based on no more than an illusion that I had seen Mr. Punch in the club car. Of course he hadn't been there! Such nonsense! I smiled at how silly I'd been.

I puttered about in the room for awhile; its front windows overlooked Fifth Avenue and had a view of Central Park. I took a shower and afterwards, cozy in a terrycloth robe, I turned down the cover of the bed, patted the pillow in anticipation and crossed to the front windows to close the curtains before my sleep. From the sixth floor, I looked down on Fifth Avenue.

As always, it was choppy with people, a seeming regatta surging on the insignias of multicolored shopping bags from fashionable stores and signalling that only gold braid rated here, the most stylish street in the most stylish city in the world, and anything else was flotsam. I came to New York a few times when I was in television and I used to admire, and feel at home with, its ruthless no-time-for-losers ethos. Now I was no longer sure I felt the same about it. All that energy, all that arrogance, all that push and shove and snarling. Even suicides can be spectator sports here and I remembered some documetary footage I had edited in which a woman stood on the edge of a skyscraper and persons in the crowd down below yelled, "Jump, jump, jump!" But such reflections as I gazed down on Fifth Avenue were no more than musings and I decided that my seeming change of heart about New York was down simply to lack of sleep.

The phone rang. Yawning, I left the window to answer it.

"Hello," I said. No reply. "Hello," I repeated. Still no reply. "Who is this?" I said. The line went dead.

And at that moment I knew who it was. *Him.* He was letting me know he knew exactly where I was. A momentary appearance on the train, and now a silent phone call: that was his style.

The phone rang again.

As I froze, I joined that company of women—until then I had regarded them as inadequates—who were intimidated by mysterious phone calls.

I let it ring four or five times while I scrambled for the lines, the delivery, the general insouciance that would mask my stage fright and project my role as a liberated woman. I picked up the phone.

"A short message," I said. "You *bore* me. A longer message. You are juvenile and pathetic and—"

"Uh?" A man's voice. Flat. Peeved. "No call to come on snotty with me, lady. I'm just a guy tryin' to get through to room six-eleven."

"That's my room. Did you call just now?"

"Yeah. It wasn't Aunt Hetty's voice who answered, so I figured I'd got a wrong number and hung up."

"With nary a word!"

"Wadya expect? The aria from *Madame Butterfly*?"

His name was Bob, he volunteered, as our ridiculous exchange went on and nudged companionability. Bob from Hackensack, New Jersey, and he was downstairs in the lobby trying to contact his aunt, Hetty Ogden from Portland, Oregon, who, when he spoke to her last night, had been in room 611.

"Well, she's not here."

"Obviously not, and I'm real sorry to have troubled you."

"And I'm sorry if I was abrupt with you."

"Hey, this is New York. Abruptness, and worse, comes with the turf. Crazy city."

"I hope you find your aunt."

"She'll be around. You have a nice day, now."

In the jumpy mood I was in—only a few hours later it was all medically explained to me and made sense—my relief as I hung up and accepted that the call had been a genuine mistake was overtaken

almost immediately by a sharp exasperation over the panic I experienced because of the phone calls. In the impatience I now felt with
myself I was no longer sleepy and decided to unpack, reasoning that
the dull order of putting clothes into drawers and on hangers would
act as a soporific. Methodically, I cleared out one suitcase and when
I opened the second one I saw the straw boater—why on earth had I
bothered to pack it?—from the club car revels and suddenly I had no
doubt that Mr. Punch had been on the train. None. Just as he was
here now, not far away, conceivably down in the lobby pretending
to be gruff but ultimately friendly Bob from Hackensack, New Jersey. Why not? Mr. Punch liked playing games.

Abjectly, I sat on the edge of the bed and pulled stray colored
streamers from the straw boater and had the feeling that I was finger-
ing my very nerve ends.

Then, impulsively, I picked up the bedside phone and called the
front desk. Was there, I asked, a Mrs. Hetty Ogden from Portland,
Oregon, staying at the hotel? The clerk politely—he had an Italian
accent—excused himself while he checked the register. Yes, he said,
there was, and did I wish to speak to her? No, I said, I was simply curious to know why I was getting calls for her in my room. He excused
himself again. When he came back on the line he said Mrs Ogden had
occupied room 611 until that morning, afterwards transferring to a
penthouse suite which had not been available when she checked in.
He apologized and said he hoped I had not been too inconvenienced.

No. Just mortified. My hand tightened on the receiver as I tensed
at the way, in that craven check with the front desk, I had buckled
yet again.

Then, a juvenile fury, I hurled the straw boater across the room
and as it spun I realized it was time to fling my hat into the ring in a
strategic way and prove to Mr. Punch—for I couldn't shake the
notion that he had followed me from Chicago—that, undaunted by
him, I was getting on with my business.

And that business, here in New York, was movie research. So I
called the Mayor's Film Office where, and it was as though a clipboard of efficiency was slapping me back into purposeful shape, a

dizzying agenda was promptly proposed for me. My first engagement was for that night, at a police precinct house in the Bronx. A limo would pick me up at the Plaza. I then changed into a lightweight blue suit, simple but stylish, which carried the label of one of Italy's top designers and also conveyed (I chose it with Mr. Punch in mind) the imprint of my persona—organized, decisive and more than a match for any man. As I fastened the buttons, though, I became aware again of the slight trembling, a sort of pulsing, in my right hand. It was nothing; lack of food, perhaps.

Sensibly, I went down to the hotel's coffee shop, ordered a glass of milk and a tuna sandwich. But I left even that modest meal relatively untouched, for I found that chewing and swallowing were rather painful; I ascribed this to no more than a minor stiffness in my neck after the long train journey. Still, the trembling in my hand had ceased, though now—a self-deprecating roll of my eyes—I was feeling alternately hot and then cold.

I remembered the spartan panacea of my gym mistress at convent school—"Wholesome fresh air, my girl!"—and I decided to take it: a walk halfway down Fifth Avenue, in a direct line to Greenwich Village, seemed a splendid idea. And so it turned out to be—for a short time. I was jostled by the crowds, of course, but I did the New York thing and jostled right back. Or I did until, in a manner of speaking, I was tripped up by Mr. Punch.

At Tiffany's I paused to look in one of the windows, which contained only a black sculpting of an Egyptian cat with emeralds for eyes. I was musing on how that slanted green gaze summed up the entirety of the feline spirit when a shadowy face prowled into view on the far side of mine in the window's reflection. A man's face. Long. Gray. The chin curved.

My reaction may have been a gasp or a sharp swallow—possibly the latter, for I seem to recall the same stab of pain as when I tried to eat in the coffee shop—and then I jerked round to face Mr. Punch.

And he wasn't there.

I saw only the emptiness of the crowd, that void mass of set faces. But he *had* been there. All he had to do was step back. Merge. Disappear. Ridiculously, I looked back at the window, as though expecting it to have retained that smudge of face.

Out on the street on my first day in Chicago my fear of Mr. Punch had dissipated, overpowered by the palpable well-meaning of strangers, but here in New York the crowds were denser and had a different constituency of humanity, a greater variety of sizes and a total commonality of cold indifference. That, however, may be no more than a facile excuse for my conviction that he was following me and that he fitted naturally into these merciless crowds.

I moved on, tried to seem unperturbed. And so I paused at other window displays, ostensibly gazing at elegant designer clothes and jewellery, effectively staring into the garish bazaar of my fears as I waited for that face to edge into muzzy view in the glass.

In my hotel room I had sought to put Mr. Punch into place with the studied neatness of my unpacking, but now I acknowledged a drawer that wouldn't shut, a drawer wedged on sheer dread.

"Watch where you're fuckin' goin', lady!" As I turned from a window I bumped into a well-dressed youngish man carrying a briefcase. And that verbal slap brought me round. Once again, I knew anger. Not at the man with the briefcase. At myself. At Mr. Punch. I had indeed to watch where I was going, to find my direction, and I knew exactly what that course should be. *Exactly*.

So I stopped at a hot dog stand, ordered one, proffered twenty dollars, the smallest bill I had, and asked for some quarters for the phone in my change. "No friggin' way," the attendant said, red-faced under a white paper hat with, insincerely, "Have a nice day" printed on it. "Make it a *dozen* dogs," I said. After he had prepared them, after he had followed my fussy instructions for how they should be variously garnished with ketchup, onions, mustard and chillies and in some cases "everything"—in messing him about, I was going through the motions of a larger plan—he handed over my change, which included all the quarters I needed. I moved off. "Hey," he called after me, gesturing at the row of hot dogs I had left behind, swaddled neatly in white paper napkins and taking up valuable counter space. "Hey, lady, what about these babies?" I turned, took out full citizenship of New York. "Put them up for friggin' adoption!" I called back.

It boosted me, that little encounter, set me up for the big move, the latest tilt of my emotional see-saw—which was to stop at the next pay phone and call Harry Korda's office in San Francisco.

After Lou Eggenberg, I had written off Harry Korda. In Chicago I had heard, and seen in print in the magazine proofs, the full story of the treachery that had claimed Johnny's life. It seemed unlikely that Harry Korda could have anything of true substance to add. And what was even unlikelier, given his refusal to cooperate with Lou Eggenberg, was that he would be willing to talk to me; the evidence was that he was a do-it-by-the-book old soldier, that kind never changes, in the mold of Colonel Crinkle.

Lou Eggenberg had called him Judas. But now I had another name for him—patsy. *My* patsy. I was damn well going to *hound* Harry Korda and in the process give Mr. Punch the runaround as I showed that he hadn't scared me off. I would plague Harry Korda's office with calls. I would not be deterred by Tony Donovan, the general manager, saying that his boss had been held up in Alaska—that story was an obvious fob-off—and indeed I would park myself outside Harry Korda's office in the cause of the high visibility expressly designed to defy Mr. Punch and restore my dignity and independence.

And that process was starting promptly. I stopped at a street phone opposite Rockefeller Center. I got out my address book, assembled an ample pile of quarters, tapped out the number and felt I had keyed myself back into self-respect.

"Korda Aviation. Harry Korda speaking."

I was quite nonplussed when he himself answered—I'd expected to deal with another evasion from Tony Donovan—though, smoothly enough, I identified myself and went into the spiel about my academic research project. He said he knew all this from Tony, and, another surprise, when could we get together?

"As sooon as possible. I'm in New York right now, but I could be in San Francisco tonight." I meant it; I *had* to show Mr. Punch.

He said he had a better idea: how about Washington, D.C. tomorrow afternoon? He was flying a consignment of computer parts to Rhode Island overnight and it would be no problem for him to detour from there to Washington and was I willing to fly down on the hourly shuttle from New York?

"You *betcha*!" My use of the Americanism expressed my triumph at trumping Mr. Punch so easily.

We arranged to meet at two in the Adams lounge of the Mayflower Hotel in the capital. "You'll have no trouble spottin' me—I'm a big, lumberin' old relic," he said, just before hanging up.

It was as simple as that. I hung up cockily. A thirty-second phone call and I had swiped Mr. Punch. I felt like swaggering down Fifth Avenue, but the crowds were too packed for that. Also, every now and then as I walked on, I felt a sense of physical swaying, not just here in crowded Midtown, but at various other locations throughout the hours that followed. It was nothing.

I was wrong. That night, in a police precinct house in the South Bronx, I had an experience I had never had before in my generally robustly healthy life—I passed out.

When I came to I was sitting on the floor with my back against a desk, my head cushioned on a police flak jacket. A young, ginger-haired cop was looking down on me, his arms folded sternly, as if I had committed a felony by passing out. A paramedic, on his knees, was shining a small torch in my eyes.

He asked if I often blacked out like this. Never, I said, and made to get up. He eased me down. My temperature was way above normal, he said, my pulse was racing and there were small swellings behind my ears. He tapped gently with his finger at a point just below my earlobe and I winced at the sudden pain.

His guess, he said, was that I had incipient glandular fever brought on by—he was probing my eyes with his torch, pulling down the sockets—sustained exhaustion.

"When did you last have some real sleep, like eight hours' solid?"

"Oh—" I shrugged.

"Yeah," he said, "and it shows. You had mood swings lately?"

"Who doesn't in New York?" I smiled. Brightly.

"Erratic behavior. Ups and downs. Impulses. Irrational fears. That kind o'stuff?"

"No," I lied.

He didn't believe me. "Apart from anything else, your ear mechanism is outa sync—it's part of the glandular trouble—and you've lost some physical balance and your emotional reactions also could be kinda uncertain. Not on drugs, are you?"

"No."

He squinted again, using his torch. "Um." He slipped the torch into a recess in his sleeve. "You go see a doctor, okay? Like first thing tomorrow. A short course o' antibiotics is all you need. For now, concentrate on serious sack time. You need rest. Lotsa rest. Like I said, serious sack time."

In the limo on the drive back to the Plaza I reflected that it was reassuring to know I was sick: it explained my recent jumpy behavior and put everything into proportion. *Everything.* It all added up. Lack of sleep, lack of food, living on my nerves—I'd *imagined* Mr. Punch. Not in Chicago, of course, but that fancied sighting of him in the streamered and honky tonk clamor of the club car—I saw now how easy it was to distort a passing face on the split second—was as vaporish as what I had taken to be his reflection in the window at Tiffany's. At least, I thought, I shopped for my phantoms in the best places! I smiled, amused in my relief, revelling in my minor illness and the proof, in the swellings behind my ears, that I had indeed been making mountains out of molehills.

Along with my key, the night clerk at the Plaza also took from my docket a sheaf of faxed press releases from the Mayor's Film Office and a long and rectangular gift-wrapped package.

I skimmed through the faxes in the elevator, found them irrelevant and glanced at the card on the package. There was no message, simply my name and room number, but the Big Apple motif on the red and silver wrapping left me in no doubt that it was a standard promotional gift from the Mayor's Film Office.

In my room, I put the press releases in the wastepaper basket, dropped the package on the bed and went off to take a long tub. It left me feeling drowsy, relaxed, quite recovered—the paramedic had meant well but I didn't need to see a doctor!

The bedside clock showed 2:55, and in a few hours I would be on my way to Washington to meet Harry Korda, though with Mr. Punch disposed of in my mind that meeting was no longer strictly necessary. But the appointment had been made and I'd keep it, if only to prove to myself that, despite the swooning at the precinct house, I was as strong and resilient as ever.

As I got into bed, the package fell to the floor. I looked down at the Big Apples on the wrapping and the way they were represented as beaming faces with U-shaped dimpled mouths. In my mellow mood, it seemed a trifle churlish to ignore this largesse, despite its commercial motives. I yawned luxuriously, stretched to pick up the package, opened it as negligently as one unwraps complimentary bedtime hotel chocolates.

What I uncovered was a plain cellophane box, padded on the inside with a swathe of white satin—and containing a long-stemmed black rosebud.

Twenty

AT LEAST MR. PUNCH STAYED OUT OF THE DREAM I HAD THAT night. A cold dream, full of the drafts of the doors I kept opening in the parsonage at Haworth. Johnny was in one of those rooms, but I didn't know which one. I blundered from room to room.

My dream derived from a hitherto forgotten memory, which took subsequent shape in my mind, of an afternoon at the parsonage when, crossly, I made it clear I was not prepared to join him in a search for a spinet.

Since the memory explains the dream, or at least part of it, I am putting down what I remember of that day. We were in the Reverend Patrick Brontë's study and Johnny had come across papers, a diary or something, referring to the spinet and the fact that it was played by the sisters on Sunday nights, after evensong, when their father had his small circle of friends round for supper.

These friends were listed in the documents Johnny had found and he mentioned them. A mill owner, the local doctor, an asthmatic wealthy widow, persons of that ilk. I snubbed them, and him, with my silent and aloof impatience. There was no stopping his enthusiasm, though, for now he was reading aloud, and with an air of *real* discovery, to the effect that although Charlotte was held to be the most generally musical of the sisters it was Emily who was accomplished at playing the spinet.

And then he had the notion of looking for the spinet, sure that it must still be in the parsonage. He wanted to start the search at once and after we left the study I positioned myself pointedly at the front door in the hall while he rummaged.

Finally, I knew he had found the damned spinet—and that increasingly was my mood—because I heard him playing it somewhere. I stood there for a minute or two and then I went off to remind him that it was getting late and it was time to leave. I had no idea where he was, whether upstairs or downstairs, so I followed the sound of the spinet.

In my dream, however, in the crazy way of dreams, I was guided not by the genteel tones of the spinet but by the record of playing "I Gotta Gal in Kalamazoo" on his phonograph. Faintly, though. And in my dream it was night and that music scratched the darkness like a match which, once ignited, would surely show his face, his smile. But pinpointing the source of that sound . . .

I opened door after door, saw only the gaunt outlines of Victorian furniture, smelled dust and camphor, the brackenish odor of horsehair sofas and the whiff of old candles—all the pungencies I had come to associate with the parsonage at Haworth. In one room a grandfather clock ticked, a stately foot-tapping to that jitterbug which flitted everywhere. *A, b, c, d, e, f, g, h, I gotta gal in Kalamazoo* . . . I chased the tune along hallways, and up and down stairs.

I reached a door where, positioned to one side, the young gingerhaired cop from the Bronx Precinct House sat, arms folded, on a wooden chair in the sputtering light from a wall gas bracket enclosed by a white globe. He didn't even glance at me and made no attempt to stop me as I opened the door and entered the room.

A woman was writing at a large mahogany desk. Her head was partly turned away from me. A scant coal fire smoldered a dull red, like a festering mood, in a black grate. The flame from a tallow candle in a long pewter holder on top of the desk flicked the woman into emerging form. She was wearing a black dress and her dark brown hair was drawn in a tight bun at the back of her neck. She wrote with a quill pen. Her strokes were quick, emphatic, fierce and the rasp of the pen on the paper made a sound like a wasp trapped in an upended glass. She looked up and saw me. The broad forehead, the hair parted in the middle, the intense eyes and the fullish, though small mouth: I recognized Emily Brontë.

We stared at one another. Then her lips parted slowly and she hissed at me. And I fled.

I rushed down a long hallway. Outside, the wind rose and the house shuffled, but suddenly it was the front-row saxes of the Glenn Miller orchestra that blew at top pitch. *A, b, c, d, e, f, g, h, I*—So near! Indeed, behind this very door before which I now stood, this door with the round glass handle spotted with painted flowers, this door where the ginger-haired cop sat in exactly the same posture as at the other one. He ignored me.

I spent a moment or two patting my hair into place, straightening my dress, recovering my breath, and it was while I was doing this I heard a woman's laughter in the room, above the music. It was a low and knowing laugh, curled in sexuality.

My hand reached out for the glass doorknob and my wrist was seized by the cop. I couldn't go in there, he said. Why not? She was in there with him, he said. She? Miss Scarlett, he said. He was on his feet now and holding both my wrists. She laughed again.

I woke up to the sound of that laughter, though after a moment or two it transmuted into the banter of a couple of maids as they vacuumed outside my room at the Plaza.

I lay there, quite still, and, a bid for cool amusement, reflected that if dreams were the cinema of the skull then what I had just experienced was a re-make of my recurring dream of Haworth. An added dash of Fellini in this version, perhaps!

No breathlessness this time, however, no palpitations—none of the usual side effects of my Haworth dream syndrome. I decided I felt fine. But as I turned my head to check the bedside clock my neck shot with pain and I reminded myself I had incipient glandular fever, or so the paramedic had said. The time was 7:55. I shifted my eyes to the right of the clock and took in another reality—the black rosebud, its stem magnified through the thick glass of the martini pitcher.

It was a real rosebud and I had affected a calm little ceremony, the night before, of unwrapping it, taking the martini pitcher out of the fridge, filling the pitcher with water and putting the flower in it. I even had fussed a little about just where to place it for best show on the bedside table. For this was my trophy, my affirmation that I was not going to be traumatized by Mr. Punch.

Then, a pleased-with-myself smile, I went back to bed—and started to tremble.

Eventually, I slept, but the trembling took another form when the dream reared and I was chasing a jitterbug through the dank rooms of the parsonage at Haworth.

Now, fully awake, I let glandular fever explain away my dream and also make a case for not taking the shuttle to Washington. My health, I reasoned, was more important than my self-respect, than cocking a snook at Mr. Punch.

I glanced at the rosebud.

Then I got out of bed, resolved to keep my appointment with Harry Korda in Washington.

It was a bumpy flight to Washington. The weather had changed overnight. In New York the skyscrapers mourned in low gray cloud, thunder rumbled and on the radio in the cab taking me to La Guardia Airport I heard that a cold front had moved in from Canada and the whole of the eastern seaboard was in a cold snap.

On the aircraft, meanwhile, I endured the tropical heat of my glandular fever or whatever it was and knew I was being stalked from somewhere in the sargasso of the crowded seats behind me.

I had dressed for Mr. Punch. *Power*-dressed. I was wearing my three-piece chartreuse macho suit—trousers slightly flared, waistcoat topped by a broad striped tie, the jacket padded at the shoulders.

Seeking height, I wore my hair piled up. I had on my antique gold necklace with the ruby pendant, a bequest from an aunt I had never known.

My *pièce de résistance*: the rosebud. I had snapped it off and fixed it at my lapel with a safety pin.

I was imposing, grand, a patently strong-willed woman who was impervious to threats. Inside, though, I was a stringbag of aches and raw nerves.

But from the moment I left the hotel I hadn't once glanced back, determined not to compromise my bearing. On the plane, though, I was burning up. I reached for the ventilation nozzle above my head and as I switched it to full its hissing reminded me of the sound Emily Brontë had made in my dream. Stupid dream! Though with that dismissal, I promptly started to think about it, wondering why I had been so agitated by the sound of Miss Scarlett's laughter when, in fact, she had never figured in my mind as a rival. That tenure had been held by Emily Brontë, my intellectual equal, my—such bletherings!

On that note of reproach I determined to clear my mind, but the way I was burning up the hising of the ventilation nozzle now brought to mind the only time I had been in a hospital bed, which was when I had meningitis as a child and oxygen had been rushed to me one night. I drifted back to that experience and then, a sick-room visitor, Mopa, Colonel Crinkle's Indian housekeeper, somehow was at my side, both at the hospital and there on the plane—at my side and reminding me I was in danger.

The plane bumped and I opened my eyes. Obviously, I had fallen asleep; it could only have been a matter of minutes, if that, but it left me feeling a little better. The plane bumped again and the safety-belt sign went on. I clicked my belt into place and promptly, as if such recall was no more than a mechanical function, I was connected with the memory of that day in the parsonage at Haworth when Johnny had searched for the spinet.

The memory gave my dream a structure, provenance, and that helped, but the real bonus was the unexpected discovery of that day

in my mind. I looked back and saw myself locating Johnny in the
attic where he was tinkling with one hand on the keyboard of the
spinet. I worked on that memory with the diligence of a picture
restorer and finally I had the spinet in full view, saw its grainy red
wood and the frieze of wood nymphs on the lid. And all the time he
played with one hand, played a scale that sometimes ventured into a
snatch of melody.

Possibly there would have been more, but the seatbelt sign was
switched off with the usual pinging tone and the spinet notes of the
past ended as if my money had run out on a nickelodeon.

Back to the present, then, and I shook my head when the cabin
crew came round with coffee and Danish—at the hotel I had tried to
eat some breakfast but had to give up because of the discomfort of
swallowing—and half an hour later I was fastening my seatbelt again,
in preparation for landing.

The plane slewed on touch-down as a wet wind gusted across the
runway. Along the corridors and into the concourse at National Airport: I walked purposefully and didn't look back. Nor did I as I stood
in line at the taxi stand, and, in the cab taking me to the Mayflower I
stared straight ahead. In spite of the wind and rain, I made an assured
entrance into the hotel and it was only when I was inside, as I
climbed the steps to the Adams lounge, that my hands started to
shake.

The lounge was quiet, empty, club-like. Sane. I sat down, about
an hour early for my appointment with Harry Korda, in a dark-green
leather armchair, under a portrait of George Washington. My hands
continued to shake. I stared down at them in my lap, tried to will
them into line.

And then I became aware that someone was standing over me,
someone who must have approached silently. I looked up. Saw the
long, gray face. My immediate instinct was to recoil. Instead I said,
"May I have a large brandy?"

The waiter—and he did indeed have a long, gray face, as do many
men—inclined his head deferentially and padded off for my drink.

And I sat there and acknowledged fully—no protest of intellectual superiority—that Mr. Punch terrified me.

It helped, that acceptance. The self-honesty gave me a kind of strength, made me realize that in spite of earlier reservations about the wisdom of that trip to Washington I was right to be there, taking steps to deal with my fear. The waiter arrived with the brandy and it helped too. The shaking of my hands diminished. Soon I was poised enough to pick up that day's newspaper from the coffee table.

There was plenty of sleaze headlined on the front page. Bribe-taking in Congress, sexual harassment in the Justice Department, a young presidential hopeful photographed secretly as he and his wife dined with prominent Mafia figures, senior welfare department officials named in a multi-million-dollar fraud involving the food stamp program for the poor.

The last time I was there was part of a television series on the world's power capitals and my script, inter-cutting between the grotesque slums on F Street and the nearby White House, had carried the coda that Washington was a city of classical architecture and moral dry rot. I meant those words, but didn't *feel* them emotionally.

Had I, I wondered, changed since then? Was I just a little less selfish, that bit more willing to give of myself in matters beyond my career and my ego? I was pondering this possibility—brandy on an empty stomach can be a profound, if specious, influence—when my name was paged and I heard there was a call for me at reception.

It wasn't, as I had thought it might be—and, yes, as I had feared—Mr. Punch. It was Harry Korda. He said he was still in Rhode Island and he wasn't going to be able to make our meeting. Engine trouble, he said.

"Really?" He didn't seem to pick up on my skepticism.

When the repair was done, he said, he would be flying to the Bahamas to start four or five weeks of contract work in the Caribbean. I said I could meet him there. He said his itinerary was an uncertain one. I said I would take my chances. And then I felt weak and dizzy, as if this little conversational zig-zagging had been too much for me.

He had an idea, he said. He would be returning briefly to the States next Wednesday. "Florida. Town called Kissimmee. It's right next door to Orlando. Disneyworld. Any chance you can make it?"

"Yes."

"Swell. The military aviation museum at Kissimmee. It's in the back of the municipal airport. The coffee shop at the museum. Say two o'clock?"

"Very well."

"Sorry to mess you about like this . . ."

Mr. Korda, I am about to do the messing about. I have a hunch, call it an intuitive insight into your shifty character, that you never intended to turn up and you are making this call simply for appearances. What's more, I have another hunch that our next appointment will be another no-show in your Judas trail. I'll be there, however, if only to prove that I am impossible to shake. Impossible. As you will discover in the fullness of time, Mr. Korda . . .

Well, that's what I wanted to say. Or something like that. But I was too disappointed. Suddenly too tired. Too achy.

But I retained my outward *sangfroid* on every step of my return journey to New York—strictly no looking over my shoulder—though once in my hotel I let it all collapse as I sprawled across the bed, uncaring about how I was creasing my suit. I unpinned my hair, kicked off my shoes. It was early evening. I decided on a nap before dinner and though I had no appetite I knew I absolutely must eat a proper meal.

I awakened two or three hours later and was dismayed by what I saw in the bathroom mirror: my eyes were puffy and my hair had tumbled from *haute coiffure* to chaos. A lot of work would be needed to make me presentable for the dining room of the Plaza. I settled for room service. An omelette. A salad. Coffee.

I persevered with that meal and found that if I swallowed very carefully and in tandem with a sip of coffee the pain lessened. I drank the whole flask of coffee, about five cups.

All that caffeine, in combination with my nap, deflected my fatigue. I showered, went to bed, and, realizing sleep was not an immediate prospect, I picked up a book on the bedside table. The book, provided by the hotel for its guests, was an anthology of essays about New York. A ten-minute read, I decided, would lull me to sleep. I read for much longer than that, for at least a couple of hours, absorbed in the book and also feeling stronger; obviously the food had helped. I fell asleep while I was reading.

And then the phone rang.

Where was I? Back in Beverly Hills? My book was still in my hands and open and from the chapter heading I saw I took a blurred map reading: New York, New York. The phone, louder now as my conciousness increased, threw in its own hackneyed contribution: *the city that never sleeps*. I had a feeling it was very late. I peered at the bedside clock. Five to three. Still not properly awake, I had a notion, as I picked up the phone, that it would be Bob from Hackensack, New Jersey, seeking his Aunt Hetty.

"Yes?"

"Cozy?" It wasn't Bob from Hackensack. It was Mr. Punch. I recognized at once his slight lisp, which seemed to drift on the line like a slick.

"What do *you* want?"

"Can't an admirer check in?"

"If you've something to say—" I was physically widening my eyes as I sought alertness and the focus on words that would cut him down.

"I'm *sayin' it. Admirer.* You got *class.*"

"There speaks a connoisseur." I shoved hair out of my face.

"Here speaks a guy with two sharp eyes that miss *nothin'*. Not a thing. And what these eyes saw yesterday was the best dressed chick in New York and Washington. I just couldn't take my eyes off you the whole time. I took in everythin' . . . includin' the rose."

"That was my finishing touch." I was a little more organized now.

"Yeah? And it was also our *final* warnin'."

"Our?" Keep him talking. It was as if I had remembered something I had read contemptuously in a self-help manual for panicked women.

"The, uh, *family* business to which I am affiliated."

"Affiliated? My, that's a long word for someone like you. What's the name of the business? Creep, Creep and Creep? If so, you'll be heading for a junior partnership one of these days." Better.

"A sense of humor yet."

"You can count on it."

"And what you can count on is that we have the last laugh. *Always*. It comes with the contract."

He gave an odd little giggle and I knew his small, cherub mouth, that design fault in the long and gray face, was very close to the phone; I wondered, absurdly, if he was still using the same mint breath freshener as he had that night in Chicago.

What next to say? I floundered. "If you for the remotest moment actually believe you have me running scared then—"

"I know I have, lady." He giggled again. "I knew it that first night in Chicago. I knew it some more on the train to New York when, like they say, our eyes met across a crowded room. I knew it the way you jerked round when you were looking at the cat in that window on Fifth Avenue. And I know it *now*. It's my job to scare people. I love my job. I take it all the way down the line. I scare people to death. *Literally*. And that's another big word I know. Ain't I full of surprises, uh?" Another giggle.

"What you are full of, let me assure you unequivocally, is—"

But it was too late. He had hung up.

I replaced the phone. I sat up in bed, my hands clasped around my raised knees. As methodically as I could, I made myself remember everything that was said in that phone call—which is why I have been able to recall it fairly accurately here—and then I analyzed it, tried to weigh up what was bluff and what was menace in his words. But it wasn't so much what he said that unsettled me as it was his giggle. It had an out of control sound as if, and this seems utterly stupid, he had uncupped those foul hands of his and released a skeetering and squeaking wild creature, like a bat.

Sheer exhaustion shoved me back into sleep, but my dreams flipped like card tricks. A pack of nonsense in which peril was uppermost. I was in my student rooms in Oxford, only they were shaking under the force of an earthquake I had once experienced in Manilla; I was punting on a placid English river, only Niagara Falls raged just around the bend; I was hill walking in the Lake District, only I was about to fall from a peak in the Himalayas.

I awakened about eight and regarded what I dearly wished to see as another absurdity—the black rosebud.

Shortened to fit my lapel for the trip to Washington, it was now in a drinking glass on the bedside table. I had put it there the night before, a symbol of my pride and my resolve; both were shredding now, though, while the rosebud was expanding, ready to bloom.

I stretched out my hand and, a token bravado, flicked one of the petals. It came off, left a little dusting on my fingertip, a dusting which smeared as I rubbed at it with a tissue. I realized, the proof was there on my finger and on the tissue, that the rosebud, far from being an exclusive and sinister mutation, simply had been dyed. As I looked at the spoiled tissue, it was as if some of Mr. Punch's cheap bogey-man makeup had been wiped away. Some. I remembered his giggle, tried to persuade myself that it was just a stock part of his repertoire.

Emotionally, I felt that bit surer as I got out of bed, though physically I was aware of my weakness as soon as I stood up and the room seemed to slope for an instant. My neck was stiff. Gently, I placed my fingers at the back of my ears and felt the swellings there, but so far there was no pain.

I knew that I ought to stay in bed and ask the hotel to lay on a doctor. But after that phone call I wasn't prepared to grant Mr. Punch the satisfaction of thinking he had scared me to stay indoors. It was Friday. I could rest up, seek a doctor, over the weekend. Today, though, Mr. Punch had to see that he had not intimidated me. I called room service and ordered a light breakfast. Then I went to take a shower.

In the bathroom I weighed myself on the scales and discovered that since I had last stood on scales, only two or three weeks ago, I had lost nearly nine pounds. I washed my hair, dried it carefully, avoiding any brisk movement that might set off the pain behind my ears. I took some time applying eyeshadow to conceal the puffiness and the dark rings under my eyes.

Room service had come while I was in the bathroom and my breakfast tray was on the bedside table, along with the *New York Times*. I sat on the edge of the bed and took a sip of coffee and a nibble of toast, but the moment I swallowed pain stirred behind my ears. I made myself drink half a cup of coffee, but I wasn't prepared to wince my way through toast and grapefruit. Once at Oxford I took part in a two-week hunger strike protesting against the jailing of a woman activist who had stabbed her drunken husband in self defense, and I hadn't come to any harm then. Nor would I now. I had some kind of little bug, yes, but it wasn't life-threatening and neither, I glanced at the phony black rosebud, was Mr. Punch.

I felt totally confident suddenly, in a fuzzy kind of a way, and I was humming as I flipped through my wardrobe to see what I should wear. As I shoved aside blouses and suits I also rejected the ready-made words of the paramedic as I remembered him asking me if I had experienced sudden mood swings. He was doing his best to diagnose my condition, but who did he think he was—Schweitzer, Pasteur? I smiled.

The weather was sunny again and the forecast in the newspaper was for highs in the low eighties. Sure of myself, I decided I had no need for the boost of designer clothes and I chose a simple lime-colored dress. I put on flat heels. No power dressing today. No special effects. Just the rosebud. I wadded the back of it with tissue to prevent dye stains and pinned it to my collar.

Out into the crowds and the noise and the competition simply to keep in step and I revelled in my adrenaline-powered progress down Fifth Avenue . . . until my mood faltered a little. It didn't exactly go into reverse, but I found myself window shopping for a face that could so easily insinuate itself at the edges of the glass and the wilderness of my fears.

But that phase was short-lived, straightened out by a schedule planned by the Mayor's Film Office and paced to a New York tempo that kept me so busy I had no time to dwell on Mr. Punch. I seemed to spin from interview to interview.

I had been looking for a cab on 34th and Broadway since finishing my final interview of the day. They all zoomed by, taken.

I decided to walk on, thinking my prospects would be better the nearer I got to the theater district, when I came across a display of horror masks at a theatrical costumery on Broadway. Until then I had been strolling, generally satisfied with the progress of the day. Thereafter, though, my steps quickened slightly and my hand signals sharpened and my easygoing acceptance that cab hunting was one of those competitive sports of New York started to erode. I became aware that I was tired and soiled and that my shoes pinched. And that Mr. Punch was out there, watching me.

I did my best not to own up to his presence, beyond assuring myself that he was no more than a nuisance and that my desire to be back in my room at the Plaza was not flight but a perfectly natural need for the rest which, apart from anything else, would set me up for the strategy of giving him the runaround.

The cabs continued to ignore my wavings and, as though unwarily I had crossed a frontier into a territory that was extreme even by the standards of this city, I was in Times Square—that howling epicenter of New York with its shock waves of noise and crowds and its chill furnace of neon.

After the relatively sedate office blocks I had traversed in the mid-
and upper-thirties and even, just back there, the fringes of the forties,
Times Square pitched and frothed on a dementia of sounds and lights
and raw smells of cooking. On top of a building an electric rooster
the size of a dinosaur shrilled nonstop against a psychedelic sunrise
and on another billboard that was bigger than an Olympic swimming
pool monster multicolored bubbles rose and fizzed audibly in the
promotion of a soft drink. The same hoarding also showed the time
(5:05 P.M.), the temperature (84 degrees), the humidity (78), the
pollen count (high), the air quality (poor) and, with a neon stork
flapping its wings to show the latest maternity addition, the up-to-
the-minute population of New York (8,147,343). I mentally noted,
and memorized, these figures (inexplicably, they have stayed with
me) as if keeping a score card of my sanity.

The population count changed to 8,147,344 and as another baby
howled its way into New York my panic whimpered. They were all
here in Times Square surely, all those 8,147,344 New Yorkers—the
sign promptly updated to 8,147,345—pushing and heaving around
me. And so was Mr. Punch. The back of my ears surged sudden pain.

I kept my hand raised, a supplicant for one of those hundreds of
yellow cabs that blared amid the gray and black stretch limousines
with the look of flashy funeral caskets and, somehow, a quintessential
New York gaze entombed in their unfeeling opaque windows.

And then I thought of my own plight, there in Times Square, the
most teeming hub in America, where any kind of violence was possible. Times Square was potentially the deadliest place in the world,
with twenty to thirty psychopaths present, or so one of my inter-
viewees had told me, in every thousand of its throngs at any given
moment. And one of them, I *knew*, was Mr. Punch.

I was tempted to turn my head to see if I could spot him. I resisted
that, but I let panic break other rules of my self respect. I started to
sweat heavily and suddenly I was breathless and as my lungs and my
heart thudded it seemed that the gusts of Times Square were the
winds of Haworth, come to seek me out. I remembered Mopa, back
in Arizona, saying I was hunted by a wind and as I recalled her flat

Indian features the slash of a quill pen promptly erased them and I was staring into the face of Emily Brontë that night she had hissed at me in my dream, her teeth showing on that feral sibilant.

Now, blundering in those crowds, I felt everyone was hissing at me. The huge cop with the toothpick at the side of his mouth. The bag lady in the stained white dress. The wild-eyed sandwich-board man yelling about apocalypse. The young blonde who was seeking to get by me as she maneuvered one of those large black artwork portfolios. Everyone was hissing. All except the bald taxi driver with the squat Greek nose.

"Ya wanna travel or don'cha, lady?" He was looking up at me, his hand tapping the steering wheel, the bored proof that even in the midst of my personal storm I had continued hailing a cab.

"The Plaza," I said, and I was surprised at how very normal my voice sounded.

At the hotel I supplemented the Do Not Disturb sign I had hung outside my room door by phoning the front desk and requesting that any calls for me should be held until further notice—my way of making sure that there was no infiltration by Mr. Punch as I settled down to taking the paramedic's advice that I needed "serious sack time."

I took a long bath and in its perfumed steam the pain at the back of my ears dissipated and I thought I could risk putting off seeing a doctor—the few times in my life I had sought medical advice I always felt I was compromising my independence—until the next day. I settled, without appetite, for another room service meal, a souffle with asparagus tips, and I chewed and swallowed tentatively and drank lots of coffee to aid that process.

Now, in bed, I brooded a little over my ridiculous behavior in Times Square; what with that and swooning in the police precinct I was really fluttering my "little woman" feathers. I grimaced, opened the book of New York essays. I read until 8:10 P.M.: I checked the time as I switched off the light.

I was awakened by a series of thuds, one of which, louder than the others, appeared to have come from right behind my door. I got up. It was daylight. The thuds carried on, a rhythm, receding now. I opened the door, and shortly before he turned the corner of the corridor, I saw a bellboy riding what looked like a power-driven golf buggy as he dropped off the *New York Times* on doormats.

I picked up my copy, surprised by how heavy it was. Then I saw, incontrovertibly there on the masthead, that this was the Sunday edition. Sunday? I had gone to sleep mid-evening on Friday and now here it was, I glanced at my watch, 7:15 on Sunday morning: I actually had slept for two whole days.

I needed both my hands to carry the paper, all twelve pounds of it, and as I let it fall on a chair another weight dropped from me as I realized, now that I was fully awake, that I felt not only rested but fully recovered. My deep snow of sleep showed no tracks of dreams and I had emerged from it feeling whole. I checked the sides of my ears. No swelling. No pain. No temperature. *And* I had a huge appetite.

I called room service and ordered breakfast. Scrambled eggs, bacon, sausages, pancakes, croissants and marmalade, orange juice, coffee. As I hung up I saw that the rosebud, and I hadn't forgotten to place it in its usual position, had opened fully and was beautiful.

I crossed to the side windows, opened the curtains and looked out over Central Park. It pulsed with joggers, young New Yorkers whose strides and dress combined the Darwinian principle of survival of the fittest with a dedication to sportswear designer chic. The running suits flowed and sparkled many colors in the sun in a tapestry that suggested a religious festival, a pilgrimage by these high priests and priestesses who had found the holy grail New York demands of its votaries—the gold-plated credit card.

After breakfast, I rustled through sections of the newspaper. New York, I discovered *en passant*, had once again emerged as number one in a poll of the most selfish and boorish cities in the world. I crossed to the window again, looked out across the park. And knew what I had to do. Jog.

•   •   •

I've always exercised and, traveling, I routinely pack a track suit and running shoes. My first steps as I left the Plaza and turned left into the park were hesitant, and I began to wonder if I had overestimated my recovery, if I had succumbed to another mood swing. I got some contemptuous glances from my fellow joggers, who no doubt not only found me guilty of poor stamina but also, I was wearing an unpretentious gray track suit, a lack of sartorial standards.

Soon, though, the style was all mine. I have long legs—dancer's legs, as Lou Eggenberg observed—and they responded to a swiftly developing flow of energy, fuelled by my hefty breakfast, in which I outpaced everyone. As I overtook them, in their fancy suits and jewelled sweat bands, I realized I was not merely celebrating my return to health—I was giving Mr. Punch a full installment of that run for his money which had taken me to Washington and which tomorrow, I made the decision on the spot, would be taking me to Florida for that *supposed* meeting with Harry Korda.

It didn't really matter that he was unlikely to turn up. What mattered was that I was in the lead, tracking him down doggedly, and, the whole purpose of the exercise, demonstrating to Mr. Punch that up against this lady he was a non-starter.

A trier, though—I had to grant him that. But why? Why all this effort to discourage me from asking questions about Johnny? All these years later, the circumstances of his death could have no possible significance. But, as Lou Eggenberg had said, bureaucracy was baroque, though against that was my feeling that Mr. Punch was in no way bureaucracy, or not in the accepted sense.

These were familiar musings. That sleepless night on the train I had tried to ponder them. Now, clear-headed on the jog, I accepted that I was unlikely to ever find the answer. I was ready to settle for my pride and, for a change, keeping Mr. Punch on the run. Simply for the hell of it, I put on an extra spurt.

I did two full circuits of the park and ended up, resting against a clump of ornamental rocks, half-watching the regular Sunday morning marionette show in the children's zoo. There I mused on the two men who had been pulling my strings—the knee jerks occasioned by one and the way the other had yanked me all the way to Washington for an appointment he had never meant to keep. *Punch* and *Judas*, I thought, pleased with my pun. From now on, though, *I* was the puppet master. And that, I knew, was no mood swing. My fever, glandular or otherwise, had broken in that long sleep and left me restored and ready to be a winner again.

In my room, after my shower, I luxuriated in a curl-up-and-read session in which I finshed the collection of New York essays.

The one I liked best was by the travel writer Jan Morris, taken from her book *Manhattan 45*, an evocation of the city as it was at the end of World War II. Jan Morris is Welsh and, like a Celtic harp strum, her elegant opening echoed the distant foghorn of the *Queen Mary* as it nosed into the misty entrance of New York harbor on June 20, 1945. The ship's passengers: the first of the GIs, 14,526 of them, to come home.

They sailed into a New York that was as effervescent as the world's most powerful fireboat as it saluted the *Queen Mary* with a liquid skyscraper of twenty thousand gallons a minute while hundreds of other craft let rip with every siren, hoot and general noise-maker at their disposal. Overhead, like a plump old admiral, a US Navy dirigible waddled and silvered in the rapidly clearing sky.

The boys *and* the gals—a woman lieutenant nurse waved a pair of black lace panties from a porthole of the *Queen Mary*—were home and New York was cheerleading them as well as its role as a place where every kind of hope and noble aspiration could settle and soar, in keeping with the skyline of the city.

The spirit of that day burst the twelve-and-a-half-mile boundaries of Manhattan island and spilled coast to coast and proved now that once there *had* been a wholesome land that rejoiced in its strength and its bounty and its potential to shape the world for the better.

New York, though, was the place to be that day; it was the mood of the nation, the setting of an unsurpassed showtime in which Camelot wasn't the plug nickel of cliche but the newly minted big silver dollar of hope . . .

"All the signs were that it would be the supreme city of the western world, or even the world as a whole. New York in 1945 saw itself . . . as representing a people 'to whom nothing is impossible.' "

There were only 1.9 million New Yorkers in those days, a manageable population, and a Gallup poll found that fully 90 percent of them were happy with their lives.

Happy New Yorkers? That today seems a contradiction.

But on that day in 1945 and for a short span of following years New York was happy, was the fountainhead of a feel-good factor, the phrase unknown at the time, that drew its strength from every part of the nation.

"The moment of grace soon passed . . . New York was never to lose its excitement, its power to move, its limitless energy; but never again, perhaps, would it possess the particular mixture of innocence and sophistication, romance and formality, generosity and self-amazement, which seems to have characterized it in those moments of triumph."

In some of those quoted words—in innocence and sophistication, romance and formality—I recognize Johnny and appreciate how much he was bound up with the ethos and the mythos of that old and fleeting New York, and what could be construed as having once been the American soul.

Could be: I insert my marker of caution, unwilling to be unequivocal about such a vast and corporate summing up.

All the same, *perhaps* if he had survived to come down the gangplank of the *Queen Mary* on June 20, 1945, or on any of the subsequent troopships, his qualities *perhaps* would have had a seminal and lasting influence. And so, here in my final night in New York, I offer up my one-word epitaph on the possibilities of his life . . . *Perhaps.*

Florida

Twenty-one

ART DECO AT ITS MOST PLAYFUL ROMPS THROUGH THE ARCHI-
tecture of Miami's skyline and fronts the roots of much of the city's
growth—the American gothic of mob money.

Those funds financed many of the fancy buildings, with their
streamlined geometry of glass and steel and their sheened legitimacy
for money laundering from every kind of racket, particularly the
business, once a sideline and now a vast industry, of shipping in
drugs from Colombia and other points in South America and the
Caribbean.

That transportation is its own art form: a nonstop legerdemain in
which, planes, usually flying at night without navigation lights and
below the level of radar, land on remote strips, and cabin cruisers,
ostensibly on charter for marlin and swordfish, cut their engines and
nose into deserted reefs.

The furtive cargoes firm up the commissioning of newer and even
more extravagant skyscrapers from inspired international architects. I
can't decry the visual style of Miami. That said, I could be writing in

this mode because another kind of blueprint preoccupies me—a design in which formerly tangent lines have joined and I now know exactly how Johnny died.

I even know the fate of Alice, or Alicia. And, all around, a very great deal more. A whole shattering pattern, which I hold numbly in my mind.

Once again, I have the compulsion to write it down without delay; once again, I am simply not up to this task, not immediately, and I must put those words on hold until they form and assume their own totality in the sequence of events. It's the only way.

Back to where I started, then, in my bid to be coolly observant—back to Miami, my first stop in Florida, with its jubilant blue tropical skies, its chorus-line symmetry of voluptuous palm trees, its gee-but-it's-great-to-see-you tourist market smiles.

And its reek of gangsters.

By which I mean a smell that seemed to be a compound of sea-soned cigar leaf and something sickly sweet, like decaying lilies, and while no doubt it was local vegetation it assailed me the moment I left the plane and became instantly evocative.

It reminded me of a holiday in my youth in Sicily. In the village where we were staying—I was there with a group of fellow students from Oxford—the mayor, a man in his eighties, died, and on the day of his funeral mourners, nearly all of them men, arrived from Palermo and Messina in limousines and even a couple of helicopters. We thought it great fun and we joked about all the dark glasses and the cardinal who was imported to lead the requiem, he was one of those who arrived by helicopter, and the awful splendor of the wreaths which were unloaded from the boots of the limousines by chauffeurs. The combined aroma of the wreaths and the burning of incense from every house swamped the village and it was something very much like that smell, though on a subdued scale, which assailed me in Miami and I was aware of it for the two days and nights I spent there. Mr. Punch, and I had no doubt he had followed me, must have felt at home in Miami. But he was no longer a cause to bother me; I, with a pigheadedness that passed for principle, was out to *bother* him.

I was early for my appointment with Harry Korda in Kissimmee (though of course I didn't really expect him to show), so, as a time filler, I joined the rest of the pilgrims, and the flight from Miami was full of them, to the latter-day Lourdes where the Disney deity delivers up its miracles.

I went there as a heretic, ready to sneer at the quasi-religiosity of the Magic Kingdom, with Tinkerbell as its resident cherub (an irradiated model of her flickered around the concourse of Orlando airport in accompaniment to a celestial intoning of "When You Wish Upon a Star") and where, surely, the marshmallow had been substituted for the communion wafer. But I ended up, if not converted, at least ready to concede that a certain ersatz sacrament had been brought off by the planners.

I tried to resist Main Street, but in the end I took to it. I took to its Victorian general stores and soda fountains and its working bank with its mahogany counters and polished brass grilles behind which mustachioed tellers wore wax collars. I took to the Model T Ford that ambled along at five or six miles an hour and to the newspaper boy in knickerbockers and a floppy button-down cap who held up his papers and piped, "Extra, Extra—the Wright Brothers Make the First Heavier than Air Powered Flight! Read all about it!"

I wondered how Mr. Punch was taking all of this. Just as I was certain that he had followed me from New York to Miami—though I hadn't seen him or heard from him—so I knew he had to be watching me now. And—good!—hating Main Street.

Main Street suited me, though. Not that I was deceived. This wasn't replication; it was the American Dream on snooze time, a forty winks to a way-back-when that had never existed, or not on those fine lines, those soft shadings. But I was content to be lulled for a while.

"And fuck you too, sweetheart!"

Suddenly there was graffiti on dear old Main Street, a rip in that lustrous drape of the past, as a young man pushing a go-kart in which a child wailed moved by me and argued with his wife.

"It was your idea to come here, shithead," she snapped back.

And then they were gone—and so was my mood. I became aware that other families—not all of them, but enough to stand out—were not having the time of their lives. Parents tetched, children bawled, and the sauntering spirit of Main Street withered in the slouch of present-day bile and boredom.

Still, having been brought up by guardians, no doubt I am an incompetent observer of the family scene and its vagaries. It simply seemed to me that fretfulness on the scale I saw had no justification in this theme park with its sweeping monorail in the sky, its lagoons and fountains, its white uniformed oompah band that promenaded every half hour.

This was the big prize for Happy Family finalists—I recalled the awfulness of a religious quiz show I had seen in Texas, with its inducements of "heaven sent" trips to Disneyland—and it had soured. On a bench in front of a bow-windowed store on Main Street I noticed a family of six or seven, mom and dad and children in a range from about five to fourteen, huddled like troglodytes as they watched a portable TV, which they had set up on the ground in front of them. They jabbed away at the remote control which they passed from hand to hand, sharing it like a reefer in that addiction which had subverted and sublimated the old restlessness of the American spirit—channel surfing. I thought of the title of a recent academic report on this mindless bondage: The Dumbing of America.

"Extra! Extra! The Wright Brothers Fly!" The newsboy chirruped away, an ignored little chorister, and it struck me that his street corner notes echoed the whole ethos of a former America. "Extra! Extra!" That once was the call-sign of this country as it used the exclamation mark as its baton in a nonstop parade of quest, audacity and style. Now it channel surfs.

I chided myself for hasty generalization and decided it was time I made my way to Kissimmee for my notional meeting with Harry Korda and the next phase in my baiting of Mr. Punch.

Twenty-two

THE MILITARY AVIATION MUSEUM AT KISSIMMEE TURNED OUT also to be an operational airfield geared to the refuelling of vintage aircraft—as well as, in the playing of World War II melodies on background tapes, the topping up of high octane nostalgia.

I sat by the window, overlooking the runway, in the cafeteria while massed squadrons of saxophones swooped and glided—Glenn Miller and Tommy Dorsey predominated on the tapes—and I watched as, now and then, old planes bumped into landings or heaved into takeoffs.

I found it all diverting enough; indeed, recognizing the tunes and one or two of the planes from the filming in Yorkshire, I had a silly sentimental sense of returning to base.

But that mellowness went into a gradual meltdown that was marked by the increasing frequency by which I began to check my watch. At three o'clock, which was an hour late for our appointment, I accepted that Harry Korda wasn't going to show, and the fact that this time he hadn't phoned through with an excuse proved he'd never had any intention of coming.

This was what I had expected, so why was I feeling so absurdly disappointed? Was it because in my heart I had wanted him to keep his word as a sort of tribute to Johnny—come on, the man was a Judas!—or was it that I had let myself down by embarking on this ridiculous stunt of hounding him simply to defy Mr. Punch? Couple of deadbeats. "Punch and Judas." They weren't worth my time, my pride, my intelligence.

These were my thoughts, and my accompanying snap decision to call it quits and return to Beverly Hills and the better class of boredom there, when a twin-engined aircraft came into view on the runway.

As it drew nearer, I saw it was a Dakota; we'd had a couple of them in Yorkshire. It trundled to the grass area, where visiting aircraft parked. Someone once said to me—I think it was Colonel Crinkle—that Dakotas were the Don Quixotes of aviation, and this one merited that description: it was the dusty color of battered pewter and as its propellors wound down I had the impression of gauntlets shed after a long trek. My interest in it was no more than a musing, something to take my mind off my previous thoughts.

After a few moments, the fuselage door was opened and a steel ladder put in place from inside. A man in a lumberjack-style tartan shirt and gray slacks came down the ladder. A tall man. He went out of sight under the wing and when he appeared, moving toward the cafeteria, I was able to see how really tall he was—at least six feet three or four. White-haired. Old. But his lank frame was in no way bent by age, though his walk seemed curiously out of date: he walked, it struck me as he came nearer, like one of those law 'n' order frontiersmen of Hollywood caricature. A paced, wary walk in which he glanced fractionally from side to side and in which his hands, his fingers flexed, hung loosely and moved back and forward in a rhythm that echoed both alertness and independence.

I think I knew at once he was Harry Korda.

And, even more surely, I knew he wasn't Judas Iscariot: he was more like, I had to smile, Gary Cooper.

•   •   •

He entered the cafeteria hesitantly, stood and looked around for a moment or two. I raised my hand slightly. He nodded. As he came forward, I tok out my tape recorder, put it discreetly on the table, pressed the play button.

"Miss?"

"Mr. Korda?"

He sat down, apologized for his lateness, said it was due to head-winds in the Caribbean and that sunspot activity over Florida had disrupted communications and he had been unable to raise Kissim-mee and leave a message for me. His voice was quiet, shy, but there was nothing tentative about his gaze—he looked at me levelly. His eyes were gray and serious and, notwithstanding the hugely grinning young man in the group photograph I had of the crew, I had the impression that he had stopped smiling long ago and that life had passed over his face like a storm, leaving a debris of hardy wrinkles in his squared face. His hair was oddly youthful, though, cut short with a fringe straggling his forehead.

I asked if he would like a coffee and something to eat perhaps and he said no thank you, Miss, and turned—a task for a man of his reserve—to the preliminary obligation of small talk: was I enjoying my experience of America? I responded with a few conversational postcards, glossy impressions of places I had visited. He listened earnestly, as though I were talking wisdom, and then, almost abruptly during a pause in my trivial monologue, he said, "You're a ringer for her."

"I remind you of someone?"

"Sure do, Miss. Johnny's girl."

"Alice," I said and wondered, peripherally, if this supposed resem-blance—Dante Centofanti and Lou Eggenberg had commented on it, though less definitely than now—somehow had been a causal influence in what happened to me in Yorkshire.

"I didn't figure on you knowin' about Alice."

"She was mentioned to me by two of the old crew. Dante Cento-fanti and Lou Eggenberg."

"Those guys are still around, uh?"

"And with highly serviceable memories."

"What do they remember?"

"Everything." I paused. "Most of all that their captain was murdered."

Those words, spoken casually, were my Judas test: if he had tensed, shuffled, blinked, looked away, showed any signs of evasiveness, he would have vindicated Lou Eggenberg's verdict about him. He merely nodded.

"Yes, Miss, he was." He was sitting upright, his hands—big, uncomplicated hands—resting on the arms of the white plastic chair.

"And you're willing to talk about it?"

"I'm here."

"Frankly, I was led to believe that you—well, that you weren't cooperative."

"I guess Lou Eggenberg might have put that thought into your mind."

"Actually, yes. He said you had refused to have anything to do with a magazine article he was preparing."

"Old men and their grudges, uh? Still, it was some bust-up we had. I just couldn't get Lou to understand why there was no way I could speak out. No way."

"Yet you're willing to talk now?"

"Sure." He leant back a little in his chair, like a man settling into the witness stand. He brought his hands together, his fingers interlocked, at his knees. I trusted those hands. "For the first time since it happened I'm—I'm open to questions. I know a lotta answers. The full story, no less."

"I'm grateful for that, of course"—I eased up the volume on the tape recorder—"though I'm somewhat surprised, after what I was told, as to why you should be so suddenly forthcoming."

"I guess because it's late in the day. *My* day. And because I was impressed by your, uh—your credentials."

"The fact of my academic research?"

"Uh? Oh, that." He shrugged, politely dismissive. "No, I saw your credentials, in a manner of speakin', when they showed me your photograph."

"My—my photograph? *They?*"

"The two fellas who called on me when I got back from Alaska for a couple of days. I'd shipped in a cargo from Nome to Seattle and I had time to spare before I went back to Alaska to see out the rest of the contract, so I flew across to San Francisco to check out a few things in the office and to see if—"

"These men," I said, and tried to cover the brusqueness of my cut-in—I was unsettled by what he had said about strangers in possession of my photograph—with an engaging smile.

"They came callin' that first afternoon. Tony was out. Tony Donovan. My manager. He said to say hi to you."

"And I to him. These men?"

"Hoods. They just walked in. I guess they'd seen too many bad movies because one of 'em just stood at the door and the other one pulled up a chair and put his foot on the desk. He said, the one in the chair—he was young, his hair done in a ponytail—that they had some professional advice to give me. I asked what profession they might be in and this kid, couldn't have been more than twenty-five, said he guessed they were troubleshooters.

"I figured it was a local shakedown, we get them from time to time, and I said what kind of trouble might I be lookin' at. At which point the fella standin' at the door said, 'This kinda trouble,' and he came across and put your photograph on my desk. The kid in the chair took over again and said for me to keep the photograph and study it real hard. Would you care to see it?"

I nodded. He had brought his flight bag with him and now he unbuckled it, took out the photograph and passed it to me. It appeared to be an enlargement, about fivefold the original size, of my passport picture and I hoped I had journeyed on in my development as a human being since it was taken for it showed me—the unsmiling set of my eyes, the haughty inclining of my head—at my supercilious worst. I looked at it for a few moments, then gave it back.

"He said, the kid in the ponytail, that you were out to make serious mischief," he went on as he returned the photograph to the bag, "and that if I wanted to stay in business and be healthy all round—he was a giant of a kid and I figure he was lined up to do most of the talkin' so he could scare the bejesus out of an old man—I should have strictly nothin' to do with you. I said for him to hold on there, sonny, and that if he wanted to make sense he could start by identi-fyin' himself."

"Did he?"

"Nope. Maybe he was riled at bein' called sonny. I was riled as well on account he thought I was a pushover old man. I told him I didn't do business with men with no names and for him and his buddy to get the hell out of my office. They did. But slowly. Like they thought they'd scared me. What they had done was made me good and mad, which doesn't happen often. Guess that's why I'm here. 'Cos I got mad. That and your photograph, of course."

"It's just a passport picture—nothing special," I said, a fill-in while I tried to adjust to that latest proof of the steps that were being taken against me.

"It was special for me, Miss. Like I said, I saw your, uh, credentials in it. I saw Alice. Not detail for detail exactly, but you've sure got her eyes. Proud eyes. Kind of Asian. She was Russian. From the far eastern part. Tashkent."

I'm half Russian. My mother was from Leningrad. She was a ballerina of no distinction whatsoever who defected when her company was on a tour of the West. I promptly dismissed my Russian links as a coincidence in the context of what Harry Korda was saying.

"Johnny and Alice figured on marriage," he said. "Only they had to keep that under wraps on account that if it became known, officially known, it seemed kinda likely she'd be sent back to Russia. She got out only because her father had the money to bribe the right people. She was a war artist."

"I know," I said, more absorbed in my own situation—two men touting my photograph—than in Alice. But Alice meant a lot to Harry Korda.

"Her father's last words to her before she left was that she must never return. I guess he knew somethin'. 'Cos one day Alice gets a message through the Red Cross that the whole family's been arrested and shipped off to Siberia or someplace. Johnny reckoned that the Russians wanted Alice as well but they hadda stay their hand because she was on a kinda goodwill loan to the Allies. He was doin' his darndest to try to find a way of gettin' her to the States. Only as things turned out they weren't goin' anywhere, except—"

He broke off and a brooding filled his eyes. At least I had the good sense to stay further questioning. He took a toothpick from the holder on the table and, methodically, began to prick the back of his hand with it, as if in some improvised acupuncture for an old pain. He kept his eyes on his hand, where the proddings were raising little white spots.

"I showed Tony your photograph," he said finally, still prodding, still with his gaze on his hand. "He said you were the English girl who wanted to see me, which I'd already figured, and I asked him if he saw anything of Alice in you. He hardly remembered Alice, which is fair enough after all this time. But I *remember* her. Guess I was closer to her than any of the others on account that Johnny and me were best buddies. We'd often go out as a threesome—that way, the RAF couldn't think Johnny and Alice were serious—and we'd usually end up at this little village that Johnny liked."

"Haworth," I said.

He looked up then, perhaps a little surprised. "Sure," he said. "Haworth."

He placed the toothpick between the balls of his thumbs—in retrospect, it seems to me he may have needed this tiny prop to express the puniness of life—and applied pressure until it snapped. He placed the two broken pieces of the toothpick carefully on the table and then sat back and considered me.

"Haworth was where Johnny bought it," he said. "Just up from the village. On the edge of the moor."

•   •   •

There is something almost commemorative about the long silence that follows on the tape—a silence of more than a minute—and then, like a ragged fanfare, the sound of an aircraft engine is heard.

It was a yellow aircraft, single-engined, newly arrived on the runway.

"That's a Harvard," he said, glancing at the plane. "Johnny and me did our flight training on Harvards."

"Really?"

"Good ship."

I went on to show a bright, too eager interest—anything to defer the question of the manner of Johnny's dying—as he essayed the maneuverability and stability of the Harvard. He clearly felt as I did, for after enthusing about the Harvard he declared that the Dakota was the best ship ever built, that it flew itself and was ideal for the vast distances and the brawling climate of Alaska. He talked about his affinity with that terrain, especially as viewed from the sky, but in the end Alaska left us circling the circumstances of Haworth—or anyway, more specifically, the chaos he found when he returned to San Francisco after the second leg of his latest Alaskan trip.

"Guess those fellas weren't kiddin' about trouble. I mean, I'd been gone only a few days and in that time the bank had been on saying they were reevaluatin' our credit, and the insurance company was threatenin' to triple our rates. A couple o' contracts we've had for like twenty years had been cancelled, just like that. Also the FAA in Washington was takin' a sudden interest in me, sendin' me all kinds of questionnaires and—point is, at my age I'm not supposed to fly as a commercial pilot. I get round this by usin' a couple of young freelance pilots. Their names go down on the flight manifest and I'm down as a flight supervisor. A lotta the time I use these pilots. But sometimes, like today, I—where's the harm? My health's okay, I don't drink when I'm flyin' and I'm in nobody's way. Except . . . except those two fellas who are out to show me how easily my wings could be clipped.

"I hadda be sure, though. So I called an outfit that specializes in electronic detection. They ran a sweep of my phone line, and there's a bug on it. There's also a couple of bugs in the office and one in the room behind I use as my private quarters."

"But—but why?" I paused. Then, wearily, I repeated the question, as much to myself as to Harry Korda. "Why?" This whole campaign to forestall enquiries into the death of a forgotten young man in an all but forgotten war: *why?*

"I think I've got the answer to that, Miss," he said. "And, in a twisted way, I guess it makes sense. Adds up. We'll get to it in due course, if that's okay with you."

In due course sounded like old-man-speak for digressions and the repetition of things already told me by Dante Centofanti and Lou Eggenberg, but I nodded and even threw in a smile.

"You got Alice's smile," he said. "Her voice too. She spoke perfect English. Upper-crust, y'know? When you called me from New York askin' to see me it was just like listenin' to Alice."

"Only," I said, "you were listening to trouble. I—I didn't mean to complicate your life like this."

"You haven't. Tell the truth, you've put things kinda straight for me. I mean, the day you called was only two or three days after I found I was bugged. I was sittin' there broodin' about the pickle I was in and the phone rang and it was you and—You know how it is when a decision comes to you suddenly and you know, a gut knowin', that it's right?"

"I think so."

"That's how it was for me when you called from New York. I knew—just knew—that I hadda carry this thing all the way through. I owed the truth to Johnny and to Alice and—and to me. That's why I said loud and clear—for the sake of the third party on the line—that I'd fly from Rhode Island to Washington to meet you the next day. That cargo could have waited a week or two, it was in my warehouse makin' money for me in storage fees, but there was no way *I* could wait.

"When I hung up I felt like I was in business again—as a man.

Those two fellas had treated me like a stooge. An old stooge who would cave in and sell his pride—and I'm not like that, Miss. No matter what Lou Eggenberg thinks of me, I'm not like that."

"I know you're not."

"Yeah?" He half smiled. "But I guess you had your doubts when I didn't show in Washington."

"Well—"

"That day, I got back from the freight office at Wilmington airport and found the fuel lines on the ship had been tampered with Very expertly. Someone was out to make sure I was grounded."

I sighed. I listen to it now on the tape: a drawn-out, bona fide sigh, the evidence of a solicitousness I once would have scorned.

"Look, Mr. Korda," I said, "this is all too risky for you."

"Only to my social life. Ship wouldn't fly I couldn't keep our date."

"Even so, I think we should shake hands now and—and leave it at that. Your safety, your business—there's just too much at stake."

"What's at stake, Miss, is my self-respect. At my age, it's time I sold the business, such as it is—it's been losin' money for years—and, more to the point, it's time I ended my silence about Johnny. Guess I knew that as soon as I looked at your photograph and saw Alice. Like I said, your credentials.

"Okay, I'm just a hillbilly pilot. But a good one. You get to be a good pilot by—by instinct. By sixth sense. And the way I see it that sixth sense got to work as soon as I saw your photograph and it's also why I know, a gut knowin', that you've got Johnny's interests at heart."

"Believe me, Mr. Korda, I *do*. I swear it." Replaying those words, I hear pledge, avowal; I had spoken from my heart and I have no reservations about using that cliche.

He then did a surprising thing. He stretched out his hand and stroked my hair for a moment, like a grandfather. I was moved, also a little embarrassed. He, too, seemed self-conscious, for he sat back, placed the fingertips of his hands on the edge of the table, as if bringing a meeting to order.

"Where do we start?" he said.

"Haworth, I suppose."

"The day Johnny was—?"

I nodded. It had to be faced. It was evidence—I tried to think legally.

In his unease, in a temporizing I empathized with, he brought the palms of his hands together, moved them up and down in a shuffle of dry, calloused sound. He turned his head, looked round the cafeteria, looked anywhere except at the past.

And then, suddenly, he was rigidly still. He stayed like this for a few moments before turning his head to look at me.

"Son of a gun," he said, shaking his head.

"What?"

"One of the two fellas who was in my office, the fella who stood by the door and then showed me your photograph, he's here—about a dozen tables behind us."

I looked. And saw Mr. Punch.

I had no doubt that he meant to be seen, for he was at a table in the middle of the cafeteria and there were plenty of other places he could have sat relatively unnoticed. He even seemed dressed to be seen. A cream-colored blazer with flared lapels. A black shirt. What looked like a medallion—something gold—at his neck.

In his telling, Harry Korda had concentrated on the young man with the ponytail and so it had simply not occurred to me that the other man might have been Mr. Punch. Besides, although my first contact with him had been when he joined the FBI agent in Chicago that night, subsequent developments had lined him up firmly in my mind as a loner.

Just as he was on his own now and staring at me—a fixed, venomous stare which for a moment or two, at least that, renewed my earlier fear of him. I looked away, as casually as I could.

"That man," I said to Harry Korda, "has been following me since I was in Chicago."

"Yeah?" He scratched the lobe of his right ear. "So let's shake him. Let's go someplace we can talk in private."

And that's how I came to be flying over Florida in Harry Korda's old Dakota. Which, I suppose, was a fitting place to hear the final truth about Johnny—a truth more terrible, more revealing and more far reaching than that told to me by either Dante Centofanti or Lou Eggenberg.

Twenty-three

"JOHNNY," HARRY KORDA SAID, "WAS SHOT IN THE BACK OF THE neck. Twice. At point blank range." The Dakota shuddered as it lifted through a strata of cloud. "He would have died instantly."

"I see," I said. Brittle and English. Inside, I writhed, wailed.

A clip of newsreel jerked in my mind for a split second. It was that moment when Kennedy slumped forward in the open limousine and bits of his brain, seen as flecks on that famous amateur footage, scattered and hope died everywhere.

I cannot explain why that scene seemed, and still does, such a natural counterpoint to Harry Korda's words. Was I projecting the promise of Johnny's future into an infinitely larger dimension, putting his murder in the context of political assassination? Or was it that in a momentary numbness in which I couldn't quite comprehend what I had heard my subconscious mind raced back for a precedent of violence and arbitrary life-taking and came up with, perhaps because recently I had been to Dallas, Kennedy? I simply have no idea.

Where I can be specific is that even now, contrary to what I once held to be my instincts as a totally ordered and self-sufficient woman, I continue to feel a sense of shock and of personal grief, a trauma as sharp as the ripped open envelope of a wartime telegram bearing the worst possible news.

And with that news comes a mental picture: Johnny sprawled dead over the steering wheel of his jeep at Haworth. A gag stuffed in his mouth. His hands tied behind his back. And the Brontë parsonage in sight of where it happened.

It's all so unreal and, in a bid for some kind of perspective, I need to go back to the matter-of-factness of Harry Korda's words when, shortly after takeoff, he said, "I guess we'd better get down to how Johnny died."

His voice was remote in the roar of the engines, we were climbing and I had yet to attune myself to their sound, and what he had just said somehow lacked impact, like small talk. I came to realize, though, that his apparent casualness was catharsis, a release from a truth he had been brooding over in total solitude for more than half a century: it transpired that he had a lot to say about Johnny—*everything*—but the beginning, for him, had to be the detailing of his death.

I, for my part, nodded, set up my tape recorder, and he went on to tell me, in the sparse words I have already quoted, the manner of Johnny's murder. And, as I have noted, I said, "I see." Cool. Disinterested. Devastated.

I remember, in the immediate aftermath, him staring straight ahead into the blue sky—an intense, almost startled blue, as if the shock waves had spread beyond the cockpit—and I remember the swirls and flickers of the needles on the various dials of the control panel and thinking vaguely that time had been set to go backward.

I thought—shock licenses all kinds of wanderings—of the headstone of Emily Brontë, a prim shrine in the parsonage graveyard, and, not far away, Johnny's crumpled body in the jeep that had become his hearse. I thought too of his wall, up on the moors and overlooking that dark village with its history, not just the Brontë sisters but also the children in the textile mill, of early death. And now—and, curiously, it seemed immediate, a tragedy of only yesterday—his own death. Two bullets in the back of his neck. The Dakota's engines throbbed. A dirge. A drum roll. A pain.

"Well, then—" I heard at once the clipped efficiency of my voice, but I seemed quite unable to change it. "Well, then, so that's how the duke settled his score with Johnny?"

Harry Korda stared straight ahead, concentrating on his flying.

"The duke," he said, "had nothing to do with it."

Was he Judas after all? Was he still selling out Johnny by stringing me along with half truths in which while admitting the facts of the murder and the way it was carried out he was also exonerating the culprit? I took a measured breath and tried to organize my rebuttal.

"I must remind you," I said, "that I talked extensively to Dante Centofanti and Lou Eggenberg. I heard from them, in precise detail, how another member of the crew—"

"Sure." He nodded. "Buddy Fanzoli. The duke and his boys strung him up. It's what some Englishmen of *breedin'* used to think they could do—get away with murder. Mad dogs with pedigrees." No, of course he wasn't Judas. "The duke was, he was plain evil, the most cold-blooded man I ever met, and all the more so because he had a kinda . . . a kinda charm. The life he lived, I guess he's long dead, and if there's a hell he's gotta be a kingpin there. Only he didn't kill Johnny."

"But—" For a moment or two I floundered; it was as if we were climbing too steeply and I needed oxygen. "But he sent a wreath with Johnny's name on it—his way of boasting about what he had done—and after the war he confessed, or as good as, to Lou Eggenberg."

"I know. Lou told me all about that when he tried to rope me in for that magazine article." His eyes stayed fixed ahead, as if the past were on the horizon.

"Good ole persistent Lou, uh? Trackin' the duke all the way to Scotland. As I see it, the duke wanted the credit for Johnny's death. Pride. As simple as that. He'd tried plenty enough before to get rid of him—to get rid of all of us—and now that Johnny was dead the duke wanted to claim the, uh, the 'kill.'"

"But on the day in question—" I broke off, self-conscious about my courtroom locution. "The day Johnny set off for Haworth the duke was seen to follow him in his car."

"Yeah. I know. And it's no big deal. Any excuse, and the duke would be houndin' Johnny. Sometimes he'd get one of his ground crew to mess about with Johnny's jeep"—I remembered the afternoon we had hurled out of control down the hill, the brake fluid gone—"but most often he'd spot Johnny drivin' off and he'd jump into his own car and start cuttin' up around him. The day you're on about, the duke's clutch gave way—he drove that car so hard this was always happenin'—and that's why he *seemed* to be trailin' Johnny. Fact was that sports job of his was clean out of power. I saw the work sheets—I saw a whole lot of things in the investigation—and his car was towed back and put in for clutch repair long before Johnny got to Haworth. Okay, work sheets can be faked. But there was other evidence, and plenty of it, that the duke didn't kill Johnny. No way."

"Then—then who did?"

He pushed a lever forward, one of three to the right of him, and the pitch of the engines changed, became altogether tighter, fiercely focused.

"An American," he said.

"American?" I wasn't sure what I felt and nor does the tape offer any interpretation: it relays only my voice, somehow stranded in this new expanse of sound.

He eased back two of the three levers and the sound diminished as the engines settled into a steady cruising rhythm.

"Fella from San Diego. A pro. A—a hit man. Brought over to— There was a contract out on Johnny."

Such nonsense! Such tawdry, B-movie nonsense! That was the voice I heard in my head, expressing the reaction I wished to have, in keeping with my self-image. My actual voice, which I have been listening to just now on the tape, acknowledges that in his simplicity Harry Korda is conditioned to speak only the truth and, in its telling, does not blink at the B-movie excesses of life. (And, wisely, didn't Lou Eggenberg have something to say about the relative norm of melodrama in real life?)

What I said to Harry Korda after he told me about the "contract" was straightforward, though my words broke away from their earlier crispness and conveyed—the tape gives me that sub-text—a confusion, a pleading, an acceptance of his veracity.

"I—I don't understand."

"It's a long story, Miss." He didn't shift his gaze from the sky. "I could try to give it to you broadside on, like I did just now with the shootin'. I just *hadda* get that outa the way. Or we could take a roundabout route, so that maybe the pieces fit together better. Up to you."

I looked out of the window. I think we were over Cape Canaveral. I saw runways and a couple of gantries and what looked like a display of rockets, from this height resembling an asymmetrical collection of fireworks. I mused, a momentary detour from mayhem, on all the time it must take for a space launch. All that planning and coordination of fine details. I turned to him and said, "Could we take the roundabout route?"

He nodded. He swung the wheel and the wings tilted in an arc that swept us out, for a time, over the Atlantic, as if he needed symbolic depths to get started on whatever he had to say.

"I guess," he said, "it's gotta start with the first time I met Johnny. That was at flight school, here in Florida. At Pensacola. I was a cocky kid in those days on account that my home life was—let's just say I needed a family. And that's what Johnny gave me. He was understandin', patient and—from the moment I met Johnny I signed up for him all the way. Y'can unfasten your seatbelt now."

As I unfastened my belt I let go, temporarily, of my angst. I suspected it would return, and it did, but for now I needed a break and it suited me to sit back in the cracked green leather of the copilot's seat and appreciate the honest smell of the Dakota—a loamy smell of wooden crates and webbing cargo straps—and listen to the words of this tall stranger as they rode the sound, now a steady thrum, of the engines . . .

Harry Korda wasn't even seventeen when he checked in at flight school. He lied about his age, though he didn't have to embellish his aptitude as a pilot. He had no license, but he had flown solo at the age of thirteen on a Curtis Jenny biplane owned by an elderly farmer, for whom he worked on weekends, in the Salinas Valley in California. The farmer taught him to fly, showing a generosity the boy had never known from his father—a retired prison warden who drank heavily and was brutal to his family. One day the old farmer toppled from his tractor and was found to be dead. Heart seizure. His simple will included a small sum of money for Harry Korda, which his father promptly took, along with the Curtis Jenny, which his father just as promptly put up for sale. One night the boy climbed into the plane with a few dollars, a ham sandwich and a thermos of coffee and took off on a course for Florida—more than 3,000 miles away.

"Crazy, uh? But I needed to get as far away as possible from my old man and Pensacola looked like a good bet. Took me the best part of two weeks to get there. Fuel stops, engine over-heatin', oil leaks, bad weather. When I finally made Pensacola I decided to take the entrance examination straight off—which I did by barnstormin' the runway. I mean, pilot trainin' was for college kids and I hadda make up for that. When I landed, they threw me in the brig. Then they thought about it—I'd shown I was pilot material in my little stunt over the runway—and they released me into the care of the most senior cadet on the course—Johnny.

"It was kinda like Johnny was my probation officer. Only I didn't resent him. We shared the same bunk section and every night, way after lights out, we'd sit there with a flashlight while Johnny coached me in math and trigonometry and all the other things a hot-shot pilot doesn't need when he's flyin' a Curtis Jenny. I picked it up real quick. Maybe I wasn't so dumb. Or maybe Johnny just knew how to get through to me."

It was good to hear his simple anecdotes—they were a polar remove from Haworth, or so I thought—and I listened drowsily, the sound of the engines, now that we were cruising, a soporific. In fact, I think my eyes were closed when he switched from the basics of camp life and he was talking of the liveried black footmen in white colonial wigs: he was, it turned out, describing Johnny's first furlough back home in Atlanta and a night in which tables were garlanded with magnolias and centerpieced with iced sculptings of swans.

"Johnny took me home with him—I had no place else to go—and I met his sister, Adelle. We figured, Johnny and me, on a few beers, a few laughs. Not this Hail to the Chief stuff at this *little* welcome home party which turned out to be a regular banquet. Johnny was at the salutin' stand, by which I mean he was stuck at the top table and wearin' his uniform, which she'd insisted on. She'd laid on strollin' violinists, the works—it was all her idea of a surprise to show how much she'd missed him."

"His sister?"

"No, Miss! Not Adelle. She didn't care for it one little bit; right from the start she was worried about the way that girl had moved in on Johnny."

"What girl?"

He took his hand off the wheel for a moment, moved it slowly across the back of his neck.

"Madge. Her name was Madge. Though she liked to be known as Miss Scarlett."

"The Miss Scarlett on the side of the B17?"

He glanced at me. "You sure do know a lot, Miss."

"I suppose I do."

"Yup. *That* Miss Scarlett. She had that drawin' done by a big-time cartoonist in New York and just took it for granted that she would be up there on the ship. She got her way in everythin'. That's what came of havin' a rich daddy. She snapped her fingers and expected the world to jump. And it did."

"Was she—" I paused, decided that the question had to be put neutrally. "Was she pretty?"

"As a picture. Though not one I'd care to hang in my house. Dark. Slim. Sort of violet-colored eyes. Had a dimple. Regular Southern belle."

"Well, fiddle de dee!" I said in a mock Southern accent meant to show Harry Korda and myself that I had no particular interest in that young woman, and as part of the amused pose I turned my head negligently and gazed down on the view. We had come in from the ocean and were following a serrated shoreline of pink and white beaches, like decorous ruffs on the sleeves of the Atlantic. It was all very pretty, I thought. And so was Miss Scarlett! I acknowledged a *certain* interest in her. I recalled the figure on the fuselage—the long legs, the picture hat concealing the face, other than the provocative peek of nose, the ringlets—and I transposed the essence of that outline to the top table at the banquet in Atlanta that night and imagined her vivid and bright-eyed and bossy while the candles flickered— there *had* to have been candles—and the iced swans melted.

That visualization of her was supposed to be some kind of a private joke, my way of putting her in her place in the chocolate box of stereotype, though my next question to Harry Korda wasn't quite within those terms.

"Were they close?"

"Too close for comfort. Johnny's comfort. The set Madge moved in—wild kids and wealthy with it. Servants. And, when there was somethin' bigger to clean up, lawyers. They were a million-dollar crowd and Johnny hadn't much more than a couple of nickels."

"So why did she bother with him?"

"Could be she loved him. In her way. Could be that she took to him on account of his one and only social connection—he knew the woman who wrote *Gone with the Wind*."

"Margaret Mitchell."

"Sure. I met her once. A real nice lady. I guess as a writer she mixed with all kinds and it was through her Johnny and Madge met up."

"A sweet all-American romance," I said, and was instantly aware of the jaded European sneer of my words.

"I wouldn't say that, Miss." He shook his head in slow ruefulness. "Johnny was on the receivin' end right from the start, and I don't just mean the gifts she piled on him. Apart from embarrassin' him, they caused him other problems. Like one day she just ups and buys him a brand new convertible and a couple of days later it was torched—totalled—by the fella she'd dropped to take up with Johnny. Fella by the name of Jake Hays. Jake hated Johnny."

Vaguely, no doubt in a bid to be detached and superior, I wondered what I was doing bumping over Florida in an old Dakota and swirling in a long-ago agony aunt saga of poor boy, rich girl and jealous ex-beau. And what bearing could such bathos possibly have on Johnny's murder, five thousand miles away in Haworth?

Harry Korda, I decided, was doing what old men do naturally—he was rambling—though, conveniently, I sought no explanations or motives for my own conduct as I went on to sound him out about Madge Slattery. He was well informed.

She was the first born, and his favorite, in the large family of Frank Slattery, an Irish-American entrepreneur. He called her after his mother.

Slattery was bad enough, but Madge too—*Madge Slattery*! In the context of Atlanta society it was a crone name that wrinkled somewhat his daughter's standing as a Southern belle. She was accepted, her father's wealth guaranteed that, but she knew of private snickers, knew that at the more formal occasions major domos would announce her arrival in relatively sotto tones or stentoriously—depending on the charity or the capriciousness of the organizers.

Frank Slattery, though I am inferring this, was too crudely simple to understand his daughter's situation, and presumably that same mentality—a blindness in reasoning right from wrong and a con-comitant ruthless energy—accounted for his money. He made his first fortune from bootlegging during Prohibition and went on to increase it vastly in cotton, cattle, paper, shipbuilding, transportation and property. The Slatterys were a classically dynastic American fam-ily. Not nearly as powerful as the Vanderbilts or the Astors, Harry Korda said, but "pretty high up in the second or third leagues."

And Madge Slattery, heiress, felt impoverished by her name.

No doubt this accounted for her passion for her theatricals and her starring roles—a donation from daddy always saw to that—in local amateur productions.

And she slipped naturally into the persona of Scarlett O'Hara—given her wiles and her selfishness, it was no more than a costume change for her—when *Gone with the Wind* was published to instant and phenomenal success and re-focused public interest in Atlanta's Civil War past as the city that was burned to the ground by Union forces in 1864.

She set out to cultivate Margaret Mitchell, prior to her success an obscure figure, who had no interest in being taken up by the haut monde of Atlanta; however, even Mrs. Mitchell could not refuse, without seeming churlish, an invitation to a Scarlett and Rhett fancy dress ball which Frank Slattery, fronting for his daughter, was giving for a children's charity to which he had pledged a check tripling the total raised by ticket sales.

Margaret Mitchell's party included Johnny and his sister, though Adelle attended reluctantly.

"She told me they were out of place," Harry Korda said. "Johnny, this wasn't long after he had met Madge at Mrs. Mitchell's house, had on a rented tux and the tie wouldn't fit properly and Miss Scar-lett—and that's what Madge was for the first time that night in her big fancy hat with its ribbons—was always on hand to fix it and every time she snapped that tie into place Adelle felt Johnny bein' tugged away into a world that would never suit him."

"An overprotective sister," I said, feeling a tone of objective brisk-ness was in order.

"No, Miss. She wanted the best for him, was all, and the best wasn't Madge and her money. She used to say Johnny had a—a destiny. A place in life. She was a wise woman, a givin' woman. Would have made a great wife and mother, only she had a heart murmur and couldn't have children. I figure she let me in on that because she guessed that, young as I was, I was head over heels in love with her."

A slow smile hauled across his face and merged into the shadows of the late afternoon sunshine now drifting into the cockpit.

"I got to know Adelle real well. Spent all my furloughs in Atlanta. We'd sit on the porch waitin' for Johnny to come home after Madge had swept him off to some fancy party or other and we'd talk about just everythin', though sooner or later it would come round to her worries about Johnny and Madge. We'd just sit there and talk our hearts out."

Drone of engine, drone of voice and now creak of porch chair in those long-gone Atlanta nights: I wondered if those digressions had any destination, any possible link-up to Johnny dead in his jeep at Haworth.

They did. Eventually.

Twenty-four

THE PHENOMENAL SUCCESS OF *GONE WITH THE WIND* DREW visitors from across America and the world to Atlanta to see the setting of the book, and one of the tourist sights—for those with the right social kudos—was Madge Slattery as Scarlett O'Hara.

In that role she hosted balls and garden parties and at-homes, ostensibly for charity. No doubt it was meant to be seen as an expression of Deep South grace, indolence and whimsy combined, and no doubt she exercised judicious stealth and decorum in shedding the crude chrysalis of her family name and emerging as her alter ego.

How she must have revelled in it! The picture hat, the gowns, the flowing guilelessness of her smile and all the rest of the camouflage of her monstrous conceit.

"The way Adelle told it," Harry Korda said, "Madge was driven by Scarlett O'Hara—a split personality we'd call it today, I guess—and Adelle mentioned one night on the porch, not out of meanness but because she was trying to explain her behavior, that it was an open secret that Madge's mother was tucked away in an asylum in South Carolina and wasn't even able to recognize Madge."

And Madge Slattery certainly wasn't prepared to recognize herself—which became apparent when, shortly after the book won the Pulitzer Prize, the movie producer David O. Selznick announced that *Gone with the Wind* was to be made into an epic and, in America's biggest screen test, he would be searching the land to find the perfect Miss Scarlett.

Madge Slattery applied. Or, rather, she told big daddy—and he just had to have been that—to buy the part for her. Why not? Her father held substantial stock in several major studios and his daughter was young and beautiful *and* from Atlanta and, effectively had been playing the part of Scarlett ever since the book's publication. That *must* have been her thinking.

The result was an invitation to go to Hollywood for a screen test and she treated it as her personal premiere. Money is its own rich tempo, and Cole Porter was commissioned to write a song for her to sing—she had absolute faith in both her musical and acting talents, Harry Korda said—at the screen test. The night before her departure there was a ball in her honor and she left Atlanta in her father's personal railcar. Johnny had the flu and couldn't attend the ball or take up the invitation to join her on the journey. She had plenty of other company, including an acting coach and a voice coach.

Just as, on another level, Harry Korda had flown himself across the country to join the Air Force, so also was her journey a quintessentially American experience of the time—or it was if you were an heiress whose cultural influences were the Jazz Age and a bestseller in which the heroine had every confidence to win by scheming.

But her return to Atlanta, a couple of weeks later, was a subdued affair. She flew back on a commercial flight, let it be known that she was exhausted after the tests and that the studio—no, David O. Selznick himself—would be in touch very soon to let her know when to go back to Hollywood for the start of shooting of *Gone with the Wind*. Meantime, she said, in apparent explanation of the dark glasses she was wearing, she had to memorize the script and so she was cancelling her whole social life. Which she did for weeks, not even contacting Johnny.

Apparently, she never did hear from the studio. Like everyone else, she read in the paper one day that the English actress Vivien Leigh had been cast to play Scarlett O'Hara opposite Clark Gable's Rhett Butler.

Some hours later, in the middle of the night, the phone rang in Johnny's home. Adelle answered.

"It was county hospital," Harry Korda said. "Seems that Madge had gone round every room in the house, and that was some mansion they had, smashin' mirrors. Then she slashed her wrists with broken glass. Now she was demandin' to see Johnny before she would let them sedate her."

Johnny spent the rest of that night and the whole of the next day at her bedside.

"She just didn't want anyone else," Harry Korda said. "Not her daddy. Not any of her other friends. Only Johnny."

I said, determined to be fair-minded, "She must have loved him."

"Maybe. Maybe also she was showin' that in spite of her slashed wrists she could still snap her fingers and get just what she wanted.

"Johnny was the only fella who wasn't crazy about her—that had worn off for him, though he stayed loyal to her—and he had to be brought to heel like all her other lapdogs. So there he was at her bedside. Sit, Johnny. Good boy, Johnny."

I wondered again how these swathes of Deep South reminiscence fitted the pattern of Johnny's death on that stark moor in Yorkshire. But, oddly, I was not impatient. I was, I do believe, the model listener and, with little more than an attentive nod here and there, I concentrated on what he said as his talk switched back to flight school at Pensacola.

Johnny graduated as the top cadet on the course, earning the traditional right to request a favor. He asked if he and Harry Korda could share the same operational posting. It was granted. They would report to Seattle to pick up a new B17 and from there they would fly the plane to England.

First, though, there was their final furlough in Atlanta. They flew there, this last time, in the Curtis Jenny, taking turns at the controls.

"That old Jenny," Harry Korda said, "she was painted red and blue and bright yellow and we were ridin' a butterfly. We just flitted here and there. Put down once in a meadow behind a farm for some milk and cheese and bread. Put down another time near to a county fair and ended up takin' a few good citizens on flips. It was a different America in those days. We saw a quiet beach that took our fancy so we just landed on the sand and had a swim. I look back down all these years and I see that as the finest flight of my life. It was a—it was a shinin' flight."

Two young men in an open cockpit and the American Dream flowing purely in the slipstream: I'm glad Johnny had that experience.

Finally, that little red and blue and yellow biplane, that medal ribbon of their youth, fluttered down into Atlanta and they were engulfed in a much grander ceremonial.

"She'd laid on a huge outdoor ball, lanterns in the trees and everything, and the moon was so big that night it was like she'd gone out and hired it special . . ."

He shook his head, seemed almost for a moment to smile at the sheer gaudy energy of her excess in which the wearing of her heart on her sleeve was done with the hand stitching of her scheming.

"The ball was supposed to honor Johnny's graduation and his goin' off to fight the war and she was out to show the world how much she loved him. It was also a ball for old man Slattery's birthday. But most of all, I figure, it was a ball strictly for herself—'cos, her bit for the war effort, she'd gone, I swear, and formed an all-ladies' orchestra to entertain the troops and this was its gala openin' performance.

"Miss Scarlett and the Sweethearts, that's what they were called. One way or another, she was *set* on being Scarlett O'Hara."

The orchestra, made up of Southern belles whose menfolk were in the services, added up to its own Confederate division, attired as its

Searching for Johnny   339

members were in the stereotyped flowing gowns and chapeaux of
that period. None of them, of course, was as resplendent as Miss
Scarlett herself—the lead vocalist.

"They looked good, I'll grant you that," he said, "but as for
soundin' good, well, let's just say they lacked a certain big band polish. Still, they had a slew of engagements at camps up and down the
country—old man Slattery was doin' well out of defense contracts
and he'd fixed that—and, like I say, this night of the ball was their
first big tryout.

"It also was the night Madge told Johnny she'd be flyin' with him,
so to speak, by which she meant that the drawin' of her would be up
on the side of the B17. Old man Slattery had seen to that as well,
though this was the first Johnny knew of it. But there were other,
and bigger, surprises to come that night. Crazy night. For the time
bein' though there was a big ice model of a B17—she had a thing
about ice, I guess—hangin' from chains in the trees and set into its
sides, Adelle said it had been done with colored spun sugar, was this
drawin' of Madge, just like it turned out to be when we picked up
the ship in Seattle. Crazy, crazy night."

He shook his head again. We had been flying for some time
across a massive swamp, it may have been the Everglades, and gazing
down at the primeval green ooze I pictured that emotionally seeped
night and saw, through the details he gave me, Madge Slattery
sashaying to the grand piano for her star performance before dinner
was served.

The piano was on a raised piazza enclosed by an arbor of magnolia
trees and she, the connoisseur of the perfect cue, waited until every
sound had ceased, until only the crazed moths spiralled in the single
spotlight that was on her. And then she began to play, and sing,
"Love Letters."

"She could play, no denyin', though as for her singin', kinda
scrawny. Still, I guess anyone can sing 'Love Letters' and make it
sound movin' if you kinda half talk, half breathe it. And that's what

she did. When she was through, even Adelle and me joined in the applause.

"Madge took her bow and then crossed over to where Johnny, and she'd been lookin' at him all the time she was singin', was sittin'. Just before she got to the table she undid the red ribbon on the wide-brimmed hat she was wearin'—always wore a big red ribbon in her hats—and kinda flicked it at Johnny. He caught it by the end and she pulled at it, kinda reeled him in, and that way eased him onto the floor.

"The whole orchestra then struck up with 'Love Letters,' it all must have been rehearsed, and the two of them were up on the floor all by themselves and dancin'. I remember that Adelle and me looked at each other at the same moment and I swear we musta been thinkin' the same thought—that Johnny was trapped.

"And just how trapped he was came through loud and clear when, after the dance, she led him by the hand up to the stage and said she had a very special announcement to make. Which was that she wanted everyone to know they were engaged and would be married just as soon as he got back from the war.

"Johnny kinda—he kinda blinked. He didn't have time for much else because just then there's a snowstorm of magnolia petals tumblin' from the ceilin' along with heart-shaped balloons and everyone's toastin' the happy couple. Except Adelle and me." He paused.

"And Jake Hays," he added.

"He was there?" I wasn't interested in Jake Hays. Not then, anyway.

"Yes, Miss, he was. He *surely* was. And with murder in his heart. There was, uh, steak for dinner."

I regarded that remark as a nonsequitur, old men's ways, then he went on to remind me that this was also Frank Slattery's birthday and the tradition was for steak to be served, prime cuts from his prize-winning Aberdeen Angus herds in Texas. Each cut, moments before it was put on the plate, was imprinted with an S by servants wielding silver branding irons—thus did Frank Slattery, ceremonially on his birthday, mark the elevation of his family name from a background in which his forebears had subsisted on potatoes in Ireland.

All of this seemed quite pointless, until Harry Korda remarked that the meal had only just started when "all hell broke out."

"Really?" It was no more than a polite response.

"Jake Hays, Miss. With a gun. Revolver. He was up on a table and with the butt of that gun he was hammerin' away at that ice model of the B17. It came crashin' down and then Jake was rushin' toward the table where Johnny and Madge were sittin' and he was firin' wildly.

"Everyone's panickin', of course. Except Madge. I know this because I had one of those frozen moments—you know how it is when things are wildly out of control and suddenly you see clearly for a split second—in which I saw she was bright-eyed and enjoyin' what was happenin'. Like . . . like passion. She'd driven that fella to that point and it—it was givin' her pleasure. I'll never forget her look. Never.

"Anyway, by now two or three fellas had hurled themselves at Jake, but he was big—two hundred pounds at least—and out-of-his-mind drunk. He threw them off. No trouble.

"And then he was right in front of Johnny. Johnny sort of half rose and Jake pointed the gun right at him, pulled the trigger and—nothin'. He's out of shots. He realized this and flung the gun at Johnny, then grabbed one of the brandin' irons—they're white hot and set out on brazier trays in front of the top table—and lunged it at him.

"That iron, Miss, went straight into Johnny's face. On the side, near his mouth. No real harm done, I guess, not when you think that if the gun had been loaded Johnny would have been dead for sure. Only he was left scarred for life."

So now I knew how Johnny got his scar. Just as I knew who had arranged for his killing in Yorkshire. Jake Hays. That judgement was confirmed by Harry Korda's next words . . .

"Even as Jake was hauled away, and it took half a dozen fellas to do that, he was hollerin' that one day he'd get Johnny, that there was no escape in Europe for him, that he'd be tracked down there and finished off, that they didn't call him Grudge Hays for nothin'.

"Grudge—that was his nickname. On account he always settled a score. Kinda fella he was, he had this great collection of firearms in his old man's mansion and his idea of tellin' a girl he liked her was to give her a pistol with her name inscribed on it. How's that for crazy?"

I nodded, fronting an indifference which suddenly seemed to be called for. Privately, shatteringly, I thought of how Grudge Hays had lived up to his name all those miles away in Haworth.

I waited for him to go on talking about Jake Hays, to supply the specific evidence of his guilt. But he didn't; not right then. He ambled off into other territories of remembrance and I decided he would get back to him, given time, and that in navigating the past in this wandering way he was following the convoluted course of his old man's memory, with all its disjointed lines and whorls; this was his catharsis and he was entitled to it. I listened, then, while he talked about anything but Jake Hays.

Inevitably, he strayed into areas that I knew from Dante Centofanti and Lou Eggenberg—the cover-up of Johnny's death, for example—though he moved along willingly whenever I reminded him I had already crossed a particular ground. But it was on the subject of the cover-up that I learnt something that was new to me—his reason for not cooperating with Lou Eggenberg on the magazine article. I have been listening just now to his words on the tape on that subject and, since they refute Lou Eggenberg's charge that he was Judas, they must take their place as evidence on the record.

"I was—well, I was looking out for Adelle. What was at stake here was her life. Lemmee try to explain. I'd kept in touch with her, even after I was married. I cared for my wife, respected her, was never unfaithful. But I—I, uh, loved Adelle. That was why I was never able to tell Jeannie, my wife, about Johnny because somewhere along the line Adelle would have figured in the story and who knows where that might have led to? So I kept my silence, though that was hard, and as often as I could I'd detour to Atlanta to see Adelle; I had my own airplane, business was good in those days—Jeannie, God bless her, saw to that—so this wasn't hard to manage.

"The hard part was seein' just how much Adelle had changed. After Johnny, her heart murmur had gotten worse and she'd aged. What kept her goin' was her belief that Johnny had died a hero's death. So for the truth to come out that he'd been murdered, which was what Lou wanted to splash all over America, would have killed her.

"I just thank the Lord that, for whatever reason, his article wasn't published. Adelle passed away in December, 1957. She was old and frail beyond her years, though she lasted longer than I thought she would. I went to the funeral. Afterwards, I decided that the only sensible thing was to stop thinkin' about her and Johnny. And I guess I pretty well did that, leastaways as much as that can be done, until you came along."

"No hard feelings, I hope," I said, and impulsively, my version of the way he had stroked my hair, I touched his hand.

He turned to me, smiled. "How could I have hard feelings for someone who looks so much like Johnny's girl?"

He paused, then reached down to his flight bag, by his side. He took from the bag a brown manilla envelope, which he tapped by its edges on the steering wheel for a moment or two.

"Alice was teachin' Johnny to draw, and I don't know why— maybe some kind of that sixth sense I mentioned back there—I brought these drawings of his along in case I felt you might want to see them. I've, uh, reached that decision."

He passed me the envelope. I opened it, removed a sheaf of sketches. And saw Haworth. The parsonage, the graveyard, the cobblestoned main street with its patched shawl straggle of cottages worn threadbare by the wind from the moors. The moors were there too of course—coarse and sweeping, the raw material of *Wuthering Heights* itself.

There were perhaps thirty or forty drawings and I must have been halfway through when it happened—when I came on the sketch he made of me on the runway that night of our first meeting.

I experienced no sense of shock—on the contrary, it was like finding something in its rightful place—though I did feel a certain dryness of my mouth.

I was aware of the soft laminate backing on the other side of the drawing and I turned it over and saw what I fully expected to see— the aerial map marked Bremerhaven bisected by three red dots. Just as it had been that first night on the runway.

Gazing down on that map in the Dakota I knew there was no point in trying for a rational explanation; time and space are quantifiable only to the most finite extent, and after that mystery takes over.

"That's a bomb aimer's map," Harry Korda said.

"It is?" My reply was a fill-in, and so were those that followed, while I adjusted to the development.

"The red dots lined up the droppin' zone."

"They did?" I turned the map back to the drawing.

"And that's Alice," he said.

"Really?"

"What you can see of her. It's the drawin' that went on the side of the ship after Miss Scarlett was, uh, jilted."

"Naughty," I said, a would-be lightness, a little conversational mint to take the dryness out of my mouth.

"Madge thought so. She raised a ruckus. Raised one almighty— she said they were engaged, which they weren't, and that no one trashed her. She said this in letters, cables and even—unheard of in the war—phone calls from the States. I was with him one night when he hung up on her. We'd been up late, playin' cards, when her call came through. I couldn't help but overhear him tryin' to reason with her. Y'ask me, he didn't have to write and tell her in the first place that he was droppin' her picture from the ship; still, that's how he was, fair and square. But this one night on the phone his patience ran out and, only time I'd ever seen him lose his temper, he plain hung up on her."

Miss Scarlett trounced! The thought delighted me. I wanted to giggle.

And my sense of triumph was boosted when Harry Korda went on to say that a major European tour, with Bing Crosby and Danny Kaye, had been earmarked for Miss Scarlett and the Sweethearts, with all the self-evident publicity of a reunion with Johnny: *Life* magazine had shown an interest in photographing them against her insignia on the side of the B17.

That insignia, the very trademark of her megalomania, also was the band's logo. It was emblazoned the full length of its luxury touring bus, Harry Korda said, replicated on the stage curtains at concerts and on the front of the musicians' pews and printed on her stationery.

It was even worked into the giveaway souvenir pencils by which she signed autographs, and I could imagine the particular flourish she gave to the writing of her name and the way it cancelled out Madge Slattery and endorsed the full and binding contract of her persona and her destiny as Miss Scarlett. She must have been having the most marvellous of wars—until Johnny, in a spirit of honor, dropped his bombshell on her monstrous pride.

Really, it was very funny. Hilarious. And then I thought of Johnny, dead in his jeep at Haworth, and of Jake Hays who had kept the threat he made in that shattered Atlanta night when the mad burn of his hatred left Johnny with the S-shaped scar on his face . . .

We were coasting across the Florida Keys when at last Harry Korda made his approach to the day Johnny was murdered.

"The weather that day . . ." I know, I know, I thought, suddenly impatient; I reminded myself that he was entitled to his memory.

"The kinda day it started out, it put me in mind of that time Johnny and me flew the Jenny to Atlanta . . ."

Beyond the Keys, I saw a flotilla of white-sailed yachts, like a spilling of envelopes on blue blotting paper. I thought of the unfinished note Johnny had been writing to Adelle. *Dear Sis . . . it's such a glorious day . . .* And he hadn't lived to see the end of it.

"Alice," Harry Korda said, "had fixed to go to York that day to spend some time with friends of her family in Russia. They were both vets, this couple she was visitin', they'd studied in Russia or somethin', and Johnny had this little black-and-white dog—"

"Heathcliff," I said, more or less to myself.

"That so?" He glanced at me. "Well, the dog needed a couple of injections so Alice was taking him along with her to York. Johnny drove her to the train station and then went on to Haworth."

"She—she didn't go with him to Haworth?"

"No, Miss."

"Are you sure?"

"She was interviewed in York by the RAF."

"I was quite certain—I inferred it from what Dante Centofanti and Lou Eggenberg said—that Johnny and Alice had gone to Haworth together. I assumed that—well, that something awful had happened to her as well."

To tell the truth, I wasn't concerned about Alice's fate per se; I raised it now, due hypocritical concern in my voice, simply to correct my misreasoning.

"Something bad did happen to Alice," he said.

His hand went to the visor above the window and he unslotted a pair of tinted glasses. He put them on; the sun was setting now, harsh in its glare.

"Alice was sent back to Russia," he said. "She was sent back to a country where the rest of her family was in prison. Gulag. Isn't that the word? I don't figure the Russians would have shown her any favors. What happened to Johnny was terrible, but quick. What happened to Alice must have been terrible, and slow."

He said nothing for the next two or three minutes, though it seemed much longer than that, a drape of silence. That lull alone makes me realize how wrenching, how almost impossible, it has been to edit and transcribe this tape, logistically and emotionally. The synchronicity of time and memory does not guarantee an easy chronology, and in his case he was trying, as the Dakota droned on, for a compass bearing between so many oscillating points of the past: all the way from, and he actually used that phrase, "magnolia-drenched" nights in Atlanta to the night in Haworth, and he got round to telling me about that eventually, when the wind blew savage tribes of sparks from a fire in an oil drum on which soldiers made tea as they lounged guard over Johnny's body, and on to Alice, banished to an even greater darkness.

The tape head rotates, supplicating facts and sequence and coordination, and, in the cause of my own confused direction, I put down what he told me subsequently—namely that as second in command of the B17 he was appointed by the Eighth Air Force in London to liaise between them and the RAF in the investigation of Johnny's murder.

The RAF, certainly at the level of the base in Yorkshire, tried to veto his role, but the Eighth Air Force, particularly in those first phases when they needed time to organize and send in their own investigation team, insisted on an immediate American presence as, I take it, a matter of protocol and even-handedness.

Though, on both sides, fair play was never in consideration.

"I was in on that investigation, but only because the RAF and the Eighth were playin' biggest guy on the block," Harry Korda said. "The RAF, and all the more so at the base, wanted no part of me, but the Eighth dug their heels in and—it was a game. And the rules of that game were who could shoot the dirtiest pool. The RAF opened the scorin' when, in the middle of the night in York, they got Alice out of bed to question her about Johnny. They said he was just fine—I saw their report—and said all they were doin' was running a routine security check on him on account that Churchill was making an unexpected visit to the base in the morning. Liars! They asked her the same kind of questions they asked me; I'll come to that in a second. Alice, when they were through, said she wanted to go straight back to the base to see for herself that Johnny was OK and they said that wasn't possible because of Churchill's visit. But as soon as the great man had gone, they said, a car would be sent for her to take her to Johnny."

"Only, of course, there was no car," I said, and I realize now, replaying them, that my words were hasty, chivvying, that I was restless with this part of his narrative and that I didn't give a damn about Alice.

"Yes, Miss, a car was sent," he said. "A regular limousine. From the Russian embassy in London. Alice was—she was manhandled into that car."

His eyes flickered behind his tinted glasses, a dazed flicker, but in a moment he found the focus of his story again and told it concisely enough.

"I know what happened from what I overheard from our investigators and what I saw in bits and pieces of reports. Alice had been told when to expect the car and she was so sure it was gonna take her to the base she even had the dog with her when she left the house. But when she saw the car she sensed somethin' was wrong. Maybe it was flyin' the Russian flag; I dunno. Point is, she tried to make a run for it. A man and a woman got outa the car and went after her. The woman was carryin' a medical bag and when she caught up with Alice she forced her against a wall and, after a struggle, she injected her with a syringe. Alice went limp. The woman and the man half dragged her to the car. Which kinda tells you what was waiting for her in Russia."

"Quite," I said. And, if I may claim that redemption, it was a heartfelt quite. Alice, I reflected, must have counted as a bonus for Jake Hays in his revenge against Johnny.

The Dakota banked over the city of Key West as Harry Korda set off back to Kissimmee and also took his final heading to Haworth: he began by telling me what happened to him the night the crew of the B17 were ordered out of the briefing.

He was put in an enclosed truck in which his fellow passengers were the base commander, four or five other RAF officers, a couple of military policemen and a British bobby (he remembered that man's black domed hat and his red-faced bewilderment).

He lingered over none of these details; his words were more direct now, as he pressed on to resolution.

"I had no idea where they were takin' me to, just that the RAF guys were askin' me nonstop questions about Johnny. The same questions, over and over again. Like was he in some kind of trouble and did he have any enemies? I said the only enemies he had, that the whole crew had, were the duke and his boys. But they weren't interested in that. Just as they weren't interested in *my* question: what had happened to Johnny? They ignored that and kept on with their grillin'. Had Johnny been himself lately? Had he confided in me about somethin' untowards in his life? Matter of fact, he had. Two or three times lately he'd mentioned that he kept seein' this car, not the duke's car, keepin' at a distance behind his jeep—civilian cars were rare enough to stand out in those days—like someone was followin' him."

"What did they say to that?"

"I didn't tell 'em. Johnny hadn't taken it seriously and, besides, that night in the truck I was—I was thrown. In a spin. I figured that maybe he'd had an accident or that the duke had put him behind the eight ball in some way. I just never for a moment thought of him as bein'—"

He broke off for a few moments and his unspoken word—*dead*—seemed to hover in the trembling cockpit. Then he got round to putting that word into place, locking it into a stiff, official sounding sentence.

"We stopped at Haworth and there I was ordered to formally identify the body as required by military law."

He let out his breath and the sound—defined by the tape—was of a slow weariness, like a man who had scaled the rock face of memory and now looked down. He went on to describe the starkness of that view. The jeep was parked in a horseshoe-shaped inlet—a spot I recognized as the start of Johnny's route to the wall—and Johnny was slumped across the steering wheel. A field ambulance was alongside

the jeep. Storm paraffin lighters were placed here and there and half
a dozen soldiers were warming their hands and making tea over a fire
they had built in a large oil drum.

"I could have sworn Johnny was just takin' a nap," he said. "It
seemed like all I had to do was tap him on the shoulder and he'd
wake up. Then a medical orderly, I remember the Red Cross arm-
band he had on, pulled Johnny's head back so I could see his face.
And I saw he was—he was dead. His eyes were open. Someone, I
don't know who, said did I identify the body and I said yes and the
medical orderly pressed his thumbs hard on Johnny's eyes to close
them. They'd, uh, kept his eyes open so I could make a full identification. Regulations."

It was dark and, as ever at Haworth, there was a wind—he recalled
the swarming sparks from the fire in the oil drum and how they
seared split-second background shapes, the parsonage and the sullen
village—and thereafter everything else must have seemed to have
gusted. Various forms and statements swirled in the village police station—"it was crazy, a regular storm of paperwork"—and an angry
senior rank police officer, summoned hastily from the nearest town,
huffed and puffed and desk thumped as he challenged the RAF's
right to interview, without police participation, witnesses to a crime
commited on civil territory.

And the night's howling then entered a new dimension, for those
witnesses, Norwegian commandos who had been training on the
moors, were back in their camp, more than fifty miles away, and
due to leave shortly for a raid on German coastal emplacements in
Holland.

"We drove on to the camp," he said. "We were there for hours.
Language problems. The Norwegians spoke hardly any English and
their interpreter, an English officer, was too drunk to be any use.
Who says war isn't mad, uh? What finally broke through was that a
squad of Norwegians had been out on the moors, in a hidden
emplacement, on a trainin' exercise. They saw what happened to
Johnny, even though they were more than a mile away.

"What they saw, through field binoculars, was a jeep arrivin' at the foot of the moors. A fella in American uniform, Johnny, got out and struck off up the moors. He hadn't got far when another car drew up. A blue saloon. A civilian, fella in a raincoat, got out and he must have called to Johnny because Johnny turned and went back toward him. They stood outside the jeep for a few moments and then Johnny got into the front seat and the other fella went and sat behind him.

"Now these Norwegians, just kids, had been stuck on the moors for hours, so they were gonna watch anything that moved. And where it became interestin' was when the fella in the back seemed— there was only so much they could see through binoculars—to tie Johnny's hands and then gag him, and where it became doubly inter-estin' was when what sounded like a couple o' shots rang out and Johnny slumped over the wheel.

"The other fella then got into his car and drove off.

"They weren't exactly sure what happened, those Norwegian kids, but they called up their unit on the walkie talkie and, honest to God, they were told off by the British for breakin' radio silence. The same English officer who was drunk when we got to their camp now told them their war game was top secret and that no one was sup-posed to know they were up there on the moors and they weren't to concern themselves with anything else. Can you believe that?"

Abjectly, all I could offer out of a deep brooding which had fallen on me when he described the closing of Johnny's eyes by a stranger's thumbs, I said, "C'est la guerre."

"That sounds kinda like the right ketchup," he said. He shook his head, took his hands off the wheel for a moment and spread them in a gesture of helplessness.

"At least those Norwegian kids did the right thing," he went on, "because when finally it was time for them to come down from the moors they changed their route, disobeyed orders, so they could check the jeep. When they found Johnny dead they raised the alarm with the village policeman.

"They took him to the jeep but, the language barrier again, what they couldn't get through to him was that through their binoculars they had a make on the other car, even part of the plate numbers.

"Still, this was a village policeman and it could be the nearest thing he got to a crime was the local poacher and maybe the sight of Johnny's body was too much for him. Who can tell? What it came down to was that he goofed up—understandable, I guess—and when the trucks turned up to take the Norwegians back to base he let them all go. And then he contacted the base. By the time the base told London and by the time they'd finished arguin' over whether I should have a part in the investigation Johnny had been up on those moors for hours! Save me from the military mind, Miss!

"But SNAFU time went on overload when the RAF reached the Norwegians' camp, got those kids out of bed and lined them up in front of a desk on which their pay books were laid out in a neat row. It was then I twigged that they were bein' questioned alphabetically! I knew that for sure because one of the kids kept tryin' to get to the head of the line—hadda piece of paper in his hand—and they kept shooin' him back, said he had to wait his turn in the, uh, *queue*.

"I went up to this kid and it turned out—we got through to one another in sign language—that he was the one who'd written down the details of the car and they were on that piece of paper. So I took him to the front of the line and tried to explain this and the RAF got very shirty. I was a bloody Yank and I didn't understand the impor- tance of doin' things by the book. Of *queuin'*.

"I guess I oughta have raised a ruckus, but suddenly I was all-in, suddenly the fact of Johnny's death hit me and I was numb all over and I just waited in line with that Norwegian kid until it came our turn to hand over that piece of paper."

Thereafter, though, results were swift. Every police station and every military police post in Britain was alerted to the details of the car. Within hours, military policemen doing a routine check of a red- light area in London came across a parked blue car with registration plates that included the three or four characters identified by the Norwegians. The car also bore the evidence, a smeared wind screen and mud splashes, of a recent long journey. The MPs waited until a man left a nearby house and got into the car. They moved in on him. He was an American.

"Henry Jackson," Harry Korda said. "Until then, I figured the duke was the culprit. I was wrong. It was plain old Henry Jackson. Hank."

I glanced across at him. He continued to gaze straight ahead and was expressionless. The sun was setting in grand opera colors which costumed the tops of the clouds and gave added resonance to the bass timbre of the Dakota's engines.

"Turns out Henry Jackson had two identities," he said, after a silence of a few moments. "There was Henry Jackson, civilian defense contractor, flown over to England from the States to check the installation of a new radar device. That's what his papers said. And there was Henry Jackson, professional hit man. That's what the FBI records said.

"I filed some of the paperwork relatin' to friend Hank—by then the investigators from the Eighth were givin' me plenty of leeway, if only to show the RAF who was boss—and that's how, among other things, I came to learn he was under twenty-four-hour cross examination at the US penal center at Shepton Mallet in Somerset.

"For days on end he stuck to his story that he was a legit radar expert and that the gun found on him, the murder weapon, was for his own protection.

"And then his prints and his picture arrived from the FBI in Washington and he cracked. Wide open. What choice did he have? There was some talk that he cut a deal—murder two, with his time done in the States, instead of the rope the US military used at Shepton Mallet for capital punishment. Whatever, his cooperation was total.

"He named the person who had put the contract out on Johnny and said the reason he hadn't got rid of the gun—which would have been the smart and obvious thing to have done—was that the, uh, party who had hired him had given him the gun and wanted it returned. As a . . . a keepsake."

Fugues of sunset, shafts of red and gold and mauve, were streaking into the cockpit and against this crescendo of colors I imposed a verdict-gray voice.

"Jake Hays," I said. I paused, tightened up the indictment in my mind: Jake, alias Grudge, Hays.

"Jake Hays loved guns and hated Johnny." I paused again, felt contrived, the stock character who explains all. But I continued, summarizing the self-evident guilt out of a conscious wish to have it all down on record. Guilty as charged. Case closed. "Jake Hays had vowed to track Johnny down all the way to Europe, to track him down and kill him. Only he made that threat in public when he was drunk and when he sobered up he had to have realized that he couldn't possibly risk carrying it out. Not himself. So the next best thing to pulling the trigger personally was to provide the gun to someone else and, after the deed, to have that gun returned to him—something he could look at, touch, gloat over. Right?"

Harry Korda nodded. "That's Jake to a tee, Miss," he said. "Or it was." He pursed his lips. "The night he busted up the banquet, Jake made off in his car. He was spotted by the highway patrol doin' near enough a hundred an hour. They took off after him. Jake was killed when his car hit a tree on a bend in the road."

I said nothing, but I remember thinking that the sunset seemed out of control, wanton in its sudden spread.

Harry Korda rolled his head slowly two or three times, seemingly to ease tension in his neck.

"The gun," he said, "wasn't the kind you'd expect a pro to use. It was small. What's known as a Lady Colt. Gold-plated handle inscribed with the owner's name. That name was—it was Scarlett."

The way it flared now, the sunset seemed to shriek.

Atlanta

Twenty-five

SHE'S ALIVE—A DEAR OLD LADY WHO RICHLY DESERVES THE SIM-
ple innocence of gazing at the lawn of flowers from the window of
her nursing home. Mr. Punch himself told me so.

His greeting card sentiments had to have been drafted by lawyers
and I contrast those words with the death sentence she drew up for
Johnny and, indirectly, for Alice. I think also of Lou Eggenberg, left
a cripple because of her. God knows what other mayhem is account-
able to her name.

But I am here in Atlanta, where she lives still, for justice for only
one person, Johnny, and if that remit takes in other names—and yes,
I suppose it has to include Alice—then so be it. Meantime, I think I
am entitled to congratulate myself on the particular devising of my
plan of retribution.

It is rather exquisite, that plan. I can appreciate its structure now
that my mind is clear and hard with purpose . . .

• • •

Such wasn't so when I set off to come here; I was somewhat frayed.

Though I believed I was in intelligent control of my emotions after Harry Korda flew me back to Kissimmee and I returned to my hotel in Orlando. I spent a week there, and brought this account up to date. Mindful of the way my health crashed in New York, I paced the work and tried to be sensible about rest (though sleep wasn't easy) and food. I swam in the pool, worked out vigorously in the gym. On my last full day I went to the hotel's beauty parlor and had their most expensive massage and facial.

And only when I was under the quasi-anaesthetic of aromatherapy did I acknowledge that I wasn't going to all this trouble to make myself presentable for my return to Beverly Hills; that was simply what I had persuaded myself to accept. What I was actually doing, what subconsciously I must have committed myself to the moment I heard it, was acting on a snippet of information from Harry Korda in the Dakota: and so I was doing my damndest to make myself look like a million dollars so I would be on a similitude of equal terms when I confronted Madge Slattery.

When my beauty treatment was through, I went straight to the front desk of the hotel and said I wanted to be on a flight to Atlanta the next day. I also requested a hotel reservation there.

I slept well that night.

Boarding the plane the next day, I stumbled on the ramp as I prepared to enter the door, felt foolish as the stewardesses reached out their hands to help me, and thereafter—so superficial had been my confidence—I hobbled on doubts.

Was I *really* doing the right thing? Supposing she was alive, and all I had to go on was a chance remark by Harry Korda, what could I say to her? How could I possibly begin to deal with her instigation of a murder so long ago? How on earth could I face her and harden hearsay evidence, old men's stories, into indictment?

The plane took off and I opened my briefcase and tried to seem efficient. I fidgeted with the editing notes I had made for Harry

Korda's tape, put them in order again and again, in so doing sought to file away my doubts. Failed.

And then, about half an hour into the flight, Mr. Punch joined me.

The aisle seat, next to mine, was vacant and he sat down in the manner of a man who had a place in my life. At least I had the presence of mind to take the tape recorder out of my briefcase and switch it on.

He said nothing for a few moments. He simply sat there, his arms folded, staring at the back of the seat in front of him. He had on a dark sheened suit; it might have been the one he had worn that first night in Chicago. The passenger on my other side, by the window, was a bald man who, in that familiar occupation of the American male airborne in business class, was absorbed in a mass of spreadsheets. I decided this stranger was a guarantee against Mr. Punch pulling a knife or a gun on me.

"You're one lucky bitch," he said at last. Softly. Without turning his head.

"You and your sweet nothings," I said.

He unfolded his arms, locked both sets of fingers together, and I realized why, for a time, he had terrified me. Those hands were primitive, the fingers malformed at the joints.

The man in the window seat rustled his spreadsheets contentedly and Mr. Punch went on to explain that I was a lucky bitch because his clients—"my people" he called them—had decided to be "up front" with me.

"Could have gone the other way," he said and, whether out of dramatic effect or reflex, his fingers tightened, twitched.

"Which means what?"

He ignored that. His people had nothing to hide, he continued, and since I was persisting in my baseless enquiries—at this stage his words switched to a text that absolutely *must* have been prepared for him by lawyers—they had decided to give me total and unhindered access to the lady in question in order to prove that my imputations against her good name were unfounded. Definitely, a lawyer's work.

"So," I said, "when do I get to see the fabled Miss Scarlett?"

"You get to see her when—" He broke off, as if the nameless lawyers had tugged at his sleeve. "The name is *Slattery,*" he said. "Miss Madge Slattery. And you get to see her as soon as her medics decide she's up to receivin' a visitor."

He went on to say that she was in a nursing home and after that came the huckstering—the lawyers in Mother's Day mode—about her age and frailty and sweetness and the simple pleasure she took in gazing at the flowers on the lawn.

"I'd be proud to call her Mom," he said.

"And what does she call you—Igor?"

He didn't respond to that, not even by so much as a finger spasm. He said he would call me at my hotel in Atlanta, soon, and give me the date and time of my appointment.

"Fine," I said. "I'm staying at the—"

"I know where you're stayin'," he said. He stood up and for the first time in our exchange looked directly at me. His eyes swarmed hatred. "I even know the number of the room they're gonna give you. Three one three. Bye."

He held up his hand in a false wave and I glimpsed the rose tattoo in his palm and, for a moment, I had another insight into why he had once intimidated me so totally.

Not anymore, though. His little visit had proved that I was winning, proved capitulation at the highest level. I was confident again—*genuinely* confident this time.

Here I am then, in room 313—he was absolutely right—waiting for his call and anticipating that moment when I administer justice for Johnny.

I am, I must confess, enamoured of the stratagem by which I will fulfill that purpose. It came to me on the plane, only moments after Mr. Punch's departure; it formed, inspiration itself, out of my sense of triumph.

My law tutor at Oxford, a crafty old barrister, had a standard pre-
cept when he lectured on the art of moving in for the kill in a prosecution: *Be simple, be direct, be devastating.*

That's what I mean to be with Madge Slattery, and I exult at the
prospect.

I muse also on serendipity, for it was no more than a conversational fill-in by Harry Korda as he flew me back to Kissimmee that
tilted me here; until then, Atlanta had no place in my itinerary. We
had discussed Johnny in every detail and our pauses were becoming
longer and perhaps a little awkward, which must have been why he
said, out of social obligation, that he had heard her singing on the
radio one night as he flew over Alaska in a snowstorm.

Along with much else, I left that out of the written transcript I
did in Orlando on the grounds of irrelevancy; very likely, I just
wanted it to be irrelevant. I'll find the passage on the tape now,
though . . .

". . . the song was 'Love Letters,' her signature tune and the only
number I knew of that she handled well. Sort of breathed it, y'know?
It was kinda unexpected to hear her after all these years. Still, this was
the golden oldies channel, which is all I listen to, and hers was one of
a whole slew of World War Two singers and bands whose records
were bein' played. Guess it was some kind of anniversary."

"Could she still be alive?" I said.

"She was then. No more than a couple of years ago. Three at the
most. Yes, Miss, she was alive and full of herself.

"I know that because after they played her record they said they
were goin' over to Atlanta to talk to her on the phone. She said she
sent her love to all the, uh, gallant boys she'd sung to in the war. My
thousands and thousands of sweethearts, she called 'em, and she sent
'em a big smacker of a kiss—like um-whaa. Y'know? She said she
still got loads of fan mail, which I doubt; I mean, she wasn't exactly
major league. That night on the radio she was just a gabby old
woman gettin' by on her make-believe."

But alive. I hadn't considered that possibility. The whole manner
of her life, the recklessness and the wrist slashing—and she'd tried

that more than once—pointed to an early death in which she, so conscious of drama, had connived wholeheartedly.

Only she had survived to a boastful old age in which she blew kisses over the airwaves. I thought of this for a moment, then tuned out on her, a natural switch-off, a sensible blankness in which I recognized that the final witness, Harry Korda, had been called and the case was now closed, the record as complete as it possibly could be.

Or that's what I thought I believed at the time. I was tired, fraught. It was only later, as I have described, that I accepted that right from the start, right from the intimation that she might well be alive, I had resolved to root her out. Pass sentence, for God's sake! How? I had no idea, not then. It was enough at that stage to be going to Atlanta where surely a search of the archives in the local paper would give me a lead on her whereabouts. And then, of course, Mr. Punch turned up and made even that simple research unnecessary.

Obviously, Mr. Punch picked up my movements from the front desk—my room number here in Atlanta was a little extra refinement—and, just as obviously, he had called his "people" and the lawyers had pow-wowed. I can imagine how often the words "proactive" and "damage limitation" came up as they reached a strategy whereby, in the event of my creating the kind of publicity I had so carelessly outlined to Colonel Crinkle, they could refute any and all allegations by citing the open-door, nothing-to-hide approach that was being taken.

It could have, as Mr. Punch said, gone the other way. I suppose I could have been judged *causus belli,* in which case my life could have ended as precisely and as impersonally as the click of a lock on a lawyer's briefcase. A traffic accident. A mugging that escalated to homicide. A—a personal bonus for Mr. Punch, that one—a fall from my hotel window. They were ruthless people.

And, in essence, I know who they are. America, contrary to myth, is not classless and in some of its dynastic families it is, I believe, more medieval—for over there they are slowly dying out—in its rites and rigid loyalties than any of its European counterparts. Power has made them inherently sinister—Medicis in Cadillacs—and though the name Slattery sits like a tinker's brooch on their various epaulets it gleams real money, the fundamental criterion of these cabals.

I doubt if there's a listing for Slattery in America's so-called "blue book" but the family's sundry heirs and surrogates—their names changed by marriage in many cases—have long since filtered into top echelons of the American establishment.

The family tree, a stump from the bogs of Ireland, has metamorphosed into a redwood and it occupies a prime site. Shake that tree and out come tumbling congressmen, generals, judges, tycoons, bishops. And gangsters. Harry Korda said as much.

I transcribed his words on the subject, and other matters, when I was in Orlando, but I held off incorporating them into the overall record; even then I must have sensed that other developments—Atlanta—were pending and that his words deserved their moment as a form of coda. That moment, I judge, is now. This is what was said.

". . . so they tell me they're posting me to Eighth Air Force HQ in London. I don't have to be a super-brain to guess that the reason for this special treatment was so they could keep tabs on me and also so I could be on hand for the investigation on which they seemed—for a while, at least—to be doin' a real thorough job. I mean, they brought in this military psychologist fella and he was doin' a, what's the word, a profile—yeah, an in-depth profile—on Madge and her family. Saw quite a lot of him, that psychologist.

"He asked me questions like did I know her family had links to crime. He was a very nice fella, but to tell the truth he was also kind of a green kid—Yale and all, but green. Guess I got more out of him than he got out of me. Which is how I came to know of the family's connections everywhere. Just *everywhere,* Miss. So Lord knows how they're spread today.

"I mean, even back then the Slatterys had their eye on the White House—that's what he told me, the psychologist—and I guess it could still be the same today. I used to kinda enjoy those sessions with that psychologist. Dave, his name was. We'd play checkers and chat and—and then it all ended. So, I gather, did the investigation. Ended when they shot Henry Jackson."

"They—they what?"

"At Shepton Mallet. Shot while attemptin' to escape."

"Handy."

"Saved a lotta bother."

"I wonder if they ever got round to talking to her."

"Yes, Miss, they did. Or tried to. This was early on. They sent down a team from Washington to Atlanta. Dave, the psychologist, told me this—on account he wanted to know if she'd ever done it before."

"Done what?"

"Slashed her wrists. And deeper than the last time, from what I gathered. She'd been driftin' in and out of a coma for a couple of weeks. Seemed she'd been depressed for some time before. Booze. Drugs."

"So she wasn't conscious to answer their questions?"

"Guess not."

"And presumably they didn't bother to press the investigation?"

"I don't know, but I guess not."

"Only when I turn up, a full lifetime later, I'm judged to be a federal case, an enemy of the US government."

"Y'ask me, the government isn't involved at all. Not broadly speakin'."

"I was warned off by an FBI agent in Chicago."

"Sure he was FBI?"

"He showed me his badge."

"Y'can get a badge out of a box of sugar pops."

Had I been so gullible? I reminded myself that I was overstretched that night. Harry Korda's voice rolled on. Folksy. Wise.

"Sure, the military covered up in the war, let it be known that Johnny had died in action. But that record just passed into time as fact, just sits there in the files.

"Y'ask me, you're up against a private government—her family. They're like any family, they don't want anyone rattling their skeletons, only they're their own power base. They're used to gettin' their own way.

"These are people, seems to me, who are out to protect their good name and are also lookin' out for their own kin—and Madge, at her age, must be that family's figurehead. If she's still alive, that is."

What he said made sense. I suppose every family is at least a freemasonry, a fireside Mafia, closed in on its secrets, only this one has the wealth and the influence to ensure its privacy, even—vide Colonel Crinkle—strategically placed correspondents to report acts of trespass.

Like her Miss Scarlett hats and gowns, the scandal must have hung in a musty old closet of the family consciousness, ignored until the alarm bells sounded—and, before me, they had last gone off, so far as I could tell, when Lou Eggenberg wrote his article and then went on to try to turn it into a movie.

I wonder who Colonel Crinkle called that night when I outraged him with my questions. A general? A senator? A judge? A bishop? A mobster?

It doesn't matter. What matters is that, albeit obliquely, I am going to remind this sweet old lady who loves to gaze at flowers that she also dug a grave in wartime England.

Only—only I don't know if Johnny has a grave. Neither does Harry Korda. All he knows is that the body was taken to the general hospital at Bradford for post mortem and transferred from there to London for further tests.

About two months after his death, Adelle held a memorial service for Johnny. It was planned as an affair of the simplest dignity, Harry Korda said, except that Madge Slattery, out of the hospital by then, bedecked the church with magnolias, read one of the lessons and, with her usual flair for center stage, sang "Love Letters" from the pulpit.

When am I going to get that call from Mr. Punch? It's mid-evening and I've been waiting here, in this luxurious but characterless room—the decor, right down to the telephone, is a rampant pearl gray—since I returned from a shopping trip this afternoon.

I want nothing more than to see her and then get away from Atlanta, for this city depresses me. Like my room, it's all pearl gray. *Corporate* pearl gray.

I feel no closeness to Johnny here. None. The quiet city he grew up in—and the elderly cabdriver on the ride from the airport assured me that time was when Atlanta was "real folksy"—has gone on to swagger, but not with the brio of its legendary carpetbaggers. Atlanta is a pearl gray pelting of salespersons on incentive trips and delegates to conventions; relative to its size, more conventions take place here than anywhere else in America.

Atlanta, though, has heroes. Martin Luther King, for one, was born here.

And so was Johnny.

The phone is ringing now, and even that has a pearl gray tone . . .

It was Mr. Punch on the phone. He gave me the address of a nursing home in the suburbs and told me I was expected there at ten the next morning. He said he could arrange for me to be picked up or—he must have been talking to the lawyers again—I could "proceed independently".

"I'll take a cab," I said.

And now I mean to do some gift wrapping. The reason for my shopping trip this afternoon was to buy a lush red ribbon, one suitable for wearing on a picture hat. I meant it when I said that in seeking justice for Johnny I would be simple, direct, devastating.

Twenty-six

I OVERREACTED, OF COURSE, BUT WHEN THE CAB ROUNDED THE curve in the long drive and I saw the white antebellum mansion I thought—Tara! She lived in bloody Tara!

The truth is that such buildings are commonplace on the outskirts of Atlanta, redoubts against the prevailing pearl gray of the city. But in those first moments of fury I made no allowances for that reality. I was aware only of the sweep of the colonnaded facade; the hitching-post statues of grinning black jockeys at the foot of the steps to the main entrance; the fat black woman (a mammy, if ever I saw one) passing a straw broom across those steps; the densely green lawns and their pirouetting sprinklers; the groves of cyprus trees; the ornamental pond and its decadence of pink flamingoes. Bloody Tara!

I cooled down when I went inside and took in the fact of a nursing home. Nurses and doctors in no-nonsense whites. An old man in a Zimmer frame. A row of oxygen bottles on a metal trolley.

I was sure Mr. Punch would be there, waiting for me. He wasn't. Or not that I could see.

I went up to the reception desk, a semicircle fronted by studded brown leather. A middle-aged woman with bluish scalloped hair sat behind the desk and, smiling, projected pearl gray Atlanta charm. I gave her my name and before I could say anything else she exclaimed, "Why, you'll be Miss Scarlett's visitor! All the way from England, I do declare. I'll just beep for her boy. For Floyd."

Floyd, it turned out, was Madge Slattery's manservant. I sat and waited for him on a long sofa, also of brown leather. I looked around at black-and-white tiled floors and light blue walls: the reception area was unpretentious, though I was sure that wealth lurked there. As no doubt did Mr. Punch, but I still didn't see him.

After about twenty minutes, and I was getting impatient, Floyd shuffled up, seemingly from the recesses of Uncle Tom's cabin. He was a long and gaunt and stooped old black man, his hair a froth of silver curls. He had on a steward's white jacket, fastened with gold-plated studs all the way up to his neck. His trousers were dark gray pinstripes, rigidly pressed, with enough space above the ankles to show he wasn't wearing socks. His feet were enormous and his cracked black shoes were sheened. He addressed me as "Missy" as he stood there, wringing his hands, imploring forgiveness for keeping me waiting.

I didn't like Floyd. I didn't like him because he was craven and crafty and his idea of dignity was to be seen as a non-uppity "colored" man and, most of all, I didn't like him because patently he was there to front his employer's reputation.

Mr. Punch had made a small point of calling her Miss Madge Slattery, but to Floyd she was Miss Scarlett and the name dripped from his sly mouth like molasses.

"Yes, um, Missy, ah grew up in the service o' Miss Scarlett and her family and ah praise the Lord for grantin' me such a golden pathway in life."

We were climbing a long and wide staircase, on our way to see her; my tape recorder, in the top pocket of my jacket, was switched on.

"The whole family was special to me, but the most special person

of all was, and is to this day—well, ah reckon you've figured who
that person is, Missy."

"Miss . . . *Slattery*," I said. "Miss *Madge Slattery*." Though I smiled
politely, I enunciated that minor triumph, that little downpayment of
truth, and for an instant, in the hardness of his glance, he looked like
a moneylender who had been short changed.

And then he chuckled.

That chuckle was straight out of the plantation and his cotton soft
words dabbed amusement at my ignorance of the situation.

"Lord bless ya, Missy, but if what you jus' said ain't the funniest
thing! Why, she been Miss Scarlett ever since ah can recall, and that's
jus' about forever. She done wear that name like a party dress made
by the angels themselves and it's a party to which *all* is invited 'cos
she's jus' set on doin' good in life." He paused, took a slightly different tack. "No denyin' she can seem willful at times, headstrong, but
that's on account she has a mind of her own and only such a woman
could do the kind o' good she's done."

He had dentures and they clicked and his shoes squeaked and his
breathing wheezed and he seemed generally to be coming apart.
Where, I am sure, he was meant to be perceived as *whole,* solid, was
as *their* witness for the defense and I wasn't surprised when he took
the oath, as it were, by declaring himself a weekend preacher.

"Our little church is done kept goin' only 'cos o' what she puts
into it," he said. "She done made us an outright gift o' the land and
any expenses we have—like a brand new shingled roof last month—
is passed on to her estate. Every Sunday we say a prayer that Miss
Scarlett, *our* Mother Teresa we done call her, will make a full recovery real soon."

"Recovery from what?" I said.

"The stroke, Missy. 'Bout a year ago. She came here two years
back on account o' old bones and the pains they bring, though she
was still sprightly in her heart. But then the stroke happened and it
was like sudden lightnin'—yes, sudden lightnin'—and, a lady like
Miss Scarlett, a free spirit, it was all the more cruel."

We reached the top of the stairs and he paused for a moment for breath, his eyes watering from the exertions of the climb. There had to have been an elevator, of course, and I decided the reason we hadn't used it was so Floyd could do full justice to the Miss Scarlett spiel. The lies.

We carried on again, Floyd leading the way down a corridor. He halted at a perfectly ordinary brown door above which a small brass plaque, not much bigger than a postcard, made a discreet announcement: *The Miss Scarlett Wing.*

Floyd, beaming, opened the door and we entered a foyer-like space that compensated for the understatement of the plaque. A huge crystal chandelier hung from a domed ceiling and its prisms dappled the highly polished circular surface of a Queen Anne table. There were French provincial chairs and elaborate urns of magnolias and azaleas. An ormolu clock presided on an alabaster column in a corner. The carpeting was blue and thick, the walls lilac-colored.

I might have been in the receiving room at the embassy of a small but immensely wealthy republic—and indeed there was a sovereign presence in the form of a life-sized portrait of Madge Slattery. I had no doubt of her identity, and I crossed to the wall for a closer look.

"Miss Scarlett when she was twenty-one years old," Floyd said, teeth clicking, eyes gleaming, head lolling in approval. "Her daddy done brought over a regular artist from Paris, France, man who done painted kings and queens."

"Daddy's little princess," I said, staring at the face that preened out from a large picture hat, a flowing red band at the brim.

"He done doted on her, Missy. Of all his daughters, he done doted on her the most and though it's not for the likes o' me to take sides I understand why. Oh, Lordy, yes. Lordy, yes."

He stood to one side of the portrait, his hands clasped prayer-like under his stringy chin, as if at a shrine, and certainly the artist seemed to have done his damndest to make her look like a goddess. A somewhat wayward goddess, perhaps, in view of the more than ample décolletage defined by her long blue gown.

She posed negligently against a peach tree, one arm raised to caress the blossom. In the background—perhaps it was sunset or perhaps it was the whole of Atlanta burning in sacrificial tribute to her—there was a reddish haze. And she smiled her lazy goddess smile out of those half-amused violet eyes and the full and perfect lips. In every detail, her beauty was total—the glossy brown ringlets, the noble forehead, the exquisite nose.

I decided, personal prejudice aside, that it was a bad portrait, that it was Woolworth values at what must have been a Louvre price, that it was over-colored and succeeded only in the terms of its commission—narcissism and ostentation.

My criticism must have showed, for suddenly I was aware of Floyd's eyes narrowed in hostility against me. His voice whined protest.

"That jus' what she done look like and anybody who think different is jus' plain jealous!" He blinked, as if taken aback by his outburst. "What I mean is"—he was trying to make amends now—"what I mean, Missy, is that some folks is heartless, even though the artist done said that no man 'ud ever look at this picture without wantin' to bow and no woman without wantin' to curtsy."

"And is that what they do here?" I said.

His smile rubbed his oily praise-the-Lord look back on his face. "They'd surely like to, Missy, 'specially on this wing, but their hips is gone and jus' about everythin' else that done holds 'em together. Only they're alive and that's down to Miss Scarlett—she done rescued 'em from poverty."

A tilt of his head, and he indicated the doors, perhaps a dozen in all, on either side of the wing. "She done opened this wing for the poor folks. This here nursin' home, it's for millionaires and beggars—and ah reckon it's the beggars get the best deal!"

He chuckled again, a regular Amos 'n' Andy chuckle, and he motioned with his hand to show our direction lay farther down the wing. As we made our slow way there he told me that the trustees of the nursing home hadn't been happy with her proposal to fund a wing for the impoverished and that a positive crisis arose when it was realized that some of her geriatric indigents were "coloreds".

"But Miss Scarlett done told 'em that if they didn't want her money—and she done put millions into this place—that was fine by her and she'd up and take her business somewhere else. Well, Missy, they mulled this over and done their sums and, praise de Lord, when they looked at the total they done decided that colored folk added up to God's chillen just like everybody else. Course, Missy, it jus' might have helped that Miss Scarlett owns this buildin'!" Another Amos 'n' Andy chuckle. "She's strong-willed, Miss Scarlett. Alus gets her way. Alus."

Johnny, dead in the jeep at Haworth, two bullets from a Lady Colt in the back of his neck: yes, I thought, she always got her way. Not for much longer, though. I touched my bag, felt the shape of the package I had gift-wrapped so carefully the night before.

Floyd led me to the door at the end of the wing. A blue door, like all the others. He tapped it with his knuckles a couple of times, then opened it. He smiled at me, held up his finger in a signal that I should stay on the threshold for the time being. Then he shambled across to her.

She was by the window and in a wheelchair. Her back was to the door. Even so, I felt I had an encompassing view of her. For she was wearing a wide-brimmed picture hat and the red band around the rim trailed down her shoulders . . .

It wasn't a big room and, for me, its centerpiece was the hat. A cream-colored hat. Like the one in the portrait. Like the one on the B17. I told myself that, metaphorically, I was about to knock that hat askew, demolish the supremacy of her self. I savored the prospect of that moment.

"How's you feelin' after your nap, Miss Scarlett?" Floyd was at her side now, bending over her. "Not that you done need no beauty sleep. No, sir, not you . . ."

He continued to humor her and I, standing in the doorway, noted the room more generally. Blue carpet, white walls. There were no pictures on the walls, which surprised me; I expected at the very least a likeness of the portrait outside. A black baby grand piano stood, diagonally, on the other side of the window to where she sat in the wheelchair. A yellow chaise longue was to my right, against the wall, and in the middle of the room was an antique-looking desk, mother of pearl insets in its spindly legs. And that was the extent of the decor—that and the dominant picture hat.

"Lordy, Miss Scarlett, if you don't get prettier every day," Floyd said. "And talkin' o' pretty, you gotta visitor. The young lady you was told about. Remember?" I neither heard nor saw any response; there was no movement of the picture hat. "She's here right now, rarin' to meet ya."

He unbent from the wheelchair, beckoned me across.

As I walked toward him I spotted the tiny red lights, one at each side of the window lintel, of concealed television cameras. I wondered if I should wink at Mr. Punch; I didn't, though.

There was a footstool alongside the wheelchair and Floyd, in his grovelling way, passed a handkerchief across its brocade surface.

"You jus' sit here, Missy," he said. I did, though reluctantly, feeling at a disadvantage.

"She done has good days and bad days," Floyd said. "Some days she done tries to talk and some days she don't. Ah's gonna leave you now. You jus' talk to her. She hears. She understands. She's as smart as she ever was."

He left, and as the door closed behind him and his wheezings I was aware of another sound—that of her breathing. The sound was slight and not rusted by the years, a measured—*calculated*—inhaling and exhaling.

The wide brim of her hat concealed her face totally. Of course, I could have shifted my stool slightly in order to see her face, but I wasn't willing to make that concession, to grant her the prize of my curiosity.

No, the plan was that she would be under *my* command, that she would be forced to turn her head as the result of something I said. But what—*what* could I say? In my hubris, I hadn't worked that out. I had relied on instinct, on the smooth spontaneity of the television interviewer, though now I realized that thinking on one's feet wasn't easy from a footstool. She had the upper ground. For now. Only for now.

Temporizing, resisting the sudden notion that I was being manipulated, I took a closer look at what I could see of her. She was wearing a long blue dress, her hands were down by its sides and tucked in its folds, though it lacked the splendor of the one in the portrait; it was a simple dress, trimmed with lace and spotted with a motif of daisies.

Only her hat was elaborate—her chapeau—with its small crown and the sweeping drape of its brim. And its red bow. Sash. Ribbon. Whatever name, it was the symbol of her banditry, her plundering, her—I tensed on sudden raw hatred of her and it came to me that it would be so satisfying, so simple to tear the hat from her head.

So simple, and so stupid. I couldn't afford the luxury of de-throning by peasant revolt. The loss of dignity would be mine. No histrionics. I was bound by my own particular jurisprudence in this matter in which somehow—*somehow*—I had to intimate her guilt, no more than that, and then follow on with the deliverance of the justice I had worked out so carefully and with such satisfaction the night before. All that stood in my way now was the framing of that *intimation*. But how?

Waiting for that answer, putting my faith in something that would form out of the ether, I found myself giving careful attention to the window. Bower window. Floor to ceiling. View of lawns. Flowers on the lawns (Mr. Punch was right). Poppies. Bandit red, those poppies. Like the bow on her hat. The sash. The ribbon . . . This wouldn't do. I had to make a start. Anything.

"Madge," I said.

She showed no reaction.

I waited a few moments; then I said, enunciating, trying to make the words courtroom austere in the spirit of the truth, the whole truth and nothing but the truth, "Madge Slattery . . ."

She remained totally still, her breathing as steady as ever, as if invoking her constitutional right to silence.

I had no choice. I had to fall back on the alias.

"Scarlett," I said. "Miss Scarlett."

And, promptly, she inclined her head.

It wasn't enough to show me her face, but it proved she had heard me, formally acknowledged me.

Even so, I remained at a loss. Tension denied me immediate words and, lacking a script, I saw only blankness on my private autocue, the neat little scenario of the night before in which I would act with such decisive finality.

But I couldn't afford to flounder. So, perhaps hoping that its very tangibility would get me going, I took out of my bag the sketch I had laced with red ribbon.

It was Johnny's Moonmaiden sketch.

My possession of it was not part of the transcript I wrote in Orlando because—because, I suppose, it was too personal, too poignant. Though at the time I persuaded myself that its exclusion was a balanced editorial judgment in which, at those closing stages, I could not afford to be too indulgently subjective. I have since changed my mind and propose a brief explanation of how the drawing came to be mine.

Harry Korda, shortly before we landed at Kissimmee, wondered if I would care to have one of Johnny's sketches as a memento of our flight.

I asked if I might have the one of Moonmaiden.

It was, of course, a sentimental choice and only later, the result of Mr. Punch approaching me on the flight to Atlanta, did it come to me that it could serve another purpose—that it would have to be sacrificed as a quasi-legal document, the Exhibit A in my case against her.

Yes, it all seems over-the-top and theatrical—though, self-servingly, I remind myself that my law tutor at Oxford kept insisting that the execution of justice was the oldest form of showmanship.

And so I count my purchase of that red ribbon as inspired, and relevant, bravura.

For Harry Korda told me that Johnny's hands, that day in Haworth, were tied tightly together with a red ribbon.

And Henry Jackson—and Harry Korda had learnt this from one of his chats with the psychologist—had said, in his anxiety to tell all and win points for cooperation, that the binding of the hands was part of his instructions.

Johnny was her property and the ribbon tied up her rights of ownership.

But now I sat in her room in the nursing home and gazed down at the beribboned sketch and wondered why my scenario seemed to be going awry.

Such a straightforward scenario too. *Be simple, be direct, be devastating.* It called for me merely to hand over the sketch, watch as she looked at it (I hadn't calculated for infirmity on the scale of a stroke) and as she reacted to what she saw. And then to tell her—with the utmost brevity—that this was the illustration that had replaced the pin-up of her on the B17. And then to pick up the sketch from her fingers and slap her across the face with it. A light slap, bearing in mind her age. A token slap. But a *pointed* slap. Both cheeks. French style. "That's for Johnny," I would say.

I had rehearsed it in my hotel room, had timed it to pre-empt intervention by Mr. Punch—I was sure then that he would be present—and, at just seven seconds, there would be nothing he could do to stop me. I thought of the slap and the attendant *coup de grâce* ("That's for Johnny") as a masterstroke. My day in court.

After which I would leave immediately. Sweep out on the lingering satisfaction of the last word. *"That's for Johnny . . ."*

Simple. Only—only it wasn't coming together. I sensed a lack of coordination. A hidden flaw. But it had to work. *Had* to. I told myself simply to get on with it.

"Johnny," I began. "Joh-nny." I repeated his name, divide it into two, the way one does with the very old and the very sick. I went on, speaking slowly, carefully. "I am here about Johnny. Do you understand? You remember Johnny? Of course you do. And you remember what you did to him. In England. In the war." I paused, then yielded to irresistible harshness. *"Don't you?"*

At first, I thought she gasped. But the sound turned out to be the whirr of the electric motor on her wheelchair. The chair swivelled slowly and we were face to face. And I was the one who gasped.

Lou Eggenberg must have had a similar experience in Scotland when the duke revealed his face, though I didn't think of that as I recoiled on the impact of that gasp. On the tape, however, it comes across as no more than a slight intake of breath, and though I would like to lay claim to such relative composure, in all honesty I cannot. Floyd was right when he described her stroke as lightning: it was forked lightning, a jagged and frozen schism in which her face was chaos. One eye was wider and lower than the other; her nose was twisted; her mouth, on the left side, gaped and dribbled. A bib was stitched to the top of her dress.

The girl in the glossy portrait had become this Salvador Daliesque study in the brokenness of age. But her eyes, though so grotesquely misaligned, were essentially the girl's eyes in the portrait, violet and sensual, and I realized, even now that her face was that shattered abstract, that her birthday artist had not faked those eyes and their potency to dwell on any kind of passion, including murder.

She was staring at me, but I couldn't tell whether her gaze held regret or gloating. I wondered if she had presented her stroke-clawed face out of defiance, out of a reflex to do what she had done all her life—flaunt. Was she doing now with her ugliness what she had done in her youth with her beauty—demanding total attention, center stage at all costs?

And then she was trying to say something, her lips—and, another daubing of tragedy, they were painted—writhing, so that her teeth were bared. A sound dragged in her throat. "J-o-Joh-" I waited, while she pulled on his name.

"Johnny."

It was there, carried by an inner strength, a ruthless will; it was there and it was clear in a voice that didn't belong to that age-wrecked face. A girl's voice.

That voice was so unexpectedly young that it made her next action—an attempt to raise her right arm—incongruous. She persevered in trying to get her arm up and I saw, on the slack and yellowish skin, the signs of slashes on her wrists, a pattern which diagnosed her mental history more cogently than any precise psychiatric case notes.

She managed to partly raise her arm and now aimed a tremulous finger at an indeterminate point in the room, trying to identify something for me. I looked round.

"Piano?" I said.

She shook her head and her finger jabbed agitation.

"Desk?" I said.

She nodded. I hesitated—why do her bidding?—then got up and crossed to the desk. On its plain mahogany surface, and overlooked by me when I entered the room, was a small apple-green phonograph, a record on its turntable. I glanced at her. She was nodding, jabbing, dribbling. I shrugged, flicked the on switch, placed the playhead on the rim of the record.

As I walked back to the window, applause and whistles were drifting into the room in a tinny, far-off way, like a long-distance call on a bad connection.

I resumed my seat on the footstool. In as much as I could tell from that plundered face she was listening raptly to the sounds coming from that phonograph. A woman's voice undulated in the echoes and rasps of an imperfect microphone.

"Thank you, boys. Thank you, thank you, sweethearts. Each and every one of you is precious to me."

A young woman's voice. A Deep South voice ("mah" for my). *Her* voice . . .

"But mah next number has gotta be for one boy and one boy only, and though ah love you all dearly—'deed ah do,'deed ah do—this song, mah

finale tonight, is dedicated, as always, to a young man who's over there in England but right here next to me in mah heart. This one's for Johnny."

A crumpled whoosh of what I took to be violins and saxes and in a static of long-gone time, from a concert that had taken place at some American camp during the war, Miss Scarlett—and even I concede her role in that context—was singing "Love Letters."

Harry Korda was right: she breathed the words. Given the langorous tempo of the tune, this worked and meant that her lack of pitch and the resultant failure of breath when she tackled a high note came out as warmth, passion.

Trying to pinpoint her technique, I inclined my head in the direction of the phonograph so I could hear better. Obviously, she worked close to the microphone, very close, and of course it would have been one of those old-fashioned long-stemmed mikes. Once or twice she got too close and the sound rasped and pinged, though even that flaw was part of the perfection of the performance.

For sheer virtuosity, for making the most of a dud singing voice, it reminded me of that occasion, many years later, when Marilyn Monroe got up at Kennedy's birthday and sang—*breathed*—"Happy Birthday, Mr. President."

The final notes of "Love Letters" were lined up like a row of candles and snuffed out softly, one after the other, on the catch of her breath.

Afterwards there was total silence on the part of those young GIs, a palpable silence in which I sensed the gathering fusion of romantic mist and raw sexual steam—and then that combustion spilled, milled into climax and an ejaculation (I can think of no other word for it) of orgasmic applause.

Schmaltz, I told myself. Sheer schmaltz.

But I listened intently, my head half-turned still, to that applause, listened until it became spent, exhausted, like the act of sex itself.

"I love you, boys. Oh, I love you, love you, love . . ." Her voice was closer than ever to the microphone, a whisper, cued perfectly to the post-coital moment, to—for God's sake!—the afterglow.

Now that it was over, the record made a hushed scratching that echoed the blankness of time past and lives that had run their grooves and had known their music and their wails.

Except that she was still here, still playing her power games. And that was what her singing of "Love Letters" was all about—power. A ruthless need not simply to move an audience, but to own it. All her life, in so many ways, she had played such games, obsessive in her assertion of ownership and deadly—*Johnny slumped in the jeep at Haworth*—when she was challenged.

And now she was playing a game with me, setting out to prove her mastery, stroke or not, by putting me in my place.

For when I turned my head and looked at her after I had listened to the record I saw that, in those few moments of my preoccupation, those stricken fingers had somehow managed to slip on dark glasses. She wore them like a gambler, a confident high roller, and now she held her head to one side with the poised arrogance of the natural winner.

I looked straight back at her, tried to make a standoff of it, though in fact I felt inadequate, beaten. And at the same time I was furious with myself for the way I had allowed her to finesse me into the whole pre-arranged setup in which, denied speech because of her stroke, she had used those lyrics as her advocacy of love for Johnny— and perhaps even as her defense of what she had ordered to be done to him after he rejected her.

For a moment I wondered if there could be tears behind those dark glasses and she was too proud to let me see them.

But no—she was preening. Thus she regarded me. Triumphantly. Mockingly. The glasses, and the confidence they restored to her face, were her winning card.

Only I had the ace. I glanced down at the Moonmaiden sketch in my lap. Now was the moment. Trump time. *Now.* I picked up the sketch. The red ribbon trailed softly, a promissory of the lashing I had schemed.

The advantage was supremely mine. And, for once in my competitive win-at-all-cost ways, I didn't take it. Something . . . supervened. I am not stretching on tiptoes for character credit marks; I am simply, and self-consciously, trying to explain what happened and why a moment's impulse became an imperative.

Something supervened and instead of the slap I kissed her on the lips, tasted her dribbles. Something supervened and when I said, after the kiss, "That's for Johnny," my words were forgiveness and not sentence. Something supervened and I knew this was what I owed him, for he had the grace of generosity, and not the showy justice I had contrived with an old sketch and a length of red ribbon.

I was clutching that sketch as I stumbled out of that room. I stumbled because I was weeping. For the first time in my self-centered life, tears . . .

Clouds. All the way from Atlanta to the present stage of my journey back to Los Angeles—the captain was on the intercom just now to say we were flying over the Grand Canyon—a near-total cloud cover. They suit me, those clouds. They somehow blur the unseemly exit from the nursing home (though, oddly, I have a clear enough picture of Floyd lounging outside the door and studying the racing form) and somehow too they clarify the landmarks I hold in my mind—the airy pinnacles of high purpose and decency represented by Johnny's generation, with its fired-up commitment to creating a better America and a better world at a point in history when this truly was possible. That generation, or at least a goodly part of it, had its head in the clouds (and why not?) as it sought moral ascendancy, strove to make war's aftermath worthwhile. Cue the cliche: a land fit for heroes. Cue the reality: a ruling status quo of wealth and greed and violence, though perhaps here I am being tendentious vis-à-vis Madge Slattery. Still, even if Johnny had returned from the war, what chance would he have had, what price his values in a society so soon to be swamped, as never before, by the dollar sign?

Oh, come now! Come! Of all persons, who am I to play moral arbiter? Who am I to express dismay over what I have found in travelling across this land? Besides, there were the good experiences, the proof of a residual resilience and the ability to bounce back—and surely a trainload of barbershop quartet singers is a sound enough reason for a tap on the straw boater of hope.

And better that as a salute to Johnny than the dirge of a drum roll. For Johnny was hope itself. Not hoopla hope, perhaps, but hope as a quiet and enduring force.

Even I, the most unpromising of candidates, feel I may have grown a little under the influence of his spirit, feel that in searching for Johnny I have discovered something about myself. I kissed Madge Slattery, didn't I? I wept, didn't I?

And that's why, needing to keep this hope alive, needing, at least for the moment, not to be solemn about him, I look to the future and quite brazenly—and that attribute, I persuade myself, also can be part of hope—I quote that original and fictional Miss Scarlett: "Tomorrow is another day . . ."

Haworth

Dear Andy,

*Finally, here it is. My journal, my memoir, my (in a way) exorcism.
My book? You mentioned that possibility when you urged me, at my
lowest point, to put it all down.*

*Still, that was some years back now and it was only the other week
when I was preparing to move house yet again (in Beverly Hills one
needs to keep reaffirming one's upwardly mobile status!) that I came
across the manuscript at the back of my shoe closet.*

*I had tucked it away because I was drained by what it revealed
and felt I needed not to see it for a while; even so, I hadn't planned
such a long hibernation for it. Another reason for my neglect, I suppose, was that I was, and still am, unhappy with many parts of what
I had written and indeed on the original read-through I did some
squirming—God, I remember thinking, should this be subtitled Emily
Brontë meets Scarlett O'Hara? Then again, though, one of the characters in these pages, and he was a wise man (he's now dead, as are
most of the principals, including a certain Madge Slattery), remarked
that life resonates with the bizarre and the melodramatic. (It is we
practitioners of the blue pencil who cut the whole process down to size
and credible trim.)*

*Anyway, when the manuscript reemerged during house moving I
observed due reunion. I sat down, opened a bottle of wine, and as I
turned the pages it seemed to me that this particular "Auld Lang
Syne" might, in a modest way, segue into the general overtones of this
so-called Spirit of Millennium. Okay, so we are well into A.D. 2000
and all that, but the consensus of the "experts" is that for years to
come society will be using the twentieth century as a compass for making sure we don't mess up the future. (Some hope!)*

*Meantime, to use that no-nonsense word one hears all the time in
B. Hills, I am trying to pitch a book at you.*

*You may think it rubbish, in which case I shall accept your ruling
as my agent and my friend.*

*Should it actually come to fruition, I would hope that the editor
was a woman and therefore likelier than a man to accept the basic*

premise of the situation—the way Johnny came into my life—without raising too strongly the kind of questions of pedantic logic of what, feebly, I can describe only as other realms of time.

Equally, given the choice, I would not want a romantic as an editor; on the contrary, my desire would be for a realist, but one with a constructive and open-ended imagination who would concede that other than a relatively few scientists—including a Nobel Prize winner at Cambridge, though he's now dead too—we are totally ignorant of time and its ineffable mysteries.

And now for an epistolary change of tone . . .

I am back in England. In Haworth, no less. My visit is a fleeting one and, knowing you are in Tuscany at this part of the year, there was no point in calling your office. My visiting card, however, is this letter and manuscript, and a Haworth postmark seems apt for the package—though my purpose in coming here was to return Johnny's dog tags to their rightful place.

I have said in the manuscript that Johnny has no known grave. Actually, he has—up there on the moors. That little private wall he built there speaks more eloquently of him than any formally inscribed headstone could. And that's where his dog tags belong.

When the manuscript reemerged and I read it again I realized that the dog tags were not mine, that in the traditional English way I had assumed ownership through plunder, and their place was up there on the moor where, just as before, they would rust and encrust and endure. As he had planned.

I felt I couldn't delay in doing this and once I rearranged my schedule with the studio I flew to London for the weekend. I rested up briefly at a hotel at Heathrow before taking a domestic flight to Leeds, from where I hired a car and drove to Haworth.

Here I am, then, in—would you believe it!—the Charlotte Brontë suite of the Wuthering Heights Guest House (the Emily Brontë suite is occupied by a pair of honeymooners from New Zealand who both wear thick glasses and look remarkably like brother and sister).

Haworth is full of tourists from across the world and has been village-England groomed as if it were a bucolic boutique (Brontë Bon Marche, The Parsonage Perfumery, the Brontë Crafts Emporium et al.).

But the innate grudge of the village is as hard as the cobblestones in the main street and tourism has not been able to temper the Haworth wind which reddens eyes and wrecks the coiffures of Brontë Stylists and Beauticians.

That wind warned me off in every step I took up the moor. I made it though, located the wall easily.

I did my very best to return the dog tags to at least the approximate spot in the wall from where I had taken them. I used a strong hand trowel, from the hardware shop in the village, to lever a slight opening between the stones. And I put the dog tags inside, returning them to him and to time . . .

But I wasn't quite through. Johnny, after he finished building the wall, scattered American coins over the site—I have mentioned this in my manuscript—in a little quasi-religious ceremony dating from Ancient Rome. And now, an impulse, I searched in my bag for change. I came up with a few dimes and quarters and half dollars, with their shared inscription of In God We Trust. Which seemed fitting for that spontaneous service of re-consecration.

As he did all those years ago, I flung the coins in the air, smiting (a good Brontë word) the face of that wind and feeling that I was zapping (a good American word!) Satan more pointedly than the Reverend Patrick Brontë had ever done in his four- and five-hour sermons down there in his ugly church.

Apart from general atonement and the restoration of balance—the dog tags returned to the wall—I felt this was my very own millennium gesture and it comforts me to know that long after I am dead the dog tags will be there, a spiritual token of one young man's short life.

In God We Trust—though not this lady, thank you. My atheism is intact. What I do have, though, thanks to Johnny, is a particular small faith, an inchoate concept of purpose and care which I would like to think transcends, or at least mellows, the vanities and selfishness of my life.

Perhaps that was why I was suddenly carefree as I made my way back down the moor, and though the wind was all for roaring, I heard it as no more than a romp.

That wind, it's true, still does a little bit of haunting in my life, by which I mean that my dream continues to recur from time to time and I see again the Misses Emily and Scarlett. I have this notion that only the thump of a book might finally shoo them away.

What do you think?

My love, as always,

A.